BLACK SUNSHINE

By

NINIE HAMMON

BAY
FOREST

Black Sunshine

Copyright © 2011
Ninie Hammon

Cover illustration by Mona Roman Advertising
Interior Design by Bookmasters

Published by Bay Forest Books
An Imprint of Kingstone Media Group
P.O. Box 491600
Leesburg, FL 34749-1600
www.bayforestbooks.com

Printed in the United States of America by
Bay Forest Books

Library of Congress Cataloguing-in-Publication Data is on file.

ISBN 978-1-936164-40-0

BLACK
SUNSHINE

*This book is dedicated to the coal miners
in the mountains of Eastern Kentucky who
risk their lives in the dirty, cold, wet darkness
every day to dig coal.
To their families, who carry the mine with
them in their hearts every minute their loved
ones are underground.
And to the memories of more than 7,000
miners who went down one day and never
came back up. May they rest in peace.*

ACKNOWLEDGMENTS

FIRST, ALWAYS—TOM.

Who is encouraging, patient, kind and irrepressibly silly—but not necessarily in that order.

Who tiptoes around the house like a cat burglar so he won't disturb me and pretends he doesn't mind watching Sports Center with the volume on mute.

Who picks me up, dusts me off and shoves me back into my writing chair when I am convinced I do not have another word left in me.

Who lives out his faith every day with a strength, courage and joy that leaves me breathless.

Who is all that and a bag of Cheetos. Couldn't write a syllable without you, Babe.

◊ ◊ ◊ ◊ ◊

IF THE DETAILS about coal mining and all things hillbilly in this book are accurate, it's because Jerry Asher told me. If any of the details are wrong, it's because I didn't listen to him. Jerry is a retired coal miner and a proud-of-it hillbilly from Harlan, Kentucky who served as my expert on everything from the temperature of a coal mine to the heart and character of mountain people. He invested hours answering my dumb questions, always told me 110 percent of what I asked—even drew diagrams for me of coal mine ventilation systems.

Thanks Jerry. Your the best.

And thanks to the sweet ladies at the Coal Mining Museum in Benham, Kentucky. Your exhibits made coal mines real for me.

Other Books by Ninie Hammon

God Said Yes
Sudan
The Memory Closet
Home Grown
Five Days in May

CHAPTER 1

October 20, 1980

A sudden clap of thunder ripped open the crisp autumn afternoon, banged harsh and loud—but not in the cloudless sky. The boom roared in the tangled roots of Black Mountain, deep in the dark guts of the earth.

In the stunned stillness that followed, time shut down. For an airless, eternal moment, not a bird cheeped, not a dry leaf rattled.

Then the earth groaned, as a man might cry out in his sleep. *Rumbled.* And the rumble swelled, became a grating death rattle like gravel in a blender. The ground shook, dogs howled, kitchen cabinets flew open, glasses, plates, and bowls clattered out and shattered in a tinkling symphony of breaking glass. Pictures and mirrors leapt off walls, clocks crashed to the floor and stopped—all of them at the same time: 12:18 P.M.

But even before she heard that first sound, Ruby Sparrow knew.

She'd been hanging up a load of laundry on the clothesline in the backyard when the knowing of it came to her. She sucked in a ragged gasp and the honeysuckle-sweetened air suddenly turned as thick as creek mud, curdled, so she couldn't catch another breath.

Not much scared Ruby. Not Joe Pritchard's old bull with the broken horn. Not the haints that hid in the graveyard mist. Not the

1

shadow of the mountain that reached out to grab her in the evening. But in that moment, Ruby made the acquaintance of pure terror. A horror beyond her sight—though not out past the knowing of her heart—had dried up all the spit in her mouth and set her hands to trembling so bad she almost dropped her husband's clean shirt in the dirt at her feet.

A scream crawled on hairy, black legs up the back of her throat, a wail as haunting as the cry of lost children wandering in the dark. She didn't give it voice though. Couldn't. She had no air to push the sound out through her lips into the world.

Ruby wasn't the only one who knew. Other wives, mothers, sisters, and girlfriends did, too. Sick dread instantly seized hearts all up and down the hollow. One of the reporters who came later, feeding on Aintree Hollow's grief and misery like crows tearing at roadkill, claimed some of the women had "sensed the first silent movement of the earth." That fool didn't know jack. What the women had sensed was the string break. The thread, delicate as a moonbeam, tough as a piece of catgut, that bound Aintree's families together, that knit the whole hollow together—they'd felt it snap.

When they did, they froze—breathless. Listening. Straining to hear and begging the good Lord to strike them deaf so they couldn't.

One heartbeat.

Two.

Then the rumble ate up the world and Ruby found herself running down the rocky slope barefoot, her flip-flops lost or torn away. She didn't notice the sharp stones, didn't feel the ground at all beneath her feet. Everything below her waist was numb; the top part of her body bounced along on churning air. Other women ran too and mindlessly dragged small, crying children along with them. Left front doors open, shirts half-ironed, goats half-milked, breakfast dishes in the sink, and stew, soup, or beans on the stove to burn.

All at once, a line of vehicles, like beads on a string, clogged the lone paved road down the hollow, passing Ruby as she ran. All the dirt roads spewed cars and pickups and farm trucks on to it, their drivers as frantic as she was. When Della Mattingly stopped and yelled, "Get in!" Ruby jumped into the front seat. She didn't shut the door, though, left it open the whole way and sat with Bowman's wet shirt bunched up tight in her hands.

Della skidded to a stop where the stampede had pulled up short in front of Harlan #7, an unimpressive hole in the base of the mountain across from the hollow.

The stunned, silent crowd stared at it wide-eyed—watched the mouth of the coal mine vomit a black cloud of dust and smoke into the bright, fall sunshine.

Words were too painful to form and too jagged to speak so nobody said anything, just made little whimpering sounds, some of them, like a baby rabbit run over by a tractor.

The bell on the Baptist church began to ring. *Dong. Dong. Dong.* A mournful cry nobody needed to hear to know disaster had struck. Every man, woman and child for 10 miles around Aintree Hollow had heard the blast and felt the earth shake. All of them understood instantly what the quaking rumble meant—and *who* it meant. The day shift crew was at work at the far end of a maze of dark shafts that stretched more than a mile into the base of the mountain. At least twenty, maybe as many as thirty miners—husbands, sons, fathers, brothers—were bent over beneath a 48-inch roof digging at a coal seam 2,500 feet below the mountaintop.

Ruby's husband was down there! Her brother Ed was too. So was Will, and her son-in-law, Jody. And the youngest of Ruby's four children, her only son, Ricky Dan. Just turned 25, Ricky Dan had finally popped the question and planned to get married before Thanksgiving. But that was before Harlan #7 exploded on a sunny October afternoon and blew him apart. Or Black Mountain crushed

3

him under a million tons of rock and dirt. Or buried him alive, maybe, left him to gasp for breath down there in the dark until there was no air left.

Twenty years later

Will Gribbins is pretty sure the creature inching on little clawed feet up his pants leg is a rat. It has to be. What other animal hangs around a dumpster behind a pizza parlor—a squirrel? That rheumy-eyed old man in the bunk next to Will's at the shelter hated squirrels. Said once, "Squirrels are nothing but rats with good PR."

The remark strikes Will as riotously funny and he roars with laughter—which doesn't appear to sit well with the rat in his pants because it bites him, sinks its sharp teeth deep into the boney flesh of his thigh. The lightning bolt of pain momentarily sobers him and Will pummels the wiggling lump with his fist as he struggles to leap to his feet so he can shake it out of his pants. But he can't stand up and is only able to rise far enough to stagger backward and collapse on a pile of black plastic garbage bags that overflowed from the dumpster.

He flops around on his back, shrieks in agony, and tries to roll over on the rat, using his weight to crush it. The animal fights back and bites him again and again. The struggle rips open one of the garbage bags and a choking, putrid stench rises from it, but Will is too drunk and in too much pain to notice. He writhes in rotted food. Pieces of pizza stick to his hair; grease and lettuce slimy with Italian dressing slather goo on his back.

Then his hand lands on something solid—a stick, a pipe! He grabs it and slams it down on the lump in his pants. The creature takes a hunk out of his leg before Will can hit it again. Then he hammers the beast over and over until it is still.

4

Will finally drops the pipe and falls back in the garbage panting, sobbing, his leg ablaze in pain. As soon as he catches his breath, he holds on to the side of the dumpster to steady himself and pulls slowly upward until he's standing—on one leg. He sways like he's on the deck in a rolling sea. With the stink of cheese gone bad and rancid marinara sauce in his nostrils, he tries to shake the dead rat out of his pants. But it's jammed in there, stuck. He leans against the dumpster, unsnaps his filthy jeans, and eases them down toward his knees until the bloody rat carcass plops out on the pavement. In the dim glow of the streetlight at the end of the alley, Will examines his leg. It's covered in blood, his and the rat's. Puncture wounds up and down his thigh from his knee to his crotch pour streams of warm liquid, black in the sickly, yellow light. Each wound is a separate agony. It's like they're on fire, like each one is a red-hot coal—

> *Will freezes.*

> "Coal," *a voice whispers in his ear.*

> *"Who said that?" Will whirls around, almost falls and has to grab the dumpster to keep from losing his balance. He peers into doorways, dark recesses and shadows, and asks again, his voice trembling, his words slurred. "Who said that?"*

> *A breeze scatters the trash at his feet, rustles newspapers, and sends them scurrying along in the darkness. An empty soft drink can rolls noisily down the alley; the clinking sound echoes eerily against the brick walls until it clunks into a fence.*

> *And the wind sighs, its voice haunting, "Coal."*

Will reached down unconsciously and massaged his thigh to ease away the shadow pain he still felt from the rat bites 9 months ago that had gotten infected and almost killed him.

"Hurt your leg, didja?" the bearded truck driver asked. Will looked over at him, startled. "I seen you rubbin' it's all. I's workin' in a dog hole mine once, seen a man get his leg mashed plumb off by a scoop."

A dog hole mine was exactly what its name implied—a hole in the ground no better than a dog could dig, a dangerous pit operated outside all the boundaries with no regard for the safety of the coal miners inside.

Will knew about dog hole mines; he'd worked in one—had barely escaped dying in one.

The coal truck bumped down into a pothole the size of a bathtub and Will grabbed the old leather seat to keep from being dumped into the floorboard. Some things hadn't changed in 20 years. Two decades' worth of weight restrictions and highway regulations obviously hadn't made a lick of difference. The huge coal trucks still tore up the roads.

"I didn't injure my leg, break it or anything. It just aches sometimes where I got bitten by..." Will edited his response at the last second, no need to gross the guy out, make him ask even more questions. "...a squirrel."

That was dumb!

"A squirrel? How in the Sam Hill'd you get bit by a *squirrel?*" The man moved to one side the plug of Skoal swelling his lower lip like a wasp sting and spit a stream of brown liquid out the window. A considerable amount didn't make it past his beard. "Musta had rabies. In these woods, you mostly got to worry 'bout rabid skunks and foxes—not squirrels."

Will looked out the dirty truck window. He knew what you had to worry about in these woods.

The steep, tree-lined Appalachians rose around him like giant ramparts protecting a castle, their autumn splendor set against a blue sky dotted with cotton-ball clouds tethered like hot-air balloons to the treetops. The medley of color splashed on the hillsides—claret-wine red, the gold of a Spanish doubloon, smiley-face yellow, the deep russet of a chestnut foal's coat or an auburn-haired toddler, cloverleaf green and an amber shade of brown—reminded Will of Scottish clan tartans. No, it was the other way around. The clan tartans he'd seen in tourist shops on the Isle of Skye had reminded him of autumn in the mountains.

Will soaked it all up, warm oil on chapped skin. There was profound comfort in the mountains' agelessness, as if time itself had been so taken by their velvet beauty it was reluctant to move on—and profound delight in the everlasting newness of crisp, clear images, their edges sharp as sabers, a wet oil painting still glistening with morning dew.

As the empty coal truck bumped deeper into the paint-splattered mountains, each twist and turn opened up a view more hauntingly familiar than the last.

They passed Pine Mountain Taxidermy Shop—"You rack it, we'll pack it." Pine Mountain—God's practical joke on the coal companies. The rock strata in that one mountain had been pushed upward so the coal seams ran vertical instead of horizontal. No way to mine vertical coal without ripping the whole mountain apart, and Will didn't think even King Coal could get away with strip-mining Pine Mountain.

The farmhouse/office of Joe Tungate's Used Cars flew past the truck window. Five vehicles, half a dozen birdbaths and a flock of concrete ducks sat in the front yard there awaiting adoption. A hand-painted sign nailed to a nearby fence post offered HAND-PAINTED SIGNS for sale. The Convenience Store around the next bend promoted Kentucky lottery tickets: "Somebody's got to win; might as well be you!" along with the Kentucky Fried Chicken Restaurant in Hazard: "Eat supper with the Colonel tonight."

The sign out front of the Four Square Full Gospel Pentecostal—pronounced Penny-costal—Church proclaimed: "You not believing in hell don't put the fire out!"

7

Trailer houses, alone or in small herds, were affixed to the hillsides with round white stickpins. Will had heard they'd declared the satellite dish the official flower of West Virginia and it was plain the seeds had blown across the state line.

The road hugged Stinkin' Creek, that spilled in a white cascade back the way they'd come. The sides of the valley rose so sharply on either side in some places there was room only for the creek, the road, the railroad tracks and the shaft of sunlight that shone down between the ridges.

Five hours of sun.

Will had grown to manhood in more shadow than light, in a hollow so deep the mountains only granted it direct sunlight 5 hours a day. The sun cleared the top of the mountain to the east of Aintree Hollow about 10 o'clock every morning and then dropped down behind the one to the west by three in the afternoon. Of course, it didn't matter if the sun was shining and it was 100 degrees in the shade, or if it was raining like a big dog or snowing a blizzard. Down in the coal mines, it was always the deepest dark ditch of midnight. Fifty-eight degrees and dawn never broke there.

Will forcibly shook off the image of headlamp beams shining out like pallid light sabers into dusty blackness and concentrated on figuring out why he wasn't moved in some intensely emotional way by what he saw. The splendor of the mountains folded protectively around the hollows was the canvass on which his dreams had been painted every night for decades. Every night the nightmares didn't mug him, beat him senseless, and leave him bloody and broken—reaching out for the blessed comfort of oblivion.

Why didn't he feel…well, *something?* The ragged ache of homesickness had throbbed like a rotted tooth in those early years, took his breath away as he stood on the deck of some ship in some ocean and stared at flat blue water all the way to the horizon. How he'd longed then to swing on a grapevine over a creek, or go sangin'—hunting for ginseng in the woods. How desperately his soul had yearned to hear his own sound, the one-of-a-kind Eastern Kentucky dialect it had taken years of concentrated effort to erase from his own speech.

So why couldn't he manage to conjure up a single emotion now?

Maybe he had mourned so long all the feelings had finally bled out of him.

No, that wasn't it. It wasn't that he didn't feel *anything*. He did, just not what he'd expected. He felt—normal. The sights that greeted him looked sublimely ordinary. Everything else he'd seen in the past 20 years—that was foreign. This was reality, like waking from a dream and seeing the walls of your own bedroom, the curtains stirring in a breeze perfumed by wisteria, honeysuckle, and the ancient outhouse in the backyard.

He'd been screwed up to feel something big—euphoric, maybe. More likely some razor-edged emotion that would slice him open if he got anywhere near it. So he gladly settled for what he felt instead. Peaceful. For these few moments as he lumbered along the rutted road back into his world, the warring factions inside him declared a truce. The weight of pain he carried every day lifted; the fear that consumed him abated; the guilt that was his constant companion faded. And the compulsion, the itch that screamed every second to be scratched—even that eased.

His eyes filled with unexpected tears and he turned his face toward the window, his own reflection in the dirty glass superimposed on the view he could see through it like one of the haints Ma Sparrow teased would slither up out of the graveyard when the moon was full. And for an instant, he could see the faint image of a ghost in the reflection—the ghost of the shattered young man who'd run away from his whole life, fled everything and everybody he knew or cared about. Then it was gone and what stared back at him was the ruin of a face. All hard lines and sharp edges—haggard, drawn, and gaunt.

Eyes once a bright, arresting ice blue were now the color of faded denim, sunk deep in hollows, underlined by dark shadows. Way-too-early furrows in his brow and around his mouth, a thick scar on his chin, skin ashen, thinning hair almost as gray as brown that hung limp over the tops of his ears. Will needed a haircut.

"Where was you at when that squirrel gotcha'?" asked the coal truck driver who'd offered to "carry" Will up the mountain when he saw him walking along the roadside of the Kingdom Come Parkway with everything he owned in a borrowed turquoise-and-black gym bag. The irony had struck Will as he climbed up into the rig—he'd left these mountains two decades ago hitching a ride on a coal truck; it was fitting that he came back the same way. "They cut its head off and test it? 'Cause rabies can stay in your guts for years, sleepin' like, then one day it'll whup up on you and you'll start to foamin' at the mouth. Wait that long, though, and it'll be too late and they cain't do nothin' 'bout it."

"Can't" pronounced so it rhymed with "saint." Welcome home, Will.

"I had great medical care," he told the driver with a smile. "Matter of fact, these bites saved my life. If I hadn't gotten bit, I'm sure I'd be dead by now." Before the man had time to question further, Will waved him off. "Complicated story and you'd be welcome to hear it, but this is as far as I need to go. If you'd pull over up there at that dirt road, I can walk the rest of the way."

The driver eased the truck to a stop. Will thanked him, sincerely touched that the generous mountain spirit he remembered hadn't faded with the years. He climbed down out of the rig and watched the big truck lumber away, dribbling little pieces of coal out the back as it bumped along.

CHAPTER 2

THE CHERRY POPSICLE the little Hayes boy'd snitched out of the dairy case on the back wall was melting—in his hip pocket. He reached his hand back and felt the sticky wetness and the look of panic that instantly spread across his little-kid features was downright comical.

"You *was* plannin' on paying for what you got there, wasn't you?" JoJo Sparrow asked him innocently and bit down on her lip to keep a straight face. When the boy started to drag the mushy mess out of his pocket, she pointed out, "Don't you think it's a little late to return it?"

"I ain't got no money right now," he stammered, his face a brighter shade of red than either his hair or the growing wet spot on his backside. He glanced out the glass door at a man pumping gas into a beat-up pickup truck. "I can't ask…I gotta go find my granny. She'll give me a dollar if'n I bring back the change."

It would be easy to let the kid off the hook, but JoJo wouldn't be doing the boy any favors if she did. The kindest thing she could do was to scare the bejeebers out of him now, before his daddy caught him stealing something else someday and beat the crap out of him. Not that thievery was a moral issue with Skeeter Hayes. He had a chop shop in the barn out back of his place. BMWs, Lincoln Town Cars, Cadillacs, Porsches, and Lexuses stolen from Lexington went in one side of that barn and untraceable car parts, batteries, transmissions, and Mag Wheels came out the other. But your own little boy stealing—now that was another thing altogether! A man had to raise up his kids proper, didn't he, teach them right from wrong—*beat* it into them if he had to.

JoJo shook her head. Skeeter wasn't smart enough to see any contradiction in that.

She stepped out from behind the counter, looked very official in the red Jiffy Stop smock she wore over her jeans, and her long, blond hair pulled back neatly in a ponytail. She stared down at the terrified 6-year-old.

"You listen here to me Riley Hayes," she said, her voice stern. "I know what you done. It's called *shopliftin'.* Stealin'. I could pick up the phone right now and call Sheriff Jack. He'd come over here, slap handcuffs on you, and haul you off to jail!"

The boy's face went from the crimson of embarrassment to the chalk white of abject terror in the space between one heartbeat and the next. He didn't say a word, just stared doe-eyed up at JoJo. The spray of freckles on his face stuck out like red sequins; his bottom lip trembled.

"Give me that popsicle," she demanded and held out her hand.

The boy dug at the slush in his jeans pocket; all he managed to retrieve was two mush-covered sticks and a wad of wet wrapper.

"This popsicle costs 50 cents. That's a lot of money." She paused for effect. "But *just this once* I'm gonna let you come back and pay me for it later, the next time you're here." The boy almost collapsed in a puddle of soggy relief. "You got to earn it, though. Feed the chickens or wash your daddy's truck." The boy shook his head frantically up and down. "Don't you bring me money somebody give you." He shook equally frantically side to side. "Now scat!"

The child turned and bolted out of the store, trailing a little red convoy of popsicle droppings on the floor behind him.

For a moment, JoJo let the thought of having Darrell's child flit through her mind like a bright blue hummingbird zipping from one flower to the next—a cute little red-haired boy like Riley.

Who'd grow up to be a miner and get killed like his daddy and his granddaddy and his great granddaddy.

Come to think of it, he'd be lucky if that's what *did* happen. There were worse ways to die than in a mine.

JoJo stepped back behind the counter, banished the image of a child from her mind and concentrated instead on figuring out where she could get her hands on a gun. Not a rifle; those were as common in the hollow as bumps on a pickle. But a rifle wouldn't work. Her arms weren't long enough. With the barrel of a rifle pointed at her head or stuck in her mouth, she wouldn't be able to reach the trigger to pull it. No, she needed a handgun—a pistol.

JAMEY SPARROW BRUSHED back the blond hair that had fallen into his eyes and wondered what his hands would decide to make today.

He picked up two lumps of coal, one about the size of his fist and one big as a small watermelon. When he did, he felt the tickly, fluttery feeling in his belly he always got when he commenced to working on one of his arts.

He set aside the smaller rock and fixed his attention on the watermelon one.

Just touching coal made Jamey feel warm all over, like he was holding sunshine in his hand. Granny said that's what the old-timers had called it, black sunshine, because coal was made of squashed-up plants, and it give off the light and heat the sun had give them plants. Jamey liked the thought of holding a lump of sunshine in his hand and a smile stapled itself to his cheeks with deep-dish dimples. He liked every kind of coal—some of it hard and brittle, dark as the night sky but shiny; other pieces, flat black like a iron skillet, softer and more crumbly. He loved the feel of coal, all slicky-like, and the smell…

Jamey's smile faltered. Neighbors said coal didn't have no smell, laughed at him when he told them it did, too. They said he was storying. Made him cry so hard Granny'd marched over there and give them what for. That was when she'd still go all the way to the fence. She'd raised her voice even, said she'd put a quietus on the lot of them if they didn't stop tormenting her Jamey Boy.

Jamey held the black rock up to his nose and breathed in. That day the Jewetts got so put out with him, Ray-Ray had sneered, "If'n coal smells, what does it smell like?"

Jamey'd told him, "Coal smells like the color black, you mow-ron." Ray-Ray just run off laughing.

He took another deep breath of the dull-as-smoke rock in his hand and his smile grew wider. Then it faded again, slipped down off his face entirely and he sighed.

Jamey loved coal and it troubled him something fierce that the other miners who spent their lives digging coal out of the mountain alongside him didn't have no fondness for it at all. They was all the time down there in the dark keeping company with it, touching it, and caring for it like he done.

"How could they *not* love coal?"

He heard his voice and knew he'd spoken his thought. He clamped his hand over his mouth! He was supposed to *think* a thought and then *decide* if he wanted to say it, not spew out whatever was in his head like spitting watermelon seeds out his mouth. Granny *said*. But wasn't nobody to hear him except ValVleen and she wasn't no tattletale.

"You ain't gonna tell on me, are you ValVleen?" he asked the bright yellow canary perched on his shoulder.

The bird cocked its head to one side and studied him, then let fly a warbling bird song full of tweets, chirps, and whistles that sounded just like she'd answered Jamey's question. Oh, how Jamey ached to understand what ValVleen said! He'd tried, struggled hard, listened close as he could, sometimes seemed he was almost there—like when you hear somebody talking in another room and you can almost make out what they're saying but not quite. Maybe if he was…what was it Granny'd told Ma Jewett?

Jamey grew very still. His only movement was unconsciously wiggling the fingers of both hands in his lap, intertwined like they were dancing. That's what he always did when he put all his energy into thinking.

Granny'd said… *They's folks quicker on the uptake than my Jamey Boy.* Yeah, that was it! He was proud that he'd remembered. So maybe if his uptake was faster, he'd know what ValVleen was saying. But then it struck him that didn't nobody else understand bird songs neither so it didn't appear being able to uptake quick, whatever that meant, was any help.

Jamey puckered up and made smooching sounds at the bird. The canary hopped over and pecked his lips and kept on singing, *chirp, chirp, chirr, tweet, chirp, rbbb-rbbb, whistle, peep-peep.* The world was full up with things Jamey loved, but coal and the sound of ValVleen's songs was so dear, his throat hurt from the joy of them sometimes— like he was about to cry.

The bird didn't sing much as she used to, though. There was a time ValVleen chirped from morning to night, didn't never stop once. All mine canaries did. That's how miners like Jamey's grandfather knew to drop their picks and run—when the birds *stopped* singing. ValVleen still sang a lot, but not all the time no more. Probably because she was getting old.

Fear spread out in Jamey's belly like icicles forming from snow runoff on the roof. His eyes filled with tears that didn't have nothing to do with joy. No! Can't think about ValVleen getting old. Next thing that happened after a body got old was they *passed.* Can't think about ValVleen...*dying*. JoJo said he needed to start considering it, get himself ready, said ValVleen'd already lived way longer than most canaries. But Jamey wouldn't do it, *couldn't* do it. Life without ValVleen would be....

He started to breathe hard, pant like a hound dog chasing a coon and broke out in a sweat even though it was cool in the shed he'd soon need a coat on to work out here.

He let out a little peep of a cry and streams of tears slipped down his face when he blinked. Then ValVleen hopped back over close to his cheek and cocked her head, like she wanted to comfort him, and Jamey pushed the awful thoughts that made him sad and scared right out of his mind. He couldn't let himself wander around out there in tomorrow; it was dark and scary and spooky out there. Today was warm, happy, and good. He'd stay right here in today.

CHAPTER 3

WITH A BALL-PEEN hammer raised high above her head—it was all she could lay her hands on quick—Ruby Sparrow got down on her knees fast as she could and eased the trash basket away from the wall. The little gray mouse hidden behind it took out across the worn linoleum as she slammed the hammer down at it, missed it by inches—*bam! bam! bam!*—all the way across the kitchen. She thought she had him sure when she cornered him up against the refrigerator. But before she could squash him, he squeezed between it and the cabinet and was gone.

Ruby sat back on her heels and brushed a tendril of curly white hair out of her face.

"Think you got away from me, do ya? Well, you got two or three more thinks comin' if you b'lieve the two of us is just gonna live here together all friendly like. You best find wherever you come in here this mornin' and go right back out the same way. I ain't gonna have me no mice in my house!"

She reached up and grabbed the cabinet and pulled herself slowly to her feet, turned and eyed the calico cat sprawled on its back in the spot in front of the glass doors where sunlight warmed the rug for a few hours every day.

"Fat lot of good you done, Crawdad," she grumbled. "You're lazier'n a Mason jar full of slugs." She walked over and nudged the cat with her foot. "Hey, you. I'm talkin' to you."

The cat opened one eye, looked up at her, then rolled over on its side and went back to sleep.

"Come Monday a week when Lloyd takes Jamey Boy's arts to that gallery in Lexington, I'm gonna pack you 'long with him so's he can drop you off at the animal shelter." She paused. "You see if I don't!"

All right, she might be bluffing Crawdad, but she had pure intent toward that mouse! She'd fairly well do *something* about that critter even if it meant Jamey Boy had to move the refrigerator out from the wall and stuff steel wool into every itty-bitty crack and cranny behind it. Most times a mouse'd move out before it'd chew through steel wool.

Of course, it was bound to happen, mice and such. Trailer houses, especially a double-wide like hers, wasn't built snug as a proper house. And this one was going on fifteen, no, more like 18 years old. It was already used when Jamey Boy set the house afire with that butane lighter he found up next to the Jewett's fence. And he was only four then.

She and JoJo'd been out working in the garden while Jamey Boy was supposed to be taking a nap. When he was little, he was always poorly and he'd been up the night crying with an earache. So she left him asleep while she and his sister dug some carrots to put in soup for supper.

The garden had been way in the back of the yard then. Ruby paused, considered how she hadn't been out that far in years. Bow'd made the garden so big the back side was right up next to the woods and the deer was all the time eating her tomato plants and pole beans. Had to tie plastic grocery sacks to sticks to flap in the wind and scare them away.

She hadn't smelled the smoke that day; wind was blowing the other direction. JoJo seen it, though, screamed and pointed. Ruby liked to died when she turned and flames was licking up out of the roof. She run back in the house and found Jamey in the living room crying, his hand all red, still holding on to that lighter.

She scooped him up and run outside and then the three of them stood there with the neighbors and watched the house burn all the way to the ground. Didn't even seem real when she was watching. It was like looking in through the window at a kitchen in hell—the table blazing and the curtains curled up, wiggling and dancing in the flames. It didn't take no time at all for the fire to eat up that brittle old wood house. Volunteer fire department from Harlan got there and wasn't nothing left but smoldering timbers.

Ruby lost everything she owned but the clothes on her back that day—not that she'd had a whole lot more than that to begin with. But she didn't mourn none of it except her pictures and their tags, Bow's and Ricky Dan's. When a miner checked in for his shift, he took a tag that had his name and Social Security number on it from the "out" side of a Peg-Board and put it on the "in" side. The Wilson Cooper Mining Company gave her and the other families the tags their men had put up on the Peg-Board the day Harlan #7 exploded. The tags was what they got instead of bodies to bury. The company never did find none of them miners, just sealed up the mine and shut it down. Said there wasn't no bodies to recover, fire that hot, burning in the coal at the face. Said there couldn't possibly be nothing left. Ruby couldn't deal with the thought of *nothing*. When she looked at Black Mountain, she seen it as a headstone over a *grave* that held her husband and son, and her brother and son-in-law.

After the house fire, her daughters Stella, Ruth Ann and Charity pitched up and got her and the little ones the trailer. If she'd known that's what they were planning, she'd have stopped them. Didn't none of the three of them have money for a thing like that, trying to keep food on their own tables like they was. Well, Ruth Ann had a little more than her sisters. After Jody died in #7, she'd married the man who run the Walmart in Somerset and he got all the trailer's appliances for next to nothing, scratched ones from the warehouse. Even got a clothes dryer so Ruby didn't have to hang out the laundry no more.

That was good; the clothesline was out past the circle.

She turned to put the hammer back in the catchall drawer, between the Duct Tape and the Bondo Lloyd used to patch the aluminum skirting around the bottom of the trailer. Her elbow caught the mail JoJo'd brought in and put on the counter and the pile dumped onto the floor. She didn't even have to bend over to see the story on the front page of the *Harlan County Daily Enterprise.*

Memorial Service Planned Friday on Twentieth Anniversary of Harlan #7 Explosion.

Today was Monday. The anniversary of the worst day in her life was 4 days away. She didn't need no memorial service to remember that.

"Why cain't they leave it be?" she asked Crawdad quietly. "Just leave it be."

◊ ◊ ◊ ◊ ◊

WILL HEFTED THE strap of the gym bag over his shoulder and looked down the dirt road in a silence so profound the air was burdened by the weight of it.

He had always been struck by the contrast of the quiet of the mountains above ground with the cacophony at the face of hundreds of coal mine shafts down in their roots. The ear-numbing, vibrating, rumbling roar of the continuous miner as it chewed into the coal seam with slashing tungsten-carbide bits as sharp as a giant shark's teeth. The thump and rattle of hunks of coal dumped behind it. The clattering of the shuttle cars and the squall of the conveyor that carried the coal away. All the sounds bounced off rock walls, fractured and multiplied in a space only 20 feet wide by 4 feet tall.

Will stood by the roadside and listened, imagining he could hear an echo of the rumble under the mountains. But there was a silence here more than the mere absence of sound. It had substance of its own, a life-form warming itself before the sun disappeared behind the ridge and afternoon shadows stretched out fingers of darkness across the valley. Then he heard the murmured music of the woods, the arthritic creak of ash, hickory, sugar maple, white, and red oak trees in the breeze—a faint screech like treading on stairs in an old house or opening a gate on rusty hinges.

A mine was never completely silent either, even when all the machinery was turned off and the vibrations calmed. There was the constant drip, drip, drip of water. And when you ripped out miles of coal beneath a mountain, millions of tons of rock, soil, and water above the missing coal shifted. Rocks cracked and fractured, layers split, the immense pressure threatened to rip open the roofs of mine shafts or rupture the sides. Then the mountain had a voice. Its groans, squeaks, pops, and rumbles spoke to the old-timers as clearly as all the fancy monitoring devices; it whispered warnings to those with ears to hear, told them to run for their lives back out into the light while there was still time.

Will put his hand up to his forehead to shade his eyes—habit—there was no glare. He figured it'd be a hike from here to Aintree—the name of both the "holler" and the little town at its base. All the way around the side of the mountain, then down into the steep valley on the other side. But he had all the time in the world. And now that he was actually here, with a clear understanding that what happened in the next few days would determine whether he lived or died, the familiar knot-in-the-belly dread returned. Only here, this close to it all, simple dread morphed into a fear as cold as a shark cruising dark currents in a night sea.

He took a deep breath and set out walking, kicked up puffs of fine dust in the road with every step. Didn't rush, though. Will Gribbins was in no hurry to make his way to Aintree Hollow. No hurry whatsoever.

CHAPTER 4

As JoJo composed a mental list of everybody she could think of who owned a handgun, the old fellow who lived up Goat Rope Ridge came through the door and flashed her a toothless smile. He was wearing a wife-beater T-shirt, blue jeans cut off at the knees, high white socks and muddy work boots with the laces untied. She didn't know the old man's real name. He'd been called Tugboat ever since his crew at the Hard Rock Mine near Hazard had cut into old works—the Boogie Man of coal mining.

There'd been somebody or another digging coal in Kentucky since 1820, so all the mountains were riddled with abandoned mine shafts—some of them mapped, most of them not. Over the years, those empty shafts, called old works, had filled up with all kinds of stuff and none of it was good. Explosive levels of methane gas. Deadly carbon monoxide. Carbon dioxide called Black Damp that left no oxygen in the air. A crew that accidentally cut into one of those old shafts usually paid for the mistake with their lives. Tugboat was the only one of his crew who made it out when they hit old works full of water. The rest of them drowned, but Tugboat somehow managed to float out of the mine hanging onto a wooden roof beam.

The old man picked up an RC Cola, two Slim Jims, a Moon Pie and a packet of Red Man Chewing Tobacco and handed them to JoJo to check out.

"Some'm wrong, Missy?" he asked as she put the items into a sack. "You got the sorrowfulest look on yore face."

His kindness left JoJo momentarily speechless.

"Looks like you could use a hug," Tugboat said, his watery blue eyes fixed on hers. "I ain't choicey no more. I don't git a hug more'n onct in a blue moon, so I take 'em where I can git 'em and I hand 'em out the same way." He hobbled around the end of the counter, wrapped the surprised girl in his arms and squeezed. Then he gave her a fatherly pat on the shoulder, picked up his sack and limped out the door.

After Tugboat left, three strangers came in to pay for gasoline. Deer hunters. One of them, a fat man whose beer belly stretched out his camo T-shirt, flirted with JoJo, but she knew how to handle herself. She just did what Granny told her to do when she was a little girl if she ever come on a rattlesnake in the woods—stand real still and don't say nothing and eventually it'll lose interest and leave.

Then two coal truck drivers stopped in to buy scratch-off lottery tickets and made little piles of rubber crumbs on the counter as they rubbed down to the numbers with their blackened thumbnails. By the time she'd waited on them all, dusted off the countertop and the store was empty again, JoJo had decided it'd be too much trouble to find a gun. Besides, guns were scary.

You're afraid you might get hurt by the gun you're going to use to blow your brains out?

There was probably humor in that somewhere, but right now JoJo couldn't see it.

She'd thought of an easier way, neater and cleaner, too. If anybody in Harlan County could lay hands on enough Oxycontin to drop a moose it was JoJo Sparrow. Not all the dealers had gotten busted in the sting that shanghaied Avery 8 days before their wedding and sent him on a 15-year, all-expenses-paid vacation in the Kentucky State Penitentiary in Eddyville.

She shivered. Sometimes the reality of what her life had become since then slammed into her like a wrecking ball—19 years old; she'd just turned *nineteen!* But whenever she instinctively backed up from what she had to do, the way you yank your hand away from a hot stove, she thought about the skinnys, witch people who clawed at the air and drooled, their eyes wild.

Yes siree, there was plenty of worse ways to die than in a coal mine. And plenty of Oxy out there to make it all go away.

As soon as Will stepped out of the woods into the meadow at the top of Aintree Hollow, he finally got the emotional wallop he'd braced himself for. When he was at sea, there'd been days his soul sang such a song of longing for this place he imagined he could reach out his hand and the melody would wind around his fingers like a pet snake. Seeing it real now, not a vision, took his breath away.

The little town spread out below him had once been home to upwards of five hundred people, but that was before Harlan #7 massacred two dozen of the hollow's own in one screaming moment of agony. Or sucked the life out of them—one strangled gasp at a time. All of the 29 miners who were digging coal together when #7 blew were still buried under Black Mountain—except Will Gribbins and Lloyd Jacobs. They got out alive.

Will's eyes followed the line of the blacktop road that wound down the valley. A handful of streets—all of them paved now!—branched out from it like tendrils of asphalt morning glory weaving up the mountainsides. He could see the elementary school about half way down, grades one through six. Harlan County School District bus #32 carried students the 45-mile round trip into Harlan for junior and senior high. He could also see three churches, a filing station, houses he recognized and some he didn't and the flag out front of the post office, which shared a building with a grocery store—at least it used to.

And down at the bottom, at the base of the hollow, sat the mine, about a hundred yards from where the road connected to the highway across a one-lane bridge over Turkey Neck Creek. From where he stood, it was an insignificant hole in the side of the highest crest in Kentucky, 4,135-foot Black Mountain, which towered more than 2,500 feet above the valley floor.

In the beginning, when he first left the mountains and realized the rest of the world got their understanding of coal mining from the movies, he'd tried to set the record straight. Tried to help the people he met understand what it really was like.

You don't sling a pick over your shoulder and ride an elevator down into a long, dark tunnel deep underground. In Eastern Kentucky, most of the coal mines aren't under the ground beneath your feet; they're under the mountain you're standing beside, so you ride straight in seated on a train called a mantrip. Get comfortable; it could be a long ride. The coal you're about to dig is at the far end of a maze of shafts that could stretch 10 miles into the mountain. *And forget about standing up and stretching when you get there. Forget about standing up at all! You work your whole shift bent over, squatting or on your hands and knees. The shaft roof is only about 4 feet off the floor—because that's how thick the coal seam is—and not a coal company on the planet would dig out the rock above the seam just to make the shaft comfortable for the miners. Moving rock costs money; miners with bad backs can be replaced.*

But the long-dark-tunnel part—you got that right! Only there's not just one of them. Imagine that a two-hundred-fifty-floor building (one that's 30 miles long and 15 miles wide) had a base of solid gold 4 feet thick. You, of course, want the gold. How would you get it out? If you just dug into it and started hauling it away, pretty soon the building would collapse on top of you. But what if you left big hunks of the gold base behind, 50-by-50-foot squares of gold every 18 feet to hold up the building while you removed all the gold around them, with shafts going long-ways and connecting tunnels called breaks going crossways. When you were finished, you'd leave a grid under the building, like a map of a city with main arteries and cross streets, a honeycomb of empty shafts and square support pillars. That's what the inside of a Kentucky coal mine looks like.

By the way, the coal companies don't leave those 50-by-50-foot coal pillars behind forever. Eventually, they send miners back in to harvest them in a process called "robbing the coal." The miners start at the face of the mine at the far end of the shafts, dig out the pillars one by one and replace them with 12-inch-thick wooden beams to hold up the roof—until the pressure snaps the beams like toothpicks and the roof collapses. Robbing the coal is the most dangerous operation in mining.

But after a while, Will stopped trying to explain. It was too complicated. And merely understanding the process didn't tell you anything that really mattered about coal mining. Nothing short of doing the job could teach you that.

He could see a flurry of activity at the entrance of Harlan #7, where a colony of miniature people scurried around, operating correspondingly small pieces of machinery.

He'd clocked a drunk Marine in Norfolk once for saying something like that. The Marine had started it, made fun of Will's accent—early on, before Will got rid of it. Called him a hillbilly. Hillbilly is a name mountain people call themselves and each other. It's not an insult when they use it; it is an insult when anybody else does. Then the jarhead had said coal miners were nothing but little boys playing with toy trucks, digging holes in the dirt.

That's when Will decked him, but his memory of the event ended abruptly a few seconds later when one of the Marine's buddies broke a beer bottle over his head.

He reached up and felt around but couldn't find the scar anymore. It had faded—unlike Will's emotional response to the view of the hollow below him. Far from fading, it had swelled unexpectedly huge in his chest.

But his reaction wasn't primarily to the sight of "where he was from," a far more important location than he ever would have dreamed when he left it. His hole-in-the-belly feeling was more specific. It focused on the meadow below him and the oak tree that stood at the edge of the woods above it. The day after Will turned 12, he and Lloyd had carefully arranged five empty Budweiser cans on the ground in front of that tree, a row of three on the bottom with the remaining two balanced on top of them.

"Like this?" he'd hollered at the figure who stood in the middle of the meadow holding Will's birthday .22 rifle in one hand and a beer in the other.

"Yeah," Ricky Dan had called back, "but hold your horses." The tall, broad-shouldered man with hair the color of corn silk and a shiny gold tooth that sparkled in his dimpled grin, tilted his head back and chugged the rest of a beer in one long gulp. "Now, you can have this 'un to set on top of them others."

Ricky Dan drank too much. Well, Ma Sparrow said he did, but in her view even one beer was too much. He cursed too—never in front of a woman, though. And the thing was, his weren't the ordinary swear words all the men used. His were…flamboyant and outlandish. Will had studied Ricky Dan's creative use of profanity for hours when the two of them were out sangin' in the woods. Then Will would go home, close the bathroom door, stand in front of the mirror and practice, sliding the words in between the syllables of normal words the way Ricky Dan did.

Everything about Ricky Dan was out there on the edge. At lease, it seemed that way to Will. He drove too fast, had too many girlfriends and laughed too loud, made a sound like a mama goose protecting her chicks. He ate his meals like he was sitting on a red ant bed, wolfed his supper down so quick Ma Sparrow warned he'd get piles from not chewing his food. Often, the meat on the table was venison; Ricky Dan dropped a buck the first day of deer season every year. The evening after the target practice with Will's .22, Ricky Dan had demonstrated for Will and Lloyd one of the rapidly disappearing Appalachian folk arts, handed down from generation to generation; he'd taught them how to light a fart without catching their underwear on fire.

Ricky Dan Sparrow was everything Will Gribbins aspired to be. Though Ricky Dan was only 7 years Will's senior, he seemed much older. That was because he'd quit school and gone to work in Harlan #7 when he was 16—2 years younger than the legal age for miners.

And if you were a miner—under age or not—you weren't a boy anymore; you were a man.

A noisy stampede of brittle leaves rattled along the autumn breeze down the road and Will stood transfixed, the image of Ricky Dan so real he was reluctant to breathe for fear movement would shatter it and send the jagged shards of it tinkling into the dirt. At the same time, he wanted nothing in life more than to escape the image, to turn and hightail it back over the mountain the way he'd come.

Mostly, he wanted a drink. No, *needed* a drink. Desire hadn't been part of the equation since…it didn't matter anymore when booze had finally bested him in the shell game. He understood now, though, knew that its seductive oblivion only magnified the squinty-eyed harshness of the reality that followed. He knew the merry-go-round of blackout-real-life-blackout was no kiddy ride, that booze held a cocked shotgun to his temple.

Only one tiny flickering light shown in the darkness in his soul that was deeper than the bowels of Harlan #7.

He shivered as much from the enormity of what he'd come here to do as from the chill fingers of the wind that tickled his neck under his collar. Then he walked resolutely down the road into the hollow, into his past and his future.

Chapter 5

J AMEY FIXED HIS mind on the lump of coal…wondering. He never knew what was hidden in a piece of coal, waiting to be set free. When he was only a boy and had just took up carving, he'd try to make the coal *be* something. An ashtray for Mr. Jewett, who smoked like a chimney even though Ray-Ray said his daddy coughed up blood. A squirrel, a duck, even a church house. But the coal didn't like being forced to be something it wasn't. Usually it'd break, crumble in his hands, like if it couldn't be what it wanted to be, what the good Lord had put it on this earth to be, it wouldn't be nothing at all. It took Jamey a long time to figure that out, but soon's he did, he didn't have no trouble with the coal at all.

Of course, he also figured out along the way that he couldn't use just any old piece of coal to do his arts because most of it was either too soft and flaky, or so hard and brittle it shattered. For his statues, he needed cannel coal, the dull, black coal you could break a piece off of and light it afire like a candle. There wasn't a whole lot of cannel coal in the shafts around here and he used to go to the railroad tracks and dig through the coal piles for hours to find pieces of it.

But over the years, word got out about Jamey's carvings. Other miners'd ask him about them on lunch breaks down in the mine. And after a while, miners started to bring him pieces of cannel coal they'd come across, hunks big as pumpkins or small as lemons. And sometimes—not very often, mind, but sometimes—a miner would bring him a piece of *jet!* Jamey hadn't never seen none of it his own self when he was working, but jet was fine indeed. It was real hard and you could polish it smooth and shiny as a piece of glass. JoJo looked it up in the encyclopedia at school, said it was a form of lignite coal. Said it was a semiprecious stone, too, and it sure enough was precious to Jamey! The biggest piece of it ever found was 21 feet long. Of course, Jamey never got his hands on *that* much of it, but when he did get pieces, he always carved images into the jet instead of carving the jet into the image of something else. It was real easy to break, but if you was careful, you could carve jet into murals—*relief* was what JoJo called it—more detailed even than his statues.

"Who are you, hidin' in there?" he asked the lump of coal. "You a dog or a squirrel? You a goat, maybe, or a skunk?"

He fixed his attention on the black rock in front of him and tried to see with his heart the image that was buried inside. He'd explained to JoJo once that carving wasn't nothing more than chipping away all the pieces of the rock that wasn't the statue inside.

As he placed the rock in the vice screwed down to his worktable, he thought of JoJo's late husband, Darrell, who had built the table for him out of two sawhorses and the back side of an old wooden door. He picked up his mallet and one of his chisels—the one that looked like a little scoop, like a fingernail turned upside down. Darrell had got him that, too, and all his other chisels and carving tools—paid his cousin who worked in a machine shop in Pikeville to make them special.

Darrell's face swam in front of Jamey for a moment, with the sideways grin he had that reminded Jamey of a pirate. He could almost hear Darrell's laugh, the kind of laugh that made everybody around him laugh too, even when they didn't know what was funny. Jamey didn't like who JoJo hooked up with next. Avery smelled bad, but it wasn't a stink you could sniff with your nose.

Jamey and Darrell had just got to be real good friends when the roof fall got him. It was a petrified tree stump, a big one. Miners was all the time finding the bottom parts of petrified trees in the roofs of their shafts because the trees grew alongside the plants that made the coal. Trees was funny looking when you seen them from the bottom side, from under the roots. And the stumps looked like they was outlined in Magic Marker because a thin coat of coal always formed around the outside of them.

There was miners found a petrified snake in a mine up Hazard one time, said the head of it was big as a basketball and there was all these little snakes around it. Jamey hadn't never run across no petrified snakes in the 3 years he'd been mining—just the ferns. The outlines of plants was all over the slate mine roofs, ferns and leaves, and such. And the stumps, of course. Jamey carried chalk in his pocket same as all the other miners did so he could draw a circle around them. Then the roof bolters would see and put a heavy metal strap across them to keep them from falling.

The stump that got Darrell had been marked and strapped proper, but it come down all the same, crushed him so's they had the satin cloth pulled all the way up to his chin at the funeral home and when JoJo tried to fold it down, Granny'd stopped her and said she didn't need to see what was underneath of that cloth.

Jamey had the growing feeling that what was hiding inside this piece of coal was a face—so maybe it was Darrell's face. But Jamey didn't think so. Only time would tell, of course, but Jamey suspected he was about to free up from this lump of coal the face of somebody he'd never met.

The chill autumn wind clawed at the side of the shed with dryleaf fingernails, then slid under the door and tickled Jamey's shoelaces. But he didn't notice. He was in that place he went to when he did his arts, that space outside the dusty shed, where he didn't hear scratchy leaves or ValVleen's song, didn't smell the coal he was working on. When he come back from that place, he'd find what he'd released from the rough-edged lump of coal, but he'd have very little remembrance of the part he'd played in setting it free.

RUBY BENT OVER slowly, picked up the newspaper off the floor and set it back on top of the mail on the counter, face down so's she didn't have to look at the headline about the memorial service.

But she hadn't got to be an old woman without figuring out somewhere along the way that ignoring a thing didn't make it go away. With the mine reopened, one of these days some suit-'n-tie from Black Gold Mining, the company that bought the property from Wilson Cooper, would come knocking on her door to tell her they'd found…something. All miners had nametags braded into their belts. Ruby shook her head, remembered how the other miners used to tease Ricky Dan because he couldn't keep up with his belt, said he'd got that gold tooth just so he wouldn't wind up under the wrong headstone someday. That hadn't been the way of it, of course. Ruby's mama'd passed first and when her daddy crossed over, his gold wedding band come down to Ricky Dan, him being the favorite grandson. Trouble was, that boy'd have lost his head if it wasn't tied on his shoulders, and he was scared he'd lose that ring. Then he figured a way to keep up with it! Went into Hazard and had a dentist make it into a gold cap over the front tooth he'd chipped when he was 8 years old.

Maybe that's what they'd bring her, that gold tooth. Ruby shivered at the thought of it. No, that's not why. She'd shivered because she knew they *wouldn't* bring her a tooth. With an understanding she'd never spoken out loud to a living soul, Ruby was one hundred percent certain that when they come, it'd be to tell her they'd found Ricky Dan. All of him.

Out on the front porch, Bucket began to bark. The dog was Jamey's—followed him everywhere he went. But he must have slept through it when Jamey left this morning because he was outside the door, making such an awful racket he woke up Crawdad. The big tomcat stretched slow and lazy, then got up and wandered toward the front door to check out the ruckus, his tail stuck up in the air behind him straight and stiff as a flagpole.

Ruby listened to the rise and fall of the old hound's howl like it was a song. Dog music. She knew all the big, lop-eared mutt's tunes and the high peel of this one was his "stranger warning." Since the near-blind animal knew everybody in the hollow, whoever was out there on the road was from away from here.

Surely, it wasn't nobody from the mining company. They hadn't even started to dig out the roof falls yet.

Ruby opened the door and looked out through the screen. A lone man in jeans and a blue shirt, a skinny fellow, walking down from the top of the hollow, a poke of some sort slung over his shoulder. She couldn't see a vehicle; he must have come down out of the woods. But he wasn't no deer hunter, didn't have a bow. Gun season was still 3 weeks off.

She watched the man as he got closer. He looked out of place and right at home at the same time, like he didn't fit a-tall and like he had leave to be here.

She opened the screen and stepped out on the porch.

"Shush up, Bucket." The hound kept barking, the high, keening sound he used to make when he chased coons in the woods. "I said hush!" She reached down and gave his collar a yank. "You be quiet now, hear."

The dog paid her no mind, never did anymore, got more ornery every year. She hung onto his collar—in an effort to shut him up, not for fear he'd attack the man on the road. You'd have to set that old dog's tail on fire to get Bucket off the porch. Wouldn't do no good if he did go after the stranger. Didn't have nary a tooth left in his whole head. But you'd never know it by the way he barked. The closer the fellow got, the more energy the dog put into announcing his presence.

A sudden, tickling chill ran down Ruby's spine. The way the man walked, long easy strides, smooth, almost graceful, but with his feet splayed out to the sides a mite, just short of a swagger.

Her heart suddenly rattled in her chest like a hummingbird fluttering around in there. She kept hold of Bucket's collar and moved around the rocking chair to the edge of the porch as if she intended to step down. She didn't, though, just teetered on the edge of the top step staring. Then she slowly raised her free hand and called out, "Hidy!"

The man stopped.

She knew.

"Well, hidy-do there…" Her soft voice began to tremble. "… Will!"

◊ ◊ ◊ ◊ ◊

WILL STOOD QUIET, lost in thought, the silence of the hollow broken only by a woodpecker in the woods and the lazy bark of a coon dog on the porch of a trailer house down the road.

It was one thing to acknowledge intellectually that everything in Aintree Hollow would be different after 20 years. It was quite another to see the changes face up, changes that shattered the mental snapshots he carried in little plastic sleeves in the back pocket of his mind.

The ruin of the house where he'd grown up had upset him. It shouldn't have. It was only his "home" by the strictest of definitions. He'd spent most of his growing-up years in Ma Sparrow's house after his mother left and his father won the Black Lung lottery, or lost it.

A lifetime of breathing coal dust didn't affect some men at all; for others, it was a death sentence. And Black Lung took a long time to kill a man.

Still, that was the house in the picture labeled *home* Will carried around in his head. An ordinary house in the shade of a mulberry tree, white paint flaking even then, distinguished only by a lone rose bush by the front porch and suicide swings in the backyard. Daddy'd made the swings from discarded tires he picked up at the filling station at the bottom of the hollow, suspended them on ropes from the limbs of oak trees facing each other across a 15-foot stretch of weedy grass. So if you timed it just right, and you got going real good in your swing and another kid got going real good in his—the two of you could smack together in mid-air.

Will remembered the time he and Lloyd had…He smiled.

The tire swings were gone now, of course. So was the house he remembered. In its place sat a battered shack with no rose bush and no front door, shattered windows and an uprooted mulberry tree dangling in to the living room through the hole its demise had cleaved in the roof.

The home place had not gone gently into that good night, though. It still fought tendrils of morning glory and honeysuckle vines and the voracious kudzu that had captured its front walls and was marching like a resolute soldier into the interior.

He wondered who owned the place now. Did *he?* Surely, the county had sold the land for taxes after his father died.

Yeah, right. Like somebody'd buy this *place!*

Didn't he give up his right to it when he never claimed it?

The sight of his own house wrecked should have prepared him for what lay down the road where the Sparrows' house was. Actually, where it *wasn't* anymore. There was nothing at all on the spot where it had sat but weeds and a few broken foundation stones that peeked up through them like a row of rotten teeth.

But was it really reasonable to expect to find anybody there after all this time? Ma would be in her 70s by now. And with the men gone, what would she do in that old house all by herself? She'd probably gone to live with one of the girls, if she was still alive at all.

What if she was dead?

For a moment, the swell of relief at not having to face her carried him along in a riptide of liberation. It was quickly replaced by a lonely ache that expanded like a Navy dinghy in his chest, growing instantly huge, as if grief were the food of giants.

Will wasn't accustomed to the flood of feelings that had clobbered him ever since he got here, one after another, with the force of a series of concrete Volkswagens dropped out a third-floor window on his head. Over the years, he had perfected a method of dealing with feelings that was simple and efficient—he anesthetized them! He had slathered varnish on his emotions, coat after coat, imprisoned them like mosquitoes in drops of amber. Every input on a caring level hit the slick surfaces and slid off.

And every output on a caring level was expressed the same way—*rage.* At what? Who did he have a right to be mad at? In any objective analysis of his life, he certainly wouldn't be labeled the injured party. *He* wasn't the victim. So why was he so furious?

Occasionally, he'd experience a moment of clarity when he was in that illusive state of inebriation where all pretense had been stripped away but he wasn't yet too tanked to think. In such moments, he knew the whole focus of his blinding rage was the watery-eyed drunk he got glimpses of now and then reflected in store windows. Or beer mugs.

The image of a frosty beer mug actually made his mouth water.

He needed a *drink!* And that wasn't going to happen. So he hefted his bag and continued down the hill. On the porch of a trailer up ahead, a coon dog's unconvincing bark started to ramp up. Will was too preoccupied to pay any attention to it.

He still had some money left. He could walk down to the mine and catch a coal truck back into Pineville, or on into Benham or Lynch, and find somewhere to stay the night. Tomorrow, he could come back and try to track down Ricky Dan's relatives—his *people*. His three older sisters would be nearby, likely still in the hollow. Families stuck close; those who left usually didn't go far or stay gone for long. His absence from Aintree Hollow might have set some kind of record.

"Hidy."

The voice fastened him in shackles. He turned slowly toward the porch where the dog was making such a racket.

"Well, hidy-do there…Will," Ma Sparrow said.

CHAPTER 6

I N A PRINT dress buttoned all the way to the neck under a blue
sweater, Ma Sparrow looked exactly like she always did. Okay,
not exactly, but she had weathered the past two decades far better than Will had. Tall, 5-10 maybe, and big-boned, she still carried
herself as erect as a plumb line. Thinner, though, fragile-looking, so
her big, strong hands, knobby with arthritis now, looked even more
man-ish. Her feet were clad in the kind of clunky black shoes Ricky
Dan had called "old-lady clodhoppers" and her unruly curls were
tamed in a braided bun at the back of her head—just like always.
They'd been the color of a 10-penny nail when Will left; now her
hair was the white of creek mist on a summer evening.

But her heavy eyebrows were still thick slashes of coal black
beneath a widow's peak on a long, narrow face—plain, bordering
on homely. Her cinnamon-colored eyes set deep inside an elaborate
spiderweb of smile wrinkles gazed at him with a look that was more
than surprise, a complicated look he couldn't read.

"You gonna stand out there in the road 'til the mailman
comes 'long tomorrow mornin' and runs you over?" She spoke so
softly he barely caught her words. For a big, raw-boned woman,
her voice was amazingly quiet and gentle, the kind that should
have made folks ask her to speak up. But nobody ever did. They

leaned in, got still and concentrated so they wouldn't miss a word. He'd always loved watching a room fall instantly silent when she started to speak.

Ma Sparrow could yell without raising her voice, could yank a rowdy boy's chain up short with a single soft word.

For a moment, she turned her attention to the barking dog she held by the collar, a big tan mutt with the woebegone face, floppy ears and doleful eyes of a coon hound on the body of a scraggly German shepherd.

"Hush up, Bucket!" She swatted the dog lightly on the snout and he yelped like she'd stabbed him. Then he plopped in a heap next to the rocking chair and fell instantly silent.

In that silence, Will finally managed to find his voice.

"You're as beautiful as ever, Ma."

She cocked her head to one side and the smile that graced her face was even warmer and more inviting than he remembered. And just as close-lipped. Sometime long before Will had come into her life, Ma Sparrow had perfected a smile that showed no teeth—because she had no teeth to show. Well, precious few, and the ones she had were blackened, broken, and twisted—like the teeth of the rest of her generation of mountain women who'd gone from cradle to grave without ever laying eyes on a dentist.

When she laughed, she always put her hand up over her mouth. He wondered if she still did. But the pleat that used to staple her dark eyebrows together whenever she was peeved about something—that much hadn't changed.

"Didn't I teach you not to story to me, Will Gribbins? You never was no good at it and 'pears you ain't growed into it none." She pulled the faded blue sweater closed around her, hugged herself against the chill in the breeze. "And it ain't Ma no more, it's Granny. Got me so many grandkids and great grandkids now they're gonna have to start wearin' nametags."

She'd knitted that sweater; Will was certain of it. He had no memory of her that her hands were still. They peeled potatoes, snapped peas, scrubbed floors, planted flowers in the front yard and vegetables out back. But they'd always looked too large for any kind of delicate work, too big to fit on a mandolin, too awkward to evoke the haunting melodies of mountain music on summer evenings as Ricky Dan played his guitar and Bowman made a fiddle sing.

Her hands had looked odd when they expertly piloted knitting needles, sewed on a button or patched a hole in a pair of his or Ricky Dan's jeans—back before holey jeans were a fashion statement. He'd watched her examine their clothes every night to make sure there were no rips or tears that might catch on something, get hung on a machine in the mine. She had cut up old shirts and sewn the pieces together for extra padding in the knees of their work pants. The knees always wore out first.

"Now, get yoreself up here on this porch so's I can have a look at you. My eyes ain't what they usta be."

He suspected her eyes were every bit as sharp as they had ever been, but he welcomed the invitation and fairly bounded up onto the porch.

Then he stood self-conscious for a moment until she reached out to him.

"Ain't you gonna give yore Granny no sugars?"

He folded the old woman tenderly into his arms. She smelled of homemade soap and felt much more frail than she looked. She hugged him back, tight, and made a little groaning sound in her throat. When he gave her a kiss on her wrinkled cheek, he could see the bright sheen of tears in her eyes.

"C'mon in this house, son," she scolded, and shooed him toward the door. "Me and you, we got us a powerful lot of catchin' up to do."

Will hated trailer houses; he had long suspected that hell itself had been designed to fit on a trailer hitch. The horrid tin boxes might be all a lot of people could afford, but in his eyes they were a blight on the landscape that stuck out on the mountainsides like pimples on an eighth-grader. If the decision were his, he'd make it a felony to bring one into Eastern Kentucky, and he'd blow up the ones already here. Mountain people would be better off in caves.

For all that, he was struck by several things when he stepped into this one. It had a large family room, separated from the open kitchen by a counter. A table and six chairs sat at the kitchen end of the room, a couch, two comfortable-looking chairs and a television set occupied the other end. A Nintendo that dangled from the television like a small tumor obviously provided entertainment for her herd of nameless grandchildren.

Neat, tidy, and *clean*. Will knew without looking that you could safely perform open-heart surgery on the kitchen floor. The room was bright too; most mountain homes were dreary. You needed a lot of windows to ward off gloominess when the sky never glowed yellow and pink at sunrise or ushered in the night in a blaze of a red-gold sunset, and when a day's 14 hours of sunlight translated into 9 hours of shadow. This room owed its cheeriness to patio doors that opened on the deck that encircled the whole structure. Will had admired its craftsmanship from the road. Whoever had built it was good with his hands.

A fat calico cat lay in front of the doors awaiting a sun that wouldn't shine through them again until tomorrow. The furniture was well-used but not beat-up and rickety. And here in the land of velvet-Elvis paintings, Granny's walls were exquisitely bare. In a culture skewed toward rubber tomahawks and Precious Moments figurines, Granny had adorned the room with striking artistry.

Simple carvings, beautifully crafted sculptures, and detailed relief murals—all made from some form of coal—were displayed like beautiful ornaments on a Christmas tree.

A menagerie of small figures—cats, goats, ducks, raccoons, mama bear and two babies—sat on shelves above the couch. An eagle snatched up a rabbit off the coffee table. A bookcase with no books was home to several busts, no one Will recognized except Granny. It was a remarkable likeness. Her face had not been glamorized; the artist had perfectly captured the simple dignity of her plain features and translated them into something like nobility.

What particularly drew Will's attention was a scene etched in relief on a slab of some form of coal that had been polished as shiny as the hood of a new car. Probably 3 feet wide, it hung above the fireplace mantle and Will stepped closer to get a better look. The detail in the artwork was astonishing. Three miners, lunch pails in hand, strode side by side toward a mine entrance in the background, so lifelike they could have been walking out of the room. Even shown from the back, each man was an individual. The one on the left had his helmet cocked back on his head and wore his pants tucked into his work boots. The man on the right wore a kerchief tied around his neck and was dressed in a T-shirt that showed his muscular arms. The man in the middle was the tallest and thinnest of the three. The shirt stretched tight across his broad shoulders was tucked into a pair of jeans rather than work pants, and he carried his helmet in his hand.

Will felt a sudden chill. The hair stood up on the back of his neck and goose bumps popped out on his arms. No, these three miners couldn't *possibly* be...

He turned to ask Granny about the mural—and the artist—but she loaded and fired first.

"Sit yourself down here on the couch. The spring's broke in that chair and it's all lumpy like, and that recliner goes all the way back if'n you ain't careful. Liked to dumped me out in the floor the other day."

She sat and patted the cushion next to her. Before Will's backside ever touched fabric, she said pleasantly, "I know what you come home for, son. But you don't. You think you do, but you're wrong."

Will collapsed the final 6 inches onto the couch when his knees buckled out from under him. Well, Granny always had been open and direct.

"You wouldn't never left in the first place 'thout you had a powerful reason." She paused. "You pro'lly don't think I understand that, but I do. What I don't git is why you stayed gone so long."

Oh, he had a reason to leave all right. But some days he had the eerie feeling that he hadn't left voluntarily at all, that circumstances had hurled him out into the darkness and he'd searched for 20 years to find his way back.

He took a deep breath. "I came home because…" Then he chickened out. "…because it was time."

Will had a speech all worked out. Had practiced it in his head dozens of times. Now, he couldn't remember a word of it. No, that wasn't true. He could remember it. He just couldn't screw himself up to actually saying the words out loud.

It was like she'd read his mind. "You and me, we got a lot to talk about. You got stuff to say. I got stuff to say. But we don't got to say none of it right now." She patted his arm. "'Cept maybe 'bout your daddy. Do you know that he…?"

"Died. Yes, I know."

"Didn't nobody have any idea where to find you to tell you 'bout it when it happened. He wasn't much of a father, but he was the oniliest one you had, and I was powerful sorry to put him in the ground 'thout you bein' here. How'd you find out?"

"I called the post office 5 or 6 years ago, said I wanted to 'verify' his address and they told me he didn't live there anymore. Said he'd been dead for 9 years."

Will had been in a hospital in Atlanta after he'd staggered out into the street and got hit by a taxi. He shouldn't have survived the altercation. But drunks were like rag dolls; they rolled with punches that would have killed the sober. Absent the blessed, blurring oblivion of alcohol, the images in his mind resolved into a focus as sharp as an assassin's dagger. As he lay on crisp white sheets that smelled like starch instead of vomit, the lonely ache had overwhelmed him and he had reached out—not to *connect,* just to peek into his world from the outside through a slit in the curtains. He hadn't been surprised that his father was dead; he had been surprised by the effect the news had on him. He had pulled out the IVs, slipped out of bed, dressed in his filthy clothes and disappeared into the night—was blind drunk in less than an hour. Booze dulled the pain of his broken ribs, but not his broken heart. He hadn't been grieving his father's death; he'd been hiding from other losses he didn't want to know about.

"Even if I'd been notified, I wouldn't have come home for the funeral—for the same reason I never came back at all." Will drew in another deep breath and braced himself. "And that was because…"

"Didn't we just agree we was gonna work up to that? We got plenty of time." She reached out and touched his cheek, her big hands soft as a butterfly kiss. "Of course, Bow always said if'n you got to eat a frog, don't look at it too long. And if'n you got to eat two frogs, eat the big'un first."

Bow. She'd always made a little sighing sound when she said his name, and she still did, even after all these years. Ricky Dan used to say his parents had "a thang," the whatever-it-was that kept a marriage a love affair through a man coming home every night exhausted, with nothing left of himself to give his family. So dirty the black wouldn't come out of his skin. And with his fingers smashed, and you felt relieved it wasn't worse. Through squalling babies, lay-offs, strikes, near-misses in the mine and always, always, always too much month left at the end of the money.

Sometimes, she didn't tell Bowman things—a bill had come they couldn't pay, the car was leaking oil or the tires were bald. She organized her whole world around making sure he didn't worry; a distracted miner was a dead miner.

Will had watched Ma pack her husband's lunch pail in the morning hundreds of times. Years later, he had come out of a black-out slumped on the back row of a Catholic church during communion, and he'd watched in a daze. That was how it had looked when Ma loaded that bucket. She had worked to make everything perfect, sparkling clean, set in that metal box with so much love, care, and concern, it was sacred.

The first thing she put in the bucket every morning was a neatly folded piece of paper, down on the bottom, under everything else. Will asked her once what it was and she'd smiled the kind of smile he wouldn't understand for years and said it was "'tween me'n Bow." Will tried a number of times to get a look at one of the notes, searched Bowman's pail after he got home from the mine but could never find one. He always wondered what Bowman did with the notes after he read them.

Will became aware that she was silent, quietly studying him. She could sit so still she didn't even appear to breathe, erect as a piano teacher, with those big, man's hands folded in her lap as prim as Cinderella waiting for Prince Charming to ask her to dance.

Will felt suddenly disoriented, like he'd been living for decades outside the province of the normal laws that governed the universe—light, dark, and gravity. And now that her presence had invoked those laws again, set the world back aright, the globe was spinning so fast he couldn't seem to catch up with it to jump on.

This, here, now, was real. Had all the rest of it been illusion?

"I've got a lot of frogs to eat in the next few days, Ma…*Granny*." He looked into her cinnamon eyes, not cloudy like most old people's eyes, but with whites as clear as snowballs. "Bigger frogs than you can possibly imagine. Frogs with claws and jagged teeth and…" He literally shook; a tremor ran through him like he'd received a low-power electric shock. "I'll get to them all. I *have* to get to them all. I'm—"

"Plumb wore out is what you are." She stopped. "And there's some'm wrong with the way you talk, too."

If his gut hadn't been tied in knots, Will would have laughed. The 18-year-old kid who'd fled the mountains two decades ago had been determined to erase his past. But to do that, he had to leave his Eastern Kentucky accent behind, too. If he'd known when he started how hard that would be, he'd probably never have attempted it. He began by teaching himself to listen, really *listen* to the speech patterns around him. Then, he practiced for hours, pronouncing words the way others did. It was way harder than creative cursing; the process took years. It would have been easier to learn a foreign language.

It also took years to accept the paradox, get comfortable with the contradiction in his sense of who he was and where he'd come from. He had desperately wanted to blot out every trace of his past; at the same time, he'd been passionately proud of his heritage. He wouldn't let anyone make fun of his beloved mountains, cracked a lot of heads defending hillbilly honor.

It was ironic—back in the mountains now—he was the one who sounded like a foreigner.

"I guess I picked up how folks outside the mountains talk," he lied.

"Well, you'd best put down whatever t'was you picked up out there in the wide world. I cain't hardly understand nothin' you say." She leaned back and sized him up. "And when was the last time you had a hot meal or got a good night's sleep?"

"It's been a while."

"I thought so. Well, the bed in the spare room—you b'lieve I got me a *spare* room now? You grew up sleeping on that lumpy ole couch I had to hide under a quilt, it was so worn out and ugly. The bed in my spare room here's got a feather mattress. You go to sleep on that and you might not wake up for a week."

Sleep in Granny's guestroom—how did we get here? I can't stay!

"That's okay, Granny. I'll get me a motel room in Pineville or…"

"You'll do no such of a thing!" she snapped in a loud voice that was whisper soft. "You ain't gonna come here after all these years and not stay in your own home." She leaned toward him. "You 'member that poem 'bout a hired man you's supposed to memorize—the one that didn't even rhyme? It said home's the place that when you got to go there, they got to take you in. This here is yourn."

If it hadn't been for the Sparrows, Harlan County Social Services would surely have taken Will away and put him in foster care. His mother left when he was 5. It was soon after his father began to cough up blood and maybe that was why she left, though most said the flamboyant Winona Calhoun was too shallow and self-centered to stick it out with a simple miner like Wade Gribbins. No one was surprised when she took to hanging out in Harlan when Wade was at work and then ran off with some coal company big-shot she met there. No one except Wade. He was shattered, never recovered, became the empty husk of a man who expected nothing from life and gave nothing back. He'd said once that Winona's leaving had sucked all the air out of the world and he couldn't catch his breath.

After Will's mother left, the Sparrows stepped in and took up the slack in the boy's life. Not in any official way, nothing was ever said about it, at least not that Will heard. He just began to eat his dinner at their house when his father worked night shift in the mine. Slept over some nights. Then most nights. Over the years, Wade Gribbins got sicker and slipped further into a darkness deeper than the mines. Granny and the other neighbors did for him the best they could; Will took up permanent residence on Granny's lumpy couch and kept his clothes in the bottom two drawers of Ricky Dan's dresser. Eventually, Wade was declared permanently disabled; he could finally quit his job in the mine and draw full workmen's comp benefits. But by that time, everything that mattered in life had long since passed him by and he wore the hollow-eyed stare of a refugee whose village had been burned and family massacred. Will saw his father almost every day, but had only a handful of memories of the man. Now and then, he spent the night in his own bed, drifted off to sleep to the rhythm of his father's hacking and coughing in the next room.

In every way that mattered, Granny Sparrow had been his mother, which made Ricky Dan his brother. The three daughters had never felt like sisters, though. The youngest was 13 years older than Ricky Dan; they were like visiting aunts whenever they dropped by. And Bowman…Bowman was the patriarch, strong, quiet, and reserved, the rock of the family—of Will's family. There was no way around it—this was Will's home.

And he'd traveled almost a thousand miles to get here so he could destroy it.

"'Sides, I got to put some meat on them bones." Granny flashed an engaging, tight-lipped smile. It crinkled the skin around her eyes like cracks in a windshield running away from a rock. "Yore so skinny you got to stand in the same place twice to cast a shadder."

Before Will could protest, she reached over and took his hand in both of hers, smooth now like maybe she didn't work in the garden anymore. She grabbed his gaze and held on.

"You got a duty to the people that cares 'bout you, son." There was a slight tremor in her soft voice. "Not to do for them but to 'llow them to do for you."

Game over.

"Of course, I'll stay, Granny. There's nowhere else I'd rather be."

The glow of delight on her face warmed him as a tropical breeze warms cold fingers. And chilled him, the way liquid nitrogen freezes everything it touches.

"But only if you promise breakfast with homemade biscuits and that white gravy you make that's got big chunks of sausage in it."

"We'll see."

Ahhh. *We'll see.* The response of infinite possibilities. As often positive as negative so you could never predict the eventual outcome.

It was Granny's habitual response to almost every question asked her. "Can we go sangin'? Can we hunt crawdads down Lizard Lick Creek? Can we go play in the traffic on the four-lane?" *We'll see.*

"Scrambled eggs and bacon too." Will continued, as he warmed to the prospect. "A plate full. I know there's just the two of us, but I promise I can eat enough to—"

"It ain't just the two of us."

Oh.

Was one of the girls staying with her? Maybe her husband died or was killed in…?

"You should have told me. I'm glad you're not alone. Who else lives here?"

She looked strangely awkward. "That there's another subject I kindly needed to work up to."

There was a sudden noise from the other side of the trailer. A door opened and then slammed shut, the sounds in rapid succession like a child running into the house from outside.

Granny called out, "C'mon in here, Sugar, there's somebody I want you to—"

But the person burst into the room before she could finish the sentence.

Suddenly lightheaded, Will watched the room expand crazily, saw the corners move backward farther than the dimensions allowed. Like a room in a freak show. Or a nightmare.

Standing in the doorway leading into the kitchen was *Ricky Dan Sparrow.*

Will probably would have cried out if he'd had the air. He might even have run screaming out of the room, but his legs would have refused to carry him.

One afternoon when Will was 9 years old, he'd come up the road from school and could hear Ricky Dan's raised voice even before he stepped up on the porch. But he couldn't catch Ma's softer words until he got close. He'd heard them argue about school before. Ma telling Ricky Dan he needed to "apply himself more"—that was what she called it—and Ricky Dan firing back that school was boring and every kid he'd met was a biggity britches.

"They all think their sh…" He'd caught himself just in time. "…crap don't stink, Ma!"

Ricky Dan hadn't adjusted well to Harlan County High School, wasn't suited for academics, and couldn't seem to catch the rhythm of other teenagers' lives. But this time, their school argument had taken a different turn.

"You ain't quittin'!" Ma said. She didn't raise her voice enough that anybody would have called it a shout, but she was louder than Will had ever heard her. "You're stayin' in school and you're gonna graduate, and that there's the end of it!"

Ricky Dan had almost knocked Will off the porch when he marched out in a rage. Will followed him over to the stump where Ricky Dan liked to sit, but didn't say anything, just stood beside him.

Eventually, Ricky Dan looked over at him and said with a wry smile, "Welcome to adventures in missin' the point."

Will didn't know what that meant so he kept silent.

"Ma don't get it," Ricky Dan said, picked up a stick and began to peel the bark off it. "It ain't just we need the money and I hate school. It's that…" His voice trailed off. Then he started again, "When I'm workin' on weekends, and I come up after my shift, dirty and wore out, my snot black and grit in my teeth—that ain't *bad*. It's feeling…*alive.*"

And Ricky Dan'd had this *look* on his face, this animated, vibrant look Will would never forget. It was years before Will was old enough to interpret it. Ricky Dan's was a look of purpose, the look of a man who knew who he was and what he was made for.

Ricky Dan had that same look on his face now as he stood in the doorway of Granny's kitchen—but only for a moment, then it morphed into a kind of childlike confusion and he turned his head and looked off to the side.

This was wrong, all wrong. How could Ricky Dan be standing here *a young man like he'd been when Will was a little boy?*

Was this…a ghost, one of Granny's haints?

Then Will noticed for the first time that there was a yellow bird on Ricky Dan's shoulder—a canary.

Granny stood up and began to speak, but it took Will a couple of seconds to hear her through the roar in his ears.

"…should have warned you. I forget sometimes how much he looks like his daddy."

His *daddy?*

Granny turned to the young man in the doorway. "Jamey, you don't know this fella, but he—"

"Oh yes, ma'am, I surely *do* know him!" the young man said and extended his hand toward Will, straight and stiff like he was drawing a sword. "I'm James Bowman Sparrow, sir, named after my granddaddy, but ever-body calls me Jamey. Well, most ever-body. 'Cept JoJo and sometimes she calls me mow-ron, but she don't mean nothin' by it. And sometimes Granny calls me Jamey Boy." He paused to get a breath. "But you can call me Jamey. The end."

The whole monologue had been proclaimed in a cheery voice, but the young man never looked at Will, kept his head down, and his gaze roamed the room like a searchlight on a guard tower, up and down the baseboards of every wall.

Will found he actually could get up, on trembling legs, cross the room to where Jamey stood and take his outstretched hand. The young man clasped Will's hand and pumped vigorously up and down like he was inflating a bicycle tire.

"My name's—"

"Oh, I know who you are," the young man said, excitement in his voice, still pumping Will's hand without looking at him. He turned to

Granny, looked at her briefly before he dropped his gaze. "You said I didn't know who he was but I do, too, know this fella—well not his name." He turned back toward Will. "What's your name, mister?"

"Will Gribbins."

"Proud to make your acquaintance, Mr. Gribbins!" The young man peeked up at Will, then dropped his gaze. He seemed to realize he could stop shaking now and he released Will's hand. "Only we ain't strangers, me and you. I know you think we are, but we ain't. I don't know yore name and the like, but we done already met. We met this mornin'. I'll show ya. The end."

After he put the verbal period on his spiel, the young man turned and bolted out of the room, the bird on his shoulder clinging tenaciously to his shirt. Will heard the back door open and bang shut again.

Granny spoke one word into the stunned silence.

"Sit."

Will sat.

Her voice was flat; she seemed to have aged a decade.

"I didn't find out until after Ricky Dan got killed that Joanna was pregnant," she said.

Will should have guessed it. That was why Ricky Dan got engaged so quick and then wanted a Thanksgiving wedding. Twenty years ago, unwed mothers were almost unheard of in the mountains. But short engagements and "premature" babies that weighed 8 pounds were as common as layoffs and disability checks.

"And Joanna…she took it hard. Her only brother had hisself a heart attack and died right after, and they was real close. So she…" Granny's voice trailed off. Then she took a deep breath and continued. "She tried for a good long while, but you could see all that hurt in her was still raw as the day we lost 'em. Then there was a car wreck. Some said it wasn't no accident. You might 'member, her mama went all crazy like, hollerin' and carryin' on, and they had to put her away.

Well, her granny done the same thing, so some folks got to sayin'
Joanna wasn't draggin' a full string of fish, neither. I cain't speak to
the why of it; only her and the good Lord knows that. All I know is
she wrapped her car 'round a tree when she was 8 months along. They
took her in one of them helicopters to Lexington and we all went
runnin' up there. She was a-layin' in that bed with tubes comin' outta'
her ever-where and machines wheezin' and beepin'..."

Will reached over and took Granny's hand.

"The doctors said her body was still alive but her brain...onli-
est thing keeping her breathin' was them machines." Granny sighed.
"She stayed like that for a right smart while, but then they couldn't
wait no longer and they cut her open."

Another pause, her voice grew quieter. She gestured with her
head toward the door where Jamey had left. "Named him after Bowman..." Her voice was thick. Then she gathered herself and continued.
"Jamey didn't breathe soon's he come out, had stuff in his lungs. One
of them nurses told me he was blue as a ink stain on a shirt pocket.
Even when he commenced to cryin' he liked to never pinked up. And
while he wasn't breathin,' his brain wasn't gettin' no oxygen so..."

The back door opened and slammed shut again and Jamey raced
into the living room. He had something round and black in his hand.
He ducked his head to the side as he held it out to Will.

"Here 'tis, mister," he said, panting like he'd been running. "See!
I told you we done already met!"

The object was a lump of coal carved into a bust.

It took Will a beat to process it all. The sculptor who'd created
all the incredible art in this room was *a mentally handicapped boy*?

Will reached out for the dark rock, took it in his hand to examine it. The room went instantly airless. Granny made a squeaking
sound and covered her mouth with both hands.

The face on the bust had been captured in the coal in painstak-
ing detail; its identity was unmistakable. It was Will.

He looked from the bust to Granny and back to the exact reproduction of his own face on a lump of coal he held in his hand. But he couldn't speak.

She could.

"Jamey Boy's done opened up a whole new can of worms here 'fore I was all the way done with the last one. Here's the whole of it, Will. Like I said, them doctors liked to never got Jamey to breathe… but the *second* baby come out a-squalling. Funny how he talks all the time now and she's the quiet one. Her name's Joanna, after her mama. But when Jamey was little, he couldn't say Joanna, so—"

"I called her JoJo," Jamey interrupted, beaming. "Ain't JoJo a fine name! Jamey and JoJo—we's twins."

CHAPTER 7

LLOYD JACOBS HAD spent his whole life with a sour look on his face, even when he was a baby. His mouth turned naturally downward at the corners; that's just the way it was built. And perhaps the person he became evolved to match his looks. Or could have been the other way around. Hard to tell. It was obvious, though, as time went by, that Lloyd's insides more closely resembled his outsides every day. His face was square, his forehead high beneath an unruly mop of black hair. A bushy unibrow rested over eyes a dark chocolate shade of brown. But his eyes weren't quite big enough, like he'd somehow been issued a size too small for his face.

Will used to call him "Pea Eye"—thought it was funny. Lloyd never thought it was funny.

For some reason, when he came out of the mine at the end of his shift, Lloyd was thinking about that—how Will'd called him Squinty and Mole Man, too. But the cool wind blew the thoughts out of his mind and replaced them with two familiar itches he ached to scratch. First, he needed a smoke! And second…oh, how he longed for a shower—scalding hot water making soapy rivers of liquid coal dust that streamed off his body into the shower drain. The raccoon mask fading away; his hands clean…no, not clean. Once you got coal dust under your fingernails, got it imbedded in your skin, it had to wear off. Took a long time. Look at a man's fingers and you could tell whether he was a working miner or one who'd been laid off.

Lloyd was a working miner. For now. But he certainly wouldn't be a month from now, or 6 months—however long it took them to dig out all the roof falls in Harlan #7.

He remembered distinctly the day he'd learned they were going to reopen the mine like you remember exactly where you was when you heard Kennedy'd got shot. He'd been in church. They'd had a fine service, lots of singing, lots of testifying, good, solid hell-fire preaching. He felt especially good. It was before Norma Jean left him, before Jesse got himself all messed up in drugs, before Amy got pregnant. The whole family stood together on the church steps. It was a spring day and the mountains rose up all around, no leaves yet, but with tiny bits of color on every tree that made it look like the mountains was broke out in a green rash. He remembered thinking that this was how it should be, the way life was supposed to be. He wanted to capture the moment and put it in one of them glass balls you could shake and snow'd fall all over everything.

Then Virgil Higgins—folks called him Tie Rod—stepped up and asked Lloyd if he had a light. Of course, he had a light. He smoked two packs a day. Everybody knew it. But he didn't smoke at *church*. Tie Rod knew the First Pentecostal Church of Aintree Hollow didn't hold with smoking. What'd Tie Rod put him in a spot like that for?

Lloyd reached into his pocket, pulled out a lighter and handed it to him, then turned to walk away.

"Whatcha' think 'bout #7?" Tie Rod asked. And a little tickle in Lloyd's stomach stopped him. He turned back around.

"What about #7?"

"About them reopening it. Where you been, Lloyd? It was in the *Enterprise* on Friday that a company called Black Gold Mining bought it from Wilson Cooper." Lloyd had taken the day off Friday to go hunting. He was one of the best shots in the hollow. He'd stayed gone until late Saturday evening, didn't even go to the mailbox.

Tie Rod spit in the dirt. "Whadda ya bet it's the same bunch, just changed the name 'cause they never paid none of them fines."

The federal MSHA, Mine Safety and Health Administration, had yanked all Wilson Cooper's operating permits and shut the mine down after the explosion in 1980, slapped big fines on the company for a whole herd of safety violations. The company had responded by going belly-up and never paid anything. In the past two decades, no other mining operation had been interested in reopening a mine that had high methane levels and roof falls all over—including half the belt line and the whole face—a mine where 27 miners had been killed. But with the price of coal higher now than it had been in years...

"Said they's gonna start workin' by the end of the year, but you know how that is. They don't never start diggin' when they say they're gonna."

It had been an amazing phenomenon, the only time anything even remotely supernatural had ever happened to Lloyd except when he was caught up in the spirit in church and spoke in tongues. He looked at his family all dressed up together in the spring sunshine on the porch of the church and the image started to run. Like it was a painting and somebody had splashed water on it. As he watched, all the color washed out of his family, the church, the mountains and the sky, dripped down into a murky puddle on the ground until the whole world was a black-and-white photograph.

And that had been just about what happened. His family did "run." Norma Jean ran off, filed for divorce the day after Thanksgiving. And even before she'd hauled off all the dishes and silverware, Jesse got busted for drugs. Amy moved in with her boyfriend. Everybody knew she was pregnant, but when she didn't start showing he knew she'd had an abortion. His whole world fell apart.

It had all started the day he learned they was going to reopen Harlan #7. But Tie Rod had been wrong. They did start digging by the end of the year. Black Gold got all their ducks in a row right before Christmas and they'd made pretty good time after that, dug a mile and a half into the side of Black Mountain. They'd bought the mineral rights to an area south of #7 and were digging out a new section at right angles to the shafts damaged by the 1980 explosion. It was a shoestring operation, though, just like Wilson Cooper'd been. They'd have to make some money before they could expand, dig out the roof falls, and open up the rest of the mine.

They'd hired a crew of about 30 men and Lloyd had quit his job at Bear Creek Mine to hire on as a boss. Took a pay cut, but he had to be there, had to stay close. Maybe if he was there when… well, maybe he could do something when they started digging out the old mine. Because the day they dug out the belt line shaft, Lloyd's life would be over. Worse than any roof fall in the mine, his world would crash down around him and crush him to death under the weight of it.

Some days he told himself it wouldn't happen. That it was like everybody thought—there was nothing left to find. Other days he knew better.

There was days on end he didn't sleep at all. He didn't think you could go without sleep that long, but whenever he'd lie down and close his eyes, he'd see the walking dead coming for him.

He knew it was dangerous to go into the mine in the state he was in. You had to be sharp—on your toes. Accidents happened when you wasn't careful. But he didn't have no choice. His belly had been tied in knots for so long now he couldn't remember anymore what it felt like not to be scared. Call it what it was. Lloyd Jacobs was scared.

A Scripture popped into his head, as passages from the Bible often did.

"Do not be anxious about anything…just present your requests to God and the peace of God will guard your heart." Something like that.

Peace? Lloyd didn't know what peace was. Hadn't since they dragged him out of Harlan #7. And he'd presented his requests to God again and again. Nothing. He probably ought to accept that was the way of it, tell the church he didn't believe it no more and resign. Well, he still believed some of it. The part about Hell waiting for sinners, he believed that part! And rewards to them that done right, he believed that part, too. Outside punishing and rewarding, though, he'd figured out God didn't want to have nothing to do with Lloyd Jacobs.

But no matter what he did or didn't believe, he *couldn't* walk out on the church. Life had whittled his world down, cut into his soul with sharp, savage strokes—took everything. The church was all he had left. He was an elder. Folks looked up to him, respected him. He was *somebody*.

Lloyd had told himself not to panic a thousand times. He still had one hope. He had a way out—Will Gribbins. Will Gribbins *dead*. He was, he had to be. Nobody'd heard so much as a peep—not a call, a letter, a postcard—in two decades. Not even when his daddy'd passed. Worse come to worse, Lloyd'd lay it all onto Will. Lloyd's word against a dead man's—who was they gonna believe?

One of the maintenance men, the short guy they called Li'l Bit, was on his way in for the graveyard shift and passed where Lloyd stood by his truck enjoying a cigarette.

"You seen him yet?" he asked Lloyd.

"Seen who?"

"You don't know?"

"If I knew, chances are I wouldn't be askin'," Lloyd snarled.

"You don't hafta bite my head off," the little man said. "I was in the Jiffy when Granny Sparrow called JoJo to tell her to bring home some crackers so's she could fix him up his favorite supper—salmon patties and French fries."

There was a sudden, huge ringing in Lloyd's ears that seemed to fill his whole head with sound. He couldn't talk. He couldn't breathe. When he didn't respond in any way, Li'l Bit shrugged. "I figured somebody told you Will Gribbins come home, figured you'd be the first person they called."

A young miner had come up behind the mechanic. "That Gribbins guy, he the one that got out with Lloyd?"

"Yeah. Them two, they's the only ones made it."

CHAPTER 8

—————

WILL SAT IN the ejection-seat recliner and watched Granny and JoJo fix supper. After Jamey set the table, he plopped down in front of the television and vanished into a game of Mario Super Smash Brothers on his Nintendo 64. Will had offered to help in the kitchen—peel potatoes or something—but Granny'd told him to put his feet up and relax.

There was a time Granny would have been indignant at his offer to help. When Will was growing up, men didn't do "women's work." Even when the miners were out on strike, men did their jobs and women did theirs. For all that strict division of labor, families were as close-knit as steel wool. You looked after your people and they looked after you.

Though Granny still wasn't likely in the running for Gloria Steinem's Liberated Woman of the Year Award, she had mellowed over the years. The old ways once held firm in this house and in the rest of the mountain culture. Girls who grew up in the hollows married young; boys who grew up here became miners.

Granny was a bride at 15 and Stella had been born a little over a year later. Granny had three little girls before she was 24 and four grandchildren before she was 40. She wasn't unique. What else was a girl in the Eastern Kentucky mountains to do except get married and have babies?

And regardless of the danger, boys went underground to dig coal. Those jobs paid the bills. Will knew a lot had changed in coal mining in two decades, but he was equally certain it still wasn't a safe occupation. There never had been and never would be a safe coal mine. It was an oxymoron, like a safe game of Russian roulette. There would always be poorly maintained machines, overlooked safety procedures, malfunctioning equipment, fatigue, inexperience and the constant pressure to produce more.

Among all the miners he knew, Will could name fewer than half a dozen men who still had all their fingertips. It used to seem to him that the more bunged-up miners got, the more determined they were to go back in—even when men got killed. The day after Harlan #7 blew, miners all over the mountains put on their helmets, grabbed their lunch pails, and went back underground to dig coal.

"You want lemon in your ice tea, Mr. Gribbins?" JoJo asked.

"Will, please. But no lemon for me."

She reached out to fill the tea glasses and her long blond hair brushed the table. Unlike the mountain girls of Will's generation, JoJo was not of the big hair and heavy makeup persuasion. Her face looked scrubbed; her hair hung straight, parted in the middle. It was the same color as Jamey's, which was a shade lighter than Ricky Dan's had been. These two were true cotton-tops. JoJo's features were a feminine version of her father's, straight nose and high cheekbones, but her mouth was heart-shaped like her mother's. Ricky Dan had been, in the vernacular of the 1980s, a stud. Jamey was innocent handsome; JoJo's beauty was fragile and haunting.

Though the two were remarkably similar, they were also profoundly different. Jamey was fire; JoJo was ashes—sunrise and sunset—the bright promise of a day and the despair of approaching darkness. Looking into Jamey's bright green eyes was like looking through a window into Disneyland, but there was a dead, vacant quality in JoJo's pale green eyes—the color of lime sherbet—that was disturbing. There was something else disturbing about her eyes. They had almost no lashes. After a while, Will noticed that she constantly plucked at them, unconsciously pulled the lashes out. She bit her fingernails down to the quick, too, and picked at her cuticles—had sores on her hands from it.

Will shook his head. Ricky Dan had *children*. How could he possibly do what he'd come here to do *now?* Jamey and JoJo made his mission here exponentially more difficult. As if it could be any harder. One look at Granny—the name seemed right to him now—and he was in a puddle. What in the world had made him think he'd be able to break that sweet old lady's heart?

And then there was the statue.

He and Granny'd agreed they wouldn't talk about it until after supper, but he couldn't imagine what there was to say that would explain the phenomenona. The boy had to have seen a picture of Will—somewhere—sometime.

That was a good, rational explanation. Trouble was, it didn't fit reality. Granny'd said Jamey had set their house on fire when he was 4 years old and the blaze took everything she had, including her pictures. Besides, Will couldn't even remember if there'd ever been a picture of him in the Sparrow home. A snapshot of him and Ricky Dan together, maybe, but it would have been stuffed in a drawer somewhere. It certainly wouldn't have hung on a wall in Ricky Dan's room! Those had been slathered with posters of Charlie's Angels. Ricky Dan had had a thing for Farah Fawcett.

But let's say there had been a photo, and let's say 4-year-old Jamey had gotten a look at it before the fire—how had he managed to age-enhance the image 20 years?

Will broke out in a sudden sweat.

The statue has the scar on my chin.

He reached up and felt the lump he'd gotten when his chin came into close, personal contact with the granite fist of an exceedingly large man in a bar in Sarasota.

There was no way Jamey could have known about that scar.

I need a drink!

The instant craving was so overwhelming it actually catapulted Will out of the chair as effectively as the broken recliner mechanism. Longing drove him toward the front door and he barely managed to bank left into the bathroom instead, where he stared at his reflection in the mirror. He saw the same haunted, vacant look in his own eyes that he had seen in JoJo's.

Will whispered through clenched teeth to the gray-faced man in the mirror over the sink, a man barely clinging to his sobriety and his sanity, "I need to talk to my sponsor—*bad!*"

Couldn't have that either. Will didn't have the money to pay Granny for a long-distance call.

He splashed cold water into his face, dried it, and walked back into the family room. Granny, JoJo, and Jamey stood at the table behind their chairs holding hands.

"We was just gettin' ready to give thanks," Granny said. Will heard the distant echo of Ricky Dan's whispered voice in his ear— "…'cause eatin' unblessed food'll make you sterile." Will smiled. Ricky Dan was forever saying things to make Will laugh and get him in trouble. A stern look from Bowman was worse than taking a licking.

He crossed the room, joined the circle between Granny and JoJo, and bowed his head with a far greater respect for what he was about to do than he'd ever had as a kid.

There was a pause before Granny spoke. Her quiet tone had always lent gravity to her words, like whatever she said was important. It was even more pronounced when she prayed.

"Thank you, Jesus, for bringin' Will back to us. And thank you for this food. We know they's folks ain't got 'nough and we're grateful for what we got. Amen."

There was nothing perfunctory about the way Granny said grace. She didn't mouth words; she talked to an old friend. But she didn't presume upon that relationship. Will had barged in on her once when she was kneeling in prayer. As she stood up, she'd told him. "You got to get down on your knees ever now and again; helps you keep in mind who it is you're talkin' to."

As soon as Will raised his head, Jamey burst out, "Please, sir, tell me 'bout my daddy. Granny said you was his best friend, knew him better'n anybody—'cept maybe her...and my mama."

Granny'd said *that?* Will's heart swelled in his chest. He'd never seen himself as Ricky Dan's best friend. Annoying younger brother, maybe, but a friendship was a bond between equals. He never considered that he was Ricky Dan's equal—though after Will turned 18, whenever Ricky Dan got a beer out of the refrigerator, he'd offer Will one. Just like that, never said anything, just did it. Granny wasn't keen on *anybody* drinking beer in her house, but she didn't get hung up on something as silly as a "legal drinking age." If a man was old enough to dig coal out of the ground, he was old enough to drink a beer.

But a beer every now and then notwithstanding, Ricky Dan was less Will's friend than his hero.

Will took the offered platter of French fries, deposited some on his plate and passed it on to Jamey. The young man's face wore that quality of expectation you see on the faces of a theater audience just as the curtain begins to rise. Will shook his head to clear it. It was way more than creepy to hear "Ricky Dan" ask for stories about Ricky Dan.

"I'm sure the whole world has told you he looked just like you, smiled like you, too." Ricky Dan's dimpled grin had been so bright the glow had probably been visible from outer space. "And he had

67

this…I don't know…*way* about him that made everybody love him."
He turned to Granny. "I remember you used to say folks wanted
Ricky Dan to be—"

She finished for him, "the groom at ever weddin' and the corpse
at ever funeral."

As far as "grooms" went, Ricky Dan had avoided capture—his
word—until he was 25, and that was *old* for the mountains. He went
through girlfriends as casually as he rotated the tires on his old Buick.
When he finally settled on Joanna, there wasn't a girl for 30 miles in
every direction whose heart wasn't broken.

"Your mama was blond, too, and Ricky Dan'd deck anybody
who called them Barbie and Ken."

Jamey's delighted, musical laugh filled the room. JoJo even
smiled. It was the first time all night.

What Will didn't tell them was that Joanna hadn't been an obvious choice, though now Will understood why Ricky Dan had made
it. She was…average. You got the sense when you were around the
two of them that she saw Ricky Dan as a prize beyond all reasonable
expectation. Will was saddened, but not surprised, that she couldn't
countenance life without him.

Will took the plate of crispy, brown salmon patties, speared one
and dropped it next to his French fries.

"I promise I'll tell you all sorts of tales about your dad." He eyed
Granny. "Some your grandmother doesn't even know."

"I wouldn't bet the farm on that if I's you," she said.

"But first…I have to know the story on that canary you got
riding your shoulder."

The bird had been there since Jamey came into the room. It had
made no effort to fly away, merely paced up and down his shoulder
like a guard on sentry duty. It was silent now, but it had sung for a
little while before they sat down to supper. Of course, that had been
when Jamey was playing video games, so maybe its sweet song was

actually a cry of excruciating pain in bird-speak. The only thing Will hated more than trailer houses was video games.

"ValVleen? She's my bestest frien' in all the world. She's a mine canary, the kind they usta take down under the ground to sniff out poison gas."

Will had heard an old miner say once that the life of a mine canary could be described in three words: short but meaningful.

"I had her ever since I was 9 years old. Lloyd give her to me. Said a boy with the last name of Sparrow had oughta have a bird."

"He told Jamey he'd asked for an eagle, but they was fresh out," JoJo said. "I b'lieved that for years."

"Lloyd Jacobs?" Will hadn't spoken that name out loud in two decades.

When they were kids, Lloyd had lived in a house on the first side street off the road that led down the hollow into Aintree. There was all manner of junk in the front yard of the house. A beat-up refrigerator missing a door; three old stoves, also missing doors; a couple of cars set up on concrete blocks, absent wheels; a wringer washing machine; washtubs and various pieces of miscellaneous, unidentifiable rusting metal *somethings*. Lloyd's miner father was a loudmouthed, abusive drunk who regularly beat his wife and son. His mother was a vacant-eyed, defeated-looking woman with a soft voice and a broken spirit. Lloyd and Will were the same age and were best friends. Lloyd hung out with Will and Ricky Dan at the Sparrows' house, ate there, played there—would have moved in just like Will if he could have. Granny welcomed him; she was always picking up strays.

But Will had often spotted something odd in Lloyd's too-small brown eyes, though he was never able to put his finger on exactly what it was. Envy, perhaps—that Will had escaped into the care of the Sparrows and he hadn't. Rage over something Will didn't un-derstand and Lloyd couldn't express. Or maybe it was simpler than that—maybe his eyes were merely the windows on a soul filled with inexplicable darkness.

"Yes, sir. Lloyd brung her in a cage with a bitty bowl for a birdbath. ValVleen takes a bath ever day, sometimes in the bowl and sometimes in the dew on the grass 'fore the sun's up. She still sleeps in the cage, but I leave the door open. And this here string..."

For the first time, Will noticed the piece of white yarn, with one end tied around the bird's left leg and the other wound around the top button on Jamey's shirt.

"...she don't need it. She ain't never tried to fly away, stays right here on my shoulder."

"Yeah, right there *crappin'* on your shoulder," JoJo said and wrinkled her nose. "In case you was wonderin,' ain't no way to potty train a canary. We tried."

Granny sighed. "That boy's spent near his whole life smellin' like the floor in a hen house."

"I don't mind," Jamey said with a wide grin, then he paused and the cheeriness left his voice. "She's real old for a canary, though. They don't usually...her bein' old and all is why she don't sing much as she usta."

"And her name is...what did you say it was?"

"ValVleen."

"All we can figure is that he heard somebody talk about changing the oil in their car," JoJo said. "And he got it in his head that 'Valvoline' was a name like Darlene, Pauline, Jolene..."

"ValVleen *is* a name," Jamey responded in a pout. "It's ValVleen's name."

Will didn't even wait until Granny and JoJo got the supper dishes cleared away. As soon as everyone finished eating, he blurted out the questions he'd ached to ask ever since Jamey placed a lump of coal in his hand that had his own face carved into it.

"Jamey, how did you do that—with that statue?" He wanted to ask where a boy who'd obviously dropped out of grade school had learned to carve at all, but he let that ride for now. "How did you carve it to look just like me when you've never met me?"

"I didn't carve it to look like nothin'." Jamey reached over and plucked the lone remaining French fry off the platter. Chewing with his mouth open, he continued. "I don't never try to make the coal be what it ain't. I usta, but not no more." He maintained eye contact for a moment, then glanced away and examined the bottoms of the kitchen cabinets as he spoke. "I carve away what's on the outside to let out what's on the inside. You was in that piece of coal 'fore I ever put a chisel to it. I just turned you loose."

Now, *there* was a conversation stopper.

"We don't know how he does it," Granny said quietly, offering an explanation that was no explanation at all. "And as you can see, he don't neither."

"But he's been doing it his whole life," JoJo said. "Used to scratch pictures in the dirt with a stick when he was a little bitty kid."

"I'm not asking how he can carve coal. He's obviously got incredible talent. There are people called…" He thought better of mentioning idiot savants. "…people with minds like Jamey's who can do all sorts of amazing things—play chess or the piano or violin. Do mathematics in their heads, paint incredible pictures. That part I can understand. But how did he put *my face* on it when he's never met me?"

Granny let out a long breath. "I done tol' you, Will, we don't know how he does it. He ain't never done 'xactly this before, carved somebody before he ever met 'em. But he's done other things…"

"What things?"

Granny and JoJo exchanged a look, then Granny spoke to the girl in an unusually soft voice. "Go get the mural off'n the wall in Jamey's room."

"You ain't gonna *tell* him, show him…?" JoJo's eyes were wide.

"He done seen this much," Granny gestured to the statue with Will's face. "'Sides, Will's family."

JoJo paused for another beat, then reluctantly got to her feet, went into Jamey's room and returned with a mural like the one above the mantle. It was an equally astonishing work of art; the photographic accuracy of the detail was stunning. It showed a basketball team— the Harlan County High School Black Bears; Will recognized the uniforms—in a gym, huddled together around a gigantic trophy.

"Jamey carved this when we was 12," JoJo said.

"Twelve?"

She nodded.

"Harlan County won the state championship that year," Granny said. She pointed to the gym in the background of the mural. "This here's the inside of Rupp Arena in Lexington with all the players holdin' up the trophy."

"Jamey wasn't at the game," JoJo said. "He's never been to Rupp Arena." Will didn't like where this seemed to be going. Didn't like it one bit.

"But he knew the team members, at least the ones from Aintree Hollow, didn't he? And maybe he heard people talk about the game. There must have been pictures in the newspaper—"

"You still don't get it, Mr. Gribbins—"

"Will."

"All right, *Will*. Jamey carved this 3 days *before* the game."

Will felt his stomach drop, like he'd plummeted five floors in a runaway elevator.

"Well…he wanted the Bears to win, right? He carved a wish, a hope, a—"

"Will…" Granny stopped him and pointed to the upper left hand corner of the mural, above the head of the tallest kid on the team. "This here's the scoreboard."

Will's elevator fell the rest of the way down and crashed into the concrete floor in the basement.

Harlan County 68; Marion County 64.

Will lifted his eyes from the mural and looked at Granny; he managed to croak, "…and that was the score?"

Granny, JoJo, and Jamey all nodded their heads with the perfect unison of a chorus line.

Later, when Will tried to reconstruct the remainder of the conversation, he discovered that order and logic stopped as soon as he saw the numbers on the scoreboard in Jamey's mural. After that, he walked out on a pier and stepped off into another world where all the elements reacted in different ways, where wind went drip, drip, drip out of the faucet in the middle of the night, where seas of flame lapped against sandy beaches and gusts of water pulled leaves off trees and flapped flags on poles.

Granny and JoJo continued to speak. But Will's mind only managed to capture bits and pieces of what they said, stories written on glass that shattered when he touched it, sent out fragments in all directions, each one exceedingly sharp. The only way to see the whole of it was to put all those little pieces back together, but he knew his hands would be sliced to ribbons if he tried.

"…Jamey was 6 when he carved his first statue. It was a goat with a bent horn," Granny's voice. "He said t'was the Jewetts' goat, only the Jewetts' didn't have no goat. About a year later, they got one, though. It had that very bent horn."

"…the time Jamey carved that mural of a wedding." JoJo's voice echoed in his head, magnified like sounds in a mine. "The bride and groom all dressed up, the minister with his Bible, even a little girl had a bouquet of daisies but didn't have no front teeth." She paused and looked at Granny. "When Granny seen it, she liked to died."

"It was *my* weddin', Will. Mine and Bowman's. But the only weddin' picture I had was burned up with everything else in the fire.

And the carvin' shows all kinda' details wasn't even in the picture. It's hangin' on the wall in my bedroom, if'n you wanna' see it."

Will shook his head. "Maybe some other time," he croaked.

Maybe some other time?

"…Miss Viola at church years ago made so over that big yella tomcat. You'd a-thought it was the onliest cat ever drew breath. It got lost and she liked to had a conniption. Then Jamey comes out with this carving…" Granny looked at JoJo to help her explain it.

"We didn't know it was a carving at first. It was a piece of coal shaped like a jelly glass, only when you looked in it, down in the bottom was a cat's face lookin' back up at you. They found Miss Viola's cat in the Peterson's well."

Finally, Will could handle no more. He feared imminent death from a closed-head injury if he took any more blows to his mind.

"Enough!" he pleaded and the two women fell silent. Jamey had grown bored with all the talk and was happily playing a video game with ValVleen perched on his shoulder, singing.

"What do the neighbors, the rest of the hollow think of all this?" he asked.

"They's plenty of folks suspect there's some'm odd 'bout some of his carvin's, but don't nobody 'cept the girls know the whole of it like we told you," Granny said. "Not even Lloyd."

Lloyd's name again. The word sounded like the drip of black water in a dark mine.

"We was afraid…oh, I don't know, that they'd come and take him away from us if folks knew how special he was," JoJo said. She didn't specify who "they" might be.

"'Sides, all most people ever see is the carvin's he sells," Granny said.

"There's a Lexington company that helps out artists, trying to preserve the Appalachian culture," JoJo said. "They got his stuff into some galleries, the Berea Art Show, The St. James Art Fair in

Louisville. Folks mail in orders after them shows. And then lots of his carvin's is sold all over the mountains to tourists in curio shops and the gift shops at state parks."

Jamey put down the video control long enough to point out, "That ain't my arts, though. Making things people wants is only 'cause we need the money." He looked at the bottom of the kitchen chairs as he spoke. "And they's only made with dead coal. Live coal won't let you do nothin' with it but open up what's already in there. The end."

Hours, though it seemed like *weeks* later, Will sat on the side of his bed in Granny's spare room trembling. He had never in his life wanted a drink as badly as he wanted one now. Of course, he had, too. Probably lots of times. But when the yearning came, it was a force so powerful you couldn't imagine you'd ever felt anything like it before and survived.

The only reason he did survive was because he was here. Granny had no alcohol in the house. Nothing in Aintree Hollow was open past five o'clock. Even the Jiffy Stop across the bridge closed at 11.

Will lay back onto a pillowcase as smooth as a pool table; Granny still ironed sheets. He couldn't think about today and he didn't want to think about tomorrow, because tomorrow he had to go find Lloyd Jacobs and have a good, long talk.

His thoughts bounced around as random as a ball in a pinball machine. Then the shiny silver ball suddenly landed in one of those big holes that make the sirens wail, the bells clang, and the lights flash. That mural above the mantle of the three miners. In a glaring moment of understanding, Will knew why the figures in it had looked so eerily familiar. A photo caption of it would read: shown here, from left to right, are Will Gribbins, Ricky Dan Sparrow, and Lloyd Jacobs.

With that, his mind went *tilt* and he fell asleep.

CHAPTER 9

THE LONELY WHISTLE of a coal train wailed a mournful cry in the gray dawn light. Somewhere out there on the flat, the sun had just cleared the horizon. An early riser, Granny had already swept the leaves off the porch. Now she leaned over to drag some stragglers out from under the rocker. She paused for a moment, looked at what light she could see in the sky and wondered as she had so many times in her life what it'd be like to watch the sun come up in the morning and go back down at night.

She wasn't like some mountain people she knew who'd never set foot outside Harlan County. She'd been shopping in Somerset and all the way to Corbin once, too. And up to Hazard that time Jamey took the croup so bad he couldn't hardly breathe. She'd been to Lexington, but the first time she went, she didn't remember nothing about the trip or the city. Alls that hung in her mind was Will laid out unconscious in the hospital bed, and them doctors saying with a concussion like he had he might not never wake up. She didn't remember a whole lot more from the trips to see Joanna—miles of white fences, shined-up horses and grass that when the wind took it a certain way, really did look blue.

When she went to get them babies up Lexington that last time, Stella drove, babbled the whole way that Granny had ought to let her or one of her sisters raise them. That was when Granny first felt it. There was a shakiness in her belly; her heart started to pound like somebody on the porch banging on the door wanting in. It got worse and worse, didn't stop until the mountains rose up all around her, protective like. Made her feel safe, the way she used to feel with Bowman by her side—strong and sturdy and dependable. Him gone, the mountains was all she had. A tall green fence between her and ever bad thing.

But as time went by, the fence began to hug tighter and tighter. She'd go to Pineville and she'd get that feeling so painful she had to hurry back out to Ruth Ann's car, say she was sick, had the runs or something, and had to go home. After a while, alls she had was the hollow. Then she didn't even have that no more.

Granny could hear folks up and stirring around inside the trailer. She'd already made the biscuits, the sausage, and the gravy. She'd have to go in directly and finish up that breakfast she'd promised Will. Bacon and eggs wouldn't take long.

A wave of sadness washed over her. Will looked so...lost. Well, he was lost—had been for a good long time now. But couldn't nobody go out there and find him and bring him back. He had to come his own self. She had to admit, though, that she had begun to think he never would.

She seen the pickup soon as it turned up her way, but didn't have to see it to know it was Lloyd. She recognized the sound of his truck like she got where she could recognize the footsteps of the different nurses in the bright hospital hallway outside Joanna's room.

The truck had been red once, a 1990 Ford F150. The front bumper was missing now and the hood was held shut with duct tape. Lloyd pulled to a stop next to the road in front of the house, stepped out of the truck but didn't come up to the porch, simply went around to the back and let the tailgate down. Didn't even say hidy.

"Hidy do, Lloyd. Whatcha' got there?"

"Piece of jet for Jamey. Big 'un. I'll carry it up the hill to the shed." He reached into the truck bed and began to scoot the rock toward the back.

"That's right thoughty of you, Lloyd, but you can do that later." Granny couldn't wait to see the look on his face when she told him Will was home! "Come up here on this porch. I got a surprise. Bet you cain't guess—"

"Ain't no surprise. I know he's here."

Lloyd didn't say Will's name, but he did let go of the rock and walk to the foot of the steps.

"How come you never called to tell me he was back?" There was a strange, cold tone in Lloyd's voice Granny'd never heard before.

"You's working yesterday afternoon. He didn't show up 'til after you went down and I'd done gone to bed 'fore you got off."

Granny was confused. "What are you just standin' there for, son? Come on in the house. Didn't you hear me—*Will's home.*"

"You don't need me for welcomin'. What I hear, you done a fine job your own self, 'bout threw him a party last night."

Again, the cold, distant tone. All the excitement drained out of Granny's voice like water out a hole in her washtub. "There was times I thought he must be dead, Lloyd. *Dead.* Now he's back—alive. He's been gone for 20 years!"

"And I been *here* for 20 years. I's the one who come and checked on you, brung you groceries, built this here deck, put up..."

"I been powerful grateful for all you done. I've told you how beholden I am, couldn't a-got along 'thout you. I..." She stopped, then tried again. "Will was yore best friend, Lloyd; you two's like brothers. Why ain't you glad he's home?"

Lloyd shook his head. "These here is rock hard times for Lloyd Jacobs and I ain't up to celebratin'. 'Sides, looks to me like you're glad enough for the both of us."

His words were so sharp and angry they took Granny's breath away. He stalked back to the truck, picked up the jet and headed out across the yard with it, his footprints chocolate drops on the powdered sugar dusting of morning frost.

◊ ◊ ◊ ◊ ◊

WILL WOULD HAVE sworn he wouldn't be able to sleep a wink here, under Granny's roof, with Ricky Dan's children—his *children,* for crying out loud!—asleep down the hall.

And he'd have lost that bet. Actually, he hadn't so much slept as passed out. He'd laid back on the bed last night and awakened in that same spot this morning. Hadn't moved. Hadn't even undressed.

After a shower, he put on clean clothes, jeans, and a pale green long-sleeve shirt. He had a red shirt, too. Three shirts and two pairs of jeans, socks, underwear, a windbreaker, and the pair of Nikes he was wearing constituted his entire wardrobe.

Will emerged from the guestroom to find JoJo ready for work and Granny set to serve his made-to-order breakfast.

"You still drink coffee, doncha?" she asked, as she set bowls of scrambled eggs and white gravy with big chunks of sausage in it beside the homemade biscuits on the table. He nodded that he did. "I disremember whether you like it black or all doctored up."

"Black."

"You clean up good, son. You looked a mite raggedy yesterday."

Jamey was engrossed in his video game; JoJo wasn't doing anything. Dressed in the red Jiffy Stop smock, she sat on the couch and stared hollow-eyed out the window at a distant nothing.

Granny called them all to say the blessing and settled into the role she loved best—caretaker of her family. She poured coffee and orange juice, fetched cream out of the refrigerator and the salt and pepper shakers off the stove.

Only when everyone else had been served did she sit down and begin to fix her own plate, but a knock at the door interrupted her. Bucket slept out on the porch and hadn't so much as peeped so whoever was on the other side of the door was no stranger. Before anyone had a chance to rise, the door opened—the knock was perfunctory; Granny's doors were never locked—and a man stepped into the living room.

He was a thick, solid man with a barrel chest and an expanse of belly that had a University of Kentucky T-shirt drawn tight across it. He took off his camouflage cap to reveal a mop of thick hair as black as shoe polish without even a sprinkle of gray in it.

"Glad you decided to come on in," Granny said and Will saw a communication of some sort pass between them.

"Smells like I'm just in time for breakfast," he said and turned to Will. "'Lo, Will."

"'Lo, Lloyd."

A smile started on Will's lips and died there; he sensed no warmth in Lloyd. Will rose, took two steps toward his childhood friend and offered his hand. Somehow, Lloyd managed not to shake it without seeming rude or even calling attention to the omission. Will was the only one who caught it; he figured he was the only one who was supposed to.

"Sit down and eat with us, Lloyd," Jamey said. "We're having this extra special breakfast 'cause Will is here. But we got 'nough for you…" Then he looked stricken. "And if'n we don't, you can have mine."

"Special dinner last night, special breakfast this morning. You must be feeling real special, ain't you, Will…comin' back like you done after all these years."

Lloyd smiled when he said it, but the smile hung as limp on his face as a surgeon's mask. The undertone was so unmistakable even JoJo looked up quizzically. But Lloyd spoke to Jamey before the moment could turn awkward.

"Guess what I gotcha, Champ."

Jamey's face was instantly filled with little-kid-on-Christmas-morning expectation. "What'd you bring me?"

"Just the best-looking piece of jet you ever seen, that's all."

JoJo had told Will that Jamey used jet to carve the relief murals on the mantle and in Granny's bedroom—and the one of the Harlan County High School basketball team that showed…Will stopped himself. Now was not the time to go there.

"You did?" Jamey squealed. "Lemme see it." He made to leap up from the table, but Granny grabbed his arm.

"Finish your breakfast, boy," she said. "It took the good Lord a right smart while to make that rock. I s'pect you can wait another 10 minutes to see it."

She stood and started to the kitchen, spoke to Lloyd over her shoulder as she went. "I'll get you a plate. I made fresh biscuits and white sausage gravy. You used to favor biscuits 'bout as much as Will did."

"I done ate," he said.

Will knew that wasn't true, in the same way he knew that Lloyd would rather swallow hot coal slag than eat so much as a bite of the breakfast Granny had made special for Will.

Lloyd settled himself on the arm of the ejection recliner with his hat in his hand. His was a relaxed pose, but he didn't look relaxed. He looked wound tighter than an alarm clock.

"I done took that piece of jet up to the shed, Jamey," he said. "Fella told me about it a week ago, said he seen it in a break in Big Sandy and figured you'd want it. Took me a whole afternoon to cut it out of the wall, but I didn't want to waste none, knew you'd use it all."

He turned to Will, "Long time no see, buddy."

"Yeah, long time no see."

"You come back to Aintree for the memorial service?"

"That was one of the reasons."

"Committee asked me to speak, but I turned 'em down. But maybe you'd want to. I could tell Justine, she's headin' up the service. I'm sure she'd be glad to let you say a few words—you being one of the only survivors an' all."

Lloyd was taunting him. Lloyd knew Will didn't want to speak at that service any more than he did.

"Kind of you, Lloyd, but I think I'll pass."

Jamey leapt to his feet. He had been shoveling food into his mouth as fast as he could, barely took time to swallow.

"I'm done!" he said, his mouth so full he could barely get the words out.

"Turkeys are *done,*" JoJo said. "People are *finished.*"

"Yeah, that, too." He chewed between words as he spoke to Granny. "Can I go see the slab Lloyd brung me? Please."

"Not 'til you do the dishes," JoJo told him. She scooted her own chair back and rose from the table. "It's your turn. I need to get goin'. I got things to do."

Will had watched her during breakfast. She had moved the food around on her plate, arranged and rearranged it, but as far as he could tell, she hadn't taken an actual bite of any of it.

"No it ain't," Jamey wailed. "It's yours. 'Member? I done 'em the other night and then you—"

"You could settle this the way your daddy, Will and I used to settle things," Lloyd cut in. He spoke to Jamey, but he looked at Will with eyes as hard, cold, and dead as the coal under Black Mountain.

"How's that?" Jamey asked.

"Every time we had to decide which of us was gonna do some'm none of us wanted to do, we'd take two black rocks and one white rock and put 'em in a hat." Lloyd never took his eyes off Will as he spoke. Will noticed Granny turn pale; his own heart felt like a jack hammer in his chest. "And whoever drew out the white rock…" he paused for emphasis, "…*lost!*"

He turned his body toward Will, the plastic smile still on his face. "We done that all the time, didn't we, Will?"

"Yeah, all the time."

"I ain't got time to wait for white rocks and black rocks," JoJo said. She turned to Jamey. "You know it's your turn to do the dishes tonight, don't you?" Jamey nodded. "Okay, you do these now, I'll do them others tonight for you. Deal?"

"Deal," Jamey said cheerfully and began to gather up the plates off the table.

"Whoa, hold on there," Granny told him. "Just 'cause you stuffed food in your mouth like tampin' down gunpowder in a muzzle-loader don't mean the rest of us is finished." She sighed. "Oh, leave these be and go on out there and see that slab of jet before you jump plumb out of your skin with wantin' it."

Jamey bolted out the door. JoJo gathered up her purse, pecked Granny on the cheek and left.

Granny turned and smiled brightly at Lloyd. "Well now, set yourself down here, son, and I'll fix you up a cup a coffee."

"Can't Granny. I got to go." Lloyd hopped up from the arm of the chair. "Got a lot of stuff to get done. I change shift tomorrow, goin' from nights to days."

In most of the bigger operations, miners worked 3-week, rotating shifts: early morning to mid-afternoon, late afternoon to late night, and late night to early morning. Shift change was the most dangerous time in a mine. The men had just gotten acclimated to one sleep cycle when they had to adjust to another. For the first few days, they were tired and mildly disoriented. That's when accidents happened.

Harlan #7 wasn't a big operation, though. It ran a day shift from 7 in the morning until 3 in the afternoon and a night shift from 3 until 11. A skeleton crew did maintenance on the graveyard shift after midnight.

"I got my bossin' papers a few years back," Lloyd said to Will. "Still go down in the mine ever day."

"But you two ain't had no time—"

"There's no hurry," Will said. He rose and turned to Lloyd. "I'll walk you out to your truck."

Lloyd led the way out the door and down the steps. Will actually held his temper in check until the two of them got all the way out into the yard.

◊ ◊ ◊ ◊ ◊

"WHAT WAS *THAT* about?" Will demanded, his angry voice quiet so Granny couldn't hear.

Lloyd opened his truck door but made no effort to get into it. Instead, he pulled a pack of cigarettes out of his shirt pocket, lit one, and blew a plume of white smoke at Will as he spoke. Will noticed that his hands shook.

"What was what about?"

"Oh, come on, Lloyd! It's me you're talking to. All that stuff about rocks and…"

Will stopped, collected himself. He hadn't meant for it to go this way, didn't want to fight. He just hadn't been prepared for this much anger, though he probably should have expected it. He cleared his throat and started again in a more reasonable tone. "Lloyd, I was going to come see you, so we could talk—just you and me. As soon as I got settled I was—"

"But you got too busy, didn't you. Come waltzin' in like you owned the place and they throwed you a party, everybody makin' over you," the venom in his voice would have killed a rattlesnake.

"It's been *20 years*. Of course, Granny was glad to see me."

Lloyd leaned toward Will and snarled. "How glad you think she'd be if she knowed what we know?" He took another long drag off his cigarette; his hands still trembled. "What'd you have to come back for? I thought you's dead that day under the mountain. All this time you been gone, everybody thought you's dead."

"I *was* dead," Will said quietly. "I have been for two decades. I came home because—"

"Home? *Home?* You *left.*" Lloyd hissed the rest through clenched teeth. "*I stayed.*"

"You want a medal, Lloyd? I'll see if I can drum you up one." Will was instantly sorry he'd said it.

"You wasn't here when the air hung so heavy with grief you almost couldn't get your breath. When women would burst out cryin' in the grocery store, or walkin' down the street, or faint dead away in church. When fifth-grade kids took to wettin' the bed. And nobody laughed about nothin'. *Ever!*"

He spoke in a harsh, near-whisper. "I was here when the only thing left of 27 miners to give to their families was the tags they left on the board when they went in." He paused, then growled, "Where was *you* all those years?"

"For most of them, I was up under a bridge somewhere, blind drunk."

His frankness stopped Lloyd momentarily.

"Well, everybody'd be better off if you'd stayed drunk. Why'd you have to come back here and ruin everything."

"What am I ruining?" Will stepped back and studied Lloyd. "Why do you care that I'm here? I'm not hurting you." Will paused, then eased into it. "In fact, I was hoping to talk to you, try to work things out between us so—"

"*Work things out?* All that booze musta' pickled your brain, Will, 'cause there ain't no working out to be done 'tween me and you. Nothin' you say or do will ever—"

"You think I don't know that! Look, I'm not trying to *earn* anything by doing the right thing or saying the right thing now, after all

this time. I know I bring absolutely nothing to the party. I'm just…
here."

"You shouldn't a-come."

Will looked out over the hollow. "When I heard they'd reopened
#7, I…Lloyd, what happened down there that day can't stay buried
under Black Mountain forever."

"What are you sayin'?" Lloyd demanded. All at once, his voice
was high-pitched and strained, his little black eyes wild. "Whadda
you think they're gonna find when they dig out them roof falls?"

"What are you talking about, Lloyd?"

Lloyd's voice raised in volume and intensity with every word.
"You shouldn't never have come back here!" He jabbed at the air
inches from Will's face with the fingers that held his cigarette. "You
shoulda' stayed away, stayed *dead!*"

Will realized Lloyd was very close to taking a swing at him.
Will was taller and quicker, and Lloyd had once been a whole lot
stronger. Not anymore, though; his muscles had all gone to fat. But
Lloyd was definitely angrier. Will determined he'd take one punch if
Lloyd decided to throw it, wouldn't fight back. Lloyd was certainly
entitled to that much.

Then he thought about Granny. She didn't need to see the two
of them duke it out in her front yard.

He took a deep breath and spoke quietly—calmly—the way
you'd talk to a wounded animal so it wouldn't bite you when you
tried to help it.

"Just about every day for the past 20 years I've wished I'd died
when you thought I did, wished I'd gone with the others. I didn't.
Neither did you. We have to live with that." Then Will's voice took on
a hard edge. "But I can tell you right now, Lloyd, I'm *not* going to live
with it for the next 20 years the same way I have for the past 20."

"Neither am I," Lloyd said, his voice just as steely. "One way or
the other, it's gonna end now."

Will knew what he'd meant by what he'd said, but he had no idea what Lloyd might be talking about. Whatever it was, though, Lloyd's determination seemed to calm him.

"Do what you got to do, Will. If you come here to save your soul, have at it. You're gonna find it's a whole lot harder'n you think it is." He turned as if to get into his truck and then turned back, tossed the cigarette in the dirt and ground it out with his heel. "And as for me and you, we're quits."

He did get into his truck then, slammed the door, and drove away in a spray of gravel. Will watched him until he was out of sight at the bottom of the hollow.

CHAPTER 10

THE SHED WHERE Jamey did his arts was in the woods about a hundred and fifty yards up a slope behind the house. The path led past the garden and a stand of poplars and around a rock outcrop. The shed sat right behind the outcrop. You could miss it if you weren't looking for it, though. The years had so aged the wood it blended perfectly into the dappled forest.

The building had been there as long as anybody could remember, a simple two-room, wood-frame structure built with rough-hewn boards that carried the marks of hand tools. Granny said it had probably been somebody's house back when folks first moved into the mountains, but it'd been abandoned for years when Bowman decided to fix it up as a place to store garden tools and seed. He and Ricky Dan patched the roof leaks, remounted a door they could put a padlock on, boarded up the building's only window and built shelves to store Granny's Mason jars full of strawberry jam, green beans, corn, carrots, and peas she'd canned for winter.

When it became obvious years later that Jamey needed somewhere to work, Lloyd had helped clear the brush away from the old building and he and Jamey had repaired the floorboards and the biggest of the wall cracks to help keep out the chill in the wintertime. There was a stone fireplace on one wall of the larger room, but Granny said not to light a fire in it, that birds had nested in the chimney.

Jamey paused a few feet from the shed door and listened. Bucket stopped, too, and plopped down in the dirt at his feet. The old dog always looked for an excuse to lie down. The woods were quiet in the autumn. Peaceful. Jamey liked this time of the year best of all, when the only sound was the sigh of the wind, the rustle of dry leaves, and sometimes a woodpecker digging for food. Summers was noisy! The squalling cry of cicadas filled the whole hollow then, buzzing loud as the chain saw Lloyd'd used to cut the brush that was all tangled up around the shed.

The piece of jet Lloyd had left for Jamey lay beside the door on the small front stoop. Lloyd couldn't take it inside because the door was locked. Jamey had a key, kept it safe and secure in the right front pocket of his jeans. After he unlocked the door and fastened the padlock back together, he carefully replaced the key in his pocket, proud that he'd been trusted to take care of it.

The lock on the door wasn't so much because there was anything in the building to steal—unless somebody had a hankering for coal carvings and sculpture tools. Mostly, the lock was to keep out teen-agers, who Granny said would use the shed for drinking and doing drugs and other things that made Jamey blush to think about.

He leaned down and picked up the piece of jet and cradled it in his arms as tenderly as he'd have held a newborn baby. Not that it'd break, of course. You had to hit it real hard with a hammer to break it, but it was a rare, precious thing so Jamey treated it like one.

He went through the door with Bucket on his heels and set the rock down on the workbench. Bucket collapsed on the old rug Jamey'd put on the floor for him to lay on and let out a sigh of foul-smelling doggie breath. Jamey's eyes hadn't got used to the sudden dark of the building, but there wasn't a whole lot in there to trip over—only his worktable and stool, and he could have found them with his eyes closed.

Jamey didn't need bright light to do his arts. Good thing, too, because there wasn't no bright sunshine here in the woods, and the building's only window was boarded up. Jamey worked by lantern light. Half a dozen coal oil lanterns sat on shelves around the room. The largest rested on the far end of the door-on-sawhorses work-table. When Jamey started carving, he'd light them all and then move the biggest one down on the table near him.

It wasn't just because there wasn't no sunlight or electricity that the shed was lit by lanterns. Jamey often worked on his for-sale stat-ues on the front porch or the back deck of the house. Those wasn't real art. But for the carvings that mattered to him, Jamey worked in the flickering flames of a lantern. The dancing light made the shiny coal sparkle like stars in the sky on a summer night. And Jamey didn't tell nobody this part—because wouldn't nobody understand what he meant—but he was certain that only lantern light revealed the im-ages in the coal it was his job to set free.

Jamey went around and lit each of the lanterns until the room was aglow in a golden light. He used kitchen matches and blew each one completely out. Stomped them on the floor, too. Jamey had learned to be careful with fire! Then he closed the door and sat down on his stool and was very still for a long time. He stared at the shiny piece of jet, studied and enjoyed it. His first task would be to chip carefully at it to remove slivers of the surface, make it flat and smooth—enough for a relief mural. Only after it was smooth, could he begin to carefully remove pieces of stone to reveal the art buried inside.

"Whadda ya think, ValVleen?" he asked the yellow bird that had perched tranquilly on his shoulder all the way up the hill. "What do you 'spect is in there?"

The bird chirped, whirred, and whistled a reply that was so close to words it made Jamey's mind itch trying to understand it. Some-times he pretended like he did; didn't want to hurt ValVleen's feel-ings, make her think didn't nobody listen to what she said.

"Yeah, I think you're right, ValVleen," he told the bird, his face serious. "I think there's a mural in there with lots of people in it."

Where did that *come from?*

"And if'n there's lots of people in it, I sure hope they's happy people."

Jamey lifted his eyes and looked at the door that led into the only other room in the building. Not much bigger than a closet, the room contained drying racks for ginseng, wooden crates that held potatoes and turnips from the garden and a handful of ratty old pillowcases Jamey used to cover his murals. But it also held a mural Jamey kept secret, one Granny said he couldn't never let nobody see—ever.

He'd carved the hidden mural right after he'd done the one of Granny's wedding that she hung on the wall in her bedroom. She didn't hang this one up, though, but she did keep it in the house for months looking at it. Didn't never let JoJo see it, and sometimes when JoJo was in school, Jamey'd come down from the shed and find Granny at the kitchen table looking at the mural...and *crying.* First time he found her like that he got real upset, too, wanted to know what it was in the mural made her so unhappy. She'd wiped her eyes and told him, "never you mind, now," and put the piece of jet back in a pillowcase and shoved it under her bed.

"I ain't never gonna carve nothin' like that ever again," he'd told her and tried real hard not to cry his own self. Granny'd come over and sat down on the couch next to him. She'd taken his face in her hands and looked so deep into his eyes it had made him dizzy.

He remembered exactly what she'd said to him that day.

"What you carved didn't come outta' yore head, Jamey." Her voice was kind of thick sounding. "So I got to b'lieve the good Lord put it in that piece of jet. And he wouldn't a-put it in there if'n he didn't intend for you to get it out."

She'd told him he had to dig into whatever rocks he was give and release what God had hid inside them. That even if folks didn't like what was in them rocks, it was still his job to carve them.

Jamey'd studied and studied that mural, looked at it ever which way, but he never could find nothing in it that'd make a person cry.

The next summer, he found out it had the power to do more than make Granny cry. It was during a big storm. Thunder woke Jamey up, a rumbling, booming sound right outside his window that near scared him to death. He was already trembling when his night light blinked out, left his room dark as a lump of coal except when the lightning lit up the sky and made scary shadows on the floor. He wanted to run fast as he could and get in bed with JoJo, but she had spent the night with her friend, Becca. Then a glow come under the door from the living room; Granny must have got out a flashlight or lit candles. He wanted to run in there and sit real close to her on the living room couch, but he was too scared to move. So he hid under the covers in his room and listened to the storm rage outside.

Then Granny'd screamed.

It was the terriblest sound Jamey ever did hear in all his life, like the cry that raccoon made when they'd backed over it that time—before Granny killed it with a rock. And scared or not, Jamey leapt out of bed, ran to his door and yanked it open. Just as he did, the electricity come back on and the light was so bright it blinded him. Out of squinty eyes, he seen Granny in front of the table, with a chair laying on the floor beside her that maybe she'd knocked over when she jumped up. She stared at the table with the awfulest look on her face, like there was a rattlesnake curled up on it or a black widow spider. But wasn't nothing on the table but a couple of candles and Jamey's mural, the one that'd made her cry. She had her hand clamped over her mouth and her shoulders shook but she didn't make no sound at all.

Jamey went up to her and put his hand on her arm. Then he couldn't help it—he started to cry, too. She turned around and hugged him, but she didn't hush up. The two of them stood in the middle of the kitchen and cried, but only Granny knew what they was crying about.

The next day, she had the mural wrapped back up in its pillow-case and she told him to take it up to the shed and hide it underneath the potato and turnip boxes in the little storage room. Said to leave it there and not never let nobody see it.

He'd asked her if she wanted him to take the sledge hammer to it and smash it—though it would have tore him up to do that. Ever one of his arts was precious to him, even one that made Granny cry. But she shook her head. "Ain't no sense smashin' the mirror just 'cause you don't like what you see in it," she'd said, and he didn't have no idea what that meant.

He looked down at the shiny black jet on the table and felt that fluttery feeling in his belly he got before he started to work. But this fluttering wasn't excited; it was something else. Felt like there was little critters with wings flying around inside him, but they wasn't birds or butterflies; they was wasps or yellow jackets, something mean and nasty.

"ValVleen, you s'pose this 'un is gonna make Granny cry?" The bird cocked its head to one side, looked at Jamey and let out a lone chirp, a single note.

"Yeah," Jamey said with a sigh. "I think so, too."

He picked up his chisel and his mallet and started to work.

CHAPTER 11

GRANNY DIDN'T PRETEND she hadn't watched Will and Lloyd, didn't jump back from the window and act like she'd been clearing the table or doing the dishes. She faced Will when he walked back in the front door.

"You 'n Lloyd was hard at it." It wasn't a question so Will said nothing. "You need to know his nose was already outta joint 'fore you got here. He's got reason enough to be acting peculiar.

As Granny described what had happened to Lloyd's family, Will watched another cherished illusion go down in flames.

When he was drunk, he'd pitied Lloyd; when he was sober, he'd envied him. And sometimes it was the other way around. He felt slobbering sorry that his friend still dug coal deep in a dark hole in the ground, still lived paycheck to paycheck, still got laid off, went on strike, got hurt, and breathed dust into his lungs every day. At the same time, he had conjured up a Courier & Ives fantasy of the loving wife and beautiful children who waited to welcome Lloyd home at night. Will had squandered two decades of living, had thrown away the simple dignity of hard work and caring for a family. Now, it was clear that wasn't always what it was cracked up to be either.

Granny mused out loud, as she had often done when he was a boy, in a stream of consciousness that covered everything and nothing and all points in between. It had been a soothing sound that he hadn't listened to then. He listened now.

"…ain't rightly sure what it was come over Lloyd," she said, in that soft voice of hers that commanded attention. "Course there was a time there in the beginning when I didn't know nothin'. When a good day was makin' it to the end of it."

Will stopped her. She'd been clearing off the table, doing the job Jamey'd bailed on, as she spoke. He motioned for her to come and sit beside him on the couch.

"I should have been here for you…" he began. "You needed—"

"Honey, what I needed couldn't *nobody* give me! Didn't matter who was here. That kind of hurtin', ain't nothin' makes it bearable." She stopped. "Was times I nearly come right out of my skin. I'd be just standin' there and I'd realize I's sobbin' and I didn't even know it."

She looked past him, her eyes fixed on a reality he couldn't see. "You cain't do it all at once. Nobody can. That much grief, you cain't take it all in one gulp. Bowman. Ricky Dan. Even Ed." She smiled a little half smile and didn't try to hide her mouth. "Poor Ed, the onliest one of my brothers I ever talked to about real stuff, heart stuff. The others'd go on 'bout how to skin a coon or catch the weasel that had got in the hen house and never said nothing that mattered."

She took a breath.

"So I grieved 'em one at a time. I'd say, 'Today, I'm gonna grieve for Bowman.' The next day, I'd grieve for Ricky Dan. Then Ed. It's the onliest thing a body can do it. Try to swallow it all at one time and it'll choke the life right out of you."

Her quiet voice got so soft it was almost a whisper. "I took to the closet. There in the beginning, I had to. The house was so quiet I could hear my own heartbeat. I'd turn on the television loud as it'd go in the living room and the radio in the bedroom. Then I'd plug in that fancy Hoover vacuum cleaner Bow bought from that nice young man come to the door." She looked a little sheepish. "And I'd take it with me into the bedroom closet in Ricky Dan's room, sit down on top of a pile of his stinky shoes, his shirts and pants hangin' down all around me. I'd hit the switch on the vacuum and that little bitty space'd fill up with noise..." There was a beat of silence. "...and then I'd *scream*. Loud's I could, scream and wail 'til my voice give plumb out. I'd beat my fists against the wall 'til my hands was black and blue." Then she whispered. "I wanted to make more noise than the roar under the mountain, because my hurt was bigger and power-fuller than the explosion that took 'em from me."

For a moment, she had the look he'd seen on her face when he woke up and found her beside his hospital bed. Her eyes—they were blasted, scorched, vacant hollows in her face you couldn't bear to look into and couldn't stand to look away from. You could see into her through her eyes, all the way down to the bottom of her soul. You could see through her, too, like she was as translucent as a piece of tissue paper. And in some way he was never able to understand or explain, he could see his own reflection in her eyes. He wasn't trans-lucent, though. He was filled to the top of his head with darkness.

"I wasn't the onliest one, of course. We's all half crazy. I looked around at the memorial service we had 'cause we didn't have no bod-ies for a funeral, and it was like I's lookin' in a mirror. Grief had marked our faces so's we all looked like family."

She seemed to realize that she'd gone there, to that place. You could see her close up, batten down the hatches as he'd been taught in the Navy, so a storm couldn't come along, pour water down through them and drown you.

She rose abruptly, continued to clean and took up her mono-logue about Lloyd where she'd left off.

"For years after, Lloyd wasn't no fit human a-tall. He run with the wild 'uns, drank and lord knows what else, got Norma Jean Phelps pregnant so he married her, and then I heared he knocked her around some. I cain't testify to that, mind, but I seen her once in the grocery store with sunglasses on." She gave him a disdainful look. "Like her wearin' sunglasses to buy a loaf of bread and a gallon of milk in Aintree Holler was any less noticeable than the black eye they was coverin' up."

She put the orange juice into the refrigerator and stood with a dish towel in her hand.

"Then it was like overnight, Lloyd up'n changed." She turned to face him. "Will, he was so different, I wanted to reach out and rip the Lloyd mask off'n him to see who was really underneath there behavin' that way. 'You need anything, Granny?' he'd say. 'Can I take the kids to the picture show, or bring you some fresh tomatoes?' It was Lloyd run me and Jamey to the hospital that night the boy had the croup so bad he liked to died. Lloyd went and got JoJo her first day of high school when she called home bawlin'."

"Ricky Dan didn't like Harlan County High School much either," Will said quietly.

Granny smiled. "No, he didn't, did he. You's the only one made it through to graduate."

They sat quiet for a moment. And it was a good quiet.

"Jamey Boy probably woulda liked it, though, if he'd got that far." Granny's smile grew wider. "You can see it, can't you, Will? How he's like his daddy, only…pure. Just light, t'hout nothin' grown-up in him to cloud it. Sometimes, I look at that boy and he near blinds me."

"Yeah, I can see it." For two decades, Will couldn't even think about Ricky Dan Sparrow without the pain of it driving him into a bottle. But after he got sober, the pain didn't go away, but he came to terms with it. And when he did, he cherished his memories instead of running from them. In his mind, he had often tried to tack words on to what it was about Ricky Dan that had made him so special. All he ever came up with were greeting-card homilies. They were true, though. Ricky Dan Sparrow was *good*. So was his son.

"How far did Jamey get in school?"

"Fifth grade. But I ain't sure how much he learned 'fore that and how much his teachers passed him on 'cause they didn't want to hurt his feelings."

"Well, at least not going to school gave him all day every day to work on his 'arts,' so—"

"Not ever day." She paused for a beat. "Jamey Boy's got a job, Will. He's a miner. I thought you knowed that."

"*Jamey?*" Will felt like someone had kicked him in the belly.

"He's been off this week, but he'll—"

"You *let* that boy...?"

Granny looked like he'd slapped her and Will instantly wished he could call the words back.

"You think I *wanted* to? Think I didn't wish I could lock him up in his room and never...?" She let out a long, slow breath. "The mines is all there is. Same now as when you's growin' up. It's what we do. He's a growed man; ain't my place to—"

"I shouldn't have said that, Granny. I'm sorry."

"Came a time I couldn't protect him no more. JoJo neither." She spread her big hands out in front of her in a helpless gesture. "And right now, it's JoJo needs protectin'."

"JoJo?"

"I ain't got no idea what's eatin' at that child, but some'm is. Oh, she's always been...fragile like. Her mama was that way—you 'member? Kindly delicate, like if you wasn't real careful, she'd break apart in your hands. And losin' Darrell like she done..."

Granny told Will the story of JoJo's marriage at 16 to a "nice young fella" who was killed in a mining accident before their first anniversary.

"She was finally coming outta that...and then *bam!* Some'm happened. She went up Lexington ever weekend the last part of the summer to see Becca, this friend of hers goes to UK. Then one

Saturday mornin' she went and come right back home 'fore supper. But the girl who come back to the holler that afternoon wasn't the same one left. And she ain't been the same since."

"How so?"

"Won't eat. I bet she's lost 10 pounds and that girl didn't have it to lose. Don't sleep, up all hours of the night, roams around the house. When she does sleep, she has nightmares, cries out all pitiful like. She picks at herself, got sores on her hands. I've done all I know to do to get her to tell me what's wrong, but she's closed up tighter'n a new boot. Won't say nothin'."

Granny stopped. "You don't s'pose...could *you* talk to her, Will?"

"Why me?" But Will had to admit he'd seen something in JoJo's eyes he recognized. Desperation, maybe. Or despair. He could relate to either one.

"I just thought maybe you could reach her. Somebody's got to."

There was such yearning in Granny's plea Will couldn't refuse. "Okay, if you want me to, I'll give it a shot. But she just met me, Granny. I can't imagine why she'd tell me anything."

Granny put the dish towel down. "And you don't have to tell *me* nothin', neither. Nary a thing you don't want to, Sugar. It's 'nough you're here; I'm powerful content with that."

That was Granny. Her train of thought would set off full steam one way and without warning she'd derail it and take off down a track in the opposite direction. You had to hold on tight when you talked to her or you'd get thrown right off the train.

He took a breath. "I *have to* tell you..."

"It's a mighty heavy load you're carryin' 'round, son." Her voice was soft, her eyes tender. "Don't you think it's time to put it in a sack and leave it sittin' by the door?"

That's what she'd always told the boys when something was bothering them that dragged down their spirits. She'd tell them to tie it up tight in a sack and forget about it. It'd be right there anytime they wanted to pick the burden back up again; they could leave it by the door so they'd know where to find it.

"Me 'n you, we got to have us a serious talk, so how 'bout we sit ourselves down in a coupla days…Friday mornin', maybe, and you can open up that sack and we'll clean it out together."

Friday morning seemed right, fitting. The truth should come out *before* the anniversary of the explosion, a couple of hours short of two whole decades too late.

"All right, in the sack it goes."

Granny nodded, didn't speak, only looked at him.

"You's like smoke, you know that, Will. You's there, but you ain't. I'm askeered to reach out my hand to touch you 'cause there won't be nothin' there a-tall to grab."

"I'm not going anywhere, Granny," he said softly. "I won't vanish on you." He almost said he'd never vanish on her again, but he was not a man in any position to make promises.

Her eyes welled with tears and she suddenly got very busy scrubbing a non-existent speck off the countertop.

"Actually, that's not entirely true," he said. "I am going somewhere right now. I'm going into town. Want to walk down the hill with me?"

There was such a stricken look on Granny's face that for a moment Will thought she must have totally misunderstood him.

"I'm not *leaving*, Granny, just walking into town. You want to come?"

"Cain't." That was all she said, and suddenly there was a whole herd of nonexistent spots on the countertop that needed to be wiped. "You go on ahead; tell me 'bout it when you get back."

Then she began a noisy redistribution of large pots and frying pans in the sink creating a clatter that was clearly Will's cue to leave.

But why wouldn't Granny go with him?

Chapter 12

JoJo stopped by the post office and picked up the mail on her way to work so the mailman wouldn't deposit it in the mailbox in front of the trailer. She'd done that every day for the past month—told the postmaster she'd ordered something as a surprise for Granny.

She took the handful of circulars and bills from the clerk at the window and tuned out his daily, unsolicited report on his son's accomplishments out there in the wide world, how he was about to graduate from the University of Louisville and was considering law school. She'd gone on a date with the guy once and figured he'd ought to take up lawyering. A more complicated occupation—like an elevator operator who had to learn the route—was way more than he could handle.

She thumbed through the small pile of envelopes as she walked to her car. Then she stopped. Froze. There it was, the envelope she'd been expecting. It was addressed to Joanna Darlene Sparrow and it had the official seal of the University of Kentucky College of Medicine Research Center. She tore it open, ignored the letter inside and stared down at the check, made out to her for $300. It was about time!

Then a little half smile played across her lips. Actually, the timing on the check was absolutely perfect. Now she had plenty of money to buy herself a one-way ticket to Nowhere At All.

The words on a poster tacked to the bulletin board near their table in the Student Center catch JoJo's eye.

Wanted:
Students to Participate in Research Study
Summer Session—$300

She nudges Becca and cocks her head toward the poster.

"That mean what I think it does?"

Becca glances at the poster. "They have those things in here all the time. The med school research center's always looking for guinea pigs."

JoJo has a standing invitation to visit her friend Becca at the University of Kentucky, and though the college campus is as foreign to JoJo as stepping off a rocket on an uncharted planet, anything's better than spending every weekend in Harlan County. And she knows it's good for Becca, too. Her life is tough. Becca had been chubby in high school; she ballooned in college. Now, she is well on her way to 300 pounds. Always shy, Becca has made no friends at school. It helps to see a familiar face and hear a mountain voice.

The two girls had been inseparable, joined at the hip their whole lives until their sophomore year in high school when JoJo dropped out of school to marry Darrell. Becca graduated and went off to the University of Kentucky in Lexington, joked that the scholarship she'd gotten paid her to be the school's "token, barefoot, toe-in-the-sand hillbilly."

When JoJo visits, Becca takes time off from her job at the cosmetics counter at the Walgreen's on Man Of War Boulevard and they wander the stores in Fayette Mall—window shopping, of course; that's all either one of them can afford—and hang out together in the coffee shops around campus. In the past 6 months, JoJo has started to flirt back with the guys she's met there.

"You ever done one of them studies?" JoJo asks.

"Once. Why?"

"What'd you have to do?"

"It was a stupid color-recognition thing. We went into this little room in the psych building and looked at swatches of fabric in solid colors—red, blue, and green. Then we sat outside for 10 minutes and went back in and had to pick those colors out of plaid fabric with half a dozen different shades of reds, blues, and greens. I think they were trying to prove that the mind doesn't have a true memory for color—at least mine didn't. But I got paid 50 bucks for one afternoon."

Becca looks at the poster and back at JoJo.

"You interested in that one?"

"Maybe. Sounds like an easy way to make $300."

"Paying that much, they'll get a lot of takers. I'd sign up if I didn't have to work."

JoJo reads the rest of the poster out loud.

"Participants must be between the ages of 18 and 30, willing to provide family medical history and submit to blood tests. Time requirement is 3 hours a week, from noon to 3 P.M., every Saturday between August 15 and September 30. Payment of $300 will be made within 30 working days after the last session. Interested persons should fill out the questionnaire below and return it to the University of Kentucky College of Medicine Research Center before July 31, 2000."

"You reckon you have to be a student to do it?"

"Why would they care? If you've got a pulse and you match what they're looking for, they'll take you."

JoJo got back into her car, tossed the mail on the front seat and drove to the Jiffy Stop. She was early, so she sat in the car and read the letter that had accompanied the check. Her lip began to tremble and a tear slipped out of her eye and slid down her cheek. When she reached up to wipe it away, the blow-up figure out front of the store caught her eye. A fifteen-foot-tall yellow tube with floppy arms and a grinning face bounced and swayed its herky-jerky dance as air was pumped up through it from below.

JoJo hated that figure! Almost went out one night after work and sabotaged the pump so it would lay there limp instead of standing out front having seizures all day.

The creature reminded her of the skinnys.

She sits in a featureless room with a table, two chairs and a large mirror on the wall. The mirror's really a window where the researchers watch what happens in the testing room. If you look at it just right, you can see the faint outlines of the people behind it, particularly when they open the door in the back of the room and the hall light shines in.

On the table in front of her are kids' blocks and simple puzzles. She's been told what to expect, but she cringes anyway when they bring in the first skinny—that's what she came to call them later because they were all emaciated, looked like escapees from a concentration camp.

The woman appears to be 10 or 15 years older than JoJo, but it's hard to guess her age the way she jerks around, flails her arms, rolls her eyes and emits a haunting wail that seems more an attempt to speak than a scream.

JoJo only makes eye contact with the skinny once. It's after they've been together in the room for over an hour. JoJo performs simple tasks, stacks blocks and puts puzzle pieces together and the skinny tries to do the same things. After the skinny propels the puzzle off the table with a jerky arm movement, she looks into JoJo's eyes. It is a pleading look, a panicked look. A look of such pain and fear it freezes JoJo's heart. It hits her then, for the first time, that there's a person locked away inside that flopping, jerking body, a prisoner who can't get out, can't even cry for help, can't do anything at all except scream with her eyes, a wail of terror, anger, fear—and disgust. Her eyes are all she has left.

After that, JoJo never makes eye contact with a skinny again.

A car horn honked and startled JoJo and she dropped the letter into her lap. A white cargo van with no windows in the back had pulled up to the gas pumps in front of the Jiffy Stop. The driver, Dough Boy, waved at her, his big idiot grin colored brown by the snuff up under his lower lip.

JoJo smiled. Yep, this was her lucky day, all right. First the check and now Frank Pillsbury. She didn't have to run all over the county to find him. The very man who could get her all the Oxycontin she wanted—or any other drug her little heart might desire—was right here. And now she had plenty of money to make a purchase.

She got out of the car and walked over to Dough Boy's van. When he rolled his window down, the cloying sweet stink of a recently-smoked joint was so strong it made her eyes water. The big man with a riot of tangled, fire-truck red hair had a deceptively harmless, cuddly look—like a fat Raggedy Andy doll. But he was neither harmless nor cuddly; he was a cold, ruthless druggie who would sell his mother's soul to feed his runaway Oxy habit.

"Ain't seen you in a while, JJ," he said. "Where you been?"

"Around."

"You ain't been 'round none of yore good friends."

Translate that: you haven't hung out in the world of totally wasted human beings who'd only wanted to get a little high every once in a while to forget about life and now they had no life to forget. Called Hillbilly Heroin in the mountains, Oxycontin was voraciously addictive. Her fiancé Avery had known that; the suckers he'd sold it to hadn't. He was one of the dealers who'd capitalized on what had become a tidal wave of painkiller addiction sweeping across Appalachia.

JoJo's and Avery's had been a whirlwind romance. She'd met him at the Jiffy, had been so lonely and lost after Darrell's death; she was ripe for picking. And he'd picked. In the beginning, she pretended she didn't know what he did for a living; by the time he got busted, she was desperate for a way out, scared he'd turn violent if she broke up with him. When he got scooped up in the drug sting, she wanted to find the nearest Drug Enforcement Agency agent and kiss his whole face.

"Been busy." She glanced around, then lowered her voice. "I need some Oxy."

Dough Boy's round face broke into a smile. "You come to the right place, darlin'. How much you want?"

She told him and he nodded. He quoted a price. It was high, but she didn't care, didn't even try to dicker. Just said, "Done."

"I'll be back here at closing time," he said, then spit brown liquid from the plug of Skoal onto the concrete. Barely missed her shoe. "Fact is, I can make this a reg'lar stop if'n you want. Come back whenever you need me to…" he smiled. "…refill yore tank."

"Nope," she said and straightened up. "I won't need nothin' next week. Nothin' at all." She turned and walked into the building.

CHAPTER 13

WILL HAD BEEN shaken by how much his home and Granny's had changed in two decades, but he was surprised by how little the rest of the hollow had.

Oh, houses had new paint and roofs, had added rooms, carports or garages, or had refurbished the collection of car carcasses and appliances in their front yards. Trailer houses had sprouted like crabgrass on every street and the bridge over Turkey Neck Creek had been moved. You could no longer go directly from town to the mine. You had to go out to the road and around. The mine was now like a lot of things in the mountains, "close as the crow flies," but a while to get there. Will thought of his sponsor, who had grown up on the other side of the mountain—in a town just 3 or 4 miles away that was probably a half-hour drive from Aintree Hollow.

But for all the changes Will saw, there was way more that was just as he remembered it. The grocery store that shared a building with the post office. Unlike the bright Jiffy Stop on the other side of the bridge, this store was dim and shadowy. The door still swung open on a long, arthritic spring, its screen so full of holes it wasn't even a psychological deterrent to the flies that cruised in and out of the building. Dusty canned goods sat on its wooden shelving above well-oiled floors, and the back of the building was devoted to clothing—steel-toed miners' boots, T-shirts, boxer shorts, work shirts, and pants. On the counter beside the cash register was a large selection of different types of snuff and chewing tobacco. Bowman and the other miners had always chomped down on a plug as soon as they left the house in the morning to oil their mouths against the black dust.

And Pete's Place was still there, too. Snuggled in between the barber shop and the only garage in town, the little café/coffee shop/bar/psychiatrist's office still had rows of tables along two narrow walls, with red plastic tablecloths and red-and-white checked curtains. Appeared to be the same curtains that had been there when Will left.

He opened a squeaky screen door that rivaled the grocery store's for holiness, and stepped inside. A man who sat alone at a table by the window lifted his deeply lined bloodhound face over the top of the newspaper he was reading to see who'd come in. Hobart Bascomb. He was smaller, with a lot less hair and way more belly, but his chocolate brown eyes still looked merry and mischievous, and his smile was as empty as it had ever been. Hob always said teeth were for sissies.

A case could be made that Will and Lloyd weren't the only survivors of the explosion in Harlan #7. In a way, Hob was, too. He'd been scheduled to work that day on the crew with Ricky Dan, Will, and Lloyd. But he'd called in sick. Everybody knew he'd been out partying the night before and was too hung over to work.

For a moment, Hob didn't recognize Will. Then a surprised smile spread over his face. "Well, if it ain't Will Gribbins," he said. His speech had that peculiar, flubbery sound common to the toothless. "I heared in the Jiffy you's in town." He put down the newspaper and gestured to the empty chair across from him.

"Have a seat. Want a cup of coffee?" Hob didn't wait for Will's reply before he signaled the waitress with a coffee-pouring gesture.

"How's the world treating you, Hob?" Will eased down into the old wooden chair.

"Better'n I deserve. How 'bout y'self. You home for the memorial doin's?"

He didn't wait for Will to answer that question either. "They got me down to speak—you b'lieve that? Like I got the smarts to say some'm anybody'd wanna hear. I never shoulda said yes. I'm all tore up over it, nervous as a nun at a penguin shoot."

The teenage waitress arrived with a cup, saucer, and coffee pot. Will started to fish in his pocket full of change to pay her, but she waved him off.

"You're the guy was in #7, ain't you?" she asked. With the memorial ceremony on Friday, the disaster was on everybody's minds. When Will nodded, she smiled and told him, "Yore money ain't no good in here," then filled his cup and walked away.

"You gettin' old, Will? There was a time you's faster with coins than that." Hob's face lit up. "You still walk a quarter across the tops of yore fingers like you usta could? I got a big kick outta you boys' magic tricks."

Will sat stock-still. His heart had begun to knock out the side wall of his chest, but Hob didn't notice.

"Jus' t'ween me, you, and the gatepost, I always thought you's better with coins than Lloyd was with ropes."

As Will draped a smile between his ears and sipped his coffee, he tried to remember exactly how he and Lloyd had gotten suckered into becoming magicians.

They'd only volunteered to work on the elementary school Halloween Carnival because the two best-looking girls in the hollow were in charge of the haunted house. They figured they'd have the girls all to themselves on carnival day while they gathered up supplies to scare blindfolded children—cold spaghetti for brains, cold grapes for eyeballs, oily rice for maggots.

But somehow their job had grown to include entertaining the crowd of children waiting in line to go into the haunted house. Will couldn't remember how that had happened, though he remembered clearly that it'd been Lloyd's idea for them to become magicians, and Lloyd who'd sent off for magic-trick kits he'd seen advertised in a magazine.

Once they got their hands on the kits, though, the whole thing took on a life of its own. Will became the Amazing Willdini; Lloyd became Jacobi the Magnificent. They practiced for hours, each determined to be a better magician than the other. He and Lloyd had competed with each other over one thing or another their whole lives.

The boys even took their magic into the mine with them. Will carried coins in his pocket; Lloyd's magic rope was stuffed down his shirt. During lunch breaks, they'd amused the other miners with their skill.

"You do magic tricks the day she blew?" Hob asked.

Yes, he and Lloyd had put on a lunch-break performance that day. They had entertained men who would be dead in less than half an hour.

Will and a dozen other miners are seated on a piece of yellow plastic curtain the shuttle operator tossed on top of the crumbled coal covering the shaft floor. The profound dark is pierced by spears of light from the miners' headlamps.

Next to Will, one of the men who operates the roof bolting machine rests against the column of coal. Will leans over, pulls a quarter out of the man's ear and holds it up for the other miners to see.

"What the…?" The pinner man feels around in his ear as if there might be another quarter in there, and if there is, he wants it out. "I wanna know how you done that."

"A magician never reveals his secrets," Will says.

Ricky Dan is seated on the other side of Will and he bursts out laughing. "If you're a magician, I'm a Chinese airplane pilot!"

Bowman is leaned against the pillar beside Ricky Dan, his legs extended straight out in front of him. As the miner man, Bow operates a machine shaped like a shoe box that runs on a thousand volts of electricity, with a revolving drum on the front studded with tungsten carbide bits. Called a continuous miner, the machine can rip more coal from a coal face than two dozen miners with picks. It also creates more coal dust and more cracks in the roof where methane can seep into the shaft. A small operator's chair—with a cage on top of it that's jammed down like a coffin lid—is located on the side. The continuous miner fits so tight in the shaft the top scrapes the roof. The operator sits for hours, his legs folded Indian style in front of him with a constant stream of dirt dribbling from the roof onto his helmet and down his shirt. Bowman relishes the opportunity to dust off and stretch out.

"Com'on, Will," Bow says, "how'd you do that?"

Will doesn't answer Bowman's question. Instead, he holds out his open right hand in front of him with the coin in his palm.

"Now you see it…" he says, and closes his hand in a fist.

Conditions in a coal mine ought to make it the perfect place to do slight-of-hand—absolute darkness, harsh light, and shifting shadows. Add to that the haze of coal and rock dust that shines in the lights from the shuttle and continuous miner 50 feet away; black dust motes in a sunbeam. There shouldn't be so much dust. The bad air means the mine's ventilation isn't working like it's supposed to. A lot of other things in this dog hole mine don't work like they're supposed to, either.

Despite the murky air, the miners' headlamps pose a problem to Will's performance. With all of them trained on what he's doing, he has to get it just right, so when he makes his hand into a fist, he's careful to leave his thumb on the inside. As he slowly opens his right hand again, he passes his left hand in front of it to hide the deft movement of his right thumb that slides the coin off his palm and down between his middle two fingers. It protrudes from the bottom side of his hand but is invisible from the top.

Palm up, his hand looks empty and he concludes with a flourish: "...and now you don't."

The shuttle driver spits out an expletive with the tobacco juice he squirts off the edge of the curtain. "That ain't right." He shakes his head. "That just ain't right."

He's a new guy, down from Hazard. Showed up this morning to apply for a job just as the outside foreman got a call from Hobart Bascomb saying he was sick. Sick...yeah, right. Hob was probably still drunk! The foreman had hung up and put the Perry County miner to work on the spot. Will heard the guy whoop and holler, "This here's my lucky day!"

Seated across from Will, Lloyd pulls his magic rope out of his shirt. It is a strong nylon rope no bigger around than his little finger that appears to be more than a yard long. In truth, Lloyd has several ropes of varying lengths, not just one; he conceals the breaks between them with his hands as he holds them out in front of him and has a long, unbroken rope stretched up his shirt sleeve.

"Here we have a rope, a single rope," he says, then lets one end of palmed rope piece drop. "Well, no, actually we have two ropes." He picks up the end of the rope he dropped and lets two other ends drop out of his other hand. "Where did all these ropes come from?"

"I seen that. I seen what he done!" the mechanic squeals. Lloyd palms the small rope pieces in his right hand as the man

reaches for the rope in his left. "See, it ain't one piece it's..." The man grabs the end of the rope Lloyd has stretched up his sleeve and pulls. A solid rope, 4 feet long, slides out through Lloyd's fingers. "Well, I never..."

"Hey, Lloyd," Will says, misdirecting the miners' attention for the instant it takes Lloyd to shove the short rope pieces up his sleeve. "You tie knots in that rope?" He knows Lloyd can; he's watched him practice.

Lloyd twists the rope into a slip knot, a square knot and a sheepshank knot in rapid succession. For a finale, he ties the rope in a vicious-looking hangman's noose.

"'Bout time to get back to work," the boss says. Will drops his coins with a clunk into his empty lunch bucket; Lloyd shoves his ropes down the front of his shirt. "I want you boys," the boss indicates Lloyd, Ricky Dan, and Will, "to go up and lay track."

As the continuous miner digs the shaft deeper and deeper into the mountain, the rails for the mantrips loaded with supplies or transporting miners in and out of the mine are left farther and farther behind. The track now ends more than a quarter of a mile up the shaft from the mile-deep face where two crews of miners are at work.

The men get to their feet, bent over under the 48-inch roof. Will shivers and Ricky Dan leans toward him.

"You okay?" he asks, but Will says nothing. It's cold and dank here. Water constantly drips out through cracks in the roof, stands 2 or 3 inches deep on the muddy floor. The damp seeps into the miners' bones, but the chill Will feels has nothing to do with the temperature.

Afraid of what Ricky Dan can read in his eyes, Will won't meet his gaze. When he feels Ricky Dan's hand on his shoulder, the small gesture almost brings tears to Will's eyes.

"You're gonna be fine, Will," Ricky Dan's voice is quiet so the others can't hear.

Will is wearing Ricky Dan's old "red hat." Shortly after he turned 18, Ricky Dan had gone to work in a huge mine that employed hundreds of miners. Big mines like that required every miner who'd worked underground less than a year to wear a red helmet to let veterans know he was a rookie, so they could watch out for him, make sure he didn't get hurt—or do something stupid that put the rest of them in danger. Since Ricky Dan had come by his two years of underground experience illegally, as an underage miner, he'd had to suffer the indignity of a red hat. In small operations like #7 where all the miners knew each other, red hats weren't necessary. But Will wore it anyway because it had belonged to Ricky Dan.

The other miners pick up the litter of their lunch—apple cores and bread crusts, but Will has nothing to pick up. In the three months he has worked full-time in Harlan #7, he has never eaten a bite inside the mine. He feeds his sandwich every morning to Worthless, Ricky Dan's coon hound. He doesn't bring anything in his lunch bucket but an extra water bottle to add to the large Clorox Bleach bottle full of water he carries with him. There are no drinking fountains in a coal mine. There is a porta-potty, though. Mining regulations require it. But the miners know they'd better not use it—servicing a porta-potty costs money.

Will glances at Bowman as the big man settles into the small seat on the continuous miner and curls his legs in front of him. Ricky Dan had been working as the miner's helper, learning to operate the coal-chewing shark from his father, the best miner man in Harlan County. Bow flashes Will a kind, knowing smile, then turns on the machine, moves the head into the face, and unleashes a screaming, vibrating, roaring rumble as the metal blades tear into the coal seam, first near the floor, then moving gradually up to the roof. Will turns and follows Lloyd and Ricky Dan toward the track shaft. He will never see Bowman Sparrow again.

"I don't remember if we did magic that day or not," Will lied, and struggled to keep his voice level. Hob eyed Will up and down.

"I ain't gonna lie to you, Will. You look worse'n folks was tellin' me you did. And you talk funny, too, got a right queer accent."

Will threw his head back and laughed.

"You don't look so good yourself, Hob."

"Yeah, but I got a 'xcuse. I got a cancer."

"Hob, I was…I didn't mean…"

"Aw, it ain't gonna kill me, least not anytime soon. But it keeps me out the mine." He paused, reached into his pocket and removed a crumpled package of cigarettes. "And ya never know—might be it's savin' my life same as my hangover done."

"Folks hold it against you, Hob—that you should have been down there and you weren't?"

Hob's face turned solemn. "No, far's I know ain't nobody's nose outta joint 'bout that. It's…I think I bother people 'cause I'm a reminder of how random it is. How a man's livin' or dyin' ain't got a whole lot to do with how good he is or how hard he works or how careful he is. If'n it's his time, it's his time."

Hob tapped the cigarette package against his finger and shook one free. He lit it, took a deep drag, and released the smoke slowly.

"'T's kid, I usta sit 'round the dinner table listenin' to my daddy and mama, and minin' was all they talked about. Daddy'd tell her 'bout what happened that day, what sections was bad, the ones nobody wanted to work, what machine broke down, who got hurt. I got so tired a-hearin' 'bout it. But soon's I went down, I understood. All that stuff—friends gettin' injured, the near-misses, smashed fingers—it gets jammed up inside a man and he's gotta talk to get it out."

He flicked ash off the end of his cigarette into a metal ashtray on the table and spoke softly.

"But 'til #7 blew, I never realized what it done to the women. It's the men work in the mines, but the women carry the mine around…" He tapped his chest. "…in here. Inside 'em."

Hob reached out and patted Will's arm.

"Ain't a soul in Aintree wishes you *had* died in #7, Will; they just wish their men *hadn't*."

◊ ◊ ◊ ◊ ◊

HOB PICKED UP his newspaper and pretended to read after Will left. But he didn't see the words on the page; he saw the faces that came to visit him in his nightmares. Faces with red-rimmed eyes and skin so pale the smudged coal dust stood out like tar. Dead-men's faces. Hob hadn't told Will the whole of it. He'd said that, far as he knew, didn't nobody in Aintree Hollow blame ole Hob for being home with a hangover the morning #7 blew.

That wasn't true. There was one person who *did* blame him. Hob did.

He had not gone a day in the past 20 years without wondering if all them men would be alive if he'd gone to work. Hob was the ventilation man on the crew, the curtain hanger. Oh, he knew the foreman had hired some guy because he happened to show up that morning. But Lloyd said they'd put the new guy to work on the shuttle.

And if the new guy was driving the shuttle, who was hanging curtains?

Hob had always figured he'd come by being a ventilation man honest. When he was a little kid, he didn't like nothing in the world more than playing in the creek. Only he didn't merely splash around in the water—he *rerouted* it, changed its course, made it go where *he* wanted it to go. He'd use rocks to dam up the creek on one side, force the water to go down some channel he'd built out of rocks on the other side. The older he got, the fancier his dams became; time he was a teenager, beavers didn't have nothing on Hobart Bascomb! Then he turned 16 and went to work in the mine and discovered that "rerouting" was the job description of a ventilation man. Only he didn't change the flow of water from one place to another; he changed the flow of *air*.

Once you'd dug more than a couple hundred feet into the mountain, a coal mine's chief issue became ventilation. The machinery that chewed into the coal seam at the far end of that hole created huge amounts of coal dust and released methane gas trapped in the ore. Methane was a bomb awaiting a spark; coal dust was the fuel. You had to get the dust and gas *out of* the mine before it reached explosive levels and you had to route good air *into* the mine for the miners to breathe. To do that you needed a fan, one big enough to move 3,000 cubic feet of air per minute across the face, the deepest part of the mine.

But the fan didn't *blow* air. It *sucked* air. The fan didn't push air *into* the mine, it sucked air *through* it.

Like most other mines, Harlan #7 was designed with three openings. The one in the middle was for the conveyor belt that carried coal from the face of the mine out to be loaded on trucks. The opening on the right was where good air was sucked *into* the mine down the supply rail line. The fan was located outside the opening on the left, sucking bad air *out* of the mine. It was a continuous loop—in the right side down the rail line, across the face and back out the left side.

A ventilation man's job was to make sure the good air being sucked into the right-hand shaft flowed *all the way to the face* where the miners were working—which in the big mines could be up to 8 *miles* under the mountain. It was his job to route the good air across the face and then back out the left shaft through the fan, carrying coal dust and poison gases with it out of the mine.

And the ventilation man routed air the same way Hob had routed creek water when he was a kid—by building "dams." Hob had to block off all the shafts running crossways in the grid of tunnels under the mountain to force the air to flow to the face long ways down the right-hand rail-shaft. The 50-foot, square coal pillars were set 18 feet apart, so the ventilation man had to build a "dam" over every one of those 18-foot gaps—called breaks—the whole route to the face and then back out the other side.

Of course, routing air was easier than routing water. You didn't have to build a dam out of rocks; all you had to do was hang a curtain.

Harlan #7 was a little over a mile deep, so there were probably 90 breaks between the mouth of the mine and the working face at the far end. It was the ventilation man's job to seal off all 90 breaks along the right-side shaft and an equal number of breaks on the left. Since he'd worked at #7 from the day it opened, Hob had personally hung most ever one of them curtains—some of them made out of untreated jute, heavy fabric like burlap, others out of thick yellow plastic. As the mine was sunk deeper and deeper into the mountain, it was also his job to go back up the line and make them curtain "dams" permanent by replacing the fabric or plastic with solid walls, seals built of concrete block and mortar.

Problem was, the company wasn't paying Hobart Bascomb to do his job—they was paying him to keep his mouth shut.

Wilson Cooper run a dog-hole operation if ever there was one, about as dangerous a mine as Hob had ever seen. They got away with it by bribing the MSHA inspectors to look the other way. The ones they couldn't bribe they tricked. Whenever there was a surprise inspection, the code words "we got a man on the property" spread through the mine. The underage miners, who got paid in cash so there was no paper trail, would quickly take cover at the far end of a remote break—with their headlamps turned off. The other miner'd fix or hide safety violations before the inspector got there. They'd all stop whatever they were doing and grab limestone dust and start dousing the walls—like they was supposed to do all along to make the coal dust inert—non-combustible. And they'd rush to put up curtains, clean rockfalls, and trash, tape frayed cords—stuff like that.

"You boys been drillin' bore holes?" the inspector'd ask. They was supposed to drill holes into the face before the continuous miner ripped into it to make sure there wasn't old works on the other side.

"Yes sir, boss," the miners'd all say. "We shore have."

Speak up about safety violations and the company'd get fined. With Wilson Cooper run on a shoestring like it was, a couple of big fines and they'd be out of business. They fold up and you don't have no job, no money coming in to feed your family.

And every miner knew if he complained, the company'd fire him on the spot.

That's why nobody said nothing when the company scrimped on everything—like permanent seals for the breaks—didn't provide proper concrete blocks so the seals Hob built were nothing more than stacks of old cinder block with rock dust on them to look like mortar. Inspector ever leaned on one, it'd collapse. Lots of places up and down both shafts, Hob left the jute or plastic curtains because he never had time to build permanent seals.

But the worst safety violation was that the curtains that hung across the breaks close to the face were all the time getting yanked down to make it easier for the machinery to move around. Curtains slowed things down; time was money.

Removing a curtain had the same effect on the air flow in a mine as removing rocks from Hob's dams in the creek. The air would flow through the un-curtained break like water through a hole in a dam and right back out of the mine without ever reaching the face. That left the miners breathing bad air and the threat of a methane/coal-dust explosion mounting by the second.

And as coal mines went, #7 was a gassy one, real gassy.

"Reckon that's what happened?" Hob didn't realize he'd spoken the words out loud until the waitress turned toward him.

"You say some'm?"

"Yeah, Sweetheart, how 'bout you warm up my coffee."

It wasn't the first time Hob had spoken the words aloud—not the first time he'd heard them in his head, neither. Did they move curtains out of the way that day, not put them back up until…?

He'd been over and over it. Truth was nobody'd ever know why #7 blew. Maybe the continuous miner dug into old works full of methane. Maybe the curtains was down and methane built up in the shafts. Maybe it was something else altogether.

But Hob always come back to the same place, the biggest maybe of all. If he hadn't been too hung over to do his job that morning, maybe…

CHAPTER 14

As long, shadow fingers reached out to grab hold of the hollow, Will walked up the hill to Granny's house. He'd wandered all over town, but couldn't seem to make the leap across the chasm of change—in the hollow or in himself—couldn't seem to reconnect. It was almost worse than being a stranger.

A car pulled up beside him.

"Want a ride?"

He'd heard JoJo's car coming up the hill. It was hard to miss the sound of the old Ford Escort, probably a 1990 model. Besides a serious knock in the engine, there was either a hole in the muffler or it had fallen off altogether.

Will nodded, walked around to the passenger side of the car and noticed a spiderweb of cracks spread out on the windshield from what looked like a bullet hole. More likely it was where a piece of coal falling off the back of a truck had nailed it. Coal trucks on the road kept windshield replacement operations in Eastern Kentucky in business. All that remained of the passenger side mirror was a rusty stump; whatever had amputated it was probably the same fence post or pole that had smashed in the side of the door.

Though seriously mangled, the door swung easily open and Will waited while JoJo moved a pile of assorted flotsam and jetsam off the passenger seat so he could get in. The interior smelled like pizza.

"You got to bang that door real hard or it won't stay shut. Catch's broke. I got a matched set. The door on this side won't hardly open."

"Your grandmother allow you to pick up strange men?"

"I know lots of men stranger'n you." She looked sideways at him as she put the car in gear and continued up the road to the top of the hollow. "And I don't think you're all that strange. Just..." she paused. "I don't know. There's some'm 'bout your eyes is all."

"It takes one to know one."

Her smile faded. "What's that s'posed to mean?"

"One alcoholic can spot another alcoholic on the other side of the room at a party, can feel the vibes. Or maybe it's not vibes at all, merely the look of mouth-watering desperation on the guy's face when the waiter goes by with a tray of martinis."

"You've noticed that, have you?"

"No, I'm the guy looking desperate. I'm a drunk.

"Just like that? 'Hi, my name's Will and I'm an alcoholic.'"

Will nodded. "I'll take What It Feels Like To Wake Up In Your Own Puke Under A Bridge for a thousand, Alex."

He could tell he'd unsettled JoJo, surprised and perhaps intrigued her.

"So, what are you saying? That you think *I'm* an alcoholic?"

"I didn't say that."

"Then what did you say?"

"I said it takes one to know one. But I wasn't talking about alcoholism. That was an illustration."

"Sorry, you've lost me." She pulled off the road and parked in front of Granny's trailer.

"I was talking about being hollowed-eyed and hopeless. I know the look, at least from the inside. And I figure what I feel like on the *inside* looks just like this…" He reached over and pulled down her visor with a mirror on the back. "…on the *outside.*"

JoJo glanced at the mirror, then turned to stare at him. All at once, the image of Ricky Dan bloomed in his head and he burst out laughing.

"What's so funny?"

"I'm sorry," he said, trying to regain his composure. "It's just… if your daddy was here right now, you know how he'd describe the look on your face? He'd say, 'That gal don't know whether to scratch her butt or take third base.'"

That coaxed a tiny smile out of her.

She reached over and picked her purse up out of the floorboard on the passenger side and slammed her shoulder twice into her door before it opened. "Well, it was good talking to you," she said. "I got to go help Granny with supper."

"No, you don't." That stopped her. "We both know Granny could fix supper for all the blue-eyed men in the Norwegian army with one hand tied behind her back. Take a walk with me."

"Take a…? I can't, I…"

"Yes, you can. You're just afraid to. You don't want to be alone with me because you know you can't con me, that I see through the everything's-dandy-in-my-world act you've been performing ever since I met you."

JoJo stared at him wide-eyed, too surprised to speak.

"I'll bet I'm the only person in your life who knows you're lying. And I'm certain I'm the only person who'll tell you the truth still in the husk, all of it, no matter how ugly it is."

It was clear nobody'd ever spoken to JoJo as he just had. Will watched warring emotions play across her face, then saw something like anger light her eyes. Good! He could work with anger.

"Fine." She gestured toward the immediate world. "Where you wanna go?"

Will got out of the car, walked around to her open door and flashed a broad smile. "It's not the destination that matters, it's the journey."

As he turned and started up the road toward the shack that had once been his home, Will eased off the full frontal assault he'd mounted and dabbled in the gloriously mundane. Did she like her job? How did she get it? What happened to Will's accent? Where and how did he lose it?

"I used to love that mulberry tree," Will said of the dead carcass that had torn a hole in the house roof.

"I did, too," she said quietly.

"Wind blow it over?"

"No. Ice storm got it."

She walked to the tree and touched the dry, brittle bark on its trunk.

"When I's a little girl, I used to come here a lot. There wasn't no little kids my age around here; Jamey and me was the only ones."

The explosion in #7 had slashed a swath of destruction through the male population of Aintree Hollow. There'd have been more children around if those miners had lived to have them.

"This tree was easy to climb because of that." She stepped around and indicated a limb low on the trunk that on the fallen tree formed something like a bench. "Even when I was little, 5 or 6 maybe, I could get up on that one, and after that it was easy to climb the rest of the tree."

"This was my favorite climbing tree, too, when I was a kid."

"About 7 or 8 years ago—I wasn't in high school, yet—we had an ice storm. Not a bad ice storm; there's been lots of worse ice storms in this holler."

"I remember one where the ice was half an inch thick on all the trees. Your daddy, Lloyd and I went up to the edge of the woods when it started to warm up and you could hear a sound like popcorn all around, a loud cracking and snapping. It was the ice breaking on the tree limbs."

"This storm wasn't like that." She turned and leaned up against the base of the tree. "There was hardly any ice at all, a quarter of an inch, maybe. Didn't even make the wires leadin' to the house sag. And then I come out here and this tree was down." She sounded sad and her eyes took on a far-away look. "A little bitty ice storm…*killed* it."

Will said nothing. JoJo seemed to be moving to a place he didn't imagine she took many people and he was afraid to inject his presence for fear she'd realize he was there with her and throw him out.

"I think 'bout that tree a lot. Why'd that little storm kill it when it'd stood up under worse? But that's the thing. You can't tell from the outside. You can't look at a big ole strong tree like that and know what's going on…down inside it where you can't see."

She lowered her head and didn't say anything else for so long Will thought she was finished. When she did speak, her voice was as soft and as intense as Granny's.

"It don't matter how much I loved that tree, I couldn't have saved it. Even if I'd been standin' right here when it started over, I couldn't have held it up. Nobody's strong 'nough to hold up a fallin' tree."

She lifted her head and looked him square in the eye.

"Ain't nobody strong enough to hold up a fallin' life, neither."

She turned wordlessly and headed back down the road toward Granny's. Will stood where he was and watched her until she had gone into the house and closed the door.

JoJo sat on her bed and listened to the sounds from the kitchen. Granny had made Jamey do the supper dishes tonight because he hadn't done the breakfast dishes for JoJo like he'd said he would. She could hear the two of them talking with Will. Not the words, but the tone of their voices. It was relaxed and cheerful. Happy.

After Darrell was killed, JoJo was a ship cut adrift in a raging sea. The pain of loss was staggering, overwhelming—all slathered over with a layer of guilt. What Granny and the other women had gone through when #7 blew—not just losing husbands but fathers, brothers, and sons at the same time. Her own sorrow paled in comparison. She was almost ashamed to cry. What right did she have to mourn—they'd all seen worse. And once she'd experienced the agony of real heartbreak, she knew she couldn't have stood up under what those women endured. There was a degree of courage and determination, strength, and stamina in all of them she flat out didn't have.

In the chaos of grief, her shame was somehow transformed into anger. She lashed out at the nearest target—Granny. Crazy, irrational, she'd hollered at her grandmother that the only possible way she could have lived through that much loss was that she just didn't care. Wasn't no way she could possibly have loved her husband, her brother, and her son. If she had, she couldn't have survived their deaths all at one time.

Granny's eyes had flashed, and for one flickering moment, JoJo had thought Granny might actually slap her. She didn't. The flame went out in her eyes.

"If I's to tell you some'm all corny like, it wouldn't do you no good." She'd reached out her big, gnarled hand and stroked JoJo's hair. "But what I know that you don't, child, is that you ain't gonna hurt like this forever. You think you will, but you won't. One of these days, you'll be able to think 'bout Darrell and it won't be painful."

Granny had stopped then and looked deep into JoJo's eyes.

"I can promise you ain't always gonna be sad. But whether or not you can ever be happy again—that I cain't say. That part's up to you."

Granny had been right, of course. Wasn't a whole lot that woman was wrong about. There come a day when JoJo thought about Darrell and smiled. She had even come to a place where she believed there might be a good life out there somewhere, waiting for her. That she could love and be loved again. That she could be happy.

All that ended—she looked at the calendar on the wall—7 weeks ago. Saturday, August 26, 2000, to be exact. That's the date they ought to put on her death certificate. It didn't matter when her heart actually stopped and the blood no longer flowed through her veins. Shortly after noon on August 26, Joanna Darlene Sparrow *died*.

She got up off the bed and walked to her dresser, pulled the top drawer open, and got out the envelope she'd stuffed in there when she got home after her walk with Will.

She didn't know what to think about Will, this man who'd barged into her life like Sherman marching into Atlanta.

She plopped back down on the bed with the envelope in her hand. She…liked Will. Yeah, she did. But she didn't like the feeling she had that he could look right through her, that he knew what she was thinking, might even know what she was planning.

Then for one fleeting moment, she wondered what it would have been like to grow up with a father like Will, a man who didn't pull punches, called them like he seen them. But the moment was over almost before it started. Didn't matter what kind of father she had, what kind of man she married, what she did or said or thought or wanted—or pleaded with God for. Wasn't *nothing* could give her a future she was willing to live in.

Will was well-intentioned. He had a good heart. He just didn't understand that the kindest thing anybody could do for her right now was stay out of her way while she done what she had to do so's she could step into eternity on her own terms. That was all she had left.

She opened the envelope and looked at the small white pills inside. When Dough Boy'd handed it to her, he'd told her to count them before she paid him. She'd give him the money and walked away. But she counted them now, held each one carefully, almost tenderly.

…22, 23, 24.

There was enough Oxycontin here to fell an elephant.

CHAPTER 15

WILL DIDN'T so much sleep at Granny's as pass out. Perhaps it was that feather mattress Granny was so proud of. More likely it was residual exhaustion. No matter where he had traveled in the past 20 years, he felt off balance, a little uncomfortable. Nothing and nowhere seemed to fit. It was like he always had sand in his shoe. But cradled tenderly in the protective arms of the mountains granted a security that eased tension out of him as gently as the sigh of a sleeping baby.

Which explained why he'd slept so late. By the time he woke up, the sun shone in his window—after ten o'clock! He lay still and looked up at the ceiling. As soon as his mind oriented to being awake and began to fasten onto reality, it slipped back out of his grasp. No matter how he wallowed it around in his head, he couldn't come to grips with the…otherworldliness of Ricky Dan's son and the incredible…gift?…the boy had. Will could wrap his arms around Jamey's talent. Surely, there were other documented cases of artistic gifts in unlikely people. And if he had to, he was certain he could go…well, *somewhere* and look it up and find them. But he was equally certain there were no documented cases of artists who could carve exact replicas of people they'd never met. Or…

He had to drag his mind kicking and screaming to the place where it was willing to countenance the rest of Jamey's gift. He'd examined the carving of Granny's wedding; she'd pointed out to him details that weren't in the original wedding picture burned in the fire, details nobody except the people who had been there could possibly have known. So how did Jamey? Will had examined the basketball carving, stared at it until he could see it with his eyes closed, like it was tattooed on the insides of his eyelids. A carving that was completed three days before either team suited up.

The goat carving, the lost-cat carving—you could chalk those up to extreme coincidence. But the *score* of a basketball game?

The only *reasonable* explanation was that the whole thing was an elaborate hoax and Granny and JoJo were lunatics or liars—so much for reasonable explanations. Though in truth, it seemed the two of them didn't have to swallow nearly as hard as he did to accept that Jamey's carvings were…what? *Magical?* Yeah, maybe so. At the very least, they came from some place not governed by the same laws of time as the rest of the world, a place where past, present, and future were mingled in a way Will couldn't even begin to understand.

He sat up on the side of the bed and sighed.

You can slice and dice it any way you want to, Pal, but the truth in long johns with the butt flap down is pretty simple: the kid can carve events and people he's never seen and a reality that hasn't happened yet.

But that was *absurd!*

Yeah, it was. It was also true.

Will got up and wandered out into the kitchen, his hair a tousled display of bed head, and when Granny turned from the sink to greet him, she laughed out loud.

"I'm that funny looking?"

She put her hand over her mouth to hide her teeth and continued to giggle.

"Aw, it ain't that, Will." For a moment, her cinnamon eyes sparkled with unshed tears. "I'm so glad to have you here, with your hair all upside down, the pure joy of it makes me wanna dance a jig or laugh out loud. And I'm too old to dance." She gestured toward the table where an empty place setting still rested. "Sit y'self down and I'll make you some bacon and eggs. Coffee's hot."

"Just toast, Granny. Thanks." Obviously JoJo had already left for work. "Where's Jamey?"

"He's up the shed gettin' a potato digger and a burlap bag so's the two of you can go sangin'."

Will was grateful Granny had her back turned when she said it—couldn't see the emotions that surely were displayed on his face. Ricky Dan had taught Will how to hunt for ginseng, showed him the kinds of places it was likely to grow and how to dig it up once he found it. Those had been the best times he spent with Ricky Dan.

"Jamey Boy was supposed to go with Lloyd," Granny said as she blew by Will's request for "just toast" and cracked two eggs into the skillet of bacon grease. "They go ever now and then, not's often as you and Ricky Dan usta. They had it set up for today, but Lloyd called this morning and said he wasn't comin', said you's here, you'd oughta take Jamey."

She stopped and turned to Will.

"Lloyd's ate up with some'm. Sounds so mad and cold I ain't even sure it's Lloyd I'm talkin' to. It's 'bout you bein' here, but for the life of me I cain't figure why that's got under his skin the way it has."

"He believes he has a right to be mad at me," Will said quietly. "And I can't say I blame him."

Before Granny could ask what he meant by that, Jamey burst in the back door and rushed into the kitchen. He held a burlap bag in one hand and a garden tool that looked like an oversized ice cream scoop in the other. For one breathless moment, Ricky Dan stood before Will, laughter in his voice as he delivered one of his famous one-liners: *Will, you got to enjoy life; it's got an expiration date.*

The image vanished as soon as Jamey opened his mouth. This was a boy in a Ricky Dan suit, a kid as excited about going sangin' as Will had ever been.

"Granny said you's gonna take me sangin' 'cause Lloyd cain't," he said. "Are you ready? Can we go now?"

"Soon as I finish breakfast."

Hunting ginseng had been a mountain tradition for generations. Though very little was used commercially in the United States, it was exported to Asia where it served as an ingredient in everything from toothpaste to chewing gum, in soft drinks, candy, and cigarettes. In Japan, ginseng was used to reduce stress, lower cholesterol, enhance strength—even make race horses run faster.

But the plant wasn't easy to find. And to command the highest price, it had to be harvested properly between August and November—keeping the branching forks of the root intact. Farmers' domesticated ginseng plants sold for two hundred to two hundred-fifty dollars a pound, but prime Eastern Kentucky mountain ginseng could bring upward of five hundred dollars a pound—at least it used to when Will and Ricky Dan had taken theirs to Somerset to sell.

"They's sayin' at the post office the other day that Wilson Fur and Ginseng in Russell Springs is payin' eight-fifty for 'sang," Granny said. "Least that's what JoJo heard."

After Will finished his breakfast, he and Jamey set out up the hill behind the house past the shed where Jamey did his arts and then north across the top of the mountain. Two men and a yellow canary. ValVleen was perched on Jamey's shoulder and every now and then she'd burst into a hauntingly beautiful melody of chirps and tweets.

Will had to scratch around in his head to find the old maps, but once he located them and blew the dust off, he used them to guide him through the woods. He knew what to look for as a place ginseng would grow—shadowed land with good drainage. But he wanted to go back to the places he and Ricky Dan had found—partly because the ginseng would still be prospering there if it had been harvested properly by anyone else who'd come upon it over the years. But mostly because he wanted to take Jamey to the places he'd gone so often with Jamey's father.

They walked together in amiable silence for about 15 minutes, made their way through bright yellow oak and chestnut trees, crimson dogwoods, fiery red sumac and orange witch hazels and listened to the crackle of leaves hurried across the ground by a scolding wind. And to the call and response of barred owls, demanding to know *Who? Who? Who's out there?*

Will carried Jamey's tattered backpack with their lunch—peanut-butter-and-jelly sandwiches and bags of Cheetos—and a water bottle. Jamey carried the potato digger in a burlap bag thrown over his shoulder. When they crested a ridge, Will paused to catch his breath. Jamey hadn't even broken a sweat. Booze had taken a heavy toll on Will's body as well as his soul.

That's when Will noticed that Jamey wore a necklace. All he could see was the thin silver chain, almost too dainty for a piece of men's jewelry.

"What you got on the chain?" he asked and pointed to Jamey's neck.

The boy smiled as he fished around in his shirt for the pendant. When he found it, he held it up for Will to see—a tiny silver cross, plain, elegant in its simplicity.

"JoJo give it to me. It's her favoritest necklace."

"If it's her favorite necklace, why'd she give it to you?"

"Because she did."

Hard to argue that.

Will pointed to a distant ridge. "I thought we'd check under that big rock outcrop on the south side of Gizzard Ridge—over by Tiresome Creek—you know the place?"

"Uh huh, Lloyd showed me."

"We'll go to the places your dad and I used to go first." It was still hard for him to use the word "dad," in relation to Ricky Dan, who was frozen forever in his mind as a young man not much older than Jamey. "Then we'll check out some other likely spots."

"First thing you look for is rattlesnake ferns," Jamey said, like a first-grader reciting the alphabet.

"Very good," Will said, struck yet again by Jamey's eyes, the same luminous green as Ricky Dan's.

"Then spleen worts, Jack-in-the-pulpits, and..."Jamey's face went completely blank, like somebody'd taken out his batteries. His eyes took on a far-away look and then he put his hands together in front of him, his fingers intertwined. Each wiggled back and forth, like the tentacles of sea anemones in a strong current. "And *ginger*, wild ginger!" he squealed. "Them's the three things Lloyd and me look for."

His face darkened, like a cloud briefly crossing in front of the sun.

"Granny won't let me go sangin' by myself, won't 'low me to go no farther into the woods than the shed 'thout somebody goes with me. She says I'll get lost."

"I got lost out here once. I'd probably still be lost if your daddy hadn't found me."

Jamey's eyes lit up.

"How'd my daddy find you?"

So Will told him the story. How he'd gone to look for wild mushrooms one morning and had been walking along a trail he knew well when his foot slipped and he slid down a long embankment. Rather than climb back up the crumbly, leafy hillside, he figured he'd go around and catch the trail at a different place. Then a windfall blocked his path and he had to go around it, a thicket got in his way next and he had to detour again. Pretty soon he was hopelessly turned around.

"I got scared when I realized I didn't know where I was and couldn't even find my way back to where I'd slipped. I wanted to keep looking, to run around until I found the path, but then I thought real hard about what I should do, got real still like you just did. And I remembered what your dad told me to do if I ever got lost in the woods."

Jamey's attention was so focused he didn't appear to breathe.

"He said, 'Will, soon's you know you're lost, *hug a tree*. And you keep on a-huggin' that tree 'til I come find you.'"

A crease appeared between Jamey's eyebrows that reminded Will of Granny.

"That don't make no sense. Why'd he want you to hug a tree?"

"So I'd stay put. If you're lost and you keep going, you get more lost, farther away from where you started. And it's a whole lot easier to find somebody who stays in one place than it is to look for a moving target. It was almost dark before I heard him calling my name."

Will had hollered until he was hoarse before Ricky Dan came over the hill and down to the dry creek bed and found him. He'd wanted to be tough, act like getting lost was no big deal, but as soon as he saw Ricky Dan he broke.

"I ran to him, threw my arms around his waist and started sobbing."

Ricky Dan had held him tight and let him cry.

"I could hear your dad's heart thudding in his chest and it dawned on me that *he'd* been scared, too."

When Ricky Dan was finally able to peel Will off, he got down on one knee, eye level with the boy and reamed him out good for wandering off in the woods alone, made him promise he'd never do anything like that again. Then he stood up and did a strange thing. He took Will's hand—like Will was a little kid and not 10-going-on-11 years old!—and he held on tight as they walked back home.

"He never told anybody that I cried when he found me," Will said.

"How come?"

"He knew it'd embarrass me. Your dad joked and carried on, seemed to make light of things, but he was…a whole lot deeper than most people knew."

Will looked hard at the young man who was so very like Ricky Dan on the outside and struggled to find words to tell him what kind of man his father'd been on the inside.

"Ricky Dan had Bowman's strength and character and Granny's humor and courage. He was brave—like you."

"Like *me?* I ain't brave."

"You go down in that mine, work there in the dark, danger all around you. That's brave." Will paused. "I couldn't do it. Tried, but I wasn't strong enough. I'm terrified of coal mines, Jamey." He worked to keep his voice level. "But your daddy, he wasn't scared. He was a better man than me."

Will turned away quickly and walked to the crest of a hill, then started down the other side. The rock outcrop and the creek he was looking for was on the other side of the next hill. Up ahead lay a small meadow.

◊ ◊ ◊ ◊ ◊

THE TARGET STOPPED right before it stepped out into the meadow at the base of the hill. The hunter moved the crosshairs slightly, fixed them squarely on the target's chest. Could go for a head shot, but a chest shot was safer. Bigger area to aim at.

The hunter drew in a breath and let it out slowly.

Then he squeezed the trigger and sent a bullet hurling through space toward the third button on Will Gribbins's shirt.

CHAPTER 16

LOYD DIDN'T SLEEP at all the night before he went to Granny's to make sure his own self that it was true, that Will was alive, that he really had shown up just in time to destroy Lloyd's life. He'd tried to rest, but he couldn't just lay there in the bed and stare at the ceiling. So he'd got up, smoked one cigarette after another and paced, watched the sky outside, saw the black become charcoal and then gray. Soon's it was light, he'd gone outside and loaded up the piece of jet for Jamey.

He didn't go to work that afternoon at three—called in sick. He'd called in sick again this morning, too, after another sleepless night. But it wasn't because he was afraid to go down in the mine with his mind muddy. He was alert, as bright-eyed and bushy-tailed as he'd ever been. In fact, he was so totally awake and...*alive*.... he wondered if this was how them people felt who snorted cocaine up their noses.

His son had told him about it. Hollered at him about it. Called him ig-nert and backward, said he didn't know nothing, didn't understand how it felt to be on top of the world—strong and powerful and in charge.

Of course, Jesse hadn't never been none of those things. He was a weakling who wouldn't have lasted 5 minutes in the mine. Lloyd had pampered him, hadn't come upside the boy's head when he'd needed it like a father'd ought to, give him too much. That boy was no more in charge of his own self than an oak leaf floating down a creek.

But what Jesse had described, the feeling he got when he was high, that's how Lloyd felt now. Only he really was in charge of his own self, and he wasn't about to let Will Gribbins write the end of his story.

He'd called in sick this morning because he had a job he should have finished that day in the mine back in 1980. But he'd thought at the time that Will was dead. He'd thought the same thing for the past 20 years, and he'd been wrong both times. Will Gribbins was alive. Least he would be until Lloyd put a bullet through his heart.

As he fastened his Browning bolt-action .30-06 rifle in the gun rack across the back window of his pickup truck, he considered how surprisingly easy it had been to get to this place.

Sometime during the second night of no sleep, the idea had come to him. His mind hadn't put up much of a fight against it, neither. It wasn't like he'd agonized over the decision. It felt like a natural progression, the next step. When the law come swooping down on Lloyd like a barn owl on a mouse, he'd tell them the story he'd been practicing in his head for two decades. But his story would only work if Will wasn't around to say it wasn't so.

And Lloyd could arrange that.

Hunting accidents happened all the time, particularly when the hunters was poachers, huntin' out of season. Poachers took chances. If they'd been the kind of people who followed rules they wouldn't be in the woods with a deer rifle the second week of October.

Will wouldn't be dressed in hunter safety gear—fluorescent orange—to go out sangin'. You wasn't likely to be mistook for a deer by men using bows and arrows. They had to get close to their prey—30, 45 yards away. Bow hunters wasn't shooting from five hundred yards out, where a tree stump or a big rock could look like an eight-point buck.

And if poachers accidentally shot somebody, they wasn't likely to come forward and man up to what they'd done, not if they wasn't supposed to be in the woods with a gun in the first place!

Lloyd got behind the wheel, drove down the dirt road in front of his house and headed out to the four-lane. He planned to go around to the far side of the mountain, park there and walk over. He knew where the ginseng was; he knew where Will would go to find it. He already had in mind the perfect spot for an ambush. As he turned down Possum Trot Lane, he calmed his frayed nerves by concentrating on his ace-in-the-hole defense. If something bad happened to Will Gribbins, wouldn't nobody come knocking on Lloyd Jacobs's door—because Lloyd was Will's best friend and he didn't have no reason in the world to want Will dead. Least not one anybody knew about.

He parked his truck off the road, deep in the undergrowth where it couldn't be seen, and struck out on foot. With every step, he felt stronger, more in control of his life, less at the mercy of other people and random events.

Lloyd had never had it easy like Ricky Dan, whose folks was good people. Lloyd's family was a train wreck. Things happened in his house when the doors was closed and the rest of the world couldn't see that…But even so, Lloyd's life hadn't slid totally off the tracks until #7 blew. What had happened down in the dark that day had colored every day of his life since.

It was hard even to remember those first years after it happened, hard for everybody in the hollow to remember. Folks was in shock, coping the best way they knew how. For Will, that was running away. For Lloyd, it meant drinking and carousing. He'd knocked up Norma Jean, then after Jesse was born, he'd beat her a time or two. Didn't hurt her bad, didn't never break nothing. He couldn't seem to grab hold of his self—got fired from two crews for showing up to work drunk with a temper that even he knew would get him into serious trouble someday.

But everything had changed in the spring of 1990; his whole world had turned upside down.

To keep Norma Jean from pressing charges against him after he blacked her eye and split her lip in a drunken rage, he took her out on a "date." Drove dang nigh a two-hundred-fifty miles round trip, all the way to Somerset to eat at Cracker Barrel and then go to the picture show. Didn't know what was showing; didn't care. He'd planned to sleep through whatever it was.

He didn't sleep through it, though. He sat riveted to his seat.

The movie was called *The Mission*. It was the story of a man who had killed his brother, and to atone for his crime, he had dragged a load of shields and armor through the jungles and mountains of South America.

That movie had a more profound effect on Lloyd's life than anything he'd ever experienced. It turned on the lights in his soul and for the first time he could see everything clearly. He had done some bad things in his life that had not caused him a moment's guilt—and never would. But what had happened under Black Mountain the day #7 blew—it had torn Lloyd apart. Now, he knew how to fix that. He understood that he had to pay for what he'd done; he had to *earn* redemption.

So he'd set out in a single-minded crusade to do just that.

For an entire decade, Lloyd was a model husband and father, and took care of the Sparrow family, too. He went to church and was so pious folks noticed. Wasn't long before he became a deacon. Then an elder! At the First Pentecostal Church of Aintree Hollow, Lloyd Jacobs was a respected man.

Like that Spaniard in the jungle, Lloyd had hauled his whole life around on his back—his wife, his kids, his church, his job. If any man had ever *deserved* absolution, Lloyd Jacobs was that man. But what had it got him? He was the best husband and father he knew how to be; now his wife was gone and his kids had turned into weak bloodsuckers. He'd spent 10 years doin' for Granny and those kids and then Will Gribbins shows up out of nowhere yesterday and they treated him like he was gold! *Will.* The man who walked out on all of them, who never honored a word of the secret vow they'd both made.

Well, Lloyd was done trying to make things right! He'd meant what he'd said to Will yesterday morning. He would *not* live the next 20 years the way he'd lived the last.

Lloyd passed silently through the woods, didn't even disturb the squirrels. He quickly found the spot he was looking for, about two hundred and fifty yards above and to the right of the meadow near the creek and the rock outcrop where he'd gone sangin' with Will and Ricky Dan. Lloyd had only gone along with them one time, but he never forgot any of the places they went that day. The experience was a good childhood memory and he had precious few of those.

He was in position in a windfall behind a stand of cedar trees 2 hours before he spotted movement on the hillside across the meadow. Two hours without a cigarette. The smell of smoke carried in the woods. Two hours of quiet. A long time to think. And at one point during that silent wait he experienced a moment of clarity. Of *sanity.* It was like a lone ray of sun suddenly broke through a raging thunderstorm, beamed down to illuminate something below so bright everything else was cast in harsh relief. In that moment, the outrageousness of the act he had plotted was laid bare, naked and steaming before him.

Lloyd was about to commit *murder.*

Time ground to a halt for a breathless instant as the realization sunk in. Then the moment passed. The dark storm clouds gathered and darkness rolled in over his soul.

With a curious detachment, Lloyd watched through the telescopic sight on his rifle. Saw Will and Jamey top the hill and followed their progress down it and through the trees to the edge of the meadow.

When it came time to put the crosshairs on Will's chest, Lloyd didn't flinch. With an icy calm, he *squeezed* the trigger, didn't pull it. It was a good shot.

◊ ◊ ◊ ◊ ◊

WILL GLANCED DOWN as he was about to step into the clearing, noticed that his shoelace had come untied and leaned over to tie it. That's when he heard the crack of a rifle and an almost simultaneous *thunk* as a bullet slammed into the tree trunk a few feet away—so close he could feel the air rearrange itself as the slug passed over his head.

"What the… !" This was *bow* season! Deer hunters couldn't use rifles until November. Why…?

Another bullet plowed a furrow in the dirt inches from Will's shoe and instinct took over. Still bent over his shoelace, he turned and tackled Jamey, knocked him to the ground, then shoved him toward a downed tree a few feet away. Another bullet clipped a chunk out of the bark of that tree as he dived behind it.

Will lay there panting for a moment, then yelled, "Hey! Are you *blind?* Hold your fire! You dang near killed us." He paused. "You hear me?"

The woods were silent.

Will looked at Jamey. The boy's eyes were bugged out, green gumdrops on snowballs. Will reached over and patted his shoulder. "It's okay. Good thing that guy's a lousy shot."

"Why's he shootin' at us?"

"He thought we were deer."

"Couldn't he see your shirt?"

Will's shirt was a bright blue corduroy; Jamey's was fire-truck red. He might not have been a hunter, but Will had gone along with

Ricky Dan often enough to know that the flash of anything blue—merely a flash of it—and no hunter in his right mind would fire. Blue was a "Sears color," a color not found in the woods. Will had been standing at the edge of the clearing. This guy didn't just catch a glimpse of blue through brush or tree limbs. He should have been able to see the whole shirt!

Even poachers—no, *especially* poachers—weren't that stupid. Shooting somebody would be a really bad way to get caught hunting out of season.

Okay then, why'd he shoot? Better question—why'd he shoot three times?

Answer—because he missed the first two.

Will felt a chill, like icicles forming in all his veins.

"I guess the sun was in his eyes," Will said, but he didn't believe that. One look at Jamey and it was plain he didn't believe it either.

Careful to remain behind the downed tree, Will peered through the brush toward the other side of the meadow. Nothing. Not that he'd expected to see anybody. A hunter with a scope could drop a deer from five hundred yards away.

"I wanna go home," Jamey said softly. The boy was completely transparent. What he thought came out his mouth; what he felt showed on his face. "I don't like it out here no more. The end."

"I'm with you, Buddy. I don't like it, either." He patted the boy on the shoulder. "Rain check?"

Jamey nodded but said nothing.

Will pointed to the hill they'd topped a few minutes earlier. "Stay down low behind the bushes until we're on the other side of that rise."

The two of them turned and made their way slowly back up the hillside, crouched down like walking bent-over in the mine. As they crested the hill, they heard the mournful cry of a coal train whistle, and Will stopped, staggered by a memory still so powerful it could make him physically sick.

LLOYD MISSED!

How could he possibly have *missed?*

Will had been right in his crosshairs; the bullet should have plowed through his chest and ripped open his heart. But at the last second, Will ducked, leaned over for some reason and the bullet had whizzed by him so close he likely felt the breeze it kicked up.

Lloyd got off two more shots, but the target was two hundred fifty yards away, hidden in the bushes instead of right out there in plain sight.

A wave of such nuclear rage swept over Lloyd that he wanted to break the stock of the rifle over a tree trunk.

He *missed!*

Now what?

Should Lloyd go after him? Will was, after all, unarmed. Lloyd could follow him back toward the trailer and try to find another spot to pick him off. Gratefully, sanity grabbed him by the collar before he could run off through the woods like he was tracking a wounded doe.

He couldn't go after Will. Jamey was with him.

It had been a calculated risk to shoot at Will with Jamey so close in the first place. It had been even riskier to keep shooting after the first shot missed the mark. You could believe a deer hunter mistook you for a buck once. But *three* times?

If he went after Will, the deer hunter ruse would be exposed for what it was. No hunter would *accidentally* shoot *two* people, and that's what he'd have to do. He'd have to get rid of the witness.

His mind pulled up short at that. Not Jamey.

He swallowed hard. No choice, he had to pack it in.

Reluctantly, Lloyd got to his feet, slung the strap of the .30-06 over his shoulder and headed back the way he'd come, to the spot on the other side of the mountain where he'd parked his truck.

He'd had the perfect opportunity to get rid of Will Gribbins. And he'd blown it. That kind of opportunity came one to a customer. Now, Lloyd had no scapegoat. When the world tumbled down, it would land squarely on his head.

He heard the lonely wail of a coal train whistle then, and a memory spirited him away to another place and another decade. He'd been stronger than Will that day, bolder, with a reckless bravery that made him invincible. At least that's what he'd thought at the time. But two decades of living had beaten all the sentimentality out of him. As a kid, he'd believed that invincibility was the product of courage. Now, he understood it was the product of despair, of not caring one way or the other whether you lived or died.

CHAPTER 17

— ⸺ —

A coal train whistle blasts out its warning and they both look back over their shoulders. The train's still at least a mile away, maybe more, but it's definitely time to get off the trestle.

A boy just on the threshold of adolescence, Will is tall for his age and lean. Lloyd is shorter, stockier, most likely stronger, too, though they have never matched up against each other all out. They've come close a time or two, but always backed away from it, as if doing so would cross some line, take them to a place they could never come back from.

Will tosses a final rock, watches it sail through the air and splash into Ugly Betty Creek 50 feet below.

"You see that 'un—kaplunk...splish!" Will says in the universal sound-effects language of young boys. He and Lloyd have sat for the last half hour on the cross ties on the side of the trestle with their feet dangling off the edge, chucking rocks—and spitting, too, of course—into the creek below. "Wish I had me one more big rock. But we gotta go."

Will stands up, but Lloyd just sits there, swinging his feet back and forth.

"C'mon," Will says. As if to emphasize his point, the train whistle sounds again, noticeably closer this time. "Race ya to the far side!"

Bootleg Trestle is almost four hundred feet long. It stretches across a rocky ravine where Ugly Betty Creek meanders among the boulders. The boys are not in the middle of the trestle; the far side—away from the oncoming train—is at least three hundred feet from them.

"What if we don't," Lloyd says.

"Don't what?"

"Get off the trestle."

"You nuts! There's a train comin'."

Lloyd looks up at Will, squints into the sun, and reaches up to shade his eyes. "That's the point. What if we stay on the trestle while the train crosses?"

Will is so dumbfounded he's rendered momentarily speechless.

"You really think we could sit here and not get knocked off the edge? This thing ain't that wide."

"I ain't talkin' 'bout sittin' on the edge."

"Then where?"

"Over there." Lloyd points to the tracks. "We could lay down 'tween the tracks and let the train pass over us."

"Yeah, right," Will says, relieved that Lloyd has been joking, isn't really suggesting they stay on the trestle. He takes a couple of steps back toward the short side, careful to step on the cross ties and not into the 6-inch open space between them. "You reckon maybe they's crawdads in Ugly Betty? We ain't never..." He realizes Lloyd isn't beside him, turns and sees Lloyd sitting where he'd left him, swinging his feet, staring off down the ravine.

"Lloyd...?"

"I'm doin' it. I'm stickin'."

Will feels an ache in his belly he has no name for.
"Lloyd, you'll get killed!"

"You think anybody'd care if I did?" *The rage and pain in the words travels across the space between them like a shock wave under the sea; when it rises up and hits Will in the chest the force literally knocks him backward a step.*

*Of course, Will has seen the bruises shaped like squeezing fingers on Lloyd's upper arms. He knows why Lloyd never wants to take his shirt off in the locker room during PE at school. He's been a party to the excuses Lloyd makes for the black eyes and swollen lips—*Will tripped me. Me 'n Will was climbin' a tree and I fell out. Will's knee got me when me 'n him was wrestlin'. *It is a wordless arrangement; neither has ever spoken of it. Will knows what is happening to Lloyd at home, but he sees the fierce pride in Lloyd's eyes and doesn't ask about it. They both simply accept what they can do nothing about and go on with life.*

But this is different! Risking your life is—

"It ain't dangerous as you think," *Lloyd says, his voice maddeningly calm. Only his eyes are wild.* "Look a-here." *He gets up, walks to the track and steps over the rail.* "Ain't nothing here but railroad ties."

"So?"

"So do you see any scratch marks on them ties, like maybe them trains drag some'm, or a piece of 'em hangs all the way down to the ground?"

The 8-inch square beams coated with creosote, spaced 6 inches apart, have no marks of any kind on them. Will says nothing.

"If'n some'm hung down, there'd be marks. You seen coal cars same as me. There's least a foot clearance underneath 'em, maybe more."

Will stares at him in stunned disbelief. Lloyd is serious. He really means to do it.

"All's you gotta do is lay still and it'll pass right over ya."

"Lloyd, yore crazy." The train whistle sings out again. Probably isn't more than a couple of minutes away. "Now com'on. We gotta get outta here."

Lloyd turns to face him. Will has never seen such a challenge in anyone's eyes. "You chicken?"

"I ain't stupid!"

Lloyd drops to his knees, shoves a couple of pieces of coal off the cross ties between the rails and Will hears them plunk into the creek below. Then Lloyd lies down on his back with his head facing the oncoming train.

Will's heart bangs away so hard he's certain you can see his shirt bounce with every beat. His knees feel weak; his mouth has a strange taste in it—like pennies.

Lloyd calls out, "Scaredy-cat! Scaredy-cat!" and starts to yell—a wild, primitive cry—almost a howl.

Will turns to bolt off the trestle just as the train rounds the corner of the mountain and comes into view, a roaring black monstrosity bearing down on him.

At that moment, two things happen at once, but time elongates, so he seems able to consider each individually, ponder them carefully.

Will stumbles, trips over his feet and goes down hard on one knee. Rocks and pieces of coal rip open his pant leg and tear into his skin, both palms are scraped raw. He staggers to his feet, wobbly and off-balance, and realizes he has run out of time. He can't make it to the short end of the trestle ahead of the oncoming train and he can't outrun the train in a race to the far end.

But the second thing is so odd that even in that desperate moment it registers as a totally unexpected phenomenon. All of a sudden, he is no longer in control of his own movements. His brain is screaming, "Run! Run!" but his body does the opposite. He throws himself down between the tracks instead, and rolls over onto his back between the rails. His feet almost touch Lloyd's feet; he can see the train coming.

He feels the shock wave of vibration as the train hits the near side of the trestle and he lifts his head for a second to look. The gigantic black engine roars at him like a charging bull. He hears the cry of the whistle as the engineer spots the two bodies on the track and the piercing shriek of metal against metal as he locks up the brakes in a futile attempt to stop the train. Will slams his head back down into the rocks, feels them cut into the back of his scalp, has a heartbeat's view of blue sky and white clouds and then the world is eaten up in a wild roar.

Shrieking, rumbling, rattling and convulsing, the train roars over him inches from his face.

The train's journey across his body lasts for hours, for a lifetime.

Sound and vibration are one; they envelop him, consume him, relentlessly bludgeon his senses, blast him with hot air, pelt him with rocks and inexorably pull at him, tug him upward, suck his body toward an instant, mangled, mutilated death. He tries to close his eyes, but he is incapable of any movement, however small, except to dig his fingers into the splintered wood of the cross ties in a frantic, desperate effort to hold on! *His vision is filled with the blurry underbelly of the convulsing, beast above him. He tries to shrink away from it, from the hurling death inches from his nose, but it is all around him, under him, beside him, over him. It squeezes tighter and tighter, smashes him, crushes him, roars…*

It is gone!

The trestle still vibrates but Will feels cool air and sees blue sky and clouds. He hears his own voice—a moaning, inarticulate mewl. Lloyd is screaming, the wild cry of exaltation now mingled with relief in a voice that is at once human and feral. That yell, not the roar of the train, is the sound Will would remember for the rest of his life.

Tears stream down Will's cheeks. He looks around fearfully, like the train might come back for him. He sits up; his whole body is trembling violently. That's when he realizes he has wet himself.

Lloyd has leapt up, eyes wild as a madman, a deep, bloody scratch on his cheek that he got who knows how. He jumps up and down, whoops, pulses energy—a maniacal smile on his face.

Will staggers to his feet, stares at Lloyd for a moment, then leans over and throws up, splashes his lunch on the cross ties and rails.

"Who-hoo!" Lloyd squeals, oblivious to everything except the adrenaline high that pulses through every nerve in his body. "Wasn't that—?"

Will turns from his vomit and lunges at Lloyd, catches him in the chest and bowls him over. The two of them tumble to the trestle floor dangerously close to the edge. Then Will starts to pummel Lloyd, crying at the same time. Lloyd covers his face with his arms and Will's blows land ineffectually, but Will continues to swing and swing until his muscles are lead and he no longer has the strength to move his arms.

Then he gets up, his eyes wet, his nose running, and staggers away down the long side of the trestle. Lloyd calls to him, but he doesn't answer. When he gets to the end, he sees two men far down the track racing toward him. It must have taken more than a mile to stop the train. Then he steps off into the dirt and stumbles away, gains speed with each stride until he is running wildly, madly, recklessly through the woods. Trailing a strange keening cry like a kite on a string behind him, he frantically tries to outdistance the terror. But he has brought it along with him in his heart, where it will take up residence, put down roots, and grow entangling tendrils into his soul for the rest of his life.

The next day, Lloyd shows up while Will and Ricky Dan are in the garden hammering posts into the ground for Ma Sparrow's pole beans. Their glances connect only once—Will's eyes issue a fiery, challenging warning; Lloyd's are confused. And that's it. They never speak of it, never mention the day again. It is as if it never happened. But no matter how hard Will tries, he is never again able to embrace the innocent friendship he'd had with Lloyd before that day.

And he never trusted Lloyd again.

CHAPTER 18

WILL AND JAMEY came down the road out of the woods and found Granny sitting in the rocking chair on the front porch. Her hands worked crochet needles, pulled thread through and hooked it over and over.

"Find any 'sang?" she called out when she saw them.

"No, but we almost got shot," Jamey replied. Minutes after the bullets whizzed by him, Jamey had completely forgotten his fear. Storm clouds never lingered long in the blue sky of Jamey's world.

Granny dropped the crochet needles into her lap. "Got shot?"

"Aw, it was nothing," Will said. "Some poacher wasn't looking where he was shooting, that's all."

Will didn't believe that for a minute, but any other explanation begged all sorts of questions he couldn't begin to answer.

He and Jamey had reached the bottom of the porch steps. "What are you making?" he asked.

Granny studied Will for a moment and he had the uncomfortable feeling she knew there was more to the story than he had told. Then she picked up the crochet needles and went back to work.

"You 'member Cora Talbot? The least of her girls—Jackie—this here's a blanket for her baby." She gestured toward the ball of blue yarn. "That girl ain't far enough 'long to be hardly showing and they already know the baby's gonna be a boy. Already got a name picked out 'n everything." Granny shook her head. "The older I get the more there is in this world that don't make no sense to me. They's gonna know that child's a boy his whole life—ain't it no fun no more to wonder for just a little while?"

As she spoke, her big hands continued to maneuver the hooks in delicate movements that should have looked clumsy but didn't, working so fast it was almost impossible to follow the hooks' progress.

"Your grandmother has probably crocheted a thousand miles of yarn in her lifetime," Will said to Jamey. "Doesn't even have to think about it—her hands do it automatically." He turned back to Granny with a big smile. "Remember what Ricky Dan said about you crocheting?" He looked at Jamey. "Your daddy said one time…" Will did his best imitation of Ricky Dan's voice. "I figure if they's to put needles and yarn in yore coffin during visitation, you'd likely make up a right nice sweater 'fore they started shovelin' in the dirt."

Jamey laughed; Granny smiled a gentle smile. You could tell the memory was poignant, but no longer painful.

Jamey held up the burlap sack with the potato digger inside. "I'll put these with the dryin' rack," he said. "Then I'm gonna do me some more work on my arts." His sunny grin went flat line. "It's a sad one, Granny. I hope it ain't another one's gonna make you cry."

He turned and headed up the hill to his shed in the woods.

"He's carved statues that made you cry?"

"Just he's so good 'n all, makes things so lifelike. Sometimes they's hard to look at."

Clearly, Granny didn't want to talk about that any more than Will wanted to discuss the poacher. So he sat down on the bottom step of the porch and patted the smooth wood next to him.

"Come sit with me, Granny." The old woman spoke so softly, you needed to be near her to carry on a conversation. And the rocker she sat in had a flat, slat seat and no cushion; the porch step would be just as comfortable.

Will looked up the hollow to the bare spot where the old house once stood. "We used to sit out on the porch at night and watch the fireflies. Remember?" When he turned back to face her there was a look of consternation on her face.

"I'll go in and get a chair out the kitchen so's you can sit up here with me," she said and began to rise. "I made some fresh lemonade if you—"

"Something's wrong, Granny. What is it?"

It hadn't escaped his notice that Granny had the rocker jammed up against the wall of the trailer so tight there was hardly any room to rock, or that she had not left the house in the three days he had been there, had not gone out to the mailbox on the road or into the garden in the backyard. He'd seen several ripe pumpkins in the garden when he and Jamey went sangin'. Why hadn't she picked them?

"I cain't." Her voice wasn't just quiet, it was small, almost like a child. He'd never heard her speak that way before.

"*Can't* what?"

"I…got me a phobia, that's what JoJo says." She immediately became very interested in the yarn and hooks that danced in her lap, wouldn't look at him. "She went out and learnt all 'bout it. It's got a name, but I disremember what it is."

She stopped, gathered herself and looked at him. "Anyway, I got to stay here. I don't go nowhere no more."

Will got up, climbed the steps and crossed to her rocker, then sat down Indian style on the porch in front of her. "Tell me about it."

In a whisper-soft voice, Granny told the story. She explained that she only felt safe in the mountains. They were like a fence, a protective wall. But then the fence had begun to close in on her.

She put down her crochet needles, leaned over, and stroked Will's hair. "I ain't never had to tie words to all them thoughts and feelings before. Sayin' a hard truth like that, it ain't some'm you can spit out simple to just anybody." She paused, considered it, then continued resolutely. "And it…" she made a sweeping gesture all around "the whole of it…scares me some."

Will said nothing, merely reached up and took her big, gnarled hand in his.

"I know how it's gonna end." Her voice was level, but Will could feel her hand begin to tremble. "I done seen it comin' a long way off. The circle's gonna get smaller and smaller until it squeezes the life outta…until they carry me out this house in a pine box."

She seemed to take off in an entirely different direction then, but Will sensed there was a connection somewhere, that it fit together somehow.

"That mural of Bow and me gettin' married. Bowman standing all stiff and tall in that suit he borrowed with the collar too tight. Me a-standin' next by him, wearin' the white dress made out of Irish lace my own granny'd wore when she got married—brought it in a trunk from the old country. We got married in the morning and Bow went back to work in the mine on the night shift at three o'clock." She sighed. "My Bow ain't here, now. It's jest me. We all end up jest us."

Will realized that the years had healed her wounds, but nothing had relieved her solitude. No matter how many children, grandchildren, or friends she kept close around her, Granny remained set apart by the emptiness of the space beside her. And none of them, however well-intentioned could bridge that gulf; nobody would ever be able to quite get to her again.

"Have you tried to do anything about your fear? There are ways to deal with—"

"Ain't nobody can do your livin' for you. Or your dyin'. That's yore job."

"But you can't let your grief make you a *prisoner*, lock you away from the world."

Granny cocked her head to one side. "Yore a fine one to talk about lettin' grief make you a prisoner. You been a prisoner for all these many years. Only difference 'tween me 'n you is my grief locked me *in* and yore grief locked you *out*."

"It was more than grief kept me away."

"Where did you go, Will? Where you been all this time?"

He released her hand, leaned back against the railing post and stared up at the wind chime that dangled by a string from the porch ceiling, silver pipes that made a haunting sound a little like an old church organ.

"Well, I thumbed a ride on a coal truck all the way to Somerset," he said, as memories dragged him back into a reality he didn't want to re-visit. "I was on my way to the bus station. Had no idea where I was going *to*, just wanted to put space between me and where I was coming *from*. I figured I'd buy as much distance as the money I had would pay for."

He stopped and looked up at her sheepishly.

"And I got distance that day, more than I ever bargained for. Across the street from the bus station in Somerset is a Navy Recruiting Center. I walked in and listened to the guy's spiel. I needed a job and a one-way ticket out of the mountains. So that day I became a sailor."

"The *Navy?*"

Will shook his head. "Granny, if I'd sat down and plotted out the single *worst* possible decision I could have made that day, joining the Navy was it."

"How come?"

"I was running away from a coal mine! From everything that even remotely resembled a coal mine...small and tight, the walls closing in and..." He shivered. Then smiled a little at the absolute absurdity of it all. "Granny, do you have any idea how *narrow* the passageways are on a destroyer? And the berth space." He saw the confused look on Granny's face. "A berth is a bunk...a bed. They're stacked so tight you have to get out to turn over!"

"Them fellas you's in the Navy with, did you get rid of your accent so's you'd sound like them, fit in?"

"That was part of it. But it would have taken a whole lot more than an accent change for me to fit in with men who actually *wanted* to be sailors, who'd dreamed their whole lives of going to sea."

He barked out a little laugh. "I'd been in boot camp at the Great Lakes Naval Station outside Chicago for almost a week before it dawned on me I'd actually have to physically *get on* a ship. That I'd have to sail out into an ocean on a ship, live on a ship."

He stopped, shook his head in wonder.

"I was horrified, but I didn't let on. I wasn't about to confirm everybody's stereotype of a dumb hillbilly. I sucked it up and…drank a lot. And started fights."

Thick with cigarette smoke and the stink of beer and sweat, the air almost resists Will as he passes through it, like it's water. He's drunk, his natural state. He plops back down into his chair as the deck is passed to him.

"Deal the cards, hillbilly," says the sailor with a big nose and a pronounced New Jersey accent who is seated across from him. "That's five each. You can count that high, can't you?"

"Aw, come on," sighs Cowboy, the guy from Texas on Will's left. They're all tired of listening to the New Jersey guy give Will a hard time. "Don't start. Let's just play cards."

Will picks up the deck and begins to shuffle. He has to concentrate hard because he's had way more to drink than the other sailors. He spends every shore leave plastered. Usually has to be carried back on board, because if he had to walk up that gangplank under his own power…

"You hollered in your sleep again last night, hillbilly." The New Jersey guy keeps at it. "Yelling all crazy. You been hitting

the moonshine? Or is it that your feet hurt because you're not used to wearing shoes?"

Will sets the deck of cards carefully on the table in front of him.

"Dealer calls the game, right?" he says. The other three sailors groan and nod. "Okay…" Then Will turns his Kentucky accent up full throttle on the name of a silly childhood game he used to play: There's a Bear.

"I call Thar's a Bahr."

"What?" says the black sailor from Detroit. The others roll their eyes and grumble.

"S'real simple," Will says. "I say, 'Thar's a Bahr.'" Will points off to the right like he's seen something and the others glance that direction in confusion. "And you say, 'Whar?'"

Cowboy reaches for the deck of cards. "Com'on, Will, we—"

"And then I say, 'The bahr's right…'" Without warning, Will dives across the table and grabs the front of the New Jersey sailor's shirt. "'…thar!'" And he slams his fist into the man's face, hears his big nose snap.

"I finally got hauled in front of my commanding officer for assaulting another sailor, broke his nose," Will said. "I thought I'd finally done it, that he was going to throw me in the brig." His voice was hollow. "I'd have lost it in there. Little cell with no windows. I couldn't have…"

Granny reached out and stroked his hair again but kept silent.

Will took a deep breath. "His name was Burkhead. Commander Leonard C. Burkhead. And he could cuss almost as creatively as Ri…" Will caught himself. "…anybody I ever heard."

Will stands at rigid attention, a steel rod down his spine, as Commander Burkhead yells at him. Will is certain he'll be

*looking at the four walls of a cell in the brig before the com-
mander's through with him. He is equally certain he will never
see daylight again if they lock him up.*

*Gradually, the commander winds down. A whistling
teapot taken off the stove, his built-up steam finally sputters
out.*

*"I've read your file, sailor," the commander says. "You've
been written up…let's see…" He picks up the folder and begins
to thumb through it. "…three…four…five…" He drops it back
on the table. "I've read every one of them. You refused to sleep
in your assigned berth. You tried to punch out Seaman Perkins
because he closed the door of the head on you. You…" He sighs.
"Besides the fact that you've got some serious anger-manage-
ment issues, there's a common thread in all these incidents. And
I think I've figured out what it is. I'm just not sure what I'm
going to do about it."*

*His eyes riveted straight ahead, Will can still see out of
the corner of his eye that the commander is studying him. The
man says nothing, looks at Will for what seems like a very long
time, then leans back in his chair like he's come to some kind of
decision.*

*"Says here…" The commander tapped the file. "That
you're from Aintree Hollow, Kentucky." He paused. "I know
what happened in your hometown a couple of weeks before you
enlisted."*

Will must have looked surprised.

*"You hillbillies don't get out much, do you? That coal mine
explosion made national headlines; the whole country heard
about it. Twenty-five miners killed, wasn't it? Or thirty. I
know only two made it out alive. I remember reading that
part, and one of the survivors had this odd last name that stuck
with me." He paused again for a beat. "Gribbins."*

159

The commander leaned toward him. "That wasn't a brother or an uncle or a cousin was it? It was you."

"Yes, sir." Will struggles to hold onto his composure—to remain emotionally as well as physically rigid.

The officer is silent for a few moments, then asks softly, "Son, why in the name of common sense did you join the Navy?"

"Commander Burkhead recommended I be transferred—to supply. I worked on the dock in Norfolk—*outside!*—drove a forklift until my hitch was up. Even went to college at night and took a few classes. In history. Thought maybe I could teach, but..."

Will was silent for so long after that Granny finally asked softly, "What did you do then?"

He didn't answer.

"Will...?"

"I crawled down into a bottle of booze and never came back out—at least I wouldn't have if it'd been up to me." He lifted his faded blue eyes to meet hers and saw such compassion there he had to look away. "I became a drunk, Granny. Not all at once. It takes a while. Lost my first job after the Navy—worked construction—because I showed up late. Lost the next one because I didn't show up at all for two days. Tried a change of scenery—the geographic cure. Hitched from one city to the next to the next, crashed in flophouses as dreary and featureless as all the nameless cities. Went from bourbon to cheap wine to...eventually I ended up a filthy, slobbering, falling-down, homeless, under-a-bridge drunk."

Granny's eyes sparkled with tears. "Oh...Sugar."

"I went as far down as you can go. It was me and a bottle and dying."

He didn't realize he was still talking until it was too late to hold it back. "There at the end, I could actually see his eyes, Granny.

A gray wolf with yellow cat-eyes circling around me, growling and drooling."

Will had never admitted that, never said it out loud to another human being. Not even to his sponsor. Granny wasn't the only one who'd bared her soul today.

He pushed resolutely ahead into the silence that followed.

"Then one day, I couldn't keep on keepin' on anymore." He looked up at her. "I was done."

He felt a little like that now; he was finished. He'd finally been honest. He hadn't said all that he needed to say, but what he had said was the truth. "My life was ending, Granny, and I was *glad* it was over."

CHAPTER 19

Will is certain he's dying. You can just tell a thing like that. It was like that time he went camping and could feel the air mattress under his sleeping bag slowly collapse. He can feel himself deflating, sinking. Out some little hole somewhere, what little is left of his life is silently whishing away, and when it is all gone, he will be, too.

And he's okay with that. He is waaay okay with that. Let's ring the curtain down on this baby so we can all go home.

All around him is white light and shiny metal and he can hear bustling activity, the swish of hurrying feet and the babble of urgent voices. He doesn't know what they're saying, though. He might be able to tell if he concentrated, but what's the point? He's dying. He wants to tell these people that there isn't any rush, they can calm down and slow down; he'll be gone soon.

But he can't seem to get all the different muscle groups necessary for speech to cooperate. So he does concentrate for a moment, tries hard to focus.

"It'd take a whole roll of duct tape to fix what's broke in me." The accent of his raising colors his speech now, slides out from under the rock he'd shoved it under, and takes over. "I'm plumb wore out now. I'm tired. S'over."

He pauses. "Shhhhhh. Listen…" He pauses again. "Cain't you hear it. I'm whizzin' away."

Then a thought brings him momentarily all the way out of the fog.

"Don't you send my body back to Aintree Holler when I'm dead! You cremate me! Scatter my ashes over Jim Beam Distillery in Bardstown. Don't you put me in a hole in the ground! I done got out of a dark grave once and I ain't goin' back."

The burst of energy is all he has. The air's almost gone.

Then a face appears above him, huge above him, the way faces used to look when he was a kid and peaked at everybody through an empty toilet paper roll.

"You's in Harlan #7 when she blew, weren't you?" a voice behind the face asks.

The words are ice water poured over Will's head and the fuzzy edges of the room snap instantly into focus.

"Figured as much." The face leans so close it fills all of Will's sight. "So tell me some'm. If you was in #7 and got out, what are you giving up for now? There's 27 dead miners wish somebody'd give them the chance you got—to pick livin' 'stead of dyin'."

Those words plug up the leak, the hole in Will's soul, snug as a gob of Bondo.

That was the day Will met Deke Asher, whose broad shoulders, heavily muscled arms, bald head, and earring had earned him the nickname "Mr. Clean"—even though he was as black as a lump of coal. It turned out Deke had grown up on the other side of the mountain from Aintree—in Lynch, "where the blade from the ventilation fan landed when it blew off #7 that day," Deke used to tell him. "Barely missed the outhouse in my granddaddy's backyard, and he was usin' it at the time."

As soon as Will'd opened his mouth, Deke had him pegged for a hillbilly. The big man with a boom in his voice and kindness in his touch was one of the EMTs who'd brought Will into the emergency room of Gulf Coast Hospital in Ft. Meyers, Florida, more dead than alive from massively infected rat bites on his leg.

"You do know we found you 'under a bridge,' don't you? I mean that literally. A homeless drunk under a bridge. That ain't very original."

Deke visited Will every day he was in the hospital. Sick from the infection and going through DT's coming off booze, Will wasn't exactly Mary Poppins to be around. That's what Deke said. And when he was at a point where he could hear it, Deke told him other things, too.

"You got a chance, man, right now, clean and sober for the first time since…you fill in the blank. While you got a clear mind, you might want to come 'long with me and meet a friend of mine. Name's Bill W."

Will didn't know that was code for Alcoholics Anonymous until Deke walked him into his first meeting, where a beat-up old man sitting by the door fixed him with a penetrating stare.

"You need to go back out there and drink some more, son," the old man said matter-of-factly. "You still got a watch."

Deke became Will's sponsor, moved Will into a spare room above his garage that had been home to countless other recovering drunks over the years. Deke's wife was a sweet woman who'd been in a wheelchair for a decade with rheumatoid arthritis. Her father owned a construction company and when Will's leg was healed, Deke got him a job there.

Will began to piece his life back together "one step at a time."

The big EMT hauled out another AA mantra one evening a few weeks after Will got out of the hospital while the two of them sat in a booth at Denny's after a meeting.

"You know, you're only as sick as your secrets," Deke said.

"Easy for you to say; you don't know my secrets."

The big black man leaned his shiny bald head back and roared with laughter, a sudden rumbling sound that always reminded Will of a bowling ball slamming into pins.

"Every drunk I ever met thinks he's got the biggest, baddest, meanest story in the junkyard." He must have seen the stricken look on Will's face. "I ain't making light of it, Will. I'm just tellin' you, whatever you got to say, I've heard worse."

So Will told him, unloaded. For the first time in two decades, he said it out loud, tacked words onto the dark night of his soul. In one, long semihysterical stream, he described in graphic detail what had *really* happened under the mountain in Harlan #7 that day.

When he was finished, Deke told him, "Sounds like you got Number Four down pretty good, and tonight you got a leg up on Number Five."

The fourth step in AA's 12-step program requires that you make "a searching and fearless moral inventory" of yourself. Number Five demands that you admit to God, to yourself, and to another human being "the exact nature of your wrongs."

Then Deke spoke in a quiet voice so intense it felt like he was shouting. "Understand this—if you never understand anything else in your whole life—booze will take everything you have and then it will kill you." He paused, leaned closer. "You work the steps or you *die*, Will. It's that simple. Work the steps or you're gonna leave this life alone in some alley, lying in your own puke. And that's if you're lucky. That's if you don't take somebody else with you."

Deke sat back like he was finished. But he wasn't.

"I got 17 years sobriety. Quit the day I went roarin' east in the westbound lane of I 90 right outside Syracuse. In a blackout. Plowed into a station wagon—a mother and three children on their way to a family reunion. I don't remember nothin' about the accident, just woke up after, and this cop yelling at me that I'd killed a 4-year-old kid. Found out later I'd paralyzed his mother, too."

The big man stopped, glanced away. "Served 7 years of a 10-year sentence for vehicular homicide."

Then he turned his gaze back on Will. "His name was Samuel. The kid, he was Sam. He'd be 21 now, about to finish college, maybe. Working nights to save up for a road trip to California or a ring so he can propose to his girlfriend." His eyes were still pointed at Will, but that wasn't what he saw. "I carry Sam around with me everywhere I go, every day of my life. I knew when he should have started first grade, when he'd have gotten his driver's license or gone on his first date."

His eyes refocused, grabbed Will's gaze, and drilled the next words into his soul. "Seventeen years, and every day, *every single day* I am only one drink away from turnin' back into the man who killed him."

Silence.

"When you're *ready*," Deke said, his voice gentle now, "I'll help you work step Number Eight."

Will knew what that step was: "Made a list of all persons we had harmed and became willing to make amends to them all."

Will did his 90-in-90, 90 meetings in 90 days, and as 3 months became six and six became nine, he began to hear the first notes of a song his heart hadn't sung in years—a melody set to the sweet music of hope.

It was Deke who told Will that they'd reopened #7. And about the twentieth anniversary memorial service for the miners killed when it blew. Deke's mother still sent him the *Harlan Daily Enterprise*. The big man didn't push, but said he'd pay Will's way back to Kentucky if he had in mind to go. And he'd see to it Will's job was waiting for him afterward, if he still wanted it.

Will knew it was time to take the eighth step. He had to go back and face the persons he had harmed, admit what he'd done, and do whatever it took to make amends.

CHAPTER 20

J AMEY GOT UP early, as the sky began to change from black to blue. Finding out what was in a piece of rock was like an itch, like his whole arm had felt that time he got into poison ivy. It was hard for him to rest or think about anything else when his mind itched so about that rock.

His breath made white clouds in front of his nose and frost crunched beneath his feet as he made his way up the trail to the shed in the woods. Though it'd warm up later today when the sun cleared Black Mountain, it was cold now. ValVleen's feathers was all puffed up but it didn't seem to bother Bucket none. The old dog followed along behind him and sniffed the frosty ground as he went.

Jamey really needed a coat instead of just his tattered blue hoodie. Of course, he wouldn't even know he was cold as soon as he started to work. Fact is, more times than not, when he finished a carving, he was soaked in sweat, like he'd chopped firewood all afternoon.

Jamey unlocked the padlock on the shed door and put the key back in his pocket. He patted it with a smile and said, "The end."

Holding the door for Bucket, he stepped in behind the dog and lit all the lanterns. Then he sat down at his worktable and leaned over the dark stone, close to it, his lips puckered up like he was about to give the carving a kiss. Instead, he blew out a puff of air that chased away the thin layer of dust that had settled during the night.

The flickering light of the lanterns brought the shiny black rock to life, changed it into something that moved and breathed.

"Reckon them folks is a-dancin' in there, ValVleen?" Jamey whispered in awe, as he stared at the light that reflected off the planes of the unfinished carving. But he knew better.

Jamey picked up a mallet and a chisel. The shed, the dog, and the little yellow canary faded away.

Perhaps only a few minutes passed; maybe it was hours. Jamey figured hours was more likely because his back ached from bending over, there was a lot of bird poop on his shoulder and his butt was numb.

He picked up a work rag and wiped his shoulder. ValVleen hopped over his hand as he cleaned. Then he scooted away from the worktable; the stool's legs made a screechy sound on the old wood floor. He stood and stretched, then stepped back and looked at the arts on the workbench.

He hadn't never seen nothing like it in his life.

"I think this here's a bad 'un," he whispered to the bird, like he didn't want the arts to hear. "Maybe even worser'n the other'n I had to hide." He glanced at the closed door of the little storage room.

Then he studied the images—the people—that had climbed out of this rock when his hands had removed what held them prisoner. And he was glad didn't none of them have faces, at least not yet. If they'd had faces, Jamey was sure the looks on them would scare him, keep him awake of a night or crawl into bed with him to hitch a ride in his dreams.

He began to shake his head back and forth, wasn't even aware of it until he heard his voice say, "No." Only the one word. He knew then he couldn't keep working on that carving.

"I ain't gonna do no more t'hout Granny tells me to," he announced firmly. ValVleen cheeped at him; Bucket was asleep.

But that didn't feel any better. To stop now, in the middle…the thought filled him with a nameless fear. All this time them folks had been buried and finally they was fixin' to crawl out. How could he leave them trapped, frozen half in and half out of the rock?

He shivered, then shook off the trembles and picked up the piece of jet, surprisingly light for all its hardness.

"ValVleen, we're gonna go ask." He nudged the sleeping dog with his toe. "Com'on, Bucket."

Jamey put the carving in one of his pillowcases and carried the stone down the path that led to the house, around the stand of poplars—where Bucket paused to leave his mark. As he passed along the side of the garden, Jamey's mind whirled around and around in his head. He hadn't never stopped in the middle of one of his arts. He hadn't never showed one before it was done. He hadn't never left an art unfinished.

Jamey didn't like nevers.

Granny heard the back door slam, knew it was Jamey Boy, but bit her tongue. He'd been slamming the back door for 15 years and she'd been telling him to close it gentle the whole time. Came a point you needed to stop beating a dead horse.

Jamey Boy went into the living room carrying something—likely a carving—wrapped up in a pillowcase. Will and JoJo sat together on the couch. JoJo didn't have to go in until noon today but she was already dressed in her red Jiffy Stop smock. Playing cards were spread out on the table in front of them and Will was trying to explain to JoJo why she hadn't ought to draw to a inside straight. Jamey Boy had missed breakfast, but that didn't surprise Granny none. When he worked, it filled up his whole head and he didn't have room up there for other things.

Granny had tried to stay out of Will and JoJo's hair so they could talk. She'd rearranged the silverware drawer, defrosted the freezer, and was about to clean the oven. Letting them get to know each other had turned into a lot of work.

She could tell Will had done what she'd asked him to, that he'd worked real hard to get past the wall JoJo always kept up between her and other people. And it looked to Granny like he'd either climbed over it or she'd let him in the gate because the two of them appeared to have hooked up in some way. Granny wasn't surprised. They both had holes in they hearts all full up with suffering they didn't talk about. Their wounds was different from Granny's, but they was deep and painful. Pain was pain. Didn't matter much what caused it.

Bad things had happened to Will. She could see into the darkness behind his eyes where bats flew around with blood dripping off their fangs. But sometimes bad things happened to you so you could comfort somebody else, and maybe that was the way of it with Will. If life had taught her anything in her 76 years in this hollow it was that God never wasted a hurt.

Will and JoJo stopped and looked up at Jamey Boy; he said nothing, just stood there with that odd look he got sometimes, like wasn't nothing at all going on inside his head. And maybe there wasn't. Granny knew he was being polite, didn't want to interrupt. But Will didn't understand how long Jamey could stand there like that. She'd never in all her days met anybody as patient as he was. That boy would sit and wait for hours for a hummingbird to show up at the sugar water jar they'd set out back.

"Jamey Boy, did you want some'm, Sugar?" she asked.

"Yes ma'am."

Silence.

"What is it?"

"It's this here carvin'." He held the piece of jet out in front of him. "I need to know what I'm s'posed to do with it." He didn't look at anyone, tucked his head, and took a deep breath. "I done part of it as you can see but soon's I did I seen it wasn't people dancin' but they's movin' an' it felt in my belly like they's hurtin' and I don't want it to make you cry like that other one done so if'n you don't want me to, I ain't gonna carve nary another piece, just give the jet back to Lloyd and tell him to put it back in the hole he dug it out of in the mountain. The end."

Granny crossed to where Jamey Boy stood, lifted the stone out of his hands, removed the pillowcase and set the carving down on the table. JoJo and Will got up and the three of them stared down at it. Jamey Boy stepped over beside Granny but he didn't look at the carving. His gaze wandered like it was following a fly buzzing around the room.

"Oh." Just the one word from Will.

JoJo said nothing at all, just put both hands over her mouth, and stared wide-eyed at the stone.

Granny got down close enough to see it and far enough away so she could make out the detail. JoJo'd said she'd ought to get glasses. Soon as it registered with Granny what she was looking at, she let out a little squeak of a gasp. It wasn't near done, but enough was finished that you could see it was like that mural of her and Bowman's wedding—a moment frozen in time. Right up front was a lone miner; behind him was a great crowd of them. The up-front miner had no details, but he was the only one raised in relief on the stone; the miners behind him were mere sketches, etched outlines not yet "pulled up outta the rock."

All the figures in the carving were flying through the air. A tangle of men, twisting and turning, and a mangled piece of machinery that was either a mantrip or a shuttle had been flung backward by some invisible force.

None of the miners had faces.

Will was the first one to find his voice.

"It's the explosion, isn't it," he said, but it wasn't no question. "This is what it looked like at the face of the mine when #7 blew."

Will was right, of course. It was plain that Jamey Boy had carved the disaster. Granny shouldn't have been surprised. All anybody in the hollow had talked about for the past month was the anniversary and the ceremony. When he wasn't in the mine or his shed, Jamey Boy hung out in town at the grocery, Pete's Place, the post office. And somewhere in that brain of his—that didn't get no oxygen so it was different and special—somewhere in there he'd seen what no other living human being had eyes to see.

Jamey Boy said nothing, just wagged his head back and forth and looked at no one.

JoJo turned to Granny. "What did he mean about the *other* carvin' that made you cry? Has he carved the explosion before and I ain't never seen it?"

Will watched her closely. He'd already heard Jamey Boy mention an arts that made her cry. Granny fumbled, then finally got out an honest answer. "No, he ain't never carved the 'xplosion." That was true. He hadn't. Then she remembered what she'd told Will when he'd asked. "Lots of what Jamey does is so powerful, I get all teary-eyed." She looked back at the piece of unfinished art on the table. "But this…"

"You don't want me to finish it, I won't," Jamey said and looked out the window. "I don't aim to make you sad."

Granny put her arm around him and patted his back.

"Life just gets away from me some days; ain't yore fault."

Will spoke slowly and quietly as he stared at the carving with the empty look of a man who can't believe he's seeing what he's seeing. "Granny, when this is finished…" He pointed to the sketched miners in the background. "…when all these are pulled out of the rock like the one in front, you'll be able to tell who…"

One of them miners was Bowman. One was Ed. One was…how could she stand to watch them die, to see the looks on their faces?

Jamey Boy spoke then. "The reason they ain't got no faces is 'cause I ain't seen none. Maybe they faces got stuck in the rock and can't get out. I can't give 'em faces if'n they don't got none." He stopped, then continued softly. "But maybe the faces is comin' later."

Granny reached out and touched the stone, ran her fingers over the lone raised miner in front and over the shadowy outlines of the others in the background.

"You 'member what I told you that time 'bout yore arts?"

"Yes, Ma'am," he said and began a first-grader recitation. "You said it was my job to dig out of the rocks whatever God put in 'em and it didn't matter if people didn't like what was there."

"Ain't no less true now than it was then," Granny said. "This here arts ain't no worse'n some of the pictures I made up my own self." She took a deep breath and turned to Jamey Boy. "If'n the 'xplosion is what's in the rock, then the 'xplosion is what you got to set free."

CHAPTER 21

L LOYD JACOBS LIVED in a house, not a trailer; Will gave him points for that. It was small and nondescript and clung to a hillside about half a mile off Frog Hole Lane. A place that might once have been charming, it had descended into trashy. Weeds strangled the garden next to the porch where an unpruned climbing rose bush had gobbled up the lattice railing as well as the trellis by the door. The yard looked like it might not have been mowed the whole summer. Lloyd's truck was parked out front, so Will knew he'd found the right house, knew Lloyd was home, and he quickly pulled off the road into the driveway. He wouldn't allow himself to hesitate because he knew if he did, he'd lose his nerve altogether, turn around and go back to Granny's without ever making an attempt to put things right between him and Lloyd.

Out of nowhere, Will was blind-sided by an overwhelming longing for a drink. His mouth watered, ached for the sweet caramel flavor and the kick of good bourbon—a taste he hadn't experienced in years. At the end, Will was down to cheap wine when he could get it and cough syrup or mouthwash when he couldn't.

A wave of self-pity swept over him and demon booze appeared out of the shadows, slipped his arm around Will's shoulders and whispered in his ear like a trusted friend.

Only one won't hurt. You're back on your feet and strong enough to handle it now. A little self-control and you can drink responsibly—in moderation.

Will broke into a cold sweat

I need to go to a meeting!

But there were no AA meetings in Aintree Hollow. Nothing here to keep him sober but his past, the people he'd hurt and the little flame of hope that still burned inside him.

Will parked JoJo's car behind Lloyd's truck. It was the only space there was, and it did preclude Lloyd's bolting—though Will knew that was absurd. Lloyd could refuse to talk to him. The two of them might even end up beating the crap out of each other, but Lloyd had no reason to run from him.

Will began to second-guess that assumption, however, as soon as Lloyd opened the door. A look of such...what? surprise? anger? No, more like *fear* washed over Lloyd's face, and for an instant, Will thought the man might actually turn and run. Then the contesting emotions at war on his face resolved into the single most powerful one—fury.

"What're *you* doin' here?" Lloyd's voice sounded odd. It had a much lower pitch than Will remembered. It wasn't a hoarse sound. More like the words came out of a rain barrel. Or from some very deep, dark place.

"I came to talk."

"'Bout what?"

"What do you think?"

Lloyd squared his jaw, his face dark with unspent rage, and said defiantly, "If you're here to accuse me of some'm, go ahead, spit it out."

"Accuse you? Of what?"

"You think you can prove it, go on, call the sheriff. Now..." Lloyd spit out the next words like the taste of them made him sick. "...*get off my porch!*"

Will didn't budge. The two men glared at each other for a couple of beats, and Will noticed the gray cast to Lloyd's skin, the black circles under his bloodshot eyes. He looked like he hadn't slept—or shaved—in three days.

Then Will spoke in a voice that sounded far calmer than he felt. "Lloyd, I have absolutely *no idea* what you're talking about. You're not making any sense. Look…" he ran his hands through his hair in frustration. "…can we just take a break from stupid for a minute? I came here because I want to talk. That's *all*. Talk."

Lloyd looked momentarily confused. Then he smiled an odd smile, a smirk.

"I done said everything I had to say. Me and you are quits."

Will sensed that something had shifted in Lloyd. He'd pulled back from some edge, appeared to relax, like there had been a competition Will wasn't aware of and Lloyd had won.

"I'm sorry, Lloyd."

"For what?"

"'Everything."

"It'd help if you narrowed that down some."

"I'm sorry I bailed on you. Sorry I left, that I stayed gone, never came back. I'm sorry—"

"Sorry, sorry, sorry," Lloyd mimicked. "You're sorry all right. A sorry excuse for a human being. Now like I said, get off my porch."

He reached to close the door in Will's face.

"Lloyd, I'm going to tell Granny," Will tossed the words out into the air like a hand grenade without a pin. It took a few seconds for them to explode.

Lloyd froze, "Tell her what?"

"All of it," Will pushed ahead. "Before the memorial service tomorrow, I'm going to tell her what happened, the whole story."

"Why?" There was no anger in the question; Lloyd sounded genuinely bewildered.

"I *have to*, Lloyd," Will's voice, his eyes and his heart pleaded with Lloyd to understand. "It's eaten me up inside. I *won't* carry it around with me anymore." Will paused, but not long enough for the stunned Lloyd to summon a response. When he continued speaking there was an edge of steel in his voice.

"And I'm not just talking about what the three of us did *together*, Lloyd. There was worse done to Ricky Dan than—"

Without warning, Lloyd lunged at Will, cried out in primeval, inarticulate rage, his lips skinned back from his teeth like a mad dog. He slammed Will backward into the porch post, seized his neck, and started to choke him.

Will didn't grant Lloyd one-swing-he's-entitled-to-it this time. His response was instinctive. Lloyd might have been bigger, but military training and years of bar brawls gave Will a clear advantage. He grabbed Lloyd's right hand with both of his and pried Lloyd's fingers off his neck. Then he continued to shove Lloyd's fingers backward onto his forearm until Lloyd cried out in pain and let go his hold on Will's neck with his other hand. Then Will stepped to the side, kept the wrist-breaking pressure on Lloyd's right hand firm, and forced Lloyd to his knees. Only then did he let go.

But there was still fight left in Lloyd and he scrambled to his feet. Before he could completely regain his balance, Will shoved him backward into the porch railing. The old wood must have been rotten because the railing and the trellis behind it gave way when he struck them, dumping Lloyd on top of them in the front yard. Broken pieces of lattice and large, sharp rose bush thorns slashed deep scratches into his arms, back, and the side of his face.

Will leapt down off the porch, straddled Lloyd's chest and drew his fist back to smash it into Lloyd's face. But he let his arm drop to his side, instead, chilled by the eerie sensation of déjà vu. Will had knocked Lloyd on his back once before. He felt like throwing up this time, too, but at least his pants were dry.

"I don't know what your problem is, man, but whether you like it or not, I'm telling Granny," Will gasped, panting from exertion and from the adrenaline dump into his veins. "If she has any sense at all, she'll toss me out on my ear and never speak to me again."

He got up off Lloyd's chest. "How she'll feel about you once she knows the truth is your problem."

Then Will marched out to JoJo's car, got in, and drove away.

It was a warm morning. The sun up above the mountain to the east ignited the autumn trees in a blaze of color. But where Will's mind had gone, there was no light. There was no color. There was only darkness and smoke and terror.

CHAPTER 22

Ricky Dan leads the way toward the rail shaft. Will and Lloyd follow him through the nearest break—one of hundreds of 18-foot open spaces between coal pillars that connect the shafts.

Halfway down the break, there should be a curtain across it, a dam in the middle that blocks the air flow and directs good air toward the face of the mine. There is no curtain.

In the absolute black, it is impossible to see more than a few feet ahead; walking bent over means they can't shine their headlamps out front without squatting down.

Will is chilled. He's always chilled in the mine—even when he's hard at work. Maybe it's because he's always sweating— even when he's sitting still. Fear sweat. The stink of it makes him nauseous. And the damp makes him shiver. There's moisture on every surface. Water constantly drips from the roof; sometimes it comes down like rain. The shuttle driver has to grease the steering wheel when he leaves on Friday or it'll be rusted when he returns for his shift Monday morning.

Cold, damp and dark. And small. He feels the walls begin to squeeze tighter and tighter; senses the weight of the mountain suspended above him. Ready to crush him…like that coal train that roared over him only inches…

Stop it!

Will grabs hold of his thoughts and forcibly wrenches them away from the spiral into panic. As long as he stays busy, he can cope. Well, busy at any job except helping the pinner on the roof-bolting machine. Drilling holes for the 4-foot-long bolts that attach the unstable slate of the mine roof to the denser layer of sandstone above it is the most dangerous job in the mine. Work under unbolted top so frightens Will he sometimes loses his breakfast—tells the pinner man he has a stomach virus. Greasing the belt line isn't nearly as frightening and it keeps his mind occupied. But just walking along in the dark like this...

He turns his head and glances over to the right as they pass the next break. The headlamp on his red helmet lights up something crouched in the shadows in the shaft on the other side of it. He jumps back, loses his footing, and goes down on one knee.

Lloyd turns around. "You okay?"

"Fine, just tripped." His voice is shaky but he doesn't think Lloyd noticed. Headlamps mess with your eyes; the dark messes with your head. Makes you see things that aren't there. Ghost images, formed out of shadows and dust and fear.

He shouldn't have been able to see all the way through the break to begin with. This is the third one they've passed with no curtain. All the breaks along the rail line are supposed to be sealed off with heavy burlap or plastic curtains or with permanent concrete-block walls, "dammed up" to direct good air to the face of the mine.

Hob Bascomb does as good a job as he can, but curtain-hanging and building permanent seals are tasks he gets around to when they don't have him pulled away doing something else.

And Hob's not here today.

The next break is sealed with a curtain. And as they go along, the rest are sealed, too. Some with curtains; others with piles of cinder block disguised with rock dust to look like concrete-block walls.

It seems to take an hour to travel the quarter mile up the rail shaft to the point where the track ends. Lloyd and Ricky Dan argue about basketball the whole way. The roar of Bowman's continuous miner fades behind them; the rumble of the second crew's miner farther down the face is a low hum. But Lloyd and Ricky Dan don't bother to lower their voices as the sounds diminish; they're already shouting at each other before the debate even heats up.

Lloyd is a rabid University of Kentucky fan, has "UK" painted in bright blue letters on the front of his helmet. Last night, Ricky Dan painted a blue "UK" on his own helmet, too—with a red X across it. Just to be ornery. When Granny saw it, she warned that Lloyd wouldn't likely think it was funny. Granny was right.

"You tellin' me you don't think Joe B. Hall's the best coach in the Southeast Conference? They won the NCAA championship 3 years ago—whadda ya want?"

"Three years ago's the Stone Age," Ricky Dan says, baiting him. "What's he done lately?"

"Well, he—"

"He ain't done squat, that's what. This year, they couldn't even take the conference!"

Lloyd stops so abruptly Will almost runs into him. There is a look in his eye, a glint of impending violence Will has seen more and more often in the past few years. Lloyd has an explosive temper and there's no longer any doubt who'd be the winner if he and Will got into it. At 18, Lloyd has powerful shoulders and massive, muscular arms. After his mother died 2 years ago, he'd quit school to work in the mine—under age—and when he wasn't on the job, he worked out, lifted weights, bulked up. His father had run off the Christmas after she died and folks said he probably left because Lloyd was so big now he couldn't beat him up anymore. Though Ricky Dan was 7 years older, he was slender like Will; he'd be no match for Lloyd, either.

"I got a plan," Will blurts out in an effort to diffuse the situation before it gets ugly. "How 'bout we just lay track, okay? And talk about…oh, I don't know—ice hockey?"

"Ice hockey?" Lloyd shakes his head, makes a humph sound in his throat, turns and stalks over to a pile of rails lying up against a coal pillar.

Because the track ends here, there are supplies stacked all around. Fifty-pound bags of lime for dusting the shaft walls, extra scoop batteries, rolls of plastic for curtains, duct tape, roof bolts, and tools.

The rails are 3 inches tall and come in 20-foot sections. The metal cross ties they rest on are flat, quarter-inch sheet metal, 6 inches wide and 8 feet long. The rails fit into notches on the cross ties with a locking mechanism that has to be hammered shut.

Ricky Dan and Lloyd begin to lay out cross ties as they argue. Will grabs the end of a piece of rail and drags it along beside the cross ties, ready to clip it down once the ties are in place.

The three complete the first set of rails. Ricky Dan and Lloyd start to lay cross ties for the next set as Will hammers one last cantankerous lock shut on the first.

There is a gap in Will's memory at this point. One minute he is pounding on a catch and the next…

His ears pop.

A tremendous, thundering boom slams into him; the sound and pressure hurl him head over heels up the shaft. His body ricochets off the roof, the floor and the coal pillar-walls like a bullet fired into a rock pile.

And then he is on his back, a ferocious roar in his ears. His eyes stare into black nothingness. Blind! Not a pinprick of light anywhere. And all around him is a stink—something's burning.

Completely disoriented, Will has no idea where he is. Did he fall out of bed? Is he in the woods—where are the stars? He sits up slowly and turns around. Behind him, 15 feet away, a headlamp shines upward through dark air—smoke!—toward the roof, lighting up the fossil ferns like fleece wallpaper. A few feet beyond, another headlamp beam shines out across the floor.

Then realization hits him harder than the force that flung him down the shaft. The mine! Explosion!

Will reaches up; his helmet's gone. He doesn't trust his legs to stand, so he crawls along the rails to the first beam of light. It's Ricky Dan on his back, his eyes closed. He's not moving.

Will calls out his name and can barely hear his own voice. It's as if his whole head's packed in cotton. He touches his ears and feels no blood; his eardrums are intact. But his nose is bleeding and he wipes it on his sleeve.

"Ricky Dan!" he cries in that strange, hollow, echoing voice. He grabs Ricky Dan's shirt and shakes him. "Wake up!"

Ricky Dan's eyes flutter open. Then close again. Will shakes him hard and when his eyes open back up they stay open. But there's no recognition in them; they stare out blankly.

Will slaps Ricky Dan's face. "Ricky Dan, we gotta get out of here. It blew. The mine blew!"

Confusion downshifts into dawning understanding on Ricky Dan's face. He rolls over on his side and Will helps him sit up.

"Come on," Will urges. "We gotta run!"

As soon as Ricky Dan sits, he begins to cough. Thick, black smoke billows at them in the darkness. He lurches to his feet, then turns and begins to stagger back down the shaft toward the smoke.

"No, Ricky Dan." Will jumps up and grabs his arm. "Not that way. We have to get out of here!"

"Daddy!" It is the cry of a lost little boy. He shakes off Will's grip on his arm. "I'm not leaving my father!"

His words punch Will in the belly. It hadn't registered. Bowman's *back there! At the face where it blew.*

"Help! My leg...help!"

The light that had shone out across the floor is now pointed at Will and Ricky Dan. They hurry to Lloyd's side and Ricky Dan sweeps his headlamp beam down the length of Lloyd's body. His left boot is missing and his foot is cocked at an unnatural angle. His ankle must be broken.

"I can't walk. You gotta help me!"

Will turns to Ricky Dan. "I can't get Lloyd outta here by myself. If you go back..." He doesn't finish the sentence because he doesn't have to.

Ricky Dan looks toward the face of the mine. The light from his headlamp reveals a cloud of boiling smoke. He stares transfixed, an expression of yearning and horror on his face.

"Ricky Dan," Will urges, "we have to go—now!"

With a strangled sob, Ricky Dan turns back and grabs Lloyd's arm. "We'll have to drag 'im."

Will grabs Lloyd's other arm and together he and Ricky Dan pull him on his back down the shaft toward the mouth of the mine. Lloyd cries out in pain as they bump him over the left rail and pull him along between the tracks. The rails are their lifeline. A straight shot out. Without them, they'd get hopelessly lost in the dark and smoke.

Will has no helmet so he keeps his head down, but his back drags across the roof as he runs down the shaft. His shirt is soon soaked and his back is quickly scratched and bruised, scraped across the rough rock surface and an occasional roof bolt or plate. The bolts are almost flush with the roof; lean over and you clear them. But running as fast as you can, it's almost impossible to stay bent over far enough.

The smoke grows thicker by the second, a black cloud of death that chokes them as he and Ricky Dan pull Lloyd behind them in the dirt.

They glance sideways down every break—hoping. But there are no seals on any of them. The concussion of the ex-plosion has blown down all the curtains and cinder block walls that direct good air down the rail line shaft to the face. Without them, the fan—if it wasn't destroyed by the blast—is merely sucking clean air across the front 50 feet of the mine and right back out the other side. The rest of the mile-deep mine will fill completely with deadly smoke in a matter of minutes.

And the three miners know they can't possibly make it all the way out before that happens.

Ricky Dan falls, coughing.

Will's head spins; every breath is a searing agony. He wants to urge Ricky Dan to get up, to keep running, but he has no air to speak and he can feel his own strength begin to fail, to leak out of him like water circling a drain.

Ricky Dan stumbles to his feet and they push ahead. Past one more 50-foot coal pillar, one more break with a blown-out seal. Their eyes burn; smoke has filled the shaft all around them. Lloyd's weight drags so heavy now they can barely stagger forward.

All at once, Ricky Dan drops Lloyd's arm, stumbles to his right and vanishes in the smoke. Will collapses to his knees, coughing violently. It's over. He can go no farther. He is so dizzy he starts to pitch forward into the dirt. Ricky Dan suddenly reappears out of the cloud of swirling dark. He grabs Lloyd's arm and motions for Will to follow; he has no breath to speak. Will gets to his feet and lurches after Ricky Dan, dragging Lloyd after him. He sees yellow in the smoke, stumbles down through the break toward it and falls. Ricky Dan grabs him and shoves him under the curtain…into air! Fresh air!

CHAPTER 23

Will lies where he has fallen, coughing. He gasps in lungful after lungful of smokeless air as Ricky Dan drags Lloyd the final few feet. Then Ricky Dan pulls a piece of chalk from his pocket, ducks under the curtain into the shaft for a moment, then back inside where he collapses against a pile of rocks, debris, and trash.

The only sounds for a long time are Will coughing, Lloyd moaning, and Ricky Dan sobbing.

Will is so light-headed that thoughts and images flit across the surface of his mind like skaters on ice. Unable to concentrate, it takes several minutes for him to figure out where they've landed. They're obviously in a break between two sets of curtains—but why would a break have curtains on both sides? And why hadn't the concussion of the explosion blown out these curtains like it had every other seal they'd passed?

He can't come up with an answer to the second question, but the answer to the first finally dawns on him.

He remembers they'd used a break between the rail line shaft and the belt line shaft as a dumpsite when they mucked out the tunnels several weeks ago, filled it with trash—pieces of broken timber, empty lime bags, bent roof bolts, and curtain nails along with debris from a rockfall and several tree stumps scraped up by the scoop. In addition to the curtain seal in the middle of the break, they'd hastily put up a curtain on the rail line end of it, too, to hide the mess during a "surprise" MSHA inspection.

Will slowly lifts himself off the floor, crawls over to the coal pillar and leans back against it. He winces in pain when the scrapes on his back come in contact with the rough surface of the coal. Then he pulls his legs up in front of him and rests his forearms on his knees.

"Reckon this seal held, these curtains didn't blow 'cause there's two of 'em?" he asks. His voice is hoarse from coughing and still rings hollow in the roar in his ears.

"Or 'cause the break's mostly solid; there's more rocks in here than air," Lloyd says.

The pile of rocks and trash stretches from the curtain seal in the back to the curtain in the front, all the way to the roof and out across the floor, leaving only the small open area they've tumbled into.

Lloyd raises up on his elbows and drags himself slowly to the pillar, turns over carefully and eases into a sitting position. Then he leans against the pillar with his injured leg stretched straight out in front of him.

"Ya'll need to do what you can to seal this off better," he says, his pain-filled voice tight and breathy.

Ricky Dan doesn't respond, doesn't move. Will looks around. The enclosure is already about as airtight as they can make it. Curtains are strung from one roof bolt to the next. Using a masonry hammer, the ventilation man drives a large-head roof tack through the plastic and jams the tack between the roof and the 6-inch-square metal plate on the bolt. Then he pulls the plastic taut, snug against the roof and moves on to the next bolt plate. Curtain plastic comes in a two-hundred-foot roll, not in pre-cut standard-sized pieces, and Hob Bascomb always cuts curtains too large. So there is plenty of excess plastic on the bottom and sides of each curtain. Will piles rocks on the bottom plastic on the rail line side, then on the belt line side. The extra 2 or 3 feet of leftover plastic against the coal pillars form good seals on the sides of the enclosure.

The only light in the break comes from Lloyd's and Ricky Dan's headlamps, so until Lloyd turns toward him, Ricky Dan's face is in shadow. When Lloyd looks at Ricky Dan, Will sees that the layer of black coal dust on Ricky Dan's cheeks has been wiped almost clean by tears. It looks like his nose bled and blood oozes out of both ears, too.

"You okay, Ricky Dan?" Lloyd asks, speaking too loud. Ricky Dan turns to him and illuminates Lloyd's face with his headlamp. It appears Lloyd's right ear has bled, but not his nose. His lip is split, though, like somebody'd punched him in the face. It's bleeding and he has managed to smear the blood all over his chin.

Ricky Dan's breath wheezes in and out in a gasping rasp. "He's gone, ain't he," he croaks. It isn't a question. "Daddy hit old works and it blew."

If his continuous miner had broken through into old works full of methane and the sparks from the bits hitting rock above the coal set it off, there'd be nothing left of Bowman or the machine—or anybody anywhere near it.

But the explosion could have been a spark that ignited methane built-up somewhere else on the face—rather than an abandoned tunnel full of it. A bomb, sure, but not as big a bomb. Or maybe the other crew hit old works. They'd all have died instantly, but there was a chance Bowman's crew…

At this point there was no way to tell what had happened.

"*You don't know that, Ricky Dan,*" Will says. "*It coulda been—*"

"*No, it was Daddy.*" He is an open wound, pours out pain with every word. "*I know.*" Ricky Dan's breathing is labored and he's seized by a fit of coughing. When he regains his breath, he bleats, "*Daddy's gone.*" He puts his head in his hands and makes a kind of strangled sound that could be crying or coughing. Likely both.

Will glances at Lloyd, who is wiping at his split lip with the back of his shirt sleeve. What is there to say? Then he leans back carefully against the pillar and concentrates on breathing without coughing. And struggles desperately not to panic. It's all he can do to sit still. He aches to leap out of this little rabbit hole and run and run and run until he is out from under the smothering mountain, out in the sunshine and the fresh air—out in the open.

But if he does, he'll die. The air out there in the shaft is a lethal concoction of swirling death, and he knows the source of the boiling, sooty black smoke that's as thick as chocolate pudding. Ignited by the explosion, the coal seam itself is on fire. And nothing short of an ocean full of water could put that kind of fire out. Will knows of a coal seam in West Virginia that has been on fire for 18 years! Along with setting the coal on fire, the explosion released methane and carbon monoxide, too. Take two or three breaths of the noxious smoke-and-poison-gas cocktail beyond the yellow plastic curtains and you'd be dead in less than a minute.

The three miners are trapped, marooned in the air bubble in the break until they're rescued—or until their air runs out. They could have made it all the way to the mine entrance, of course, if they'd each had a self-rescuer—an 8-inch metal container with a charcoal filter and a mouthpiece. Self-rescuers *provide more than an hour of breathable air and are standard issue in most coal mines. But not in Harlan #7.*

Time falls off the clock. Will has no watch to measure the seconds as they tick away. His heart bangs in his chest like a lunatic piston, thump, thump, thump and he can't do anything to slow it down. He gasps for air he knows he should try to conserve, but he continues to suck it into his lungs in great heaving gulps anyway. Terror, like swarms of dark, winged things, buzzes in his belly and makes his head spin.

Ricky Dan breaks the silence that may have lasted for 5 minutes or 5 hours—Will honestly does not know.

"I'm gonna turn off my headlamp," he says to Lloyd. "Save battery power." A charged headlamp will last about 12 hours, but both of theirs have been on since they came on shift at seven this morning—at least 6 hours ago. "We'll swap out."

Lloyd removes the headlamp from his helmet and hands it to Ricky Dan, who props it on a rock so it shines at the roof and bounces pale illumination out into the rest of the enclosure. Ricky Dan reaches up and switches his own light off. His breathing is still noisy and ragged, his voice a hoarse bark. Though Will is wheezing from the smoke he inhaled, Ricky Dan obviously got a worse dose. But other than his noisy breathing, Ricky Dan seems remarkably composed. The young man who sobbed brokenheartedly over the loss of his father just minutes—was it hours?—ago has vanished into a dark, untouchable calm. His damaged voice is level when he says, "We need to do the math here, boys."

They know the arithmetic problem he's talking about. In fact, Will has been trying to work it in his head but he can't concentrate, gets more lost and confused with every effort.

All miners know the simple cave-in principle: one cubic yard of air will last one miner 1 hour.

The mine roof is a little over 4 feet off the floor. The distance between the coal pillars enclosed by the two curtains is 18 feet, and the back curtain has been placed where all seals are placed—halfway down the 50-foot pillars. So doing the math should mean multiplying 4 feet by 18 feet by 25 feet. Then divide the result by 27 to convert the number to cubic yards.

Except there are two critical variables here. To keep it from getting tangled up in the scoop, the front curtain was set back five feet into the break, which reduces the 25 feet of length to 20. But much more important are the rocks piled up to the roof and all the way across the far pillar. The pile takes up way more than half the enclosure.

"What's the open area we got to work with? Four by twenty by…what?" *Ricky Dan picks up Lloyd's headlamp off the rocks and shines it around.* "Ten feet, maybe?"

"More like eight," *Lloyd says.*

"Ok—help me out, I never was no good at ciphers—4 times 20 times 8—

"I already done it, worked it out," *Lloyd says. His voice sounds hollow, but not because of the ring in Will's ears.* "Seven hours. With three of us breathin' it, we got 7 hours of air." *Lloyd looks at his watch and when he speaks again, his voice is shaky.* "Had 7 hours of air. That was almost 2 hours ago. Now we got 5."

Terror as real as a gust of wind passes among them; the chill ruffles Will's hair as it blows by.

Two hours! They've been here 2 hours already! Will is almost more shocked than frightened. Where did the time go?

But he doesn't ponder the mystery for long. There's an even more important one to consider: if 5 hours is the time they've got, how much time do they need? Lloyd has been a miner for

2 years, Ricky Dan for almost 10. As the rookie, Will has only a vague idea how long it takes to conduct a rescue operation.

"How long...the rescue team...how...?"

"Two to three hours on the front end," Lloyd says. "Let's say three." *It's clear he's already added and readded the numbers in his mind.* "Gotta send out the call and gather up a rescue team. Some—probably most—are down in a mine somewhere workin' and they gotta get 'em out and then get 'em here."

Only the large coal companies have on-site rescue teams, but when an alert goes out that there's been an accident anywhere, teams from every mine around converge on the scene. Harlan #7's outside foreman had most certainly been on the phone to the federal and state mine inspectors, the Harlan County sheriff and rescue departments and the Kentucky State Police before the ground stopped shaking after the explosion.

"And if the fan's gone..." *Lloyd exchanges a glance with Ricky Dan.*

Will looks from one to the other. "What?"

"If the explosion blew out the ventilation fan, they can't do nothing 'til they fix it," Ricky Dan says. "Or put in a new one. Remember what happened in Scotia."

Four years earlier in the Scotia Coal Mine in Letcher County, 15 miners at work 3.5 miles underground were killed in an explosion. Later that day, 11 miners sent to rescue the first crew were killed when methane build-up caused an even bigger blast than the first. A mine explosion releases methane from the coal and fills the air in the shafts with coal dust—making subsequent explosions much more likely. Without a functioning fan to suck out the smoke and gas, it would be too dangerous for rescue workers to set foot in Harlan #7.

"Then...?"

"Say it takes 'em three—" *Lloyd begins.*

"Four," Ricky Dan corrects.

"Four hours to get the fan up and runnin'...well, there it is. Seven hours gone and they ain't even started to look for nobody yet. It'll take 'em another 3 or 4 hours to put seals back in, working their way down the shaft from the entrance to the face so's the fan's suckin' bad air outta—"

"We ain't gonna make it, Will," Ricky Dan says quietly, still strangely disconnected, like he's just told Will his ice cream cone will melt before he has time to eat it. "We ain't got enough air to last 'til they get to us."

Will feels like he's falling. Down, down, down into some dark place, into deep black water, cold water, cold as death. He's nauseous, but has no food in his stomach to throw up. He hears himself begin to pant. He breathes faster and faster, but he still can't seem to get in enough air to keep from choking.

Then a memory skitters across his mind on small, clawed feet.

He was probably 5 or 6 years old the one time, the only time, his father ever took him fishing. They'd slung cane poles over their shoulders and walked 3 miles to a sandbar in the middle of Lizard Lick Creek. Will hooked a catfish. It was the first fish he'd ever caught and not very big, but he was pumped up and proud he'd landed it. His father took the fish off the hook and tossed it over into the grass while he threaded another fat, black worm onto Will's hook. Will watched the catfish flop around in the grass, saw its mouth open and close as it struggled to breathe. He was both fascinated and horrified by the fish's fight for life. It seemed to take forever for the fish to stop struggling and lie still in the grass. Still and dead.

"But...isn't there anything...? I mean, there must be something we can do." He hates the pitiful, whining tone in his voice. He sounds like a frightened child. Feels like one, too.

"What? We wouldn't last 30 seconds out in that." Ricky Dan gestures toward the front shaft. "I chalked 'Men Here' on the curtain. Rescue team will come in down the rail shaft. So they'll find us. When they do come, they'll find us."

"Can't we—?"

"There ain't nothin' to be done, Will. I'm sorry." There is a flat finality in Ricky Dan's words, like the ominous peal of a bell. A death knell.

Lloyd speaks then, his voice still shaky. "Well, there is one thing…"

Chapter 24

LOYD SLOWLY ROLLED off the shattered trellis into the dirt. The thorns and broken boards had torn the skin on his back and arms and left deep, bleeding scratches. He remained on his belly for a long time. There was a buzzing sound in his ears he couldn't turn off, like the hum of an old refrigerator. It wasn't from a blow to the head, though. He hadn't hit the trellis or the ground that hard. Probably lack of sleep. He hadn't slept more than a couple of hours in the past three nights, ever since Li'l Bit told him Will Gribbins was home.

Will.

His mind refocused. He'd been so surprised to see Will standing on his porch, he'd about wet himself, like Will done that time they lay under the coal train on the trestle. He'd been certain Will knew he'd shot at him in the woods yesterday afternoon, that somehow Will had seen him, knew he was the "poacher" who'd *accidentally* fired three rounds at him from a 30.06.

Lloyd sat up slowly. He was so tired it was hard to think, hard to keep his attention focused. His thoughts were like water spiders on a still pool. They flitted around from one spot to another, never stopped long enough for him to make sense of anything.

When he'd opened the door and there stood Will, Lloyd was sure Will had come to settle the score; actually wondered if he could get to his gun before Will pulled whatever weapon he'd brought with him.

But that's not why Will had come to see him. In fact, Lloyd still had no clear understanding of why Will had come. It didn't have nothing to do with the shooting yesterday, though. Will didn't even mention it. He'd just said the same thing he'd said out in front of Granny's trailer the first time Lloyd had seen him in two decades. Talked about working things out between them. Like *that* was possible. Lloyd'd stayed here and done what was right; Will had run off and now he was being treated like a king because he decided to come back.

Of course, that was only a small part of why Will's return had turned Lloyd's world upside down. And not the most important part.

Lloyd got slowly to his feet, like a man who'd had his bell rung good when in fact Will hadn't hit him at all. It wasn't until he was standing up that his mind fully registered what Will did say when he was here. He'd come to tell Lloyd that he planned to confess! He said he was going to tell Granny the whole story, tell her what happened in the dark under the mountain—where what's done in the forever-night needs to remain buried with the dead.

Lloyd rubbed his hands over his face, dug his knuckles into his eyes the way he used to do when he'd awakened with a headache after a Saturday night of partying.

It was all over now. Lloyd was done for. He would go to prison, maybe to death row.

And everybody'll know!

A chill sank through his body at that thought, freezing him all the way down. Everybody would *know!*

What could he do—run? Where? The mountains and hollows were the known universe. There might be a big old world beyond them, but he was too old to pull up stakes and make a new life out there in it. He'd always harbored a mild curiosity about life outside the mountains, but he had never entertained for a minute the notion of moving away. This here was Lloyd Jacobs's world, and his world *believed in him.* His church had made him an *elder!* What would they do when they knew he'd…

And his kids?

Well, yes, and Norma Jean, too. She was still his wife after all, wasn't nothing final yet. How could he face her?

He shook his head, muttered, "No."

He couldn't do that, wouldn't live with the looks he'd see in people's eyes when they found out Lloyd Jacobs was not the man they thought he was.

So?

He couldn't concentrate, couldn't get a line of thought going and keep it going long enough to figure nothing out. But it seemed obvious even from where he sat now that there was only one way to avoid prison. And it wasn't by shooting somebody else!

How could he possibly consider…?

It felt like he stood on ice, like what formed a couple times on the deep pools in Ugly Betty Creek when he was a kid. Only it wasn't strong enough to hold him, he could hear it cracking and breaking and any minute it would shatter and dump him into the cold, dark depths.

He used to have nightmares about that.

"Am I going crazy?" he wondered aloud. No, he had heard once that only a sane man would question his own rationality; a crazy man would be convinced there wasn't nothing wrong with him.

He wasn't no madman. He seen reality clear as a dewdrop on a rosebud and there wasn't no getting around it. Either he'd spend the rest of his life in prison—with everybody knowing what he'd done—or…

Or what?

Die.

Some reasonable, rational part of his brain immediately protested the mere consideration of that option. But the rest of his mind, the black despair, understood with chilling…what?—relief!—that it was time for Lloyd Jacobs to leave this veil of tears.

Tomorrow would mark the twentieth anniversary of the day that set him on the course that had led here, that had funneled his life, squeezed it in tighter and tighter until he was as trapped as he'd been in that break all those years ago. Only there, he'd struggled to figure out a way to stay alive; now he intended to design the method, manner, and time of his own death.

And the time of his death must be tomorrow. Yes! He'd cheated death out of a victim on that day two decades ago; maybe it was time to pay up.

Take a bunch of 'em with you.

Lloyd actually turned around, looked behind him to see who had spoken. He could feel his pulse begin to throb in his temples; his mouth went dry. Somebody had spoken words. Out loud. This wasn't like in church, when people said they heard the voice of God, but what they really meant was God spoke to them in their heads or hearts. Not out loud.

He'd heard a voice, an audible voice…or had he?

Take a bunch of 'em with you.

There it was again! *Out loud.* But it wasn't the same voice. The first had been high-pitched, like the simple suggestion of a small child. But the second. The second had been no small child. It had been deep and rumbling, as if it had bubbled up from the very bowels of the earth.

And maybe it had.

All at once, Lloyd sensed the presence of an evil that thickened the air, made it difficult to breathe. It had risen from a deep cavern in his own heart, thrown off the chains that had shackled it all these years and now it walked free in the world. Lloyd knew it was of his own making, his to rein in or release. But he sensed its kinship with forces he couldn't restrain or control.

He had spent more than a decade of his life in a single-minded, determined effort to *please* God—worked so hard to atone for what he'd done, to earn redemption by living upright and moral. But obviously all he had to offer wasn't near payment enough. He was still looking down the barrel of a shotgun—loaded and cocked.

If his life wasn't good enough to earn redemption, to convince God to let him off the hook, maybe it was time to try to please somebody else.

And in that moment, a simple, ordinary moment, Lloyd Jacobs crossed over.

Take a bunch of them with you. What did that mean?

Then Lloyd smiled, an ugly, crooked smile that looked like it had been cleaved in his face with a hatchet. All those people mourning what happened 20 years ago in that mine. Well, Lloyd would give them something to memorialize 20 years from now.

He knew how, too! It had all appeared in his mind in a flash, as complete and detailed as the assembly instructions for a backyard barbecue grill. Insert Tab A into Slot B and the whole world would go *boom!*

He burst out laughing, then. Howled harder and harder until he had to put his hands on his knees and gasp for breath. After a while, he wasn't sure anymore if he was laughing or crying.

Chapter 25

WILL SHIVERED AND pulled his windbreaker tighter around him. The light jacket had been fine in Florida, but didn't cut it here in the mountains. It was all he had, though, and he'd wanted to see the night sky. He needed to stare into the depths of it to clear the day's clutter out of his head.

He had driven from Lloyd's house this morning straight to the grocery store in Aintree, put a quarter in the slot of the pay phone on the back wall and called Deke—*collect*.

His hand trembled on the receiver. What if Deke wasn't home? The store sold beer, cold, out of a big cooler by the door. His gaze was drawn to the cooler like a bee to honey…no, more like a maggot to death.

"Well, hello there, Will. You all right? No, of course you ain't. If you were all right you wouldn't be callin' me collect."

"I…, Deke, I…" He had no voice, which was fine because he no longer had anything to say.

"You don't have to talk. The silence tells me everything I need to know. You're hurtin', man. Wantin' a drink so bad the blood in your veins feels like it's drying up."

"Deke, I don't think I can…" The desperation he heard in his voice frightened Will more than the words he said with it.

"Listen to me, Will. You don't have to go the rest of the day without a drink. All you gotta do is get through right now, the next 5 minutes. Are you with me? I'll talk you through it. Just 5 minutes."

And so it went, 5 minutes by 5 minutes.

Then 15, 20. Deke calm and firm, as easy-going as a Golden Retriever on Valium.

By the time Will's hands stopped shaking, he'd been on the phone for almost 2 hours.

"Deke, I'm sorry. Your phone bill will…"

"Not a problem. I can take out a second mortgage on the house."

Will managed a small smile.

"Thanks, man."

"Just pass it on."

Then he let the little smile take over the rest of his face.

When he left the grocery store, he drove JoJo's car to the Jiffy Stop and did what Deke had told him to do, *exactly* what Deke told him to do. That's what sponsors were for—to think for you when you were too sick to think for yourself. If the big, black man had told Will to strip naked, put on a Mexican sombrero and stand in the median of the four-lane whistling "Tiptoe Through the Tulips," Will would have started puckering.

That's not what Deke said. He told Will to walk.

Keeping to the edge of Turkey Neck Creek, Will headed upstream. He didn't go into the woods, of course; the poacher/sniper would have to find somebody else to use for target practice today. When he came to a dirt road that crossed the creek, he took it. He banked left at the next one and then aimlessly wandered the dirt roads that wound up through the mountains for the rest of the afternoon.

As he walked, he soaked up the autumn colors like a paper towel absorbing water off a countertop. Breathed in the aroma of cedar and pine trees and the damp, foresty smell of wet leaves. Slowly, the tension began to drain out of him, the itch that so desperately needed scratching eased. At least for now, and that was enough.

He stayed gone all day, just like Deke told him to, and later sat on the bottom step of Granny's porch in companionable silence with the night. The darkness kept its own counsel. Spread out above was a sky as black as one of Jamey's arts, and the chill wind had polished it until it sparkled. This should be a place to find peace if there really was such a thing in the world.

The door squeaked open and JoJo stepped out onto the porch carrying a Snoopy coffee mug. She was smiling. No, she had stretched her lips like a clothesline across her face and pinned them at both ends with dimples, but it was plastic and lifeless, a Miss Kentucky smile.

She came down the stairs and handed Will the mug.

"Granny said to bring you this." It was hot chocolate. Granny used to fix it for him and Ricky Dan in the fall when they'd come home from sangin' or deer hunting. "She couldn't give it to you her own self, you know, couldn't come all the way down to the bottom step."

That was true, but Will knew it wasn't the only reason JoJo had been dispatched with the steaming mug. Granny'd wanted Will to spend time with the girl. She had mentioned again this morning her growing concern for JoJo. "That chile is burdened some'm fierce. It's like there's mist all around her. She's hid in it and I cain't find her."

"Have a seat," Will patted the step beside him. When she handed him the mug, he got a close look at her cuticles, raw and bleeding where she'd picked at them. "Has Granny been like this for long, where she can't even leave the porch?"

"It's been comin' on my whole life, but here lately seems like it's gettin' worse faster." JoJo sat down beside Will. "On the Fourth of July, we us had a potluck doin's, a big crowd and all kind of food."

"The girls and their tribes?"

"You do know they're coming to Sunday dinner, don't you—to see you?"

Will nodded. Granny had told him she planned to "gather the family for a proper welcome." He also knew she wouldn't be anxious to celebrate his presence after tomorrow morning.

"In July, it was more than my aunts, uncles, and cousins, though. Granny invited the whole holler. There was people everywhere, kids underfoot and runnin' around like wild Indians. And Granny played! You ever hear Granny play the mandolin?"

"Once or twice."

The aroma of roasting meat floats over the house from the backyard where Bowman and Ricky Dan have dug a pit and filled it with hot coals. The deer suspended on a spit above the coals is the doe Ricky Dan shot yesterday; it's been cooking since late last night.

Women in aprons bustle around. They arrange on two big tables made of boards and sawhorses the covered dishes they brought from home. There are bowls of potato salad—both the mustard and the mayonnaise kind; crisp, brown, fried green tomatoes; turnip greens with big hunks of ham hock; deviled eggs lined up in neat rows on platters; beans—green, brown and navy; black-eyed peas, ears of corn cooked in the husk, fried okra—both cornmeal and batter-dipped, plates of cookies and brownies and every pie and cake imaginable.

Squealing children thread their way through the crowd of grown-ups, teenage boys stand around awkwardly, pretending not to gawk at equally awkward teenage girls. Men talk and spit, the low mumble of their voices mingling with the clang of a game of horseshoes.

But all the commotion stops at the first clear, high note from Bowman's fiddle. He is a master. The big man stands on the porch beside Tugboat and his banjo. Earl Calhoun, the stand-up base player, is seated off to the side watching wistfully, his arm in a sling, broken in four places by a roof fall. Ricky Dan is perched on the porch railing with his guitar; Ma sits in a straight-back kitchen chair cradling her mandolin. Bowman taps his foot— one, two, three, four—and the music starts. Foggy Mountain Breakdown. Salty Dog. Orange Blossom Special. *The pure, haunting sound of bluegrass floats from the porch up into the mountains, its melodies as much a part of the listeners as the blood in their veins and the accent on their tongues.*

And the rhythm in their feet. Within seconds young and old are clogging.

When the picking and strumming is done, Will is at Ricky Dan's elbow.

"Teach me to play," he begs, "please!"

"It ain't fun as you think; them strings hurt your fingers." Ricky Dan holds his pick between his teeth, the gold one sparkling, as he lifts his guitar strap over his head. He leans the instrument against the porch railing and threads the pick in between the strings on the neck. "Soon's you're a little older, we'll see."

"You said that last year. I'm 9 now."

"Like I said, we'll see."

"Did you know your daddy taught me how to play the guitar?"

"No, but I knew he played; his guitar burned up when Jamey caught the house on fire, though. You play much?"

Will had not touched a guitar in the two decades he'd been away from Kentucky.

"Not much."

"We borrowed Maude Tackett's mandolin, and it took forever to get Granny to agree to play it. But she could flat make that thing sing! After dark, she sat right here on this bottom step and watched Jamey set off firecrackers for the littl'uns."

JoJo shook her head. "Now, she can't even step off the porch. I hate seein' her boxed in like that where she can't hardly do nothing."

"I told her she shouldn't let her grief keep her a prisoner like that." Will picked up a rock off the ground and pitched it at a bug crawling across the shaft of porch light on the dirt. "And she fired right back that I was as much a prisoner as she was. Only difference was her grief had locked her *in* and mine had locked me *out*."

"She don't let you get by with much, does she?"

"Nope, and she doesn't miss much either." He turned and looked at JoJo.

"Meaning?"

"Meaning what's going on with you hasn't escaped her notice."

JoJo started to get to her feet, but he put his hand gently on her knee.

"Granny's been hammered by life harder than anybody I ever met. But she hangs in there." He leaned closer. "You might want to watch how that's done. Take notes, maybe. I'll loan you a pen."

Anger flashed in JoJo's eyes. "What gives you the right to show up here outta nowhere, like some big bird crapped you on the roof, and jump right into telling me how to live my life? I hardly know you!"

"But I know *you*. Better than you know yourself."

"How you figure that?"

"What I said the other day—it takes one to know one. What's going on inside you, the same thing's going on inside me.

"You don't have no idea what's—"

"You're scared. I don't know what you're scared of, but scared's scared."

"What do I have to be afraid of?"

Will shrugged. "Beats me. But whatever it is has got you by the throat and it's choking the life out of you. That's the other thing we have in common, you and me—the choking-the-life-out-of-us part."

She said nothing, just glared at him.

"From what I can see, you're half a mile down the road past scared and choked, though. You've crossed the border, set up house-keeping in…different people give it different names; I called it the Pit." He leaned toward her. "I know that's where you are because I recognize the scenery—not exactly a tour bus destination. I spent most of the past 20 years there…built a house, white picket fence, planted tulips next to the porch—"

"The light on that porch of yours may be on…" she snapped, "… but ain't nobody home!"

She got to her feet and started up the steps, but he grabbed her by the wrist and spit the words at her.

"Okay, Sweetheart, here it is without the hollandaise sauce. You've given up. You're just waiting for somebody to bring the curtain down and turn on the houselights." He pulled her toward him. "You're ready to die, aren't you?"

He'd only said it to get her attention, for shock value. But Will was the one who got his bell rung. The sudden, caught-with-her-hand-in-the-cookie-jar look on JoJo's face stopped him cold.

Well, he had her attention.

"In fact, you're not just ready to die, you've planned it, got your exit strategy all mapped out."

She tried to wrench her arm out of his grasp, but he held firm.

"What's it going to be? Slit your wrists? Put a gun in your mouth? Drug overdose?"

Her eyes got huge and Will realized he'd stumbled onto the truth. His pulse kicked into a gallop; his mouth was instantly drier than a dust bunny. "You plan to down a bottle of pills, go to sleep and never wake up—don't you?"

He shook her by the arm and fear turned his voice harsh. "Don't you?"

"What if I do? What business is it of yours? You're not my father."

"No, I'm not. I'm the reason you don't have one."

"You're what? Let go of me!" She yanked her arm free. "And butt out!" She turned and started up the steps.

"Why?" No anger, no confrontation. A simple question, asked softly. She stopped but didn't turn back around. "Can you tell me that? A beautiful girl like you. Your whole life ahead of you. What could possibly be so bad that…?"

He watched all the air whoosh out of her. Her shoulders sagged, her head drooped. He said nothing else. She'd tell him or she wouldn't.

When she turned slowly back around, the girl who faced him wasn't the same one who'd yanked her arm out of his grasp. This was a scared, broken kid. Granny'd said she'd lost JoJo in the mist; Will had just found her.

"Okay. You want to know so bad, I'll tell you. But you're the only one. I ain't told a living soul and I don't intend to. You got to swear you won't tell nobody, neither."

Will had made a similar promise to her father a long time ago and he'd kept it all these years.

"I won't tell anybody."

Tears welled up in her eyes and slipped down her cheeks. "I guess somebody needs to understand, to explain it all…after."

Will swallowed hard. She wanted to unburden herself so he could explain it to Granny and everyone else in her family when she was dead! It suddenly hit him—that's why she'd given Jamey that necklace. JoJo wasn't just contemplating suicide; the clock was ticking.

She sat back down on the step beside him, looked like she almost collapsed on it. She wasn't wearing a sweater, but when she started to tremble, he didn't think it had anything to do with the cold. He took off his windbreaker and draped it over her shoulders; she didn't appear to notice.

"Do you know anything about Huntington's Chorea?"

"I think I may have heard the name of it, a disease, right?

When she spoke again, her voice was flat, emotionless, like she'd been asked to read aloud the ingredients label on a can of Spam.

"It usually shows up when you're about 40. It causes certain cells in your brain to waste away. They just…die." She turned and looked at him. "First you walk funny—herky-jerky like. Then you start to shake and twitch all over, arms fly up, legs kick, and you can't do nothin''bout it. You scream, holler, make weird, awful noises. You lose your memory, your personality and in the end, you lose your mind, go completely insane—have to be looked after like you's a baby."

"Somebody you know, someone you *care about* has Huntington's, don't they, JoJo?"

She turned away from him and stared out into the darkness.

"Yeah, that's right. Matter of fact, I know lotsa skinnys. I signed up to be part of this research project at UK—paid good, $300—and I met all kinda people with Huntington's. The disease is hereditary, so *of course* they come to the University of *Kentucky* to study it—'cause everybody knows all us hillbillies up in the hollers is married to our cousins!"

The spark of anger flickered and died, left her voice flat and lifeless again. "I ain't really surprised they come here. Them blue people up Troublesome Creek, that's no old wife's tale, you know. They were real."

The blue people of Troublesome Creek were descendents of Martin Fugate, who settled in Eastern Kentucky in the early 1800s and brought with him a genetic disorder that turned the skin blue. Isolation, a limited gene pool and time did the rest and the disorder spread through the mountains around Hazard. The people whose skin was blue—a dark shade, almost purple—kept to the hollows. Men, women, old people, and children hid there from the world; outsiders thought the stories about them were myths. Finally, in the 1960s, a hematologist from the University of Kentucky searched them out and discovered they suffered from an easily treatable enzyme deficiency.

"So UK is studying the spread of Huntington's Chorea among mountain people and—?"

"They was gonna get around to that part." She turned and faced him and cried fiercely. "But the study I was in, wasn't lookin' for nothin'. Not *nothin'!* They needed college kids to use as a control group so they could measure the effects of Huntington's on hand-eye coordination."

"I'm sorry, I'm not getting the connection between..."

Her voice grew soft. "They wasn't looking...but they found it all the same. Huntington's goes down through families and they know how. They know what gene carries it."

A remark Granny'd made began to flit around the outside of Will's memory like a moth around a porch light.

"And they can spot that gene with a blood test."

JoJo took a breath and in that moment a sudden horrible foreboding came over Will, a sense that something had been hurled at him, something he couldn't duck because he couldn't remember what it was.

"They did blood tests on all the people in the study. The control group, too—for comparison." Her voice fell to a whisper. "And they *found* it. In my blood. That gene. I got it. I got Huntington's."

She turned to him, her face slathered with silent tears. "I'm gonna turn into a *skinny*." There was disbelief in her voice. "Me, a skinny." Then her voice hardened. "I'm gonna jerk 'n holler and slobber...and then I'm gonna go crazy and die!"

The fluttering moth of memory landed and Granny's voice rang clear in Will's mind: *"You might 'member, Joanna's mama went all crazy like, hollerin' and carryin' on, and they had to put her away. Well, Joanna's granny done the same thing…"*

"Oh, JoJo!" That was all he could say.

He reached out instinctively and pulled her to him and she let go and began to cry, great gulping, heaving sobs that went on and on. Will held her tight, patted her back, and gently rocked her. It took a long time for her to cry herself out. When she did, she was exhausted and shaky, but calm. Will reached into the pocket of the windbreaker draped around her shoulders, fished out the red bandanna he'd found in the bottom of the gym bag he'd borrowed from Deke, and handed it to her.

"Only I ain't gonna do it," she said as she wiped tears off her face. Her voice was quiet and rational. But when she looked out into the darkness, her hands trembled. "I ain't gonna let that happen. I'd rather be dead."

"But I thought you said…40, that symptoms appeared at about age 40. You're not even 20 yet!"

"I said it's *usually* about age 40. But…" She stopped and her voice went dead again, mouthed words off a teleprompter. "A defect on chromosome number four causes a part of the DNA to repeat too often. In normal people, it repeats 10 to 35 times. In people with Huntington's, it repeats up to one hundred twenty times. The more times it repeats…well, big number, bad case! And the bigger the number, the younger you are when you get it."

She stopped, looked at him, and almost whispered the rest. "You can only pass it on if you have it, and when it's passed down in an unbroken line through the same family, each succeeding generation's DNA repeats way more times than the last."

Will's mind spun. Joanna had died young, but she'd had it or JoJo wouldn't. JoJo's grandmother'd had it, too, and so had her great grandmother. Four generations—*that he knew about*—in one family, from her great grandmother to JoJo and…

"Jamey!" Will croaked the name, then looked a question at JoJo he couldn't wrap words around.

JoJo nodded slowly, her face an expressionless mask.

"He was s'posed to get a physical 'fore he went to work in #7 but he never done it. I used that as an excuse, took him up Lexington." She managed something that resembled a smile. "But his ain't nowhere near as bad. His number ain't even half as big as mine. Maybe all that time when his brain didn't get no oxygen…maybe that was a good thing. 'Course, he didn't understand where we was or what they's doin' to him. He don't know nothin'."

JoJo and Jamey! Will could barely process it.

"I didn't ask to know neither," she continued. "Didn't want to know. But there ain't no way to un-know the truth." She turned to Will and her voice colored her next words with a dozen different shades of loathing. "And knowin' what's waitin' for me in…a few years." Then she gasped out, "Maybe just *months*…" She stopped, gathered herself. "How am I s'posed to live with the knowing of it hanging over my head? Get through every day and *know* what's comin'?"

"You don't have to get through every day. You only have to get through one. I couldn't stop drinking every day for the rest of my life, but I can not drink today."

She gave him a withering look. "Thanks so much for your words of wisdom, Mr. Rogers. But I don't live in the neighborhood. I live in the real world. And I will *not* die like that."

"So you're going to kill yourself because you don't like the way you're going to die? Does that make sense to you?"

She stood up, a little unsteadily, her knees weak from the outpouring of emotion. "I didn't tell you this so's you could try to talk me out of it. This ain't no debate. I've made up my mind and you can't stop me!"

Will stood slowly, too. "You got that right. I can't stop you. You said it yourself. Nobody can hold up a falling tree. Or a falling life."

That unsettled her. "Well…good then." She slipped his windbreaker off her shoulders and handed it and the bandanna back to him. "Now you understand why you can't say nothin', not even after…'cause if they know about me, they'll figure out about Jamey. But once Jamey starts to…" She couldn't say it. "Once it's clear he's got Huntington's, then you can explain what I done so—"

"No."

"What do you mean no?"

"How many things can no mean?"

"The only reason I told you was—"

"I don't care why you told me. I can't help you. I can't make somebody else understand what I don't understand myself."

She gaped at him.

He managed a shrug. "It takes one to know one—I told you. I threw away years of my life; you're about to do the same thing. See, we're just a—"

"No, we're *not!*" She was instantly so furious all she could do was sputter. "How dare you stand there so smug, so… so…" Then she chanted in a squeaky voice, "Oh, JoJo, I know *just* how you feel!" She made a humph sound in her throat. "You don't have no idea what it feels like to—"

"Want to die? I *was* dying! I was lying on a gurney while my life drained out of me and I was *glad!*"

His intensity drew out for a breathless moment before he continued, softer. "Then Bill Cosby in a Mr. Clean suit showed up, got right in my face, pointed out that I was chucking a life 27 miners in Harlan #7 wished they'd had. And that…ding, ding, ding…was my wake-up call." He shook his head. "But you, Darlin', don't even have an alarm set."

He could tell she had no idea what to make of him. And that was good. His only hope was to throw her off her game. He reached out to take her hand in both of his…and she was gone again. Vanished. Lost in the fog. The hand he held was cold and limp, felt like a dead fish on a stick.

He held on and kept talking anyway. "One of those miners was your daddy. You never knew him, JoJo, but I did. He was my hero. He was…" Out of nowhere a wave of emotion choked him. He gritted his teeth and cleared his throat, but all he could manage was a ragged whisper. "…the best of all of us."

He paused, got his voice under control. "And I guarantee you, young lady, that your daddy wouldn't have given up even one hour of living because he was scared of how he was going to die."

She pulled her hand out of his. "I'm sorry—"

"Honey, you don't have anything to be sorry—"

"I'm sorry I told you!" she snapped. "I should have known better. I should have kept my mouth shut." She turned and hurried up the steps and into the house.

CHAPTER 26

I T HAD GROWN late, but Jamey didn't notice. It had grown cold, too, and Jamey didn't notice that, either. He was in that place he went when he worked on his arts. He'd told JoJo once the place was "more in my head than in my shed"—and that *rhymed!* Jamey was so proud! He liked rhymes, but he almost never made up his own.

In fact, Jamey didn't seem to have as many words in his head as other people and he didn't see that as a bad thing at all. Surely, it must be a lot of trouble to carry all them words around with you all the time, like a bucket full of rocks. The more rocks in the bucket, the heavier it'd be. He didn't think his bucket was nearly as heavy as the bucket most folks carried and he thanked God for that. Granny said all good gifts come from God so Jamey was all the time thanking God for one thing or another because his life was so full up with good things—most times he couldn't even enjoy one before another one come along.

Only tonight wasn't all full up with good things. It was sad and scary, and Jamey asked ValVleen again and again to sing so he couldn't hear the fearful thoughts in his head. And he reached down and scratched Bucket's head over and over because with the old dog there at his feet, he didn't feel so alone.

Tonight didn't neither one of them do much good, though, because what his hands was making was scary. There was sad, hurtful images in that rock and the longer he worked on it the more he wondered if a rock could be bad. People could be bad. He hadn't never knowed nobody who was bad, but Granny'd talked about bad people and the Bible had stories about bad people so there must be some somewhere. They must be the folks who lived out on the flat because wasn't no bad hillbillies.

But if people could be bad, then maybe things could, too, and if things could be bad, maybe this piece of jet was one of them bad things.

"How would you know that a person was bad?" he asked ValVleen. The bird studied him as if she was considering the question and trying to come up with an answer. But Jamey figured out the answer first. "It'd be 'cause they looked bad, right, or acted bad? That's how you'd know!"

So if looking bad meant a person was bad, then that must be the way you could tell that a thing was bad, too. And this piece of jet looked bad, least what he'd seen of what was hidden down inside it did.

Jamey stopped carving and sat stock-still. You don't suppose he was committing a sin to turn the bad things in this rock loose. He wasn't exactly sure what a sin was, but he did know he didn't never want to do one. A sin was bad. If this rock was bad, maybe the rock was a sin.

He put down the chisel in his hand and fat tears leaked out of his green eyes.

"ValVleen, I think I've made a sin arts. But I didn't really make nothing. I let' out what was in there, so I guess I let a sin out of this bad rock."

He scooted his stool back and looked at the shiny piece of jet. It glistened in a thousand points of light from the flickering flames of the lanterns.

Had to be a sin, because didn't feel right, none of it did. Nothing about setting the images free in this rock had felt like it was supposed to. When Jamey come back from that place he went when he worked on his arts, the big miner in the front was all done, everything just right. But there was all those other miners outlined in the background to pull up out of the rock. And he couldn't manage to get back to his place to do it. It felt a little like when he first started to carve and he tried to force the coal to be what he wanted it to be. Only, he hadn't tried to force this piece of jet to be nothing. So why wouldn't the images come on out of there like they was supposed to? Was it his job to *drag* them out?

He sighed. He didn't have no choice; it was his job to finish it. Jamey wiped his tears and his nose on the sleeve of his shirt, picked up the chisel, and went back to work.

The moon was a white bone in the black sky before he put his mallet and chisel down on the workbench for the last time. He was done. He shouldn't have been. Should have taken him a whole lot longer to finish it, seeing as how there was all them miners to set free. But the arts didn't turn out like he figured it would.

He sat back and looked at the images in the shiny black rock and began to wonder if it was a sin after all, because now that it was finished, it sure was pretty. Scary and sad and ugly and pretty all at the same time in a tangled up way Jamey didn't have enough words in his bucket to describe.

There was so much detail in the explosion frozen there in the piece of jet it was like Jamey was there and could see it. Rocks flew, helmets was knocked off, roof bolts and lunch pails in the air. You could make out the pockets on the miners' shirts, the holes in their pants, the laces on their work boots. The big miner in front had lost his helmet; his hair went ever which way. The right sleeve of his shirt was torn beneath the string thing tied on his arm and all the buttons was missing so it flapped open. Two other men was tangled together and one didn't have no shirt on at all and Jamey stared at it, wondered where it went. Could a explosion blow your clothes off?

The longer Jamey looked at the carving, the more grateful he was that there wasn't no faces on none of them people.

He'd told Granny he didn't think there was any faces in the rock but he'd been wrong. There was probably faces all over it. You just couldn't see them. All them miners had they heads turned away, or there was somebody's arm or leg blocking their face, or a helmet or piece of rock.

As he stared at the carving, he felt himself drawn into it, like it was a pool of shiny black water instead of shiny black rock. Then he seen what was in there, deep down in the bottom of it. And soon as he did, he laughed right out loud.

"Look at that, ValVleen." He pointed into the depths of the rock and laughed again. "Ain't never seen nothin' like that 'fore in a rock."

The bird didn't chirp, didn't make a sound. Jamey didn't think nothing of it at the time, how she acted. But later he understood.

ValVleen had looked into that rock and seen what was coming.

CHAPTER 27

WILL WOKE UP early Friday morning, probably just as the sun cleared the horizon. But he didn't get up right away. For a long time, he lay in bed and listened to the birds perched on the old clothesline pole outside his window. His mind was calm, the way he'd seen palm trees on a beach grow still and expectant as the boiling black clouds of a hurricane hurled at them across the sea. As if in response to his thought, thunder rumbled in the distance.

When he heard JoJo's muffler-free car roar louder than the thunder as she left for work, he got out of bed and dressed. After he startled Granny with a quick peck on the cheek, he headed to town. Her voice called after him from the porch that he ought to get a coat, a storm was on the way. A few fat raindrops fell from high in the steadily blackening sky and landed with a splat on the ground as he crossed the yard to the road, painting a camouflage pattern in the dust.

There used to be a barber shop located in the converted living room of a house next door to Pete's Place. Will was outside when it opened at nine o'clock. He really did need a haircut, but it still felt like getting all cleaned up for his own funeral. Today, he would do what he'd come all this way to do.

As the barber snipped at his hair, he tried to keep his mind firmly in the present. If he inched out there into the future, he wanted a drink so bad he feared he might grab a bottle of aftershave and chug it down in one, long gulp.

"I reckon you'll be going to the ceremony at lunchtime," the barber said. "I's telling Maude this mornin' that it'd sure be a good time to break in and steal whatever it is you been covetin'. Ain't gonna be nobody left at home in the whole town—everybody's going."

"Wouldn't miss it," Will said. That was a lie, of course. Will couldn't have been dragged to that ceremony by a team of Clydesdales and the Budweiser beer wagon. But if he'd admitted that, he'd have had to explain why not.

Another customer came in as the barber dusted talcum powder on Will's neck. The man had a black armband tied around his upper arm with the number 27 printed on it in silver.

"Where'd ya get that?" the barber asked, indicating the armband.

"Handin' 'em out down at the Jiffy and the filling station, and there'll be more at the ceremony."

"I wanna get me one. My sister's first husband was killed in #7."

The approaching storm edged into the hollow as Will sat in the barber chair. In a brief, hard downpour, raindrops scampered across the windowpane with the sound of running feet. The rain had let up by the time Will left, spit a few drops now and then that shattered the mirror puddles on the blacktop.

Will's windbreaker was "water-resistant," rather than "waterproof." In a serious storm, that distinction would matter, so he needed to get back inside quick. He jogged the final quarter mile to Granny's trailer and could hear the rain crank up behind him. As he reached for the doorknob, his teeth began to chatter, but that wasn't from the chill in the air. It was from the chill in his heart.

His teeth had chattered in #7 the day she blew. Fifty-eight degrees in the mine; that was cold. But his teeth weren't chattering from the chill in the air that day either.

When Lloyd suggests there might be some way out of the sentence of death by suffocation, Will begins to tremble. Even before Lloyd says a word, Will is shaking all over.

"What do you mean there's one thing we could do?" Ricky Dan says. "Like what?"

"Maybe the explosion didn't blow out all the seals."

"Every break we passed, the seal was blown—except this one. What's your point? Even if some of the seals didn't blow, it will still take the rescue team—"

"That's not what I'm talkin' about," Lloyd coughs and loses his breath. Will and Ricky Dan say nothing, just wait for him to continue. "You know they had me greasin' the belt line last week. I got way up past this here break."

The rail line is located in the shaft in front of their enclosure and the belt line is located in the shaft behind it.

"So?"

"So when we worked up here in September, we parked the scoop on the other side of the belt line, in the next break up from this 'un. You 'member—Hob had a pile of cinder block stacked in there and he parked the scoop in front of it so wouldn't no inspector see he wasn't usin' concrete block. And just for good measure, he put up a curtain to hide it all. You 'member?"

Ricky Dan nodded, but Will couldn't tell if that meant he remembered or just that Lloyd should continue.

"Well, last week when I was greasin', I noticed Hob moved the cinder block but never took that curtain down. I come this close to yankin' it down my own self, but I forgot about it."

Will feels his heart begin to labor in his chest. He thinks he understands what Lloyd is driving at.

"You're sayin' that—?" Will begins.

"I'm saying that on the other side of the conveyor out there," Lloyd points toward the curtain on the back of the enclosure, "and 50 feet up is another space just like this 'un, only it's got a wall on the back side 'stead of a curtain." He pauses for effect, but he doesn't need to. "And it's empty—'cept maybe a couple of broke cinder blocks Hob never used. Ain't got no rock pile nor nothin' like that in it."

Empty of rocks means it is full *of air. Air that's been sealed off from the deadly smoke and poison gas that now fill the whole mine—4 feet by 18 feet by 25 feet of good, breathable air!*

"The air's there if the curtain on the front didn't blow," Ricky Dan says. "And if the block seal on the back didn't blow. And if nobody else come along and yanked that curtain down since you seen it last week. That's a lot of ifs."

"There'd be more'n 20 hours of air for all three of us," Lloyd blows by Ricky Dan's caution; his voice louder, more strident. "Com'on! 85-90 feet away is..."

"Not 'is' Lloyd. 'Might be!' There might be another sealed-up break over there. You ask me, I bet ever seal in this whole mine blew."

"This 'un didn't!"

"This 'un was full of rocks! That's what kept it from blowin' and you know it."

"I don't know no such thing. Maybe this 'un didn't blow 'cause it was far 'nough away from the 'xplosion that the blast didn't get it. Maybe ever seal from here to the mouth's still there."

"Maybe. You wanna bet all our lives on maybe? 'Cause that's what we'll be doing if we try to get from here to that

next break." Ricky Dan shakes his head as he warms to the argument. "Think 'bout what you're suggestin', Lloyd. There ain't no way on earth we could do that, even if it was a lead pipe cinch there was good air over there."

Ricky Dan leans back and ticks off the reasons on his fingers.

"We'd have to hold our breath the whole way." One finger.

"We'd have to climb over the conveyor—just by feelin' of it. So much smoke out there even with a headlamp you couldn't see a thing." Two fingers.

"And then we'd have to feel along 50 feet of coal pillar 'til we come to the curtain. An' all the time holdin' our breath, remember, 'cause if we breathed just once, we'd start coughin' and it'd be all over." Three fingers.

"You could swim underwater that far if you had to, holdin' your breath the whole way," Lloyd fires back. "What's the difference?"

Ricky Dan pauses. That's a good point. Then he gestures toward the swollen, distorted lump that sticks out of Lloyd's pants leg. "Could you swim with a broken ankle? Me 'n Will dragged you here or you'd still be in that shaft snuggled up to a piece of bent rail. How you figure to climb over the conveyor with a broke ankle?"

"I figure if I don't, I'm a dead man—that's how!" Lloyd shouts. He stops, collects his temper. "Don't you think we'd oughta at least try?" He is pleading, now—because it is a foregone conclusion that whatever decision is made, it will be Ricky Dan who makes it.

"Tryin' means dyin' if you ain't right, son." In that moment, Ricky Dan sounds so much like Bowman it's creepy. "Cause even if we could get there—and I don't b'lieve we could—but sayin' we did, once we was there and didn't find no

curtain, ain't no way in the world we'd make it back here alive. We go and it's a one-way ticket."

"What if only one of us went?" Will says. The words fall directly out of his brain and through his mouth with no conscious thought. He is actually surprised to hear his own voice. "What if one of us went to see if the seal and the curtain are still there? If they are, he could stay there long enough to catch his breath, then come back and get the other two. And if the seals are blown…well, don't all of us get killed, only one."

"And the other two'd have a better chance to make it with only two men breathin' the air in here 'stead of three." Lloyd leaps with both feet onto Will's bandwagon. "Fact is, if the two of you was to leave me here by myself, I'd have plenty of air." He stops for a beat. "That's the way it'd have to be if you find more air—leave me here alone and you two go. We all know ain't no way I'd ever make it over that belt line."

Ricky Dan looks from Lloyd to Will and then speaks to Will.

"So you're thinking one of us, either you or me, oughta go out in that smoke and gas and try to make it to the next break?"

Ricky Dan's words punch Will in the belly. He had just blurted out the idea, hadn't thought it through. If he had, he'd have factored in a game-changing consideration: no power on earth could force him back out into that poison air to die, to gasp and choke and flop around like that fish on the creek bank! He didn't want to die, but if that's what he had to do, he'd die here. Folks said suffocation was like fallin' asleep. The lack of oxygen eventually made you pass out and you never woke up.

"I don't know what I was thinkin'," Will says despondently. He leans back and stares up at the pattern of fossil ferns on the roof. "We can't—"

"Cause just one of us goin' makes sense to me," Ricky Dan says. "Either way, live or die, the man who leaves is helpin' the other two." He pauses, then continues fiercely, "He ain't leavin' 'em behind."

Miners live by a code. They stick together. One miner would never abandon his friends to save himself, and Ricky Dan is a miner to the core.

Will, on the other hand, has not a speck of miner's instinct. He hates everything about digging coal. The terror of it is more ferocious than any emotion he has ever known. He's just been unwilling to admit it, to himself or to anybody else, because of some stupid, little-kid need to be just like Ricky Dan. He'd thought that if he could gut it out for a while, his fear would lessen. The opposite has happened; every day, it is exponentially harder than the day before to get on that mantrip and ride into the dark depths.

Ever since Ricky Dan extinguished his hope of rescue, Will has been struggling to figure out how to die like a man. In the process, he has made a solemn vow. If by some miracle of God he gets out of here alive, he will never set foot inside another coal mine again as long as he lives.

"So which one of us is it gonna be?" Ricky Dan says, then begins to cough again. He has hacked and wheezed since the moment he fell into the break of "clean air"—which is only clean by comparison to the poison soup outside. They brought smoke in with them; the enclosure smells like a charcoal grill ready for steaks.

Ricky Dan continues to cough; his watering eyes spew tears down his face.

"You can't go, Ricky Dan," Lloyd says. "Yore lungs is all tore up. You couldn't suck in enough air to last you, wouldn't make it 6 feet 'fore you started to cough."

The terror that drills into Will is more powerful than the 300-volt electric shock that temporarily blinded him once when he touched a frayed cable.

He can't. He won't! Put a gun to his head and he'd still refuse to crawl through that hallway in hell clasped in the savage embrace of instant death. No!

"We ain't gonna just decide it's Will and that's it." Ricky Dan clears his throat, then manages a limp grin. "We'll decide it the same way we decided who had to crawl under the porch and get that dead cat out. Rocks in the hat."

For as long as Will can remember, disputes have been settled and decisions made by randomly drawing rocks out of a hat. Two black rocks, one white. The one who draws the white rock loses.

He'd drawn the white rock on the dead-cat carcass. It reeked so bad under that porch, he'd puked down there and made it worse. Granny liked to never got the dead-animal and vomit smell out of his clothes.

Of course, in this case there will be only one white rock and one black rock. Not one chance in three. One in two. Fifty-fifty. Will doesn't like those odds. Doesn't like them one bit!

CHAPTER 28

L LOYD SQUINTED. EVERYTHING seemed too bright. He cut off the light over the sink in the kitchen because it hurt his eyes. All the lights had shiny circles around them like headlights seen through a car windshield in the rain.

Reckon his vision had been messed up somehow because he didn't sleep Monday, Tuesday, or Wednesday nights? He'd slept last night, though. Fell into a deep, dreamless sleep the second his head hit the pillow. Soon as he decided what he was going to do, his mind stopped racing, his heart stopped pounding, and he relaxed.

As he dressed for work, his mind was peaceful as a still pond, one where you could see all the way to the bottom, watch the turtles swim with the minnows. His heart beat comfortably, slow and steady, pumping blood around and around his veins for the last few hours before it could rest, before *he* could rest.

His mind was not just peaceful, it was clear and fiercely crisp, sharp, supremely *aware*. His sense of his surroundings was in such a heightened state he could see the individual lines in the black lace pattern coal dust had created on the skin of his fingers and hear each individual drop of rain go *splat* on the roof. The glorious aroma of his last pot of coffee was so intense it took his breath away and drawing cigarette smoke into his lungs was as smooth as inhaling the clouds that hung above the mountains on a summer day.

It was only his vision that was screwy. Circles around lights and everything so bright he felt like he needed sunglasses. He ached for the velvet darkness of the mine, the absolute blackness. The total silence, too, except for the echoing drip, drip, drip of water. And even that was peaceful. The mine was a place where being dead was really more appropriate than being alive. Quiet. Dark. Preparation for eternity.

A sudden fierce chill gripped his whole body, as if someone had poured ice water on his head. No, *into* his head, so the cold sunk down inside his skin.

How had it come to *this?* To planning something so monstrous?

How...?

Before he could consider further, a door banged shut in his soul, as a man might slam a door in the face of an intruder on his porch, some bald, stinking terror come to murder his family in their sleep.

Only it was wrong-side-out. The intruder was *inside* the house. It was *reason* that stood outside knocking. But it was too late now, the terror was already poised. It drooled as it awaited the kill. There was no way to put the Boogie Man back in the closet. He was in charge now. Lloyd was just along for the ride.

He pulled his pickup into the parking lot of the mine and killed the engine. The pace of his heart had picked up. It thumped hard now, but not with fear or dread—with excitement. He was going to enjoy this.

◊ ◊ ◊ ◊ ◊

GRANNY, WILL, AND JoJo listened to the rain beat a staccato rhythm on the metal trailer roof as they nursed cups of coffee at the kitchen table. Will hadn't expected JoJo to be home. He'd thought she'd gone to work when he heard her drive away earlier, didn't know she had Fridays off. With no makeup, a paint-splattered UK sweatshirt and tattered sweatpants, she looked like a high school freshman. Except for her eyes. They held a look as old as time.

Jamey was working day shift in Harlan #7. He had finished his arts last night, came down from the shed late—tired but apparently satisfied with how it had turned out.

"I's done with it and it's wrapped up in a pillowcase on the workbench," he'd said as he wagged his head from side to side and his eyes roamed the bottom 3 feet of the room. "I's feared it'd be scary and bad and I thought maybe it was a sin rock and I shouldn't set free what was down inside of it, but I done it 'cause Granny said, and wasn't no sin rock a-tall. Wasn't bad. Down in the bottom, it was smilin'. The end."

Since it was raining off and on, JoJo had dropped Jamey at the mine on her way to the Jiffy to pick up the jug of Tide she'd forgotten to bring home last night. She was telling Granny about what had happened there when Will tuned back in to the conversation. He'd sat on the periphery of the women's chatter, waiting…okay, putting off what he had to say.

JoJo held out one of the black armbands. "Tugboat looked at it, turned it over in his hand, then reached up and tied it 'round his neck!"

"Don't guess it matters where you tie it," Granny said with a chuckle. "Long's it helps you remember."

"I don't need an armband to help me remember," Will said quietly, seizing the opening. "What happened in the mine, it plays on a movie screen in my head every day. It has for 20 years."

The room went instantly silent. Obviously, Granny'd told JoJo that Will had something he needed to say. Granny sat up straight in the chair. Will couldn't read the look in her eyes, but from the firm set of her chin it seemed she was ready, like she had screwed herself up for this.

So had he.

"Guess you're gonna eat that frog, now, ain't ya?"

JoJo started to rise. "If you two want to—"

"Sit down, JoJo. You need to hear this, too," Will said.

She shot Granny a questioning glance, then settled back into her chair.

"I've rehearsed what I'm about to say a hundred times," he began quietly. "Granny, I…"

The words were suddenly choked with emotion and he couldn't deliver his canned speech. The truth was wrapped in razor blades—no way to get at it without being sliced open. So he just said it, plain and simple.

"It wasn't only Lloyd and me who survived the explosion, Granny. Ricky Dan did, too."

Granny slowly raised her hands to her mouth and her eyes filled with tears, but she kept them fastened on Will's face, locked tight, didn't blink.

"My father was alive? Then what—"

"He died so Lloyd and I could live. He gave his life for us."

The tears began to spill silently down Granny's face.

Will described the explosion as simply and clearly as he could. Granny gasped—a little sound—when he told her that Ricky Dan had wanted to go back for Bowman, but helped him save Lloyd instead. He painted for them a vivid picture of the panicked, nightmare race through the shaft as it filled with deadly smoke faster than they could run, told them how Ricky Dan had found the enclosed break.

"We collapsed in the break panting, coughing and crying!" Will hadn't realized that to describe the scene he'd have to relive it, endure here in this warm kitchen the worst moments of his life. "The air outside in the shaft was *death,* inches away on the other side of a piece of yellow plastic not much thicker than a garbage bag." His voice dropped to a ragged whisper. "And I was *so scared!*"

"I understand, Sugar. You—"

"No, you *don't* understand!" He hadn't meant to bark, but it had all come back—so *real*. "I wasn't just frightened. I was totally panicked. Granny, I *hated* every second I spent in the mine. My stomach was tied in such knots I never ate a bite of the lunch you packed me, fed it to Worthless so you wouldn't know."

He remembered, *remembered* it all. "Eight hours of terror every day. I was exhausted, wrung out. But I couldn't sleep, lay there every night dreading…and then I'd have to get up and do it again the next day. It was a nightmare that wouldn't end."

Will realized he was shouting. He clamped his jaw tight shut and gritted his teeth to get control of himself. JoJo stared at him with wide, shocked eyes. Granny looked like she was in as much pain as he was.

When he could, he reached out and took Granny's hand. "Ricky Dan knew how I felt. I didn't tell him, but he knew. He tried to help. And that day, he knew I was about to crawl out of my skin."

Will described the hours in the dark and the realization that they would suffocate before help could reach them. He described their decision to send one of them out to find good air.

At first, JoJo was merely stunned by the revelations, by the horrific scene she could see through Will's eyes. She'd never known her father, had never loved him, so she had nothing like the emotional investment in the story that Granny had.

But as Will spoke, he watched a gear shift in JoJo. She was riveted to his every word. And he realized he had brought her father to life right there in front of her, the essence of him, condensed and purified by the intensity of the final events of his life.

Will didn't see Granny take a single breath the whole time he spoke. She stared at him with such ferocious concentration he knew she could see into him, see the darkness inside.

"So we decided to pick rocks out of a hat to decide who had to try to make it through the smoke to the next break."

"Like Lloyd was talking about the other day," JoJo said eagerly. "Two black rocks, one white. The one who draws the white rock loses."

"Uh huh, but remember, Lloyd had a broken ankle; he couldn't climb over the conveyor belt. It was just Ricky Dan and me. Two rocks."

"And my father got the white rock, right?" JoJo said. Granny reached over and patted her hand.

"Shhh now, Honey. Let Will talk." She turned back to him with tears in her eyes, her face wet with them. "Will has to tell it."

CHAPTER 29

Even though they've decided, nobody moves. Lloyd is leaned against the coal wall beside the back curtain, Ricky Dan is seated next to the pile of rocks and Will rests against the coal pillar across from Ricky Dan. It's as if the deed is so huge, the decision so momentous, they can't quite take it all in at once. They have just decided to send Will or Ricky Dan to an almost certain death.

Will grits his teeth and a sudden icy calm settles over him. He can do this. He has no choice. He has counted all his emotional reserves, cashed in all his chips of courage and come up way short. But he must do it now, right now, before he loses his nerve.

"Okay, rocks in a hat," he is surprised that his voice, though ragged and hoarse, is level. "I ain't got no hat. We'll need yours, Lloyd."

Lloyd removes his helmet without comment and passes it to Ricky Dan. Lloyd's light is resting on the pile of rocks, though it is dark, turned off to conserve the battery. The lone beam of Ricky Dan's headlamp casts precious little illumination.

On his knees, Will locates two rocks the same size—a little lump of coal and a small piece of white slate from the rock pile—and holds them out for the others to see. Ricky Dan hands him Lloyd's helmet. He lifts it up to the roof where neither he nor Ricky Dan can see into it, then drops the rocks inside. One plunk. Two. He shakes the helmet around, rattles the rocks.

The three exchange glances. Nobody speaks.

"Who's gonna draw first?" Lloyd asks.

Will looks at Ricky Dan and tries to attach a grin to his face, but it instantly falls off. "Age before beauty," he says. Ricky Dan nods. He can't manage a grin either.

His hand steady, Ricky Dan reaches up and shoves it into the hat. He grabs Will's gaze, but Will quickly looks away. Then he withdraws his hand in a fist. He holds the fist out into the light from his headlamp and slowly opens it. Lying on his palm is a white rock.

He gasps. Will lowers the helmet and sets it on the rock pile. Nobody speaks.

"That's it, then." Though Ricky Dan's voice is raspy and damaged, it is strong. He coughs briefly but quickly gets control of his breathing and silences the cough. All of them are dry, so dry.

"Shame nobody bothered to bring a water bottle along on this little field trip," Ricky Dan says.

Neither Lloyd nor Will responds. Lloyd sits quiet, obviously aware that his injury has saved his life. And luck has saved Will's. With only Lloyd and Will in the enclosure, they've got a good shot at survival. But Ricky Dan…

"That seal and them curtains is out there," Ricky Dan says firmly. "Makes sense they would be. The curtain and seal here didn't blow; they wouldn't a-blown, neither. All's I gotta do is climb over the conveyor and grab hold of yonder wall, follow it till I see yellow—or feel plastic, probably won't be able to see 6 inches in front of my face."

"Na, it didn't blow," Will says. "You're gonna get there and have so much air to breathe you might quit coughing."

Ricky Dan pokes Will's arm. "You get yore bags packed, son, 'cause I'm comin' back for you! Soon's I get my wind back and make sure everything's okay, I'll be back to lead you to the promised land so Lloyd here can have all this fine air to himself."

Lloyd works at a smile but can't pull it off. Ricky Dan points his finger at him. "You 'member to tell them guys where we're at! Rescue team'll come in down the tracks. They's chalk markin' on that curtain." Ricky Dan nods to the front piece of yellow plastic. "I smeared it some when I come under." He glances at a white chalk mark on his left shoulder. "It's readable, though. When they get to you, you're gonna have to draw them boys a map to me 'n Will."

"I can do that, Ricky Dan," Lloyd says, his voice unsteady.

The three fall silent. Nobody moves. When Ricky Dan speaks again, there is no bravado in his tone. It is quiet and sincere, but Will can hear neither fear nor self-pity in his words.

"If I don't make it, you guys gotta make me a promise... no, two promises."

"Anything," Will chokes.

"First, you gotta promise me you'll never tell a living soul about any of this. Far as you ever say, you two was the only ones made it out of the 'xplosion."

"But—" Will begins to protest.

"Promise!"

Will and Lloyd exchange a glance, then nod.

"Why don't you want nobody to know?" Lloyd asks.

"'Cause I want Ma to think I died with Daddy!" The end of the sentence is a choked sob. "I want her to think I went quick, like he done."

He pauses, looks into Will's eyes, then Lloyd's. "And I don't want nobody second-guessin' what we decided to do here today. Folks is all the time doin' that, but we was here and they wasn't and we done what we had to do. I ain't gonna have none of this comin' back on you two."

"We won't tell nobody," Lloyd says. "Ever. We swear."

"What's the second thing?" Will asks.

"Look after Ma!" Ricky Dan turns away, his shoulders shake for a few moments, then he turns back, tears in his eyes. "It'll be real hard on her...losin' Daddy and me both." Sad awareness spreads over his face, like he hadn't put it together in his head until now. "Uncle Ed and Jody, too, likely." His uncle and brother-in-law had been on the other crew working at the face. "She's gonna need you two. Not for a week or a few months. She's got the girls but ain't the same as a son. She's yore mama now. Don't you let her fend for herself."

"I won't," Lloyd says.

Ricky Dan turns to Will and speaks with a quiet intensity louder than a shout. "You take care of her, hear! You take care of my family from now on."

Will can't speak, just stares dumbly into Ricky Dan's green eyes. His heart has been sliced open, torn apart. It is a pain he never knew existed, an agony so excruciating he cannot suffer it for long or it will kill him. He doesn't know now that he will never again be free of it. Except when he's drunk.

"Joanna." Just the one word. Then Ricky Dan takes a breath. "You guys need to know. Joanna, she's..." He stops. Then seems to think out loud. "Young like she is and pretty, she'll find somebody else. Somebody to help her—"

"Joanna ain't gonna have to look for another man 'cause you're gonna take care of her your own self," Lloyd says adamantly. "You ain't goin' but 25 feet out to the shaft, across the

belt line—15 feet—then 50 feet up to the break. Ninety feet. It ain't in the next county. Only 90 feet, that's all."

Ricky Dan shakes it off. "That's right. I'm just sayin'..."

He is seized by another coughing fit and it is a long time before he can breath properly again. By then, he is all business. He seems intent now on simply getting the job done.

He stands, bent at the waist and moves to the back curtain, has to step past Lloyd who is leaned against the coal pillar next to it. He scoots away the rocks Will piled on it to seal it to the floor.

"You put them back fast as you can," he says. He picks up Lloyd's headlamp off the rock pile and hands it to him. Lloyd fits it onto his helmet. Ricky Dan turns to Will but doesn't make eye contact. "I'll be back for you in a few minutes. You be ready."

Without another word, he leans over and takes the bottom of the curtain in his hand. "See ya," he says, takes a deep breath, lifts the curtain, and plunges out into the shaft.

Will and Lloyd stare at the empty spot where Ricky Dan just stood. Will is seized by an almost uncontrollable urge to rush out into the shaft and drag him back. But he sits, watches Lloyd replace the rocks and lean back against the wall beside it.

Still on his knees, Will slumps forward onto his belly and his elbows, his eyes fixed on the back curtain. Lloyd's headlamp casts out a single pallid beam; all the corners are attended by shadows, but Will doesn't allow his eye to stray to the corners. The light will play tricks on him. And he's certain there are things in the corners of this ever-shrinking prison he doesn't want to get a good look at.

He waits, almost holds his own breath. Without a watch, it's hard to tell how long. Five minutes. Ten. Half an hour.

After a while, Lloyd wordlessly reaches up, turns off his head-lamp and plunges the two of them into blind-man darkness. Together they wait in the silent, inky black nothingness of the unborn—or the dead.

While the world outside continues to revolve, time slows down and eventually stops completely in the darkness of Will's grave. But his focused attention does not waver. It remains fixed on the curtain he can no longer see.

Ricky Dan never comes back through it.

"That darkness never ended," Will told Granny and JoJo. "I didn't find out until later that sometime after Ricky Dan left, there was another explosion or aftershock or something that knocked loose a pretty good sized piece of slate in the roof above Lloyd and me. I was stretched out on the floor so it fell several feet before it hit me in the head, and I wasn't wearing a helmet. That's when I got the concussion." The concussion that sealed him in darkness until he awakened in the hospital two days later.

"And you didn't do it," JoJo said. Will looked at her quizzically. "My daddy said, 'You take care of her. You take care of my family from now on.' But you didn't. You didn't do what you promised."

Will looked down at his hands. "Technically, I *didn't* promise. I couldn't speak, couldn't say a word. But I didn't do what your father asked me to do."

"And you ran away. That's what's been eatin' at you all these years, ain't it?" She turned to Granny. "And that's why Lloyd was acting so funny 'bout Will, like he was mad at him. He was mad 'cause he done what my daddy asked him to do and Will didn't."

"JoJo, you need to be still now, child. They's things Will's got to say and you got to hush up and let him say 'em."

"All right, I won't interrupt again. But I have to ask—why?"

Will saw a tangle of emotions wash across her face as the chill of déjà ran through her. Last night, on the porch, the same guileless, uncomprehending question. Why? Why do you want to end your life?

Granny turned back to Will and he couldn't read the emotion on her face either. It wasn't just one, though. Her reaction wasn't a single, simple emotion. It was all tangled up, too.

"Why?" Will repeated softly and looked down at his hands again. "Why didn't I stay and do what Ricky Dan asked? Why did I run away?"

It seemed like a thousand years passed between heartbeats, though his heart was banging in his chest like a lunatic woodpecker. His mouth was dry as the rock dust they spread in the mine.

His next words would shatter relationships and destroy the place he called home. But he had to say them. It was say them or die.

Will lifted his head and looked Granny in the eye. He owed her that.

"I ran away because I cheated," he said. "I rigged it so Ricky Dan would draw the white rock and not me."

◊ ◊ ◊ ◊ ◊

Will is on his knees, searching for rocks to put into the hat. He needs one white and one black. What he picks up are two white rocks and one black.

A plan formed in his head as soon as Ricky Dan suggested they determine who would go out into the poisoned shaft by drawing rocks out of a hat. It wasn't something he thought about, worried around in his head and then figured out the specifics. The plan simply dropped into his head, like a gift-wrapped package addressed to Will Gribbins. All the elements were in place; he didn't have to design any of it.

He must switch the rocks. If he can pull a coin out of somebody's ear undetected, he can replace one rock with another unseen. He will stack the deck so Ricky Dan wins the white-rock prize.

It is simple, really. He turns back around to face the others. In his left hand, he holds one black rock. In his right hand, casually out of sight behind his back, he holds two white rocks. He palms one, reaches around and drops the other into his left hand, then holds his hand out for the others to see—one white rock, one black. When Ricky Dan hands him Lloyd's helmet, Will lifts the helmet above his head and appears to reach up into it with his left hand and let the two rocks in it drop through his fingers. What he actually does is palm the black rock. Then he drops the white rock from his left hand and the other white rock from his right hand into the helmet. Now, there are two white rocks inside the helmet instead of one white and one black, and Will has a black rock safely palmed in his left hand.

If Ricky Dan chooses first, he can only draw out a white rock because there is no black rock in the hat. If Will draws first, he will reach into the hat with his left hand and draw back the black rock he has palmed in it.

Once the drawing is complete, he will quickly put the hat, bottom side down, on the rock pile, where whatever rocks are left inside will vanish.

But he's sure he will be able to get Ricky Dan to draw first. All he has to do is say…

" '…age before beauty,'" Will said. He couldn't hold Granny's gaze, so he dropped his eyes to the table. "That's what I said to get Ricky Dan to draw first. He never had a chance."

For an agonizing, thousand-year moment, no one made a sound. No one breathed. It was as if they'd become figures in one of Jamey's arts, frozen in one spot, with one look on their faces for all eternity.

"I was a coward." Will's voice was tight with restrained emotion. "I couldn't go back out into that shaft full of poison air. So…I sent my best friend…my *brother* out there to die in my place."

He lifted his eyes to meet Granny's. Her face was absolutely blank. No emotion, no expression of any kind. In a ragged voice, Will whispered, "I'm so *sorry*, Granny. I know you could never forgive me—"

"I already did."

Her voice was even, and her frozen face dissolved into a look of such compassion the light of it blinded Will and he had to look away.

"You already—?"

"I said I done forgived you. I forgived you years ago, Sugar."

The room spun, whirled around and around Will in a dizzying blur of motion. Utterly alone in the middle of the tempest, he and Granny stared unblinking into each other's eyes.

"How could…?" The rest of the words hung in his throat and he couldn't finish. He wondered if she'd even heard him, if his small voice had carried above the roar of the raging wind.

"I've knowed what you done for a long time, son."

"You…*knew?*"

Granny reached out and squeezed his hand, then let it go. "First, I cried and carried on, my heart tore all to pieces from the pain of it. Then, I got up one mornin' and I forgived you. I got up the next mornin' and forgived you again. And the next." She sighed. "The Bible says you got to forgive seven times seventy times, and folks think that means forgivin' that many hurts. But that ain't it a-tall. What it means is that it takes that many times and more to forgive *one* hurt, 'cause you got to do it over and over, ever day. Until one day, the forgiveness comes down outta your head—outta your mouth where you been sayin' it but not meanin' it—and it lands in your heart." She patted her flat chest. "When it lands here, the forgivin's done."

Her eyes filled with tears again. "I been waitin' all these many years for you to come home and tell me what you done—not so's I could forgive you but so's I could tell you I already did."

Will and JoJo spoke at the same time.

"Granny, how could you *possibly*—?" Will gasped.

"How did you—?" JoJo asked.

Granny ignored them both and spoke with riveting intensity to Will.

"You been out there wanderin' the earth all eat up with guilt and you was already forgiven; you just didn't know it."

Granny stopped, took a breath and completely changed gears. "I want you to do some'm for me, Will. I want you to go up to Jamey's shed." She fished in the front pocket of the flowered apron tied around her waist and pulled out a key. "I got half a dozen spares; Jamey's all the time losing his." She handed it to Will. "Underneath the potato boxes in the store room of the shed is one of Jamey's carvin's wrapped up in a pillowcase. I want you to bring it back down here to me."

"But Granny, I don't underst—?"

Granny waved him off before he could finish. "Be patient and do as I ask." She smiled a little smile. "Jamey'd pitch a fit if he knowed you was gettin' it out of there. I told him a long time ago to hide it and not let nobody see it. He's kept it hid all these years…'cause it made me cry. But it's time now."

CHAPTER 30

LOYD COULD HEAR thunder in the distance and it had sprinkled off and on as he drove to work. A fine mist hung in the air when miners began to pull into the parking lot beside the Harlan #7 entrance at a quarter after eight. Only in union mines did your hourly wage start when you showed up for work. Non-union mines didn't pay you until you got to the face and started to dig. It would take more than half an hour to travel the mile and a half to the face, and half an hour to get back out. All that time was on your nickel, not the mine's.

Because they were anxious to get to work so the meter'd start running, the miners didn't stand around and jaw. Like Lloyd, they all carried their coveralls, steel-toed rubber work boots, helmets, and work belts with them and put them on in the chill air, standing beside their cars or pickup trucks. Some mines had lockers where miners could leave their gear; this one didn't.

As he pulled his work belt around his waist, Lloyd glanced at the small piece of metal with his name and his social security number that was affixed to the belt with brads. He remembered how it had upset Will that he had to wear a label so they could recognize his body if he was crushed or burned beyond recognition. Lloyd never could figure why it mattered in the first place. Dead was dead. What difference did it make what family got which unrecognizable body to put in a box and stick in the ground?

Lloyd stepped into the office, took his nametag from the "out" board and placed it on a hook on the "in" board. Only one shaft was operational. A second crew was scheduled to go to work as soon as Black Gold had the money to dig out the shafts that had collapsed in the 1980 explosion.

The words printed on the back of his bossing papers came to his mind: You are responsible for the health, welfare, and safety of the men in your crew.

Well, he'd keep them all safe and healthy. Until he blew them all up. He paused, held his emotional breath and waited for the opposition chorus to rail against what he was about to do. Not objecting to the killing-himself part, but crying out against the take-other-people-with-you part. What had these men ever done to him? They were regular guys trying to earn a living. Why kill them? Why shove Aintree off a cliff into another black pit of despair it'd likely never climb out of?

He waited. Nothing. He had silenced all internal protest. Was he about to cause a world of hurt in this hollow? He was for a fact. But at this point, Lloyd Jacobs just flat out didn't care.

"How you gettin' 'long, Lloyd?" said the short, cheerful shuttle driver as Lloyd stepped up beside him in the lamp house and picked up his headlamp and battery off the charger.

"Can't complain. You?"

"If I's any better, I'd be twins."

The man leaned over and picked up something out of a cardboard box on the floor by the Peg-Board. It was a black ribbon with the number 27 printed on it in silver.

"I see you ain't got one of these yet. If'n anybody'd want to wear one, I figure it'd be you."

Lloyd reached out wordlessly and took the ribbon. The shuttle driver helped him tie it on his right arm above his elbow so the 27 was plainly visible, then the man gathered up his Clorox bottle full of water and his lunch bucket and headed outside. Lloyd had brought neither water nor lunch with him this morning. What was the point? He intended to time the explosion to go off at the same time as the mine blew two decades ago. Right at 12:18 P.M.

Hob Bascomb had been talking to another miner, then turned and smiled at Lloyd.

"Lose a fight with a bobcat, didja?" Hob asked, indicating the scratches on Lloyd's arms, neck, and face from the thorns and broken trellis.

"Some'm like that. What are you doin' here?"

"I come early for the ceremony." He looked sheepish. "*Real* early. Couldn't sleep." Then Hob noticed Lloyd's missing lunch bucket. "You on a diet, Lloyd?"

"Na, I'm s'posed to speak at the service out front, so I'll have to leave the face 'fore lunchtime."

Hob looked startled. "You're speakin' today?" He began to say something else then fell silent. He was probably just surprised Lloyd would be coming out of the mine, him being a boss and all. Bosses were not allowed to leave their sections.

Lloyd reached down and picked up the mine safety lamp called a possum light he'd set on the floor. Every boss had one. It was a special lamp, looked like a small lantern, with a flame that went out in the presence of CO_2, Black Damp, and burned with a bright blue cap if the methane concentration in the air was higher than 2 percent. Lloyd planned to blow up Harlan #7 with methane, but none of the other miners would know it had reached an explosive level because the gas was odorless, tasteless, and invisible. The boss was the only man on the crew with a possum light to detect it and Lloyd planned to take the lamp with him when he left the face "to speak at the ceremony."

"You okay, Lloyd?" Hob asked. "You look like yore wife left ya and the dog died."

"Matter of fact, Norma Jean did leave me," he snapped. "And I ain't got no dog."

Hob's face flushed. "Lloyd, I'm sorry, I didn't mean nothin'…"

"Hey, Lloyd," said a cheery voice. The sound hit Lloyd in the belly with the force of a cannonball. He turned around slowly and there stood Jamey Sparrow.

The boy always looked strange in his work clothes, like a little kid playing dress-up. His face was too innocent and earnest, his blond hair too clean for a miner.

"What are *you* doin' here?" Lloyd barked with such force two miners turned and looked. Hob Bascomb gawked at him like he'd lost his mind.

Jamey was so surprised the smile vanished from his face and he stared at Lloyd. Folks didn't speak harshly to Jamey; that'd be like kicking a puppy.

"I…well. I'm—"

"You said you's off for a week. Today's Friday. You ain't s'posed to come back 'til Monday."

The boy looked confused for a moment, then his face cleared and he spoke as if he was reciting a poem in front of a class at school.

"'Take next week off, Jamey, but I need you in here for the half day Friday,'" he parroted. "That's what Mr. Murdock said." Jamey turned and pointed toward the office building where the outside foreman stood in the doorway. "He's right over there if you wanna ask him."

Lloyd didn't follow Jamey's gaze.

"You ain't s'posed to be here." His mind spun. "You're s'posed to be home with Granny and JoJo."

"I couldn't stay home. I had to come to work. But they ain't by theirselves. Will's there."

Will. Yeah, they're home with their precious *Will!* At first, Lloyd had mourned the fact that Will would escape the fate of the other miners today. Then it occurred to him that surviving this explosion would be way worse than dying in it. Let Will find out what that kind of grief feels like!

Jamey stood before Lloyd completely still and blank, like a radio you'd left turned off—like if you didn't say something, he'd still be standing there waiting for you next week.

Lloyd stepped up to the boy and spoke urgently.

"You listen to me, Jamey Sparrow. And you do what I tell you. You go home. Right now, hear me. Go home!"

"What for?"

Jamey looked confused and other miners had turned now to listen to the conversation. Lloyd realized he had to back off, bad as he hated it. He couldn't risk his whole plan to save one kid. It was a shame. But a lot of things in this life was a shame. Lloyd wasn't at all sad to be leaving it.

"Oh, never mind," he growled.

He left Jamey with a stricken look on his face, stormed over to the mantrip, climbed aboard, and leaned back. The machine carried miners into the mine sitting backward and out again facing forward. Lloyd wouldn't be making that return trip. Neither would any of the others—including Jamey.

As the mantrip started toward the entrance and the dark tunnels beyond, Lloyd looked up at the clouds. Too bad it was stormy. He'd have liked to have seen a bright blue sky one last time.

Then the machine and the miners passed through the entrance into a darkness that matched the black depths of Lloyd's soul.

◊ ◊ ◊ ◊ ◊

WILL, GRANNY, AND JoJo were again seated around the kitchen table. In front of them lay the dusty pillowcase with a lump in it that Granny had asked Will to retrieve from Jamey's shed. As soon as he saw it stuffed behind the potato box, a chill ran down Will's spine. When he actually touched it, he had the strange sense that he almost knew what was inside. Understanding beat at the edge of his mind like a loose shutter banging in the wind. He could have opened the pillowcase and looked, of course. It's not like there was a padlock on it. But he didn't want to see. He was certain that whatever it was, he wouldn't like it.

As he'd turned toward the door in the shed, Will spotted Jamey's newest arts, the one he'd completed last night. Wrapped up in a striped pillowcase on the worktable lay a carving of the explosion that killed 27 miners two decades ago. Will sighed. Might as well get that over with, too. He set the hidden mural down carefully on the bench, placed the new one on top of it and carried the two of them back to Granny's.

When he placed the two carvings on the kitchen table in front of Granny and JoJo, they scooted to the side the one Jamey had just completed and stared at the other one. No one spoke for a moment, but the air was charged with energy. JoJo had figured out that whatever lay inside that dirty pillowcase was some of her brother's magic and she looked at it with last-Bingo-number intensity.

Granny turned to Will and said gently, "I think you know what's in here. Jamey carved it years ago. 'Course he didn't know what any of it meant, but I studied on it and figured it out."

Without another word, she pulled the pillowcase down off the carving to reveal a shiny piece of jet about 30 inches across. She lifted it, tossed the dirty pillowcase over on top of the striped one and then set the jet back down in the center of the table.

Will gasped. JoJo looked confused.

The relief mural showed three miners in a vast darkness. The darkness alone was a masterpiece—far from empty and featureless. Jamey had painstakingly etched into it an intricate, detailed network of tiny lines that displayed the cracks and texture of coal. A miner without a helmet was leaned up against the wall with his feet extended out in front of him; two other miners were on their knees. One could be seen from the side, the other from the back. Even though the faces of two of the men were visible, they weren't recognizable because all three of them were looking down, their attention fixed on what lay on the ground in front of them—a miner's helmet, turned upside down.

JoJo finally broke the silence, spoke in an awed whisper.

"That's when you was gettin' ready to draw rocks, ain't it?"

Will didn't answer. He couldn't speak. His eyes were fixed on a particular detail in the mural, a detail that stood out on the black surface like headlights coming at you on a lonely road at night.

JoJo's eyes were drawn to it, too, and recognition registered on her face. She looked up and said to Granny, "That there's how you knew, ain't it?"

Granny nodded.

The detail that gripped their attention was the right hand of the miner whose back was turned. The man held his hand casually behind his back, palm open. And lying there, clearly visible, were two white rocks. *White* imbedded in the black surface of the jet.

"I asked Jamey about them soon's I seen 'em," Granny said quietly. "He said they was *in* that piece of jet, that lotsa times they's other rocks stuck in the jet he's carvin' and he has to chisel them away. But he said the white rocks in this 'un was a part of what he dug out of the rock. Said they was right *there* and he just carved the hand around 'em."

"How did you know…how did you figure out what all this meant?" JoJo asked.

Granny took a deep breath.

"I knowed it was Ricky Dan right there." She pointed to the miner on the right. "Recognized him right off 'cause of his helmet—where he painted the UK thing with a X across it. And

I knew this had to be the day of the 'xplosion 'cause Ricky Dan painted that thing on there the night before."

She stopped, gathered herself and went on. "That there's Lloyd's helmet, see?" She reached out and put her finger on the UK symbol on the helmet lying in the dirt, then pointed to the miner leaned against the wall. "And that's Lloyd, cause you can tell some'm ain't right with his foot and his boot's gone."

The miner's left foot was twisted, lying at an odd angle.

"That's how I knowed this was *after* the 'xplosion, cause that's how Lloyd broke his ankle."

Her voice got so quiet it was little more than a whisper on a breath. "Which meant Ricky Dan hadn't got killed in the 'xplosion. He was alive after #7 blew."

It was quiet then. Again, the three seemed to be frozen in one of Jamey's arts. Finally, Granny dropped soft words into the silence.

"This one had to be you, Will," she said, pointing to the miner with the rocks in his hand. "Who else could it be? All the other miners got blowed up."

She sat back, said nothing. Will couldn't look at her. JoJo didn't speak, either. Finally, Granny took up the story where she'd left off.

"I studied on it for the longest time, got it out ever night and looked at it for hours sometimes. I knowed them white rocks right where they was in that piece of jet—that wasn't no accident. After a while, it finally come to me what musta happened." She turned to Will. "You boys was decidin' who was gonna do something none of you wanted to do. I didn't know what it was 'xactly, but whatever it was...it got Ricky Dan kilt. 'Cause when all was said 'n done, you and Lloyd was the onliest ones come out of that mine alive."

She reached out and patted Will's hand. He still couldn't meet her gaze. "I studied and studied on them white rocks you was holdin'. Two of 'em. I knowed you only needed *one* white rock to pick the loser. So what was you doin' with *two*—hiding 'em behind your back?"

Her voice was soft as duck down and hard as bone. It laid Will's soul open as effectively as a surgeon's scalpel—or a warrior's sword. "I watched you practicin' them coin tricks. It'd a been a simple thing for you to switch rocks like you done them coins."

She took a deep breath, obviously intent on getting it all said, on eating her own frog.

"In the end, one thing was clear. Some'm happened down there you boys wanted to hide 'cause neither one of you ever told a soul Ricky Dan was alive in that mine after it blowed." She squeezed Will's hand. "And you run off. You wouldn't a-left your whole life less'n you'd done some'm you's powerful ashamed of."

Will finally lifted his head, forced himself to look into her eyes.

"What I did, Granny, it was unforgiva—"

"Ain't nothin' unforgivable."

She smiled a little, not enough to show teeth even if she'd had any. "You 'member them potlucks we usta have when you's a kid?"

Will nodded. Granny's eyes shifted to a scene her mind painted out in the air in front of her.

"Ever woman in the holler fixed up her best recipe—us all tryin' to outdo each other—and we'd have food laid out on them long tables, ever good thing you could think of, and you could load up your plate with whatever you's partial to." She paused and the smile got wider. She didn't put her hand up to her mouth to hide it. "An' then we'd play music. Me and my mandolin, Ricky Dan with his guitar, and Bowman on his fiddle."

Bowman. She spoke his name in that special sighing way she had. Will had never heard another woman say a man's name the way Granny said Bowman's. He never expected to, either.

But he had no idea what her point was with the story, if indeed she had one. He'd tried to catch the train of her thought but it had pulled right out of the station without him.

Will's face must have shown his confusion because she stopped. The scene she'd painted in the air vanished and she connected the dots for him and JoJo.

"Honey, the Bible ain't no potluck dinner! It ain't like you're 'llowed to be choicey, pick only the parts you like—nothin' but cherry pie—and ignore the hard parts. Either it's all true or ain't none of it is. And the Bible says we *got* to forgive. Not it'd be *nice* if we did. Or we'd oughta if'n we *feel* like it. Says we *got* to. That there's the beginnin' and the end of it."

The room was quiet. Will could think of nothing to say and didn't think he had the air in his lungs to say anything even if he'd wanted to.

Then Granny spoke into the stillness. Like rocks pitched one at a time into a creek, each word landed with a separate plop in his heart.

"I forgived Lloyd, too."

"What did Lloyd do that you had to forgive, Granny?" JoJo asked. "He didn't cheat."

"And I waited for him to come to me and man up to it, so's I could tell him I'd already forgive him, too. But he never come. All these years, ever day, and he never said a word."

"What are you talking about, Granny?" Will had that feeling again, like something was hurling at him in the darkness.

Granny sighed.

"I's sittin' here one night, lookin' at this carvin', studyin' it. Cryin' over it. And there come up a storm; lightning knocked out the 'lectricity."

She looked at JoJo. "You might 'member it. You's spendin' the night at Becca's."

JoJo shrugged and Granny continued. Her voice was level, but Will could hear deep undertones in it—of what he wasn't sure. Sadness, perhaps. Grief. And something else, too. Something very like fear.

"So I lit me some candles 'cause Jamey Boy was askeered of the dark. And after I got 'em all lit, I sat back down at the table and looked at this here arts."

She stopped again and the silence grew, stretched out like the shadow of the mountain in the evenings.

"Then I seen it," she whispered, her voice ragged. "I screamed and jumped up. And Jamey Boy come runnin' and then the 'lectricity come back on and I's standing there cryin'. He started to cry, too, but he didn't know why we's cryin'."

Will had no idea what she was talking about. He looked at JoJo and didn't think she did either.

Granny came back from the memory, squared her shoulders and said firmly, "I done opened up this can and we're gonna eat all of it."

She stood and picked up the white-rock carving. "I want you and JoJo to take this here arts up to Jamey's shed. I want you to close the door and light the lanterns. Then look at it real hard, stare at it, study it and see what you see." She took a deep, trembling breath. "Lotsa times over the years I've wondered my own self if it's really there. I only seen it the one time."

Chapter 31

A s Lloyd bounced along on the mantrip deeper and deeper into the forever night of the mine, he considered again the mystery. He had wallowed it around in his head for years. Why had he been able to work out what had to be done the day #7 blew and come up with a way to do it when the other two wasn't even thinking those thoughts? The best he could figure was that he had a more well-developed sense of self-preservation than they did. Years of beatings had honed his instinct to survive, sharpened it to a razor edge.

Will is leaned up against the coal pillar. Lloyd can see him shake even in the dim light, can tell he's so scared he's about ready to jump out of his own skin.

Ricky Dan sits on the pile of rocks mourning his daddy, and Lloyd don't blame him one bit for that, but the thing is, there ain't time to worry about dead people when the three of them's on the edge of joining them.

Maybe the agony in his ankle has kept him alert, won't let his mind pad itself in cotton and look away from hard truth. Maybe he's just seen more brutality and meanness in life than they have. If you understand—no, not just understand—experience random brutality and aimless violence, it clears all the clutter out of your mind quick, helps you focus instantly on what you have to do to keep from getting killed. Whatever the reason, he looks around and sees he's the only one of the three intent on figuring out how to stay alive.

He measures the room with his eyes—20 feet of width, 4 feet of height. Pile of rocks sticking out 8 feet. Twenty times 4 times 8. Six hundred and forty. Divide that by 27. The answer's roughly 24. Twenty-four hours of air. Divide that by the 3 of them and you come up with 8 each. Be conservative, say 7. Seven hours of air.

The number kicks him in the belly so hard he's seized by a fit of coughing that shakes his whole body and lights a flame of renewed agony in his ankle. By the time he gets his breath back, his face is wet with tears. Well, some of it is blood from the his split lip. He reaches up and tries to wipe the wet—tears or blood—off his face with his sleeve.

Seven hours ain't long enough! He's already done that math in his head, too. Need 10 hours at least. Twelve is safer. But with 7…the 3 of them will be long dead before the rescue team gets here; won't be nothing for them to do except haul out the bodies.

But Lloyd refuses to accept some inevitable end, roll over and die because there ain't nothing to do about it. If he'd had that attitude, he wouldn't have survived long enough to be sitting here with nothing between him and certain death but two pieces of yellow plastic.

So what's to be done?

Only two things you can do. You either got to find more air or reduce the number of people breathing what you already got. Three men got 7 hours. Two men would have 12. Well, less than that. You'd have to divide up whatever air you had left after you got rid of the third man.

He comes up short at that thought, like he's outside himself watching and listening and he's surprised by what he sees.

Why Lloyd Jacobs, will you listen to yourself! "Get rid of" one of your two best friends…your two only friends? You put either one of them out in that poison air, you'd be commitin' murder.

A cold, reptilian voice in his soul reminds him calmly that it wouldn't be the first time.

A small, private smile spreads over Lloyd's face. Even here, in the pit of a mine, his life dangling by a thread, he is still warmed and cheered by the memory of killing his father. Soon as Mama died, that man's days was numbered. Lloyd believes his father saw it coming, is convinced he saw fear in his father's eyes every time Lloyd entered the room, fear like his father'd seen in his eyes all those years. Maybe not, but there was certainly fear in his eyes at the end, fear and pleading as he begged for his life. Every time he cried out for mercy Lloyd hit him again with the claw end of the hammer, over and over until the man lay in a pool of blood quiet and still. The day he chucked his father's body down that old mine shaft was the first day of real freedom Lloyd Jacobs had ever known.

It wasn't hard to kill his father; it was a delight beyond all thought and reason. But it will be hard to kill Will or Ricky Dan. Hard, but necessary. Self-preservation. One of them dies or Lloyd dies, and Lloyd doesn't intend to die. He has avoided the Reaper before; he can do it again.

Lloyd looks from Will to Ricky Dan. Ricky Dan is in a bad way, must have got a extra dose of bad air somehow or for some reason it's affected him worse. His breath wheezes in and out like a buck that's been lung shot. And that ain't good, him panting like that. He's using up precious air with every breath.

But Lloyd must be patient, come up with a plan. He won't save himself with brute force; it will require cunning. And he understands on a fundamental level that he is the only one of the three of them who is capable of cunning.

By the time Ricky Dan and Will start to do the math, Lloyd already has his strategy mapped out. He describes the escape hatch "only 90 feet away," plays the hand very carefully, doesn't push. And for all he knows there might actually be a break full of air. The curtain nobody bothered to remove—that part's true. Trouble is, Lloyd has no idea where he saw it. It was somewhere along the belt line, in this area as he recalls, but he couldn't pinpoint it to save his life—or to save anybody else's.

When Ricky Dan plunges out into the dark, smoky shaft in a futile act of heroism, Will stares longingly, expectantly at the curtain. Waiting. Hoping. Lloyd knows he will never see Ricky Dan again.

But Lloyd is wrong.

◊ ◊ ◊ ◊ ◊

WILL AND JoJo went down the back porch steps and headed toward the path that led around the garden and up into the woods. The rain was holding off—for the moment—and there was a biting chill in the air, the kind that announced winter was packed up and ready to return—just hadn't got the car loaded yet.

Any minute now the dirt trail would get another good soaking and turn into what Granny'd always called a "lob-lolly". Will would have to return to the house through sticky, ankle-deep goo, and he was wearing the only pair of shoes he…

The thought skittered away and was gone.

All his thoughts were like that. Mundane thoughts. Profound thoughts. Painful thoughts. All jumbled together, spinning around in his head like they'd been tossed into a blender set for puree. He'd try to grab one and think it, but before he had a chance it would…

Granny had known all along. *For years.* Her words from that first day came back to him: "I know what you come home for, son. But you don't. You think you do, but you're wrong."

He'd believed he'd come home to ask for forgiveness. But he'd actually come home so she could tell him he already had it.

Will had played out in his head a thousand times how Granny would react when he confessed, admitted what he'd done to her son. And how she did react certainly hadn't been on his list of conceivable outcomes! Oh, it wasn't that her response was out of character. It was just unimaginable. Because it wasn't possible that she *knew. Nobody* knew he had cheated Ricky Dan. Or so he thought.

"I ain't mad at you, if that's what you're wonderin'," JoJo said. Will turned and looked at her blankly. His mind was like Deke had described a heart in fibrillation; it wasn't really thinking, just quivering uselessly. "I ain't got no dog in the fight. I never knew my daddy so there's no reason for me to harbor ill will toward you for some'm you done to him."

Will shook his head to clear it.

"Now Granny…that's another thing altogether. My daddy was her little boy and that woman can love some'm *fierce.* The force of it near knocks you over sometimes."

"And losing them all like she did, it's remarkable she survived," he heard himself say. Where was he going with this? "An old woman can only take so much heartbreak and loss, though…" Then he figured it out. With a grinding mental effort, he silenced his inner turmoil, slammed the door on it and focused on JoJo. "…only so much *dying—*"

"Don't start! We ain't talkin' about that."

"Have you thought about what it will do to Granny to lose—?"

"You think I ain't concerned about Granny! That I ain't worried about her. That I…" She paused and he watched her grab hold of her temper. "You got all the answers, you tell me. What's it gonna do to that old woman to watch me go crazy 'fore I die? To have to look after me like I's a baby, worn out as she is? To know Jamey's *next?* If my mama'd lived, she'd have turned into a skinny, but her dying like she done, we all got spared—"

He exploded on her.

"*Spared?* Are you actually telling me that you'd trade a childhood full of…of scraped-knee kisses and putting bows in your hair and calling out your spelling words and…holding your head while you threw up for not having to—?"

"I said I ain't gonna talk about that!" She sounded like a little kid with her fingers in her ears chanting, "I can't hear you; I can't hear you."

Before Will could continue, she changed the subject, shifted the focus back on him. "Did it ever occur to you, Mr. Gribbins, that my daddy had a 50 percent chance of gettin' that white rock even if you *hadn't* cheated?"

"Yeah, but I stole his chance at life." He stopped and turned to face her. "Now you, on the other hand, are chucking *your* chance—"

"You say one more word to me about what I'm fixin' to do and I'll…" She realized she had no bargaining chips.

"You'll what? Mark my name off your Christmas card list?"

"I'll let you go look at this rock all by your own self." She turned and marched up the path toward Jamey's shed. Will caught up with her in a couple of strides and they walked together in silence, made their way around the top edge of Granny's garden where squash and gourds peeked out from under dripping foliage and big round pumpkins waited in orange patience for Charley Brown and Snoopy.

The trail snaked through a stand of poplars up the hill, and when they passed the rock outcrop, JoJo asked, "You got any idea what we're s'posed to see in this arts?"

"Not a clue. I'm still in shock at what we've already seen in it. I'm stunned that Jamey can…" Will had no words to describe how Jamey could carve the past, the present—and the future. "…do whatever it is he does."

"It is pretty special, ain't it. When I's a little girl, I used to be jealous he could carve, mad that I couldn't. I tried. I'd take a hammer and chisel to a piece of coal, and 'course it'd shatter." She paused. "And the rest of it, the part that's more than just carving—I done seen it so often it don't shock me no more. But I guess it should. It's magic, ain't it?"

"I wouldn't call it magic—that's dark and Jamey is all light. But it is unmistakably supernatural. And I've never believed in that. Always thought there was a rational explanation for everything. Jamey and his…*gift* fly in the face of everything I know or understand. I don't know how to respond."

"You don't got to respond to everything in life, do you? There's some things that just…are. And you ain't no part of it."

They'd reached the shed. When he'd retrieved the carving from behind the potato box, Will hadn't reattached the padlock. He reached out, turned the knob and shoved the door open for JoJo. She stepped past him into the building, then turned to face him.

"There's one thing about Jamey's carvings I *have* figured out over the years, though. Whatever message they got, you need to listen to it. 'Cause *somebody* went to a whole lot of trouble to deliver it."

The shed was dark. Dull shafts of gray sunlight filtered through the wall cracks and stuck like pale arrows in the floor. Their faint glow barely lit the dust motes in the air.

With their eyes unaccustomed to the darkness, they had to leave the shed door open while they located the box of kitchen matches to light the first lantern.

Then they did as Granny had directed.

One after another, they lit all the lanterns. Then they closed the door and plunged the small room into a darkness relieved by flickering, golden light. Will put the piece of jet down on Jamey's worktable, where a large lantern provided the best illumination. Then the two of them stared at the shiny surface that sparkled in the dancing light.

Will had no idea how long they stood there. The storm finally struck, mounted a ferocious assault on the hollow. Thunder cracked and boomed, wind slammed into the side of the shed and rain battered the roof. The combined cacophony was so loud it would have drowned out normal conversation.

But it didn't drown out JoJo's scream. Her shrieking wail pierced the semi-darkness in the shed and drove an ice pick of agony into Will's left ear.

CHAPTER 32

LLOYD SQUATTED BRIEFLY so he could focus the light of his headlamp out in front of him. The rumble of the continuous miner filled all the cavity around him. He breathed the roar into his body with every breath, could feel the vibration in his teeth. The machine operated at the end of what was essentially a really long extension cord. Lloyd picked up the heavy power cable and moved it out of the way so the miner man wouldn't run over it when he backed up.

Looked like the miner'd already got the cord once. Its plastic insulation had been scuffed so deep one spot was just shy of bare wires. Probably the result of constant dragging across the mine floor. It needed to be fixed, though, could give somebody a nasty shock if they touched it wrong. Inspector seen that, he'd write them up sure.

But after today, wasn't no inspector going to care about a worn cord; there'd probably never be another inspection in Harlan #7. With the storm outside, the explosion might bring the whole mine down. Lloyd knew once why that was, but he'd forgotten the specifics. Something about how the low barometric pressure of a storm allowed more methane out of the coal and the moist air the fan sucked into the mine weakened the roof.

"Need to get some tape and fix that."

Lloyd didn't know the miner's assistant was behind him until the man shouted in his ear.

"Yeah, I'm on it," Lloyd said and pretended to look concerned. Like he'd pretended to look concerned as he watched the back curtain for Ricky Dan's return.

Lloyd stares at the piece of yellow plastic, tries to muster the same look of yearning he sees on Will's face. Time passes and the look on Will's face doesn't change, but the feeling behind it does. It's like those cicadas that shed their skins, leaving them stuck to the bark of trees every summer. Will has left his face behind, frozen in a look of anxious anticipation. But the person who is Will Gribbins has given up all hope, is utterly despairing. And devastated.

Finally, Lloyd reaches up and turns off the headlamp so he doesn't have to look at Will's face anymore. In the utter darkness that envelopes him, he struggles not to get disoriented, unable to think clearly. He needs to do the math again. He tries and fails. The problem has become too complex for him to get his mind around. How much of the six hundred and forty cubic yards of air did the three of them use breathing it for...what, 3, maybe 4 hours? How much was left for him and Will? Would it be enough?

The longer he frets over the numbers, the more anxious he becomes. Suppose the three of them had used up so much there wasn't enough left to sustain him and Will until rescue came? Ricky Dan spent almost the whole time coughing his head off. Did that use up more oxygen? Or less because he couldn't breathe deep? Almost the whole time they've been imprisoned in the break, Will has been panting in terror. That certainly used up more air.

It's the dark that makes figuring so difficult, that sends racing, panicked thoughts through his brain. The dark and the silence. Will hasn't spoken a word. The moment Ricky Dan plunged out into the poisoned shaft, Will fell silent, like he'd been struck dumb.

Lloyd can't stand the dark any longer. He reaches up to turn his headlamp back on when the second bomb goes off. His ears pop as a sudden thunder rumbles all around him, roars louder than the coal train pulsing above his body years ago. The ground shakes, the curtains flap. He smells dust, hears the clatter of rocks nearby, and puts his hands over his head in a ridiculous effort to protect himself as the mountain falls down on top of him.

This is it! All his scheming has been for nothing. Terror seizes his guts harder than when he heard the first explosion. He didn't have time to process it then, didn't understand what was happening, what it meant. But he does now. He's going to die here in the dark!

Then the rumble subsides. He begins to cough; dust chokes him. He fumbles for the switch and turns on his headlamp. There has been a roof fall inside the break. Will is stretched out on the floor under a fresh pile of rocks with a widening pool of blood spreading out from his head. For a moment, Lloyd is too surprised to react. He starts to crawl to Will, but the instant agony in his broken ankle shoots up into his belly and makes him nauseous.

He settles back, panting, tries not to cough in the dusty air. He shines his headlamp the best he can on what he can see of Will. There is no movement. Without a helmet to protect him, Will's head has been cracked open by the hunks of slate. He is dead.

Lloyd's initial rush of sorrow is quickly short-circuited by relief. Then joy. Will is dead! And that's a shame, it really is. He liked Will a lot; he was like a brother. But so was Ricky Dan. And with both of them gone, all the air that's left in here, dusty as it is, belongs to Lloyd. Just one man breathing. He can last for hours, longer than it will take a rescue team to reach him. He's going to make it after all. He's going to live!

His giddiness quickly passes. The roof fall sent some rock down on his side of the enclosure as well. Dust and gravel slid off the back of his helmet into his shirt and down his back. Now it has mingled with his sweat to form an itchy goo. He leans forward carefully, unbuttons his shirt and eases it off. And his magician's rope plops out into his lap. He'd forgotten that he stuffed it down the front of his shirt at lunch—which seemed a hundred years ago. The short ones he stuffed up his sleeve are gone.

He picks up the rope and looks at it, still tied in a hangman's noose, and wonders if the disaster would cancel the Halloween carnival. Duh. Of course it would! And he hated that. He'd worked so hard to...

There's a noise outside the curtain next to him. Lloyd freezes. Why would the rescue team come down the belt line shaft?

The rocks that hold the curtain to the floor suddenly roll away as it is pulled up from the bottom. And Ricky Dan Sparrow falls through the opening right into Lloyd's lap.

Gasping, choking, his helmet gone, he tries to speak.

"...'xplosion knocked...curtain down..." he gasps.

He'd found it; he'd actually made it to the other pocket of air!

"...couldn't fix..." Then he begins to cough—hacking and gagging. He's half in, half out of the enclosure. The curtain's not completely sealed and smoke pours in around him.

"Ricky Dan, you gotta—"

He keeps coughing, won't move, probably can't move. The air inside the break begins to fill with smoke!

Lloyd has no memory of thinking before he acts. His movement is simple reflex, pure self-preservation. In one quick *motion, he slips the hangman's noose around Ricky Dan's neck and pulls it tight.*

Ricky Dan reaches up and claws at the rope. His eyes wild, he struggles frantically to get his fingers around it to pull it away. Then he jerks upward and Lloyd realizes he has woefully misjudged Ricky Dan's remaining strength. In panic, in deadly fear, Ricky Dan raises up onto his hands and knees and yanks backward, and he and Lloyd tumble out of the break into the poison air in the shaft. Lloyd squeezes his squinty eyes shut against the burning smoke and stops breathing. He holds tight to the rope. The big muscles in his arms bulge as he pulls with all his strength. Ricky Dan jerks and flops. And then is still. Lloyd holds on for a moment longer then knows he has seconds to get back into the enclosure before reflexive coughing will kill him.

He lets go of the rope and plunges back under the curtain, the agony of his ankle a remote pain, like the throb from a pulled tooth as the novocaine wears off. Everything feels distant, disconnected. In a dazed, spinning dream he forces himself to belly crawl the rest of the way in so the curtain drops back onto the floor behind him. He drags himself a foot or two farther, then he begins to cough. There's so much smoke and dust. He coughs and coughs and…

When he opens his eyes, there is no bad air. There is a mask over his face that delivers blessed, cleansing, clean oxygen. He closes his eyes again and drifts away.

Lloyd moved the cord again to give the miner man slack to dig deeper. Already 20 feet into the cut, he just kept going. Wasn't supposed to dig more than 20 feet without letting the roof bolter insert screws to hold the rock layers together. But that slowed down production and production trumped safety concerns every time. Company didn't care that the miner man and his helper was working at the end of a 30-foot tunnel of unsupported roof. Long's that black sunshine stacked up on the belt line, nothing else mattered.

The air here was already bad; ventilation was lousy for the same reasons now it'd been bad in 1980. New owners didn't do nothing but put lipstick on a pig; Harlan #7 was still a dog hole mine.

Lloyd coughed. It was a shame he had to suck in coal dust with his last breaths on earth. It had felt so good to breathe the oxygen in that mask. He'd spent the first half hour of consciousness with his eyes closed, savoring the pure joy of good air.

Then he'd heard voices, men, not nurses, and he knew he had to return to the world. Inside two minutes, he realized that the time he'd spent innocently enjoying fresh air would be the last moments of innocent enjoyment he would ever know.

"He's awake," somebody says. Lloyd squints and the face comes into focus. It's Beau Grissom, the head of Big Sandy Mine's rescue team. He's all cleaned up, nice shirt. Lloyd is confused, not completely certain where he is or how he got here.

"What…happened?" he croaks, and the effort to speak sends shards of glass through his raw throat.

"I know it hurts to talk," Beau says. "You just listen."

Then Beau describes the rescue effort and in a sudden rush powerful as a rain-swollen creek, it all comes back to Lloyd.

The explosion.

The break full of rocks.

Will.

The hat.

Ricky Dan!

Lloyd's afraid he's about to be sick. Surely, he dreamed it. He didn't really…but he knows it's no dream. And when a full understanding hits him, it feels like he's been gut shot.

He had killed Ricky Dan Sparrow! Strangled him with his magician's rope.

But even more important—he had left the rope around Ricky Dan's neck!

Lloyd hasn't heard a word Beau has said. Even in this fresh air, he can't catch his breath. There's an iron clamp around his chest squeezing tighter and—

"...got a pretty bad concussion, I ain't gonna lie to you. And he ain't woke up yet. But Will's a fighter. My money says he'll come out of this fine."

"Will is...?" *Lloyd tries, but the words won't form.*

"Alive? Yeah, he is." *Beau thinks Lloyd can't talk because of the pain in his throat.* "We need to let you get some rest." *He nods to another rescue squad member, a man Lloyd can't place, standing on the other side of the bed.* "You need to know the good Lord was watchin' over you 'n Will. We almost didn't see that smeared chalk on the curtain, and wasn't long 'fore it all went."

"All...?"

"Yeah, it blew big, bigger'n the first two times. While we was gettin' you boys out, the team from Hard Scrabble got close as they could to the face and seen... After that, wasn't no reason to send in more men. Glad we didn't, 'cause a couple hours after the big blow, the roof let go in your section. Collapsed. Good news is looks like the blocked shaft put out the fire in the coal."

"Ricky Dan...?"

Beau and the other man exchange a look. Then Beau reaches out, touches Lloyd's arm and speaks softly.

"Lloyd...there's just you 'n Will. You're the only two got out. All the rest...I'm sorry to have to say it, Lloyd, but they's all gone. Twenty-seven men lost and we didn't recover a single body. That coal fire at the face, it was burning hotter'n...

there couldn't a-been nothing left of none of 'em. There ain't no open shafts on that side of the mine no more, neither. Roof falls everywhere."

And for the next 20 years, the first thought in Lloyd's mind every morning is the same: Someday somebody's gonna dig out the belt line shaft in Harlan #7. When they do, they'll find Ricky Dan Sparrow's body. With Lloyd's magician's rope—a hangman's noose around his neck.

CHAPTER 33

G RANNY STOOD AT the back door as Will and JoJo went down
the porch steps. She smiled at the memory of the look on
Will's face when she told him. Shock. Disbelief. Wonder.
And in the end, she'd seen the beginning of... joy. Or hoped she had.
Will probably wouldn't even recognize the feeling; it'd been that long
since he'd had anything to be joyful about.

She watched the two of them until they were out of sight in
the trees beyond the garden, and she wondered what they would
see when the lantern light flickered on the piece of jet they carried with them. She also wondered if Will had got anywhere with
JoJo. That child was wrapped up tighter than an ear of corn in the
husk.

Granny sighed, turned, and almost tripped over Crawdad.

"You hadn't oughta sneak up on me, you fat thing." She reached
down and picked the cat up in her arms. "Good way to get a paw
mashed." She petted him gently and his motor instantly turned on.
His purr sounded like the hum of that old freezer they used to have
before it broke. "Yore feeling lonesome 'cause Will's here and ain't
nobody payin' no attention to you, ain't you, boy?" She scratched the
big cat behind his left ear. "Well, Granny still loves ya, even if you are
worthless as wings on a goat."

She carried the cat to the kitchen table, sat down, and put the cat on the floor at her feet. He rubbed back and forth against her leg. But when she wouldn't pick him back up, he strolled over to his favorite spot in front of the double patio doors, circled three times and then curled up on the patch of worn brown carpet that would have been warmed by sunshine if there'd been any.

Granny looked at the chair where Will had sat as he took his heart right out of his chest and handed it over to her. Bleeding, but still beating. It was a brave thing he done. Brave to come back here and face her. She was proud of him.

Now Lloyd? She sighed again. He'd been harder. *Way* harder. But God had give her the strength to forgive Lloyd too. It had taken a long, *long* time. Years and years of getting up ever morning and forgiving him all over again. Lloyd had been right here in the hollow. He could have come to her anytime, told her the truth. But he hadn't let life humble him, like it done Will. Hard times had just made Lloyd bitter. When they was youngsters, she used to look up from planting or weeding the garden and watch all three boys tumble around in the backyard like bear cubs. Even then, Lloyd didn't seem to know his own self what he aimed to do one second to the next. But he'd already got too close to the fire and she couldn't pull him back.

Bucket gave a disinterested, half-hearted bark at something, probably that badger lived in a hole across the road. If Bucket hadn't been so old, he'd a-got that badger a long time ago. But it had started to rain and wouldn't nothing get that dog off the porch in the rain; he hated to get wet. Granny hoped Will and JoJo'd made it to the shed before the rain hit. She looked in that direction as if she could see through the walls. And she wondered again what the two of them would see in Jamey Boy's arts.

Speaking of Jamey Boy's arts…

His latest one lay on the table in front of her, wrapped in a pillowcase with pale blue stripes the same color as the ragged blue hoodie that hung on a hook beside the front door. The hoodie Jamey Boy should have worn to work. Fifty-eight degrees is a mite nippy if you ain't dressed for it. But he was a man full growed, she reminded herself, even if he'd always be a little boy. Had to let him do for himself.

She reached over reluctantly, moved the dirty pillowcase she'd tossed on top of it, pulled the bundle toward her and braced herself for what she'd see. Jamey Boy'd said he didn't think the miners in the rock had faces. But what if he was wrong? What if they did? What if she lifted the pillowcase off the rock and there was Bowman all tore up, his face a mask of pain? How could she stand to look at a thing like that?

When they first married, Bowman had come home one day with his hand all mashed. Got it caught between a roller and the belt on the belt line. It was the horriblest wound you ever seen, the skin on his fingers split open on both sides, mashed open the way an orange would split if you stepped on it. Soon as she seen it, she begged him to go to the doctor and get it seen to, though she knew they didn't have no money for doctors. They was poor. But at least they didn't live in a company town where one of them big coal companies owned your house and you got paid in company script, had to shop at the company store. And the company kept you always in debt so you couldn't never leave. Her and Bowman, they was better off than that!

Only, truth was, they's just as much prisoners as them company miners. They had nowhere to go, didn't know any other way to live, and even as she begged Bowman not to go back down in the mine, she knew for total certain that's what he'd do. She wondered he had any stomach for it, but what him or her wanted didn't matter. Bowman'd go back same as every other miner got hurt at work did. He had to. They had three little girls to feed.

So she'd bandaged his hand up best as she could. She remembered the look of agony on Bow's face as she seen to it, knew the pain was fierce. And ever after that, when her mind went to that bad place the minds of miners' wives went if they wasn't careful, she'd see his face with that look on it. The roof would be falling on him and he'd have that look. Or the miner would be backing over him and he'd have that look. Or…

She pulled the pillowcase away so the jet lay naked on the table, but at first she looked at it out of the corner of her eye—just enough to see if there was any faces you could recognize. But the arts didn't look at all like she expected it would and she turned—surprised—and studied it.

When she'd seen it the first time, only the lone miner in front was pulled up out of the rock, "in relief" JoJo called it. All the other miners behind him was just outlined, like a sketch, still stuck down in the jet waiting for Jamey to set them free. Now, the arts was finished, but Jamey hadn't pulled them miners in the back out of the rock. They was all just images scratched into the jet behind the one miner in front.

But even though Jamey Boy hadn't carved them so's they stuck out, he hadn't left them sketches, neither. They was as detailed as photographs, though nary a face did she see on any of them! Somehow the tangled bodies flung backwards by the blast was situated so every face was covered up. All them miners, and not a one was anybody she could call by name.

She let out a breath she didn't even realize she'd been holding—felt almost giddy with relief. Oh, it was an awful sight, a terrible sight, but it was an *anonymous* sight. Them people could have been anybody, unless you could identify them by a helmet, or a shirt…

No!

Granny's hands flew to her mouth. But she didn't scream. She was too surprised, too horrified to make a sound. Her heart kicked into a dead run, threatened to tear a hole in her chest; her mouth went dry as the bottom of a flour sack. She sat frozen, her eyes fixed tight on the shirt of the big miner in front who'd been raised up out of the rock.

Wasn't no mistake; wasn't something she'd imagined. It was right there, plain's day.

She leapt to her feet and almost tripped over Crawdad. The cat had left his nap spot in front of the door to rub up against her leg, but she hadn't felt it. She couldn't feel nothing at all below her waist; it was like she was numb.

Granny'd had that feeling before.

She lurched across the room to the couch, lifted the cushions and tossed them aside; she threw pieces of newspaper into the air. Then she turned to the coffee table. There it was. She picked it up with trembling fingers and staggered back to the kitchen table with it clutched tight in her hand.

It was the same. *They* were the same. Wrapped around the arm of the miner in the front of that mural was a band with the number 27 on it *just like the one she held in her hand.*

Granny wanted to scream, but she held the wail inside. Gritting her teeth, she balled her hands into fists and forced herself to stand absolutely still.

What did it *mean?*

She knew the answer to the question before her mind asked it, of course. *Wasn't no miner wearing an armband with a 27 on it when they went down into Harlan #7 that day in 1980!*

Them armbands was just for the twentieth anniversary service. The only time a miner'd be wearing one was today.

The explosion Jamey Boy'd released from the rock wasn't the one that happened 20 years ago; the explosion in the carving was *today!*

Her thoughts started to run crazy, jump ever which way. She'd only felt this scared one other time in her life and that time 27 men had died. She'd known then, too. A few seconds before the boom and roar, she'd known.

But maybe she had more than a few seconds now! Maybe there was still...

Time!

The big miner in front was wearing a watch. She squinted at it, could just make out the detail. It said 12:18, the exact time Harlan #7 had blown the first time.

She looked at the clock. Straight up eleven-thirty. Forty-eight minutes.

She could warn them!

How?

Wouldn't no phone call work. What would she say? That she knew there was about to be an explosion because…because what? Wouldn't nobody in they right mind believe a crazy old woman talking about carvings and armbands!

What could she…?

Will!

Will could…No, he couldn't explain it, neither. Wasn't time and nobody'd believe him any more than they'd believe her. Will'd have to *go there*. He'd have to go get them miners out his own self!

Then her racing thoughts screeched to a halt.

Go into the mine? *Will?* Wasn't no way in the world Will'd go back into #7, askeered as he was of it!

She sucked in a breath that was a ragged sob.

Well, he'd *have to,* that's all. Will had been askeered to tell her the truth, too, and he done it. It was either go into that mine or…

But Will and JoJo was up the hill in Jamey's shed. They wasn't in no hurry—no telling how long they'd be. She didn't have time to wait for them to come back down to the house so she could send Will to the mine.

Granny's heart stopped hammering. It beat slow, now. Everything around her slowed down, too, like the air was thick as pancake batter. It seemed to take a long time to think the thought; it also blew through her mind like a cannonball.

Granny would have to go up to the shed and get Will!

If she didn't... if she *couldn't,* Jamey Boy and all the other miners in #7 would die.

◊ ◊ ◊ ◊ ◊

THE GOOD LADIES from the Coal Mining Museum in Benham had compounded Hob Bascomb's misery by telling him he couldn't smoke inside the tent they'd set up for the memorial ceremony. So on top of being nervous, he was about to have a nicotine fit. All he could do was fidget, stand on first one foot and then the other, jumpy as spit on a griddle.

Them ladies wasn't standing around, though. They was hustlin' to get everything finished up for the ceremony that was supposed to start right at noon.

Hob looked out over what the ladies had put together and he had to say they'd done a right nice job. The best thing they'd done, of course, was borrow the big tent from Wheeler's Funeral Home in Pineville "just in case" it rained. It had sprinkled off and on since around three o'clock this morning. Hob knew because he'd been up at three. And now it was coming down like a big dog.

The ladies had set a flatbed tobacco trailer, like a raised-up stage at the far end of the tent they'd pitched in the parking lot in front of the mine entrance. They'd put some kinda material—looked like white bedsheets—all around the bottom of the trailer. To hide the wheels, he guessed. And then they'd got red-white-and-blue streamers and draped them around the trailer on top of the sheets like popcorn strings around a Christmas tree.

There was steps—one of them porch things that fit on a trailer house—leading up to the back of the stage. Up on top, all they had was a couple flower arrangements, a black music stand and a stand-up microphone. You got up on that stage all by yourself, folks wouldn't have nothing to look at but you, like you's an ant they was trying to set afire with a magnifying glass.

Hob's stomach rolled. He'd already took enough Pepto-Bismol to turn his eyeballs pink; couldn't take no more or it'd set up in his belly like Sackcrete and he'd never have another bowel movement as long as he lived.

Out front of the trailer-stage, the ladies had made displays on bulletin boards where they'd arranged pictures of the 27 miners, with their names underneath. Blurry snapshots or school pictures, a lot of them, but you could mostly tell who the men was. They even had some of the tags the miners'd put on the board that morning. The coal company had give those to the families, but some of them got lost. Or got burned up—like Bowman's and Ricky Dan Sparrow's tags.

The most impressive thing the ladies done had been installed on the concrete at the mine entrance a week ago, but nobody except the miners had seen it yet. It was a plaque—kind of like a tombstone only made out of metal—that said something like: "Twenty-seven miners lost their lives in Harlan #7 on October 16, 1980. May they rest in peace."

A crowd had begun to gather in front of the tobacco-trailer stage—maybe 25 people. But it was early yet. The ladies had lined up preachers to open and close the doin's in prayer, of course. Then they'd got the Harlan County Judge Executive, and the county's state senator and representative to speak. You could pick them out; they was the only ones here had ties on. They'd also got the outside foreman who'd been on duty that day to talk and Beau Grissom, head of Big Sandy Mine's rescue team who'd pulled Will and Lloyd out. Them ladies being from Brenham, they probably didn't know Will was home or they'd have asked him to talk like they done Lloyd.

Yeah, Lloyd.

Hob couldn't make no sense at all of his run-in with Lloyd the morning. Justine Hinkle told Hob more than a week ago that she'd asked Lloyd to talk at the memorial and he'd turned her down. But this morning, Lloyd'd told Hob he hadn't brought his lunch to work *because he was going to speak at the ceremony.*

Soon as Hob seen Justine, he'd asked her about it again, didn't let on Lloyd had said nothing.

"Lloyd said no," she'd said. "'Bout bit my head off, too."

And speaking of biting heads off, Lloyd near decapitated Jamey Sparrow soon as he seen him. Didn't *nobody* yell at Jamey. He'd hollered at the boy that he shouldn't be here, that he'd ought to go home.

What was *that* about?

More than anything else, though, was how Lloyd had looked. Hob couldn't put his finger on what it was exactly, but something was off, bad off. Lloyd's little bitty eyes was…was the eyes of a crazy man! Hob didn't know better, he'd swear Lloyd Jacobs'd done lost his mind.

Hob lifted the sleeve on his starched and pressed dress white shirt to reveal the face of his watch. Here it was less than half an hour before this shooting match was supposed to start and he still hadn't come up with a speech. If something didn't come to him when he got up there, what he had to say wouldn't have to be shortened none to fit on his tombstone.

A squalling sound that set Hob's teeth on edge blared out from the stage. The suit-and-tie judge executive stood like a rooster in front of the microphone and a too-loud voice boomed into the fresh autumn air.

"Testing. Testing. One, two, three. Is this thing on?"

Hob glanced toward the mine entrance. He'd read somewhere that soldiers felt like he sometimes did. Called it survivor's guilt. Miners was like soldiers. They was tight because they risked their lives together every day—depended on each other. Hob had lived all these years with the memories of fellow soldiers he should have died with.

There was days he wished there was some way he could make up for that. This here was one of those days.

CHAPTER 34

G RANNY DIDN'T GIVE herself time to think about it. If she'd thought about it, she'd have froze up solid—wouldn't have been able to move nary a finger.

She turned from the table and ran fast as she could to the back door and out to the porch. The rain was coming down hard now, so heavy she could barely see the back of the garden. Thunder cracked, then rumbled like somebody was rattling a piece of tin. Fat raindrops battered the roof of the trailer, the ground and the trees, making a noise like applause.

Soon as she stepped down off the porch to the top step, two things happened. The rain hit her, and she hit a wall, real as a brick fence. So real she liked to fell back from it and landed on her backside.

Her heart rattled in her chest, raced like a coal train heading down the valley. For the first time in her life it occurred to her she was an old woman and if ever there was a time to have a heart attack, now was it. She fixed her mind on taking just one step. She put her foot out and bit down so hard in concentration a tooth caught a bit of her lip and she tasted blood in her mouth.

She made it down off the first step to the second and was instantly soaked to the skin. The sudden chill of the cold rain raised goose bumps all over her body.

Why didn't you get a raincoat, you mow-ron?

Water poured down off her head into her eyes so she could hardly see. Then she noticed a funny, mewing sound like the Jewett's cat made that time it had kittens on Granny's back porch. Where was that sound—?

Why, it was from her own throat, that's where! She was making it, whimpering, about to cry. She had to grab hold of the railing alongside the steps to keep herself from jumping right back up on the porch.

She didn't bother to try to convince herself this was all foolishness, that there was no *real* danger, nothing to be askeered of. She'd told herself a thousand times it was all in her head. Of course, it was all in her head—where else would it be? Everything was in your head; it was being in your head that made it real.

This was *real*.

She shook so hard she could barely hold onto the railing, but she put her foot out to take another step. Then pulled it back like she'd stuck it in hot oil.

Now, she was panting. Tears probably ran down her face, too; no way to tell with the rain coming down like somebody was pouring water on her out of a washtub.

She put her foot forward again. Made it down one more step and her heart pounded even faster. She was down far enough now that the wind hit her, blew the rain at her like bits of gravel and wrapped her soaked dress around her like a wet sheet.

This wasn't getting easier; it was getting harder! The farther she ventured from the top of the porch, the farther out past the circle she stepped, the bigger the terror grew.

She started to cry, sob, but the roar of rain around her ate up the sound. Then she threw her head back so the raindrops smacked her in the face and hollered out in a tear-clotted voice. "Please, God. *Help me!*"

A heartbeat later, she felt a warm presence beside her. No, it wasn't no angel, unless angels stunk like a wet dog. It was Bucket.

He just stood next to her, right up against her leg. The dog that *hated* to get wet, used to hide under the bed he was so scared of storms... just stood there.

With a trembling hand, she reached down and took hold of the dog's collar.

"Jamey Boy," she gasped. "Bucket, go find Jamey."

The dog started down the steps; Granny held on and was dragged down the steps along with him. He splashed into the puddle at the bottom and turned toward the trail around the garden. When Granny stepped into the puddle, water came up past her ankle and the mud sucked her shoe off. But Bucket kept going and so did she.

The wind lashed her with raindrops like a cat-o'-nine-tails. It was so open, empty and vacant out past the circle. Like her heart and her life and her soul felt when she come back home alone for the first time after the explosion. She had wandered from room to room like an old dog looking for its master. Then it got real bright in the house, as if all the lightbulbs was car headlights. She went into the kitchen and she could smell fried chicken. And there was Bow! He sat at the table, his napkin tucked into his shirt at the neck, a fork in his fist the way he always held it, like he planned to attack anybody tried to get to the chicken breast before he did.

In the living room—a little bitty thing with a lumpy couch— Will and Ricky Dan had the pieces of Ricky Dan's shotgun on the floor all around them. Ricky Dan was showing Will how to clean the gun. And they was laughing. Them boys was always laughing.

Why had she so dreaded coming home? Home was where she was belonged. Home was where Bowman and Ricky Dan and Will was at. And as she stood there in the middle of the living room, the pain in her heart faded and was gone. For five seconds, maybe ten, everything was right with the world. She let out a huge sigh of relief.

And then it vanished. Poof. With a little sparkle like a soap bubble, the fantasy was gone and she stood alone in the living room.

It was dim and chilled and wasn't no smell of nothing except wilted flowers. Her Bow wasn't waiting in the kitchen. Ricky Dan wasn't there on the living room floor. They never would be again. Not ever. They was dead. Gone. Vanished under Black Mountain.

She'd stood frozen as the realness sunk in; sickening pain punched her in the belly hard as it done when they said they wasn't looking for survivors no more. They wasn't even looking for bodies. They wasn't looking at all. After the mine blew that last time, it was too dangerous, wasn't right to risk a live man's life to find a dead man's body. And there wasn't no bodies to find, anyway. The rescue team from Hard Scrabble seen that much before they run back out. The fire in the coal seam at the face of Harlan #7 was burning twice as hot as a crematorium.

The raw, ragged pain had sliced her open like she'd only that minute felt the ground commence to shake under her feet. She'd felt absolutely empty; all her insides was gone. Wasn't nothing at all in her belly, under her bones, except wind blowing through with a whistling sound. And the empty had terrified her.

The empty terrified Granny now. But it wasn't the empty inside her this time; it was the empty *outside*. The big, empty world was so huge she couldn't breathe.

With every bit of will and strength she possessed, she gripped Bucket's collar and staggered along through the storm beside him, around the edge of the garden and onto the mud-slick trail leading to the shed.

She was certain that if she let go of Bucket's collar even for an instant, she would die.

◊ ◊ ◊ ◊ ◊

JAMEY SET VALVLEEN's cage down in the break next to the end of the belt line just as the steel teeth of the continuous miner dug into the coal seam at the face. Two shuttle cars waited to haul the coal from the miner to the feeder, where it would be crushed and slowly fed onto the conveyor belt for transport out through the center of the mine's three shafts. The belt line was like a rubber band stretched on rollers that ran in a continuous loop. As the belt line greaser, it was Jamey's job to keep those rollers lubricated; the friction of a belt sliding across locked-up rollers could cause a fire. He also shoveled up coal that had fallen off the belt and loaded it back on.

It wasn't the most high-risk job in the mine, but it was more dangerous than it might appear. Mashed, broken and mangled fingers were common among belt line greasers who didn't watch what they were doing around the five-pound rollers. Jamey knew better than to get distracted, but he couldn't help it today. He couldn't stop thinking about Lloyd. Why'd he act so funny? He didn't want to hear about the arts Jamey'd made with the piece of jet he'd found in Big Sandy—how come? It was like Lloyd didn't want to see him at all, like it upset him something fierce that Jamey'd showed up for work.

Jamey put down his grease gun and stepped over to ValVleen's cage. He didn't like closing her up in there like she was in jail, but without she was in a cage, they wouldn't let him bring her into the mine.

"You think Lloyd's mad at me about some'm?" he asked her, his voice loud to carry over the rumble of the miner and the clatter of the coal. She'd been particularly cheery today, sang to him and JoJo in the car all the way down the hill. "Maybe I'd ought to say sorry even if I don't know what I done. Ya think?"

She cocked her head to one side and tweeted. But the noise ate her reply. Jamey shrugged and went back to work. The noise in the mine didn't bother him. Like static on the radio, it filled up his mind so there wasn't no room for thoughts. And sometimes thinking was tiresome; it was good to let go of it for a while.

His mind was all full up with static when the shuttle driver arrived with a load of coal for the feeder. But Jamey's headlamp happened to land on the right spot and he seen it. The surprise jolted his mind awake.

Must have been some trick his eyes played on him. Headlamps did that in the dark, made you see things wasn't really there. Still...

He put his grease gun down again and moved where he could get a better look. And his eyes hadn't played no trick on him. It was there, just like he thought it was. He made his way around the feeder, turned down the last break, came up behind the shuttle car, and spoke to the driver.

"Can I be so bold as to ask where it was you got that thing?" Jamey pointed to the ribbon tied around the miner's upper arm.

"You didn't get one?" the man said. "They's givin' 'em out all over town yesterday. Folks is wearin' 'em to the memorial service today. They was a box of 'em sittin' inside the door of the lamp house this mornin'. You didn't see it?"

"No sir, I didn't for a fact. Could I see yourn?"

"Shoot, you can have the thing, Jamey." The shuttle man reached up and untied it and held it out to him. "Your daddy and granddaddy was two of the men died when she blew 20 years ago. You'd oughta be proud to wear it."

Then the man put the shuttle in reverse, backed up and turned around, and headed toward the continuous miner for another load.

Jamey sat down with a plop in the dirt and stared at the ribbon. It was black, with the number 27 printed on it in silver letters. And Jamey'd seen that ribbon before. Oh, yes sir, he had surely seen that ribbon before! In the arts he finished last night, the one he made from the piece of jet Lloyd give him. The miner in it wore an armband just like this one.

Only that didn't make no sense. That arts showed what it'd looked like that October day in 1980 when his daddy and granddaddy and all them other miners got blowed up.

He got up slowly and went back to where he'd left the shovel and grease gun, but he didn't go back to work. That wasn't like Jamey.

He didn't never sit around doing nothing. But he did today. He sat down beside ValVleen's cage, picked it up, and talked to her.

"ValVleen, I got me a confusion. How did that miner in my arts get one of these here armbands? Shuttle man said they give 'em away yesterday and this mornin'. Wasn't nobody givin' armbands away 20 years ago."

ValVleen sat in the cage looking at him. She didn't make a sound. Jamey's heart began to pound and he didn't know why. The longer he thought about the confusion, the more upset he got. It didn't make sense, but it *had* to make sense. It was important that it make sense—maybe the most important thing in his whole life.

CHAPTER 35

UCKET WAS AN old dog but he was big and still strong and the sheer force of him in motion kept Granny moving, too, long's she held onto his collar.

Her eyes was pinched so tight shut the tears she cried could barely squeeze out from under her eyelids to disappear in the rain that washed over her face. Her knuckles were white from her grip on the leather strap and her breath hitched in and out of her chest—like she was a little kid who'd been sobbing for hours.

Though she couldn't see with her eyes shut tight, she could *smell*—wet leaves and damp earth. Even through the rain. Part of her love of the garden was the smell of it, and now she fancied she could smell the tomato plants, pole beans, squash, and pumpkins on the back side of the garden that she'd seen from the back porch. She could smell watermelon, too! Couldn't be imagining that; it was so *real.* Must be one broke open somewhere near.

Granny's eyes fluttered open instinctively for an instant to see the watermelon. What she seen instead was emptiness. And herself exposed in it, outside the circle. She gasped, her legs collapsed out from under her and she went down in a heap on the muddy ground. Her knee struck a rock and pain shot up her leg—almost paralyzed her.

And she lost her grip on Bucket's collar.

She was all alone now. Out here in the open. She curled up in a tight ball in the mud, whined that kitten mewling sound as the rain battered her. She hadn't felt this lost and hopelessness since Will left. They'd had him in bed for nigh on a week and by the time they let him go, it was all over. The rescue had shut down; the mine had closed. And Aintree Hollow staggered from one minute to the next with holes all over it where men was supposed to be but wasn't no more, holes you was all the time stepping in. Them holes was black pits of despair that the women folk had to get out of, and go *around* them next time so they didn't keep falling in again and again until they was so wore out they couldn't climb back out.

Will'd come home for one night. The next morning he was gone. She didn't even hear him leave. She'd took to staying in bed late, until almost seven o'clock, because she didn't sleep but a couple hours a night, lay there buggy-eyed as hot tears run out the sides of her eyes and into her hair. She'd expected to see Will asleep on the couch, looked forward to getting his breakfast, was glad for some company in that too-quiet house where you felt like you'd ought to tiptoe because it was so still.

But when she cut on the light in the living room, she seen he wasn't on the couch. Wasn't nowhere. Hadn't took nothing with him; all his stuff was still there in the bottom two drawers of Ricky Dan's dresser. She could have believed he'd just gone out for a while, that he'd be right back. She didn't, though. Soon's she seen the quilt on that lumpy old couch and him not lying there underneath of it, she knew. Will was gone and he wouldn't come back for a long time, though she never dreamed it'd be 20 years—until later. When she figured out why he'd run, she feared he never would come home.

Something round and warm nudged her neck; something wide and warm wiped across her cheek. It was Bucket, poking her with his nose and licking her face. He barked a single "woof!" right in her ear. Granny reached up, felt around in her self-imposed blindness until she located his collar. Clasping it tight in her left hand, she used her right to push herself up out of the mud to her knees, then staggered to her feet.

Bucket stood quiet, as the rain soaked into his shaggy coat, until she had her footing, then he started out again for Jamey's shed. The old dog seemed to understand she couldn't move very fast. Usually, he'd bound up the hill, his tail wagging. Even old as he was, that dog'd run through solid rock and tree stumps to get to Jamey Boy.

Jamey!

Down there in that mine and it about to…

Oh please, Lord, not Jamey Boy.

He was just a little boy all dressed up to look like a grown-up. He'd put on them miners' clothes of a morning and she'd watch him through the window as he walked down the hill with his lunch bucket clutched up tight in his arms like he was askeered somebody'd steal it. She couldn't lose him, *too.*

But even if she got to the shed in time, would Will really go into #7 to get him?

Granny's foot caught on a piece of wet tree trunk and she went down again on one knee. She wasn't sure how much farther she could go. Then she heard a scream. JoJo! Her eyes flew open and there was the shed, right in front of her. Bucket had brought her the whole way.

Maybe there was still time! Maybe his arts was a warning to keep Jamey Boy safe. Maybe…

"Will!" she cried, loud as she could holler. "You got to come quick!

◊ ◊ ◊ ◊ ◊

WILL GROANED, PUT his hand up over his ear and reflexively stepped back from JoJo. The explosion in #7 hadn't ruptured his eardrum like it had Lloyd's, but it had done some damage. Over time, it healed, but like duct tape on a hole in a snare drum, the scar tissue kept his eardrum from vibrating properly. He could hear—well enough to get into the Navy—but sudden loud noises, particularly high-pitched ones close to his head, caused excruciating pain.

JoJo neither noticed nor cared that her wail had hurt Will's ear. Her attention was riveted to the piece of jet on the table. Her eyes were open so wide they looked like whitewalls around a hubcap and the look on her face…it was a mixture of surprise, fascination and horror. In the end, horror won out.

Will hadn't been examining the mural as carefully as JoJo had. He still couldn't look at it straight up. He'd had a hard time even glancing at it long enough to see what Granny'd seen, what Jamey'd "seen" with his strange, timeless vision.

But Will did look at the rock after JoJo screamed, his eyes washed over the scene Jamey had frozen in time and he could see nothing in it that would elicit that kind of response.

"What…?"

"Right there—*there!*"

JoJo didn't point to the portion of the sculpture where the raised, relief characters were frozen. The relief was off center, with about 5 inches of border around it on the left and 10 on the right. The area outside what Jamey had carved in relief had been carved as well, an intricate web of lines that showed the strata of coal seams in the rock pillar behind the three men gathered around a helmet upside down in the dirt.

JoJo reached out and touched the coal wall that formed the background of the scene. Her finger shook.

"Don't you see it?"

Will saw nothing.

He hated those optical illusion pictures that showed two different images. One was obvious. But to see the second, you had to work at it. He'd only once been able to see any other image in a picture, and had it not been for that time, he would have contended the people who saw two images either needed glasses or long-term psychiatric care.

"I don't see—"

"The lines. Will, look at the *lines!*"

JoJo was near hysteria. Whatever she saw in the rock, or thought she saw there, had so upset her he could feel her whole body tremble beside him. Will studied the crosshatch of lines Jamey had painstakingly etched to form the texture of the coal seam on the pillar. But he couldn't see anything. If there was an image of some kind in there, he couldn't find it.

He bent down closer, then slowly pulled back, farther and farther away, tried to keep his eyes unfocused. The flickering light played with his vision; an image formed in the lines on the rock. But it was gone again before he could make out what it was. Before he could move back into the position where he'd seen it, he heard a voice right outside the shed. Someone called his name.

Granny!

◊ ◊ ◊ ◊ ◊

GRANNY WAS WET and chilled to the bone, shivering, too, but not from the cold *outside*. There was a deeper cold *inside,* spreading out from her belly into the rest of her body, down her legs to her feet, out her arms to her hands, up her chest to her head. If the cold terror got all the way to her fingers, her toes and the top of her head, she would die.

She held onto Bucket's collar and shouted above the wind and rain, called out for Will, hollered loud as she could, which might have been nary a whisper in the real world. She was past being able to tell such things.

It seemed to take a long time for everything to happen, like it was half an hour between one eye blink and the next as if the terror inside her had chilled time so it couldn't move proper, made the passage of seconds slower than a herd of turtles.

The door to the shed suddenly burst open. Will and JoJo stood there, shocked, then Will jumped out into the rain and wrapped his arms around her.

"What are you doing here?"

She swayed; her knees were about to collapse like a folding chair and dump her on her backside into the mud.

"Is some'm wrong, Granny? Why…?" JoJo asked from the doorway.

Will didn't wait for Granny to answer. He swept her off her feet like she didn't weigh nothing at all, turned back to the shed, set her just inside the door and stepped in after her. Then the three of them stood together in the flickering lantern light of Jamey's shed while Granny gathered her wits about her to speak.

"You got to go!" she gasped at Will.

"Go where, Gran—?"

"To the mine! You got to warn 'em." She dragged in a great lungful of air. "You gotta tell 'em to run, to get out of there!"

She looked up in terror into his eyes. "Oh, Will! She's gonna blow! Number seven's gonna 'xplode."

"Explode? How do you—?"

"Jamey's arts you brung down a little while ago. The one he made outta the jet Lloyd give him."

"Was there faces in it?" JoJo asked. "You told Jamey to finish it anyway, even if Granddaddy's and Daddy's faces was there—'member?"

"'Course I 'member," Granny snapped. "But we was wrong. You got to listen to me. Jamey's arts wasn't the 'xplosion happened 20 years ago. It was a 'xplosion *today*."

She turned back to Will and clutched his arm so tight she felt her fingernails dig into his skin like the talons of an eagle.

"Them *armbands!* The ones with 27 on 'em they's handin' out yesterday and today. They's one of them armbands on a miner in Jamey's arts! That 'xplosion's happenin' *today!*"

Granny watched the color drain out of Will's face as understanding dawned.

Then he and JoJo spoke at the same time, both their voices anguished.

"Jamey!"

Granny let go of Will's arm and took his hand. She looked up into his eyes and spoke in a voice barely loud enough to be heard over the rain on the roof.

"One of them miners gettin' blowed up was wearin' a watch that said 12:18. There's still *time.* Will, you got to go down there and get Jamey and them other miners out."

He froze, still as one of Jamey's statues. Didn't even breathe. But Granny could see emotions fighting on his face, all tangled up like a pair of JoJo's pantyhose in the dryer. He seemed to stay frozen for the longest time, but it probably wasn't more than a few seconds.

Then he turned to JoJo. "Your car keys... I need your car!"

"They's in the ignition."

Without another word, Will turned and bolted out the door of the shed and down the hill in the pouring rain, his long legs pumping like they done when he and Lloyd and the neighbor boys played football out in that field at the top of the hollow.

In the silence Will left behind him, Granny heard JoJo whimper.

"It's all right, child," she said, reached out a wet, trembling hand to stroke the girl's fine blond hair. "Will's gonna warn 'em. He's gonna get them out 'fore..."

But Granny read in the fear on JoJo's face the thoughts she'd refused to listen to, the voice whispering in her ear that she ignored as she held onto Bucket's collar and climbed the hill. When Jamey carved something, *it always happened just like he carved it.* Every time. Was it possible to change what the good Lord had put in that rock for Jamey to dig out?

"You got to get back to the house and into some dry clothes," JoJo said. She picked up Will's rain jacket off the hook and draped it around Granny's shoulders. "This ain't much, but you don't need to get no wetter than—"

"Ain't no such thing as wet-*er*, child," Granny said, still trembling all over. "Either you's wet or you ain't. I'm wet. Let's git."

She stepped out the door into the downpour with JoJo right behind her. Instantly drenched, the girl took Granny's arm to steady her and they made their way through the mud and puddles down the hill.

The soggy hound dog followed along behind, stopping every now and then to look back at the shed wistfully.

CHAPTER 36

WILL SPRINTED—FLEW down the hill as fast as his legs would carry him. It felt more like swimming than running, though; how could there be any air to breathe in the gush of water from the sky?

Shrapnel sharp fragments of thoughts rode the breaths that exploded out of his straining lungs.

Armbands.

Today! 12:18.

Jamey!

He rounded the corner of Granny's trailer and headed toward JoJo's car. But the water that ran in rivers down his face blinded him and he didn't see the 6-inch picket garden fence until it was too late. It grabbed his ankle and his momentum carried him forward. Now, he really was flying through the air, diving through the water in it. He landed belly-first in a puddle, surfed through the mud and slid into the gravel beyond it. The sharp little rocks shredded the skin on the palms of his hands. He had already scrambled to his feet before he came to a complete stop, then slipped down on one knee, leapt back up, and finally staggered the final few steps to JoJo's car.

He yanked on the driver's door handle. The door was locked.

◊ ◊ ◊ ◊ ◊

Jamey was sitting with ValVleen, trying to puzzle things out when the rumble of the continuous miner ground to a halt. He looked down at the watch JoJo'd give him for Christmas. It was a Mickey Mouse watch. Had an alarm on it you could set and when it come up that time, the watch would play, "M-I-C, K-E-Y, M-O-U-S-E." When both hands on the watch pointed straight up, it was noon, time for lunch. The long one wasn't there yet. Miner man had stopped early today.

Jamey picked up ValVleen's cage and made his way down the belt line shaft back toward the face where he'd left his lunch bucket. Granny'd packed him a peanut-butter-and-jelly sandwich, made the special way she done that didn't have no crusts on the bread—Jamey didn't like crusts—and had butter underneath the jelly. Grape jelly—that was his favorite.

Usually his mouth would start to water just thinking about that sandwich. And an apple, too, if there was any in the house. A banana, for sure. He loved bananas and Granny always put one in his bucket even if sometimes JoJo had to go down to the Jiffy to get it for him.

But his mouth didn't water today. He wasn't hungry. The onliest thing in his belly right now was scared and wondering. He couldn't understand the confusion of the arts, and not being able to puzzle it out spooked him bad. Wasn't nobody to ask about it neither, not Granny or JoJo—or Will. Jamey liked Will! Having him around was almost like having a daddy.

The other miners had already started to dig into their lunch buckets by the time Jamey got to them. They were arguing over football and whether the University of Kentucky had a chance to win the game Saturday with the University of Louisville. It was the biggest rivalry in the state and the only thing anybody wanted to talk about.

Jamey didn't join in. Even if he'd understood football—which he didn't—even if he'd knowed what the score would be like in that basketball arts, he wouldn't a-said nothing. The confusion had set Jamey's mind on a merry-go-round like the one in the playground at the elementary school and his thinking was going around and around in circles. Understanding was right there, but soon's he concentrated hard, it was gone and he was still spinning. The answer was a butterfly and every time it lit, he'd try to grab it and it'd flutter away.

His fingers danced furiously in his lap and he didn't pay no attention to Lloyd when he started talking to the other miners.

The explosion that happened in the mine 20 years ago was down in that piece of jet and he had set it free. But that miner'd had a armband on—Jamey seen it big as life. And them armbands wasn't give out until yesterday.

How could there be a armband in his explosion arts?

His fingers twined and untwined, moving faster and faster as he focused hard as he could.

Suddenly, Jamey gave a little squeak of a cry. Nobody noticed because Lloyd was leaving. Jamey's bright green eyes grew wide. He had caught the butterfly.

That arts... it ain't 'bout no 'xplosion 20 years ago. It's about a 'xplosion today! That's why the miner's got on a armband. It's today!

◊ ◊ ◊ ◊ ◊

No, JoJo's CAR wasn't locked. The driver's side door was just hard to open. Will had had trouble with it when he borrowed the car to go see Lloyd. He yanked on the door handle again but it was too wet for him to get a good grip.

Cupping his hand in an umbrella over his watch, he checked the time. Straight up noon. There was no time for this!

He raced around to the other side of the car and that door came open so abruptly he fell backward into a puddle. Scrambling to his feet, he dived into the front seat and slammed the door behind him, then forced himself to calm down enough not to pump the gas pedal and flood the engine when he turned on the ignition.

It caught on the second attempt and he roared away, fishtailing in the little bit of gravel between the house and the pavement.

He fumbled around, tried one knob and then another until the windshield wipers finally turned on. But with rain pouring down like the sky was an open fire hydrant, the wipers barely cleared a space before it was covered up again. Will hunkered down low and peered through the part of the windshield that was the clearest.

His range of sight extended only a few feet in front of the car, but he didn't slow down, just roared through the waterfall, a missile fired down the rain-slathered street. If a car pulled out of one of the side streets in front of him, Will would hydroplane on the wet asphalt and plow right into it.

He was betting his life that he was the only person in Aintree Hollow stupid enough to drive in such a deluge.

As he swerved around parked cars and squinted at a scene that appeared and disappeared in rhythm with the wiper swipes across the glass, the fragmented thoughts of the dash down the hill were replaced by an amazing clarity. His thinking was reasoned and methodical.

What exactly did he plan to do once he got to the mine? Run up to the outside foreman and say, "We gotta get the men out of there, #7's gonna blow again today"?

Right. And the foreman would say, "And exactly how do you know that, Mr. Gribbins, sir?"

No, there was only one way to get Jamey and the other miners out. Will would have to go in there himself and say…well, *something*. Or do something. He'd figure that out once he got inside the mine.

Inside the mine.

A sense of horror passed slowly down through his body the way cold water sinks because it's heavier.

Inside Harlan #7.

He'd *sworn*. If God got him out of that mine alive he'd *never...*

Who was he kidding? There was no way on earth he'd be able to force his unwilling feet to carry him underground.

Jamey.

Could he do it for Jamey?

◊ ◊ ◊ ◊ ◊

LLOYD LOOKED AT his watch. Straight up noon. Time to go. He'd been seated on the edge of the group of miners eating lunch and arguing about football. Didn't say nothing. Just listened.

He had that same peculiar sense of brightness that he'd had this morning, like all the lights were headlights with circles around them. But this time, it was more than that. There was light coming off the miners themselves that was so brilliant he squinted and had to look away.

Was that light the glow of life, maybe? Them men was shining with every breath they took in. An ordinary moment, and their lives produced a light bright as the detergent blue of those funny lamps in the parking lot at Walmart in Pineville.

Warmth, too. Lloyd could feel heat radiating out from the knot of men. In the mine's 58 degrees, it felt like standing next to a wood stove.

And Lloyd Jacobs was about to put it all out, make each of those warm, bright beings cold corpses. Cold and dark. But cold was better than warm. Warm never lasted. Cold was permanent, like the surface of the moon. Cold was the natural state of eternity. Wouldn't need no air conditioners in heaven. Wouldn't get none in hell.

Lloyd pushed his mind away from that thought and from Jamey, too. The boy wasn't eating, hadn't even opened his lunch bucket and

Lloyd knew Granny'd made something good for him. Fruit and sometimes a cookie or a brownie. She always done that for Bowman and Ricky Dan and Will, and for him, too, when he was around.

Instead of eating, the boy sat there thinking. Lloyd could tell by his dancing fingers that Jamey was trying to figure something out or remember something important. And his heart went out to the boy. So innocent. He didn't deserve to die with the others; he was Ricky Dan's *son*. Seeing's how Lloyd had killed Jamey's father, didn't he owe Ricky Dan a life? Jamey's life?

For a moment, he seriously considered sparing Jamey. Alls he'd have to do was think of some excuse to send him back outside, away from the face and the explosion that was only minutes away. Tell him to go fetch something. Or give him something to take to the outside foreman. Jamey'd never hurt a fly, was a gentle, kind, *good* soul. He didn't deserve to…

No, and neither did the rest of them. Lloyd hadn't deserved what happened to him his whole childhood, neither. You played the cards you was dealt. That's all you could do.

He couldn't rescue Jamey. The others might notice, get suspicious. It was luck of the draw he come to work today. He shouldn't have been here but now that he was, there was nothing Lloyd could do to make it right.

Lloyd got to his feet and dusted his hands off on his pants.

"Got to go, boys," he said, interrupting an impassioned sermon by the scoop driver about the lineage of the University of Louisville's quarterback. "They need me out front for the ceremony."

Lloyd knew the other miners had been thinking about the ceremony, or more accurately what the ceremony represented. He suspected the argument about football was nothing more than whistling in a graveyard, a way to get them past the event so they wouldn't have to deal with the emotions attached to it. When it was announced there'd be a memorial service, the miners had decided to conduct their own, to pause at 12:18 for a minute of silence in memory of the men who'd been killed. Most every man seated here had lost somebody that day—a father, brother, uncle or cousin. Aintree Hollow was all family.

Digging coal in Harlan # 7 was a little like working in a haunted house, not that any of the miners would lay claim to seeing ghosts in the shadows. But it was impossible to be in the place where so many had died and not feel their presence in some way. It was equally impossible not to be scared, given that the dead men had been killed doing the same job you were doing. Miners wouldn't own up to nothing like that, least not while they was in a mine. But they talked about it to their wives. And when they got drunk.

"You got a speech all planned out, Lloyd?" asked the jovial shuttle car driver, but there was no cheer in his voice. "Seems to me like it'd be hard to come up with the proper words for some'm like that."

That was precisely the reason—well, one of the reasons—Lloyd had refused when he'd been asked to speak. He didn't have nothing to say and if he'd tried to get all pious-like, the audience would have made him for the phony he was.

"Yeah, got it memorized," he tapped his temple. "It's all up here."

"Well don't let it get lonesome all by itself up there," said the loud-mouthed miner man.

Lloyd ignored him.

"Be back in an hour or so. Might take a little longer." He looked at the shuttle driver. "And trust me, I would rather be right here cuttin' up with you guys than have to go do what I got to do. I hate it, I really do. But I ain't got no choice. I'm…sorry."

He could tell they thought that was an odd thing to say. But they'd figure he was talking about leaving the face. The boss wasn't never supposed to leave his section. Nothing short of a once-in-twenty-years memorial service was reason enough to break that rule.

Lloyd looked at Jamey one last time before he turned and plunged into the darkness. And he saw recognition wash over the boy's face, watched his fingers grow still in his lap. Whatever he'd been trying to figure out, he'd come up with the answer.

◊ ◊ ◊ ◊ ◊

JAMEY SAT VERY still. His eyes were huge. Understanding had taken his breath away.

What should he do?

Whatever it was, he'd better do it quick. The arts said the mine would blow up *today!* And the watch on that miner, it'd said 12:18. Jamey's Mickey Mouse watch was sometimes slow and sometimes fast but it was *at least* noon now. And it took about half an hour—close to that, Jamey'd never timed it—to get from the mouth of the mine to the face in a mantrip. It'd take longer to run all the way back out on foot.

He let out a little whimper of fear. Not of what the arts had shown. Fear that he wouldn't be able to figure out what to do about it.

He looked pleadingly at the little yellow bird in the cage. ValVleen looked back at him as if she knew what he should do and would tell him, but it wouldn't do no good because he wouldn't understand her.

He had to figure this out on his own. Even if his uptake wasn't fast as some people's, he had to come up with a answer, it had to be the right answer and he had to come up with it now!

Jamey's hands began to do their little dance in his lap again. But they didn't have to dance long. The answer to the what-should-he-do? question came quickly and clearly.

He had to warn the other miners. He had to get everybody out of the mine *right now!*

A smile of satisfaction started and then died on his face.

How could he do that?

His fingers twined more, wiggled frantically.

Well, he'd have to tell them the mine was going to blow up.

No, he couldn't do that. They wouldn't believe him.

How could he get them out of the mine without telling them it was going to blow up?

He thought hard as he could. Sweat popped out on his forehead and upper lip. Tears of strained concentration leaked out of his eyes and made clean streaks in the coal-dust smudges on his face. His fingers twirled around and around each other.

Think, Jamey! *Think!*

Then it came to him. The answer dropped into his head as if someone had whispered it into his ear.

There was a way to get the other miners out without explaining how he knew the mine was going to blow up.

Only one way.

And once that way became clear to Jamey, his heart broke right in two in his chest.

◊ ◊ ◊ ◊ ◊

WAVES OF THUNDER crashed against the mountainsides like surf against the rocks, then rumbled up the hollow with a roar so like an explosion Will sucked in a ragged gasp. Before the rumble had rolled all the way to the top, a sharp, distinct clap went off with a deafening *crack*, and a white spear of lightning stabbed down out of the sky into the woods off to Will's left.

But even the bright bolt of lightning couldn't erase the image that filled the screen of Will's mind. The image had appeared there as soon as Granny'd said Jamey's arts had shown a miner wearing an armband. It was so vivid it filled his whole mind, almost pushed the task of keeping the car on the road out of his consciousness.

It was the image of the scoreboard in Rupp Arena.

Harlan County 68; Marion County 64.

The score in the relief sculpture Jamey had created years ago of the Harlan County High School boy's basketball team with their state championship trophy. The sculpture that showed the *score* of the game three days before it was played.

The score was correct; the numbers, accurate. Jamey had released them from the rock where they'd been "engraved in granite" so to speak. At least engraved in jet.

What he'd carved came to pass, exactly as his arts had shown it.

So if Jamey had sculpted an explosion in Harlan #7 today, wasn't that event as "engraved in granite" as the basketball game? As immutable as the score?

As Will careened around a pickup truck stopped on the roadside to wait out the storm, his thoughts were unhurried. Almost pedantic.

He would have to go into Harlan #7 himself to warn the miners of the imminent explosion, but in his heart of hearts he didn't believe that a warning would do any good. The explosion was a done deal. As soon as Jamey'd released it from the rock, it was…destined to be.

Will didn't understand that. He couldn't have explained it. But he did believe it. According to Granny and JoJo, Jamey had never carved a future event that didn't happen.

So if Will went into that mine to warn the miners, he would die in there with them. He would become one of the figures in Jamey's arts, blown backward by the force of a massive explosion.

His was a suicide mission. Which, of course, begged the question—was he prepared to go into Harlan #7 knowing he'd never come back out?

CHAPTER 37

ABOUT 35 FEET from where Lloyd crouched on his heels was a bright yellow curtain over a break along the rail line. Lloyd got to his feet and made his way to it, grabbed the right side and in one great yank, pulled it free from the roof bolt plate it was attached to, sending one of the roof tacks pinging off the side of the nearby coal pillar. He yanked again and again until the curtain was a pile of yellow plastic at his feet. He'd already removed the curtains over the previous three breaks up the line.

Now, all he had to do was wait. Just like water, moving air took the path of least resistance. It would turn after the last curtain it came to and move in the shortest unblocked path out toward the fan sucking it through. Without curtains to route air to the face, the clean air would never get that far and gas would quickly begin to accumulate there.

Lloyd had a methane detector as well as a possum light. The methane detector was a hand-held gauge that read out the percentage of air-borne methane. Right now, the possum light was burning low. Lloyd pushed the button on the methane detector; it read 1 percent. But it would only take a few minutes with no ventilation for the readings on both meters to change dramatically.

He continued along the break past the belt line shaft to the bad air shaft at the far end. He went around to the back side of a coal pillar, sat down and leaned against it. Reaching into his shirt pocket, he removed a pack of Marlboro's and a butane lighter and set both down in the dirt beside him. Then Lloyd barked out a small laugh. Ever since the first day he went underground years ago, he had longed to smoke in the mine. It was hard on a smoker to go down for a shift and not have a single cigarette for 8, sometimes 10 hours—hard to wait until you was back outside to light up.

Though he was certain he'd never even get the cigarette lit, let alone take a drag off it, Lloyd intended to try.

◊ ◊ ◊ ◊ ◊

JAMEY WAS CERTAIN he had never felt and would never again feel any pain hurt bad as this. It felt like somebody'd took a stake and drove it right into his belly, pounded it *bam, bam, bam* with a sledgehammer.

No! I can't do that!

But even as he thought the words he knew he had to.

The solution had dropped into his head so clear he couldn't argue that it was right, that it was the onliest way in the world to get the miners out of the mine before the explosion.

It was like a voice had spoke it into his head. But the voice hadn't used words, least Jamey didn't hear words the way you do when somebody leans over and tells you something. It was just a voice and the thought. Not a mean, hateful voice, neither. A sad voice. A voice it didn't seem like wanted to say it, but had to say it anyway.

Wasn't but one way to make them miners run out of that mine, the voice had said: Jamey had to kill ValVleen.

The continuous miner would shut off automatically if the level of methane got higher than 2 percent, but it wasn't running right now and the miner man wouldn't try to crank it up again until after lunch. By then there'd be no machine to crank and no miner to crank it.

305

ValVleen was a mine canary—the best methane gauge there was! Old timers still said one bird was worth half a dozen pieces of fancy equipment. A dead mine canary would cause its own explosion, scare the bejeebers out of them miners. Wouldn't nothing convince them quicker that they'd ought to run for they lives.

And they'd already noticed the air was bad.

"Dang, it's dusty in here," the miner man said. "Can't hardly get my breath." He turned to the pinner, an old fellow with a white beard that turned black in the mine. "You need to call and tell 'em we got bad air."

There was a phone box on the wall by the power station four hundred feet back from the face that you could holler into—"outside, outside, outside!"—and soon's the outside foreman heard you, he'd answer.

The driver of the continuous miner was a big fellow. Too big to be working in a coal mine, the others always said when he wasn't around. Must have been 6-feet-4 or thereabout; leaning over was powerful hard on him. And he never let nobody forget that for a minute! He was all the time complaining about how his legs went to sleep on him, all cramped up like they was in that little operator's cage on the side of the machine. Never shut up about it from the minute he went to work until they rode out together on the mantrip when the shift was over. Wouldn't none of the other miners listen to his complaint about bad air because he was all the time moaning about something. Fact was, him saying they'd ought to call up about the air was the surest way in the world to make sure nobody did.

Seemed like Jamey was hemmed in, like everything was forcing him to do what he couldn't bear to do.

The others was seated on a piece of old curtain, scratchy burlap, had they lunch boxes open and was eating sandwiches. Jamey was seated off by himself in the dirt, away from the others. He done that sometimes, got off by himself and they didn't think nothing of it. They sure didn't notice today because soon's Lloyd left, they took up right where they'd left off arguing about the game—and the quarterback for the University of Kentucky's football team.

"Jared Lorenzen's all icin' and no cake," said the shuttle car driver who'd give Jamey the armband that had set him to wondering. "Startin' quarterback as a freshman…shoot, he's just a kid, couldn't find his boxer shorts usin' both hands and a flashlight."

"U of L's fool quarterback got sacked twict last week," said the pinner. "Coach Mumme knows how to protect Lorenzen so's he can take his time findin' a receiver."

The argument heated up as Jamey's heart stampeded in his chest. It whacked away so fast he was askeered he was gonna puke. He wanted to cry. He wanted to scream. He wanted to grab hold of ValVleen's cage and not let nobody get near her ever. Couldn't bear the thought of anybody hurting her, least of all his own self!

I ain't gonna do it!

But I got to!

No!

The voice spoke again in his head without using words.

You can't save ValVleen, Jamey. She's going to die either way. The explosion will kill her if you don't. What you have to decide is if you're willing to die with her.

Jamey started to interrupt the voice, say yes, he was sure enough willing to die with ValVleen! But the voice wasn't finished.

…and if you're willing to let all these other men die, too.

The voice got real sad again. Sad but stern, too.

Jamey, you have to decide if you're brave enough to save these miners. And you have to decide *right now.*

No, I ain't! I ain't brave enough…

Will had said he was brave. Brave like his daddy. And Jamey *did* have the courage to give his own life for the other miners if he had to. But ValVleen's life? That was harder.

You don't get to pick your choices, Granny always said. You just got to make them best as you can.

Giving his own life wasn't one of his choices. His choice was kill ValVleen or let all these men die. And he couldn't do that. She was only a bird, after all. His bestest friend in all the world, but a bird. An old bird, too, who'd die soon her own self no matter how hard he tried to save her.

Least this way she could give her life for something that mattered.

Jamey picked up the birdcage and turned away so the other miners couldn't see. He cried silently, huge gulping sobs that didn't make a sound. He opened the door, put his hand inside and ValVleen hopped onto his open palm. Then he lifted her right up close to his face.

And she reached out and give him a peck on the lip! A *kiss*. She'd always give you a kiss if you smooched at her, but never before in all her life had she kissed him all on her own.

Kissed him goodbye.

"I love you, ValVleen," he whispered.

Jamey could see in her eyes she understood. She knew he had to do this. She cocked her head to one side and chirped, a sweet mix of chirr, chirp, chirp, cheep-cheep-cheep, and a string of beautiful warbles.

And Jamey *understood* her! All these years, he'd listened so careful, tried so hard to understand what she was saying, and he finally did!

"This is a fine way for a mine canary to die," ValVleen told him sweetly. "Doin' her job. Savin' miners' lives.

Jamey put his finger and thumb around her tiny neck and squeezed gently. She didn't flutter around, try to get away or nothing. Just held real still, never made another sound.

◊ ◊ ◊ ◊ ◊

THE BLANKET OF rain erased the landscape, the houses, even the parked cars along the street. But that was not a totally foreign sensation for Will. He had been on a destroyer once in a driving storm on the North Atlantic. Standing on the deck as the ship pitched up over 30-foot waves and crashed down into the troughs behind them, he couldn't see more than a few feet beyond the rail he clutched in terror. Then he felt a hand on his arm that yanked him free from the rail and the next thing he knew the boatswain's mate had thrown him through a hatch and secured the door behind them.

The instant change was startling, from wind and rain to still and dry. And he felt that same sensation now. Not only inside the car as the storm howled outside it, but inside his head and heart as the storm of circumstance raged all around him.

Ragged panic had swelled huge in his chest when he'd first been plucked off the bench and shoved out onto the court to play. Even now, 15 minutes before the final buzzer, Harlan #7 was ahead 27 to nothing. Will knew he had absolutely no chance to win. But he wasn't afraid anymore. When he came here he knew that if he didn't make amends, he'd die. So if he had to die in order to make amends… well, that was better than letting booze kill him.

Once he'd made peace with what he had to do, Will was calmed and strengthened by his determination. He would go into that mine after Jamey with the full understanding that he couldn't save him. He owed Ricky Dan that. He owed fate or God or the mine a life. He'd been paying interest on that debt for 20 years. Today, he'd pay off the note.

Will only realized he was on the Turkey Neck Creek Bridge when he heard the tires on the metal surface—several seconds before he could make out the railing through the rain. But by the time he'd crossed the length of it, the rain had let up enough for him to see a few feet out into the road beyond it. The rain continued to let up as the brunt of the fierce storm passed over the mountain behind him. Will could see a car length in front of him. Then a couple. By the time he came to the turn-off to Harlan #7, he could make out the entrance of the mine through the rain, and the white tent that sat next to it.

Will skidded to a stop and yanked upward on the door handle, but the door remained fast until he slammed his shoulder into it.

The flap on the white tent was open, and he caught a glimpse of the people gathered inside as he raced past it to the lamp house. He jerked the door open and collided head-on with the man on the other side coming out. The force of Will's body slam knocked the man backward and he crashed into a pile of old helmets, chargers, and broken headlamps. The cigarette he'd been smoking sailed through the air like a meteor.

The man was Hob Bascomb.

"What the—?"

Will ignored him, grabbed a headlamp and a battery pack, then looked around frantically. He spotted a bunged-up old helmet Hob had knocked to the floor. It was red. Well, that's what Will was, a red hat. He picked it up and turned to run.

Hob had staggered to his feet and stood between Will and the door.

"Will, what in the world—?"

"Get outta my way, Hob."

"But—"

"I gotta get Jamey!" Will knew he must look and sound like a madman.

"What for? Some'm wrong at home? Is Granny or JoJo—?"

"Move!"

Without waiting for him to respond, Will shoved Hob aside and bolted out the door into what was now a heavy drizzle. He paid no attention to Hob's cries.

"We can call the face, Will! Get 'em to send him…"

Will didn't bother to put the headlamp on the helmet, just put the helmet on his head and fastened the battery pack to his belt as he ran.

He thought he'd already fought all the emotional battles in the car, but he was wrong. As he ran toward the mine entrance—a black hole like the gaping mouth of some great, toothless monster—Will couldn't catch his breath. He began to gasp. The open maw loomed closer and bigger with each running step; it waited there to swallow him whole, to gulp him down into forever darkness and crush the life out of him.

I can't do this!

Will stopped running, planted his feet to skid to a stop.

Only he didn't.

The déjà vu was so profound it would have knocked the breath out of him if he weren't already unable to breathe. Will's mind thought one thing; his body did another. Just like that day on the train trestle with the black locomotive bearing down on him in a roar of shrieking metal. He'd wanted to run. He'd intended to run. But he'd laid down between the rails instead.

It was the opposite now. He wanted to *stop* running. He intended to stop. But his legs continued to carry him forward into the hole in the mountainside. All he could do was hold the headlamp out in front of him to light up the rail line he would follow to the face. And to Jamey.

GRANNY STOOD ON her front porch shivering, from cold or scared one, she didn't know which. JoJo'd tried to get her to stay in the house and dry off, of course, and when she wouldn't, the child wrapped her up where she stood, went and got the old chenille bedspread off Jamey Boy's...

Jamey Boy!

Only one other time in her life Granny'd ever been too scared to pray, and memories of that day began to bark around her heels like angry dogs.

She shooed them away best as she could, but she didn't have the strength she once had. It took a powerful effort not to fall into one of them black pits was all over the hollow after #7 blew, one so deep you couldn't never crawl back out again. Effort like that plumb wore a body out, and for the first time in her life, Granny had a sense that she was just flat running out of gas.

Everybody come to the end of it eventually. What was it Bowman used say? "God pours life into death and death into life 'thout never spillin' a drop." Was that it? Was her time come? Is that what happened to a body, they strength run out and they just stopped breathing?

If that was it, she was ready as she'd ever be. It was a whole lot better than dying of heartbreak, and she was askeered that was exactly what she was fixing to do.

Jamey and Will. Would the good Lord really take them both like this? Snatch them away so's there was only her and JoJo and a empty house where voices echoed in the dark of night. Dead-people voices.

"Granny, yore shakin' so! You need to sit yourself down."

The love and fear Granny heard in JoJo's voice was so tender Granny liked to started crying her own self. Couldn't do that, though. If she ever started, she might never stop.

"I'll pull the rocker right up here to the edge of the steps so's you can see..." Granny knew JoJo'd caught herself before she said *the explosion,* but that's what she meant.

"Leave me be, child."

Granny never took her eyes for a second away from the black hole in the base of the mountain with a white tent snuggled up next to it. The rain had let up to a drip and a plop here and there. It'd been raining so hard as she was trying to get back to the house from Jamey's shed she couldn't see far as she could reach out her

312

hands. When she finally got inside and shut the back door, she leaned against it and hugged herself, relief washing over her in a such a warm flood it made her need to go to the bathroom.

Didn't last but a second or two, though, before it all come crashing down on her again and she run out to the front porch to search through the pouring rain with eyes couldn't see good as they once could. Looking for smoke. No, that'd come after. When it was too late.

The pain of them two words liked to stopped her heart. *Too late.*

She backed up from them words like they's rattlesnakes' fangs dripping deadly poison. But truth was, she was already bit. They all was. Soon's Jamey Boy started carving his arts, it was already too late. Jamey Boy's arts didn't never lie.

◊ ◊ ◊ ◊ ◊

Jamey held ValVleen's limp body in the palm of his hand; her head dangled the way JoJo's Barbie's head done after he accidentally broke it. His whole face was slathered in tears, like somebody'd dumped a bucket of water over his head, and he trembled so violently he could barely hold onto the tiny yellow bird. Warm, but still. So very still. And at that moment, James Bowman Sparrow didn't want nothing in the world but to die right there his own self.

Wasn't no experience in his whole life prepared him for the hurt in his chest right now. Then it occurred to him that if life wasn't done with him yet, he wouldn't likely get out of it without something else that hurt like this. So maybe he'd ought to have sat down with ValVleen and let this here be the end of it for both of them at the same time.

But he couldn't do that to the other miners.

He wiped his face on the back of his shirt sleeve. All them thoughts seemed like they took a long time to think, but he knew only seconds had passed since he…

And he had to *hurry!* The whole lot of them only had minutes. He cast one more loving glance at the dead bird in his hand. ValVleen had give her life; he had to make it count!

Jamey took a deep, shaky breath and started to holler.

"ValVleen! Wake up, ValVleen!"

The pinner, who was almost shouting his own self about the UK quarterback, shut up in mid-yell and all the miners turned to look at Jamey. He held the bird's dead body out for them to see.

"ValVleen's dead!" he cried. "Lookit! Some'm killed ValVleen."

There was a heartbeat of stunned silence. Jamey watched fear spread from one face to the next like a fire catching the twigs and bark under the big limbs when Lloyd come to roast hot dogs.

"That there's a *mine canary!*" the big miner man said, his voice all airy like he couldn't quite catch his breath. "A *dead* mine canary."

The others all started to talk at once.

"Now, wait a minute—"

"Don't get all—"

"You don't know what killed—"

"Where's the possum light?" asked the pinner man.

"Lloyd took it with him when he went out to talk at that memorial ceremony," the shuttle driver said.

The words shocked them all into silence. *Memorial ceremony.* For 27 *dead* miners. Killed here, in this mine. In an explosion.

◊ ◊ ◊ ◊ ◊

THERE WAS A mantrip parked inside the entrance out of the rain. A mechanic was down on his knees beside it with the lid up working on something—had tools spread out on the ground all around him.

Will momentarily considered asking for—or commandeering— the machine to ride down the rail line to the face. But he quickly discarded the idea. It didn't appear to be operational and even if it was, the guy working on it didn't look like somebody Will could reasonably expect to win a fistfight with.

"Hey, red hat," the man barked as Will raced past him down the rails. "The headlamp goes on the helmet, not in your hand!"

An instant before Will plunged into the utter blackness, he shot a final glance at his watch. It didn't have a glow-in-the-dark dial. Eight minutes after twelve. An explosion would rip through the mine at 12:18; he had 10 minutes. He was certain 10 minutes wasn't near enough time, but he was okay with that.

He surprised three miners eating lunch in the fourth break, where the shaft turned south. The men were seated up against a coal pillar talking.

"Get out of here!" Will shouted as he approached them.

"What?"

"Methane level's more than 3 percent at the face," Will lied, but didn't stop, only slowed down to speak. "They just called." He swerved around the outstretched legs of the miner at the far end and kept running.

"Then why're you—?"

"Get out—now!" Will called out over his shoulder. He didn't look back to see if they'd done what he told them.

Running as fast as he could between the rails, his back scraped painfully across a bent-down strap of metal between roof bolts, most likely holding up a tree stump. He cried out in pain but kept going. And even before he'd gotten deep enough into the mine for the velvet blackness to devour the light from the entrance, Will had figured out that his noble posturing and grand pronouncements, his lofty motives and willing self-sacrifice didn't mean squat.

His feelings about being in a dark rat hole in the ground hadn't changed a speck in two decades. If anything, his claustrophobia was far more well-developed now than it had been when he was 18. After all, he'd been exercising it for years—in the narrow passageways and jammed-tight berths of a destroyer. He'd practiced it in drunk tanks in the jails of countless nameless cities, and perfected it waking from blackouts huddled shivering in a drainage pipe or up under somebody's porch.

But nothing he'd ever experienced held a candle to the weight of an entire mountain hanging inches above his head. Hovering there, breathlessly suspended, eager to stomp down with a massive stone foot to splatter his body in unrecognizable...

I'm not wearing a belt tag.

No belt tag? And he was *concerned* about that? Under other circumstances, the absurdity of that would have made him laugh. If the mountain came down again, they'd close the mine permanently and never dig any of the bodies out. All the miners—tagged and un-tagged alike—would lie there in the dark until Judgment Day.

He tripped, went down hard on one knee, staggered to his feet and kept running. His shirt and pants were soaked, but he didn't know if it was with rainwater or fear sweat. Either way, the wet against his skin chilled him, made his teeth chatter in the cold, dank air. His legs ached, his back screamed, his breath raked in and out in heaving gasps, but at least the stitch in his side helped keep him doubled over as he ran. But not far enough. His back scraped over a roof bolt, firing white hot agony down his spine. Will's shirt was ripped now, his back bleeding, but he kept running.

There was nothing but total, black-ink darkness all around him now, broken only by the bouncing, pallid glow of the headlamp he carried in his hand. In that darkness, he couldn't gauge his progress. Dark behind, dark in front, he was running on a treadmill down an endless track, getting nowhere, passing one break after another the way a merry-go-round kept passing the same popcorn stand over and over again.

And it was quiet, except for the sound of his scrambling feet. Silent as a tomb.

No, actually it wasn't quiet. The mountain spoke to him. And Will didn't want to hear what it had to say. It groaned, squeaked, and popped. It rumbled in anger now and then; once Will actually saw a ripple move across the roof behind the mosaic of ancient ferns. The mountain was outraged by the intrusion of man. It whispered its anger in his ear, hissed its loathing. Taunted him. Threatened him.

But he kept running.

All at once it occurred to Will that he'd never been totally alone in a mine before; there'd always been other miners around. And as panic crawled up the back of his throat on little rat feet, he discovered he wasn't alone now either.

Out beyond the farthest edge of his light, he saw them. Ghost images. Silent miners, their headlamps as dark as the black holes of eyes in their expressionless faces.

He swung the headlamp beam off to the right and left; the light splintered and fractured off the shiny black coal pillars. There in the darkness down the break they crouched on their heels and stared at him—watched him.

He heard himself begin to whimper, a sound like a kid awakened by a nightmare who's afraid to call out for Mama because he's certain the Boogie Man's still in the room, lurking somewhere there, waiting for a sign of life before he pounced.

A particularly low roof bolt cracked Will's helmet hard, knocked it off his head and sent him tumbling into the dirt. He instinctively reached out his hands to break his fall and the headlamp he held hit the ground hard.

The light went out. The world went black.

Then Demon Darkness came for him in a rush, eager to do all the nasty things it had always threatened to do.

CHAPTER 38

"WE GOT TO git!" the big miner man cried, jumped up, and without a backward glance began to run down the rail line shaft as fast as he could.

"Watch your helmets!" somebody shouted as the others leapt to their feet and raced after him, ducking low so their helmets wouldn't scrape against the roof. The helmets were made of plastic, of course, only piece of metal on them was where the headlamp hooked. But still…a spark, the littlest spark…

Jamey ran, too, but had no memory of getting to his feet. Though they was crowded together as they ran, the miners just grunted and panted, didn't say nothing. But Jamey knew they seen the same thing he did—there was curtains down! No wonder the air was bad. They was running past breaks with no curtains. That was when Jamey felt the first stab of terror in his belly and all of a sudden he was more askeered than he'd ever been in his life. His heart boomed in his chest and he couldn't seem to move fast enough. It was a long way to the mouth. A long way to run bent double in the dark with an explosion about to get you from behind.

He couldn't see nothing but his feet and the feet of the scoop driver in front of him, who cried out when he caught his back on a bolt.

The pinner hollered over his shoulder, "They's a mantrip loaded with lime bags on the track about—"

"You nuts?" roared the scoop driver. "You can't—"

"It's faster'n trying to run all—"

"The switch on that thing's got a short," the scoop driver panted, "You get near it and the explosion won't have to kill you—I will!"

They passed by the mantrip and kept running.

◇ ◇ ◇ ◇ ◇

WILL LAY ON his belly in the dark. His fingers fumbled frantically around the headlamp, tried to feel—*Ouch!* He drew his bleeding finger back and stuck it in his mouth. The plate was broken. So was the bulb.

The enormity of his loss hit him so hard he groaned and rolled up in a ball. It felt like a bully had kicked him in the belly with steel-toed miner's boots.

The light's gone!

Any minute now the mine would blow. He'd have to coon the rails to find his way in the inky blackness. Cooning the rails meant getting down on all fours and feeling your way along the rails, your hands out in front of you like a raccoon's paws. In a darkness as profound as being locked inside the coal itself, he couldn't possibly crawl fast enough to get to Jamey in time—or to save himself, for that matter. They were all going to die down here. Just like the image Jamey had released from the coal.

He hadn't seen the mural, so he didn't know any specifics. Did the arts show men blown apart, burned up...or dying alone and afraid, curled up in the dark?

Will lay in a fetal position, whimpering. He had fallen through a crack in the universe in to his own worst nightmare. In his wildest imagination, he could have conceived no horror greater than this. In a coal mine. In the dark. Alone. And doomed.

He was instantly nauseous, rose up quickly onto his hands and knees, and vomited noisily, splattering his breakfast on the ground and his hands. He crawled away from it—*which way?*—but he could still smell it, mingled with the stench of his own sweat. He kept crawling until he bumped into a coal pillar—edged along it until he couldn't smell the vomit anymore. Then he felt the contour of the damp rock with his hands so he could turn around and lean against it.

He was blind! Disorienting blind! Up, down, right, left were concepts of the light. Here they meant nothing.

In the profound silence, his panting breath sounded like a winded draft horse. He heard his heart slog away in his chest, banging like a panicked fist on a locked door. He scooted his knees up and wrapped his arms around them. He trembled violently; his teeth chattered. But not from cold air and wet clothes. A rusty, notched hatchet of ragged panic had hacked into his belly.

The mountain spoke in the darkness. He heard it creak and groan, a sound like the one his father had made in his sleep, an aching moan of despair. He buried his head in his knees, held tighter, tried desperately not to hear the mountain, not to feel the weight of it above him, bearing down on him, crushing him.

His head snapped up. The ghost miners he'd seen as he ran in the dark—they were out there! Right here in this shaft. Moving silently toward him. Their cold, dead hands reaching out for him, their chilled breath...

He clamped his teeth down on the scream in his throat, grabbed hold of his emotions the best he could. He didn't want to...*cry.* But he was so alone and so...

This is the way Ricky Dan died.

That thought slapped him hard in the face.

When the oblivion of alcohol failed to obliterate the images, or when his mind conjured them up in nightmares, Will had envisioned every detail of Ricky Dan's death. He'd seen him feel his way along the coal pillar on the other side of the belt line, his lungs bursting, straining to draw in a breath. He'd watched him reach the curtained break at last, seconds before he would be forced to gasp. And the curtain was down, the seal blown. He'd seen Ricky Dan sink to his knees, then fall forward on his face. Watched him gasp and suck air and death into his lungs. One breath. Maybe two or three. Coughing violently...*flopping around like that catfish in the grass*...until finally he lay on his back still. His headlamp barely penetrating the black smoke; his open eyes staring at nothing.

Alone in the dark. That's how Ricky Dan had died; that's how Will would die, too.

◊ ◊ ◊ ◊ ◊

LLOYD LOOKED DOWN at the possum light. The flame was more than an inch tall now with a bright blue cap. He punched the button on the methane meter. It read 4 percent. Of course, the concentration would be higher in the bad air shaft, but he was sure it'd reached an explosive level at the face. If he didn't light up soon, something else would set it off before he had a chance. It wouldn't take much. A tiny spark from an exposed wire on some cable would do it. But it wasn't time—not yet 12:18. By then, the level would be 6 or 7 percent. This wouldn't be just any ole explosion. It'd be a big one!

An image flashed into his head. A giant shark lifted out of the sea and chomped down on the back of a boat, *eatin'* it, and one of the men in it!

He'd taken the kids to see that movie *Jaws* years ago. One of the dumbest things he ever done. It scared Norma Jean so bad she didn't even want to get in the bathtub no more. Jesse started wetting the bed again and they liked to never got him to stop.

But Lloyd enjoyed the movie, would have seen it half a dozen times if he could have. The way he saw it, the shark was a pure being.

That fish knew what it wanted and didn't let nothing nor nobody get in its way. No hesitation, no second-guessing. Lloyd hadn't never admired nothing in the world more than he did that shark.

And it was a great white, not no little tiger shark. That's the kind of explosion Lloyd was going to set off. A great white. One that would erase everything in one great ball of fire. One that would produce a lightning bolt he could ride all the way to the gates of hell.

He reached up and switched his headlamp off and watched the darkness leap in to fill up the light space. Then he leaned back and looked out, like a blind man at an absolutely starless night.

He searched around in himself to see if he could find fear. It was all right to be afraid; he'd still do what he come here to do even if he was so scared he wet himself, like Will done that time on the railroad trestle. But he wasn't afraid—felt nothing at all but an icy calm.

Good. Then his hands wouldn't shake when he lit the lighter.

◊ ◊ ◊ ◊ ◊

THE HAIR ON Jamey's neck stood up like a mad dog was after him, a beast he couldn't see that would jump up on his back, knock him down, and eat him alive. He could run faster than the scoop operator in front of him, but he didn't go around him, just stayed where he was—which was at the tail end of the line of scrambling miners. They'd got out ahead of him and most of them was old men—35, maybe more—and Jamey could probably have outrun them all. But he wasn't about to blow by the others just because he could. He stayed where he was, moving fast as they was.

And he held a small, limp bird tenderly in his hand as he ran.

The pinner stumbled over a small rockfall, went down, and the scoop operator collided with him, staggered off to the side and kept running. Jamey reached down and grabbed the pinner's arm, yanked him to his feet. and shoved him forward ahead of him.

"Go'on," he barked. "It's comin'. *Run!*"

Jamey could feel the approach of the explosion the way a bird senses a storm coming and takes shelter before the wind and rain hit. The air felt thicker, and not because of the dust in it. The pinner gasped so hard he spit with every breath, washed the black coal dust right out of his white beard. He slowed down and Jamey ran up beside him, took his arm, and pulled him along faster. His back dragged across the wet roof because he had to stand a little taller to keep hold of the pinner's arm.

"Can't slow down now," he sputtered between breaths. "Ain't no time left."

And there wasn't.

$$\Diamond \; \Diamond \; \Diamond \; \Diamond \; \Diamond$$

LLOYD FLIPPED THE switch on his headlamp and looked at his watch: 12:18. He pushed the button on the methane gauge. It read 6 percent.

Let's do this.

He shook a cigarette out of the pack of Marlboros lying beside him on the yellow curtain and ran it slowly under his nose. But something was wrong with his sniffer; he couldn't smell the cigarette. Things was shutting down, he supposed.

He tried to remember how he'd felt exactly 20 years ago today, huddled in that curtained break, figuring hard as he could how to stay alive. But his mind wouldn't go there. It was like all them thoughts had been erased. Ever time he looked for the memory, all he could see was a bright white light that near blinded him and he had to look away.

He didn't know anymore what it felt like to want to live, to yearn for one more breath, one more sunrise, to be so desperate to survive wouldn't nothing stand in your way. He'd been that person once, though he couldn't find any actual memories of how that'd felt. He had schemed and then murdered his way out of dying and he was certain there had been a terror-driven desperation in him that made him do what he done. But he didn't feel that desperation no more. The only thing he was desperate to do now was to conceal his crime, to hide his shame. And to end it. Yeah, he was desperate for it to be over, desperate for the cold darkness of the mine to seep into his ears and eyes and nose and mouth and fill him up like still black water— until the Lloyd Jacobs inside his chest was cold and dark and dead.

His mind had got all herky-jerky on him, like the movements of a bird on a branch; he had trouble putting thoughts together. And he did want to think. I mean, he needed to think of something important as the last thoughts ever was in his head. He tried to remember the words and the melody to his favorite song so maybe he could hum it, but he couldn't even recall what his favorite song had been. Or his favorite food. Or what the faces of his children looked like. Or how the sun on his back felt when he sat on the creek bank fishing.

Fact was, he couldn't seem to find nothing at all in his head, no memories, no wants, no regrets, no fear. Just one great big ole empty.

And then he figured it out. That's what happened to a man at the end. Wasn't none of this seeing-your-life-pass-before-your-eyes stuff folks talked all dreamy about. When you come to the last of it, wasn't nothing left at all. You's completely used up. So when the cold dark flowed into you, it didn't have to push nothing aside. There was a nice vacant space waiting for it. And wouldn't no worms eat up his outsides after he was gone. He'd come from dust, and he was going to return to dust. Poof.

Lloyd scooted away from the coal seam and stood up tall as he could under the low roof. A man had ought to go out of this life standing on his own two feet. He smiled a joyless smile, put the cigarette between his lips, lifted the lighter to the tip of it and flipped the switch.

Everything went white!

His body was hurled backward from the blast for a fraction of an instant before Lloyd Eugene Jacobs was no more.

◊ ◊ ◊ ◊ ◊

Boom!

A mighty clap of thunder, like when lightning struck that stump in the front yard, roared up from the guts of the earth and Granny's double-wide trailer house began to shake like it had a palsy. Only this time, it wasn't just her dishes that broke. Her heart broke, too, shattered into a thousand jagged pieces along cracks it had taken all these many years to heal.

The rumbling went on and on, bellowing in a rage beneath the ground in a merciless roar of destruction and despair.

Then it stopped and it was quiet, except for Bucket and the other dogs up and down the road howling.

Granny shook her head slowly back and forth to make it not so, the tears in her eyes blurring the world like she was looking at it through a glass of water.

Smoke began to belch out the mouth of Harlan #7. When JoJo seen it, she put her head in her hands and started to sob. But Granny's hurt was too deep for something simple as tears.

Her face twisted in a monstrous cramp of grief and she cried out, "No!" She lifted her eyes toward heaven and begged, with a wail of such yearning it must surely have broke the heart of God to hear it. "Oh, please no. *Not again!*"

◊ ◊ ◊ ◊ ◊

The explosion roared out in every direction from the flame on Lloyd's lighter with a force like dropping a lit firecracker into an empty Mason jar. Empty except for the miners running for their lives up the rail line shaft. Blowtorches of flame shot out, too, rode the coal dust in the air out hundreds of feet in every direction, flames hot enough to ignite solid coal in a couple of seconds and incinerate the pieces of equipment at the face. The miners, too, if they'd been there.

The force of the explosion chucked charred shuttle cars across the face and slammed them into the wall, crumpled them up like tin. It rolled the blackened continuous miner over onto its side and scooted it after them, and jammed them all together in an unrecognizable pile of scorched and twisted metal. The blast instantly melted the rubber on 75 yards of belt line and glued it to the rollers. It ripped the power station off the floor and smashed it against the coal pillar on the other side of the shaft, left the high line cable that brought in electricity from the outside a mass of exposed wires that sparked and snapped like a den of cobras.

A mighty fist of super-heated, expanding air sucker-punched the fleeing miners from behind. It hammered them to the floor, bounced them off the roof, slammed them against coal pillars and each other and fired pieces of coal, loose rocks, shattered cinder blocks and beams at them like missiles. It burst their eardrums, bloodied their noses and left them injured, dazed, and gasping. But alive. At least until the cloud of noxious fumes caught up with them, the poison gas and black smoke that trailed the explosion like a tail on a kite.

All around Jamey it was silent and dark. He lay on his side, jammed up against a coal pillar with something soft—some*body*— shoved up against him. There were pale shafts of headlamp beams shining out in odd directions, from helmets knocked off their owners' heads or from heads in strange positions. Jamey tried to move, grunted from the effort and could barely hear the sound he made through a roaring in his head. He reached up and felt blood coming out of his left ear.

He hadn't lost his helmet, but lying on his side, his headlamp shone out across the floor and didn't light up nothing. Jamey turned and seen that the man shoved up against him was the shuttle operator. He pushed and the shuttle man rolled away and began to move, feeling around with his hands, trying to get up.

"Who's here?" Jamey heard a voice call out, but he couldn't tell where it'd come from. "Call out! Who's here?"

A little farther down from Jamey, a light moved up off the floor of the shaft, righted itself like a miner crouched down on his knees. Then other lights started moving slowly as their owners tried to get up, too, or figure out why they couldn't.

"Com'on!" the voice called, and this time Jamey could tell it was the miner man yelling. He cursed—Jamey heard that!—and then yelled, "Holler out your names. Who's still alive?"

Voices come from the dark or out from under headlamps that were now shining out at eye level all around. Jamey had trouble telling where the men were, his hearing messed up like it was. His own voice sounded funny when he yelled, "Jamey Sparrow."

The miner man must have been keeping track because he said, "Everybody's 'counted for 'cept Bradley. Anybody seen—?"

"I'm right here," yelled a voice that come out of the dark farther down the shaft than the others. Headlamps turned and shone that direction and lit up shining eyes probably 30 feet away. "Lamp's busted."

Jamey started to cough. The smell of smoke was all around them.

"We got to run," the miner man said, but he didn't need to because everybody was already rising to their feet. "Anybody hurt? Check each other out."

Headlamp beams washed over the miners, revealing bleeding ears and noses, and blood on clothes, too. The pinner man couldn't hardly talk. He'd hit something smashed his mouth and broke out most all his front teeth. The blood had run down and turned his white beard red. The miner man's helper had blood all over the bottom of his pants leg. The shuttle driver's left arm was bent funny and he was holding it against his chest with his right.

"Can you walk, Jamey?" the scoop operator asked and Jamey looked at him like he was a fool. Of course, he could walk; he wasn't no baby. Then he followed the light from the man's headlamp and seen the splinter sticking out of his own leg halfway between his belt and his knee. It was a piece off a wooden beam, maybe 2 inches thick and stuck out of his leg 6 or 8 inches. He was surprised to death because he didn't feel nothing. It didn't hurt, but it was bleeding so's his pants was getting soaked.

"I can walk."

"Can you *run?*" the miner man asked. "If you can't, we'll carry you. We ain't leavin' nobody behind."

The smoke was thick now; everybody had begun to cough.

"Can you make it?" the scoop operator asked.

"Sure I can!" Jamey said, but soon's he moved, pain shot through his leg so fierce he was afraid he was gonna throw up. "You go on, I'll be right behind you."

Wouldn't none of them leave, though, until Jamey got to his feet—foot—and started hobbling down the shaft. Soon as they seen Jamey could move, they all took off running.

Then Jamey remembered and stopped cold.

ValVleen. Where was ValVleen?

He'd had her in his hand, was cradling her little dead body as he run down the shaft and then the explosion hit and…he must have *dropped her.*

He turned and swept his headlamp over the floor. The smoke was getting thicker and it stunk! It didn't smell like the bonfires he built to burn leaves. It made his eyes all watery so's it was hard to see, too, hard to find ValVleen!

Jamey eased carefully down on his hands and knees and searched the floor, crawled back and forth, the pain in his leg an agony he could barely stand. Blood had soaked the whole bottom part of his pants and was dripping off, making a bloody snail trail as he crawled.

He called out to her—"ValVleen! ValVleen, where are you?"—in a strangled cry, though he knew she couldn't hear him. "I ain't leavin' here 'thout, you, ValVleen. Where are you?"

Jamey looked and looked but he couldn't find her anywhere.

CHAPTER 39

A SUDDEN DEAFENING ROAR reverberated in the shaft around Will and inside his head, too. A thunderous boom that sucked all the air out of his lungs was followed by an invisible force that knocked him backward against the pillar and banged his head painfully.

She'd blown! Just like Jamey's art...*Jamey!*

The boy was gone. Will was too late. He'd tried to save Ricky Dan's son, but the mine had gobbled the boy up just like it had his father.

Will sat stunned. He shook his head. Maybe he was crying; his face was wet. He caught a whiff of smoke that quickly grew into the stench of a coal fire. But he wouldn't run from it this time. This time, he's sit here and...

Voices!

He turned—his eyes searched frantically. Left, right, like the tap of a blind man's cane. Then he saw something, or thought he did. Yes, pale light far in the distance down the shaft. Of course, they'd come out the rail shaft. The survivors would...*survivors!* Jamey!

Will got to his feet and stumbled off in the darkness toward the growing pinprick of light in the distance.

◊ ◊ ◊ ◊ ◊

Jamey's headlamp blinked out, then back on again. He was glad the other miners weren't here to see that. They'd have teased him. They'd have said his girlfriend was cheating on him. That's what miners always said: a flickering headlamp meant your girl was two-timing you. Jamey understood cheating. You said you didn't have no queens in Go Fish when you really did. But he had no idea what two-timing meant.

The light flickered again. He must have messed something up on the lamp or the battery when he fell down. He turned his head careful, like he was balancing a plate on top of it, and continued to sweep the floor of the shaft with the light, searching for the body of his friend.

He had begun to feel funny, though. Dizzy and weak. The splinter stuck in his leg had begun to throb along with his heartbeat. It still didn't hurt bad, though, unless he touched it or moved. But when he looked down at it, a wave of nausea almost made him upchuck. He knew he'd ought to go, run toward the entrance the way the other'd done. But he had to find ValVleen!

And besides, he was tired. He'd have to rest up some before he could run off anywhere. By the time he was rested, he'd have to coon the rails to find his way in the smoke.

He began to cough violently, so hard he lost his breath for a minute. And it occurred to him that he might already have waited too late, that the smoke would take all his air away before he could make it to the entrance.

Well, if that was the way of it, wasn't no use to pout about it. But if he was going to die here, he wanted to die with…

There! A speck of yellow showed out from under dirt and rocks. A piece of curtain or…

ValVleen!

He crawled to her quick as he could, dusted the rocks and dirt off her tiny body and lifted her tenderly. She wasn't warm no more, warm and soft. Her body was cold and kind of stiff. She felt like a stuffed animal, the kind JoJo had piled on her bed.

His eyes watered and her image swam in the sudden tears. Well, she was still his ValVleen, cold or not.

"ValVleen, I been searchin' ever where for you. Looks like me and you's gonna stay here…" he coughed so violently the shaking sent a wave of pain from the splinter in his leg all the way to his knee. "I wish you's here to sing to me while…"

"Jamey!"

His ears was so messed up he thought he heard somebody callin'…

"Jamey!" Again. Louder. He looked around, uncertain of the direction. Then seen a headlamp off in the smoky distance, dancing like somebody was running with it.

He tried to get from his knees to his feet, but his legs was all rubbery and didn't want to hold him up. And the smallest movement stabbed a dagger of pain down his whole leg. So he sat down carefully in the dirt.

The light coming at him got bigger and brighter. It had this circle around it, like a halo, that Jamey thought sure was pretty. The voice under the light kept calling his name, and it sounded like…

Will?

It was Will. What was Will doing here? Jamey couldn't puzzle that out in his head. In fact, his head swam so crazy-like he had trouble thinking at all—or even sitting up for that matter. And then he was on his back, his light shining on the roof. They was lots of leaves and flowers and such up there, the outlines of them anyway. They looked kind of like the wallpaper he'd seen in the lobby of the hospital he went to when he had the croup that time.

He wanted to reach up and touch the flowers but his arm was too heavy to lift.

◊ ◊ ◊ ◊ ◊

WILL DROPPED TO his knees beside Jamey. The boy lay on his back between the rails and he wasn't moving, didn't even appear to be breathing.

"Jamey!" he cried.

The green eyes opened and Jamey smiled at Will.

"Whatchoo doin' here? Yore askeered of coal mines. You said."

"We gotta get you out of here, Jamey." Will looked down at the wound on Jamey's leg and his heart sank. The scoop operator who'd given Will his helmet and headlamp said the boy'd been right behind him, running even though he had a splinter in his leg. So Will didn't think the wound would be this severe. Jamey's pants leg was soaked and there was a puddle of blood settled into the dust around him. "Can you stand, Jamey? Can you run?"

Will's words were punctuated by a fit of coughing. The smoke… They had to go *now!* Jamey's eyes filled with tears and he held his hand up for Will to see. Lying in his open palm was his pet canary—dead.

"I killed her, Will. I killed ValVleen. But I hadta. I—"

"Later, Jamey. Get up, we got to get out of here."

Jamey rolled to his side and tried to rise. He cried out in pain and slumped back down on the ground.

"I'm tired, Will. Let me rest a spell. You go on and I'll be 'long directly."

Will leapt to his feet and grabbed the back of the collar on Jamey's work shirt.

"This is going to hurt, Jamey. I'm sorry."

Then Will turned and took off toward the mine entrance dragging Jamey between the rails in the dirt behind him. Jamey cried out in pain but Will kept going. The power of déjà vu was so intense it was disorienting, almost overwhelming. Will tried to ignore it, just bent his head down and struggled forward as fast as he could go—which wasn't very fast at all. The last time he'd dragged an injured miner down the shaft he'd had help. All by himself, it was slow going.

As he struggled for every step, the smoke in the tunnel got thicker and thicker.

◊ ◊ ◊ ◊ ◊

JOJO GAPED AT the thick black smoke that boiled out the entrance of the mine. She could see the people who'd been in the white tent huddled together staring at it, too. A gray Kentucky State Police cruiser, lights flashing, siren screaming, had joined two brown Harlan County Sheriff's Department cars, and the officers blocked off the entrance road to the mine and quickly began diverting traffic around it. But folks just abandoned their vehicles on the side of the road and ran the rest of the way to the mine on foot. None of the officers tried to stop them. Most of Aintree Hollow was already there, anyway.

She couldn't tell for sure, but it looked like the explosion doors on the fan had blown—and that was good. The doors were at the *end* of the metal enclosure that housed the ventilation fan, in a straight line from the bad-air shaft. The force of any blast coming from the shaft would blow the doors away and release the pressure, rather than destroying the fan, which was attached to the enclosure at right angles to the doors. From what JoJo could see, the doors were gone but the fan unit was still there. That mattered. With a fan to suck the bad air out of the mine, the rescue teams…

The teams weren't even here yet.

She swallowed hard not to be sick and turned toward Granny. The poor old woman looked like a groundhog JoJo'd seen once swimming across a rain-swollen creek. Her hair had come undone and hung down to the middle of her back, a tangle of long, muddy curls and pieces of sticks and twigs.

Granny stood tall and straight, though. She stared unblinking down at the mine. But her lip trembled. JoJo couldn't begin to imagine what she must be thinking, what nightmare horrors she remembered, what agony ripped open her heart now with Jamey—*Jamey!*

He couldn't be…not *gone.* No! The thought took her breath away with a different kind of pain than she'd felt when they'd come to tell her about Darrell. Jamey was…it was like losing a child.

Just like Granny'd done.

How had she stood it? How had any of them? There'd been a time when JoJo was barely old enough to understand the tragedy that had befallen Aintree Hollow, that she couldn't make sense out of the people who'd survived. They'd just…gone on. She hadn't seen the beginning, the first few years, of course, but all those people were still around when she was growing up. They taught school, delivered mail, and raised kids. The men still went down in the mines. And the women still waited every day for them to come back out.

At the time, she'd thought it was cold and unfeeling to behave like nothing at all had happened. Now, she saw it as a kind of courage she could barely get her arms around.

A sudden, shattering roar shook the roots of the mountain, bigger and louder than the first one. The trailer wobbled like it was a toy sitting on the top of a washer on spin cycle. As JoJo watched in horror, the ventilation fan exploded off the side of the metal enclosure. The huge blade whirred up into the sky like some kid's Frisbee, sailed over the treetops, and disappeared into the woods.

Granny grabbed the porch railing, no color at all in her face. She swayed and JoJo reached back and dragged the rocking chair over behind her.

"Sit down, Granny, 'fore you fall down."

But Granny stood where she was, watched the crowd scatter, backing up and to the sides to get out of the black cloud that boiled out the entrance like smoke out a chimney.

Tears streamed down Granny's cheeks. She mouthed words she didn't give voice to, but JoJo could read her lips. She was silently repeating: Will. Jamey Boy.

CHAPTER 40

WILL'S BREATH SEARED his throat. His legs screamed in agony. He ran blind down the never-ending shaft, dragging Jamey behind him. The boy was no longer moving, hung there, limp.

Oh, please not dead!

Will didn't stop to examine him. Just kept going.

Without the rails to guide him, Will would have gotten hopelessly lost. The smoke was so thick the headlamp on his borrowed helmet cast only a pallid glow, illuminating nothing but his own feet. Now and then he spotted the bright yellow of curtains across the breaks he passed. A few seals had held; most hadn't. But he wasn't looking for double curtains, a place to hold up and wait it out. Not this time. They'd make it or they wouldn't out here in the shaft. Jamey would bleed to death if they stopped.

Several times, he coughed so hard and long he could only stagger forward. He went down to his knees once—coughed until he heaved. But lower down, beneath the ever thickening blackness, the air was a little better and he grabbed a breath, lurched to his feet, and struggled forward.

On and on in the endless, airless dark. Down through the deepest, black ditch of his worst nightmares. Through the smoke-filled antechamber of hell.

Time had no meaning here. Will imagined that the hands of his watch spun wildly round and round in opposite directions. Or dangled broken in a permanent six-thirty. At some point, he realized he had stopped moving forward. His head spun; his ears buzzed. The mine floor swayed and lurched like the deck of a ship in a storm.

Stop fighting it.

No!

He shook his head frantically to clear it and the movement pitched him forward face-first into the dirt.

Don't get up. Rest.

No.

He rose to his elbows, his lungs on fire, lifted his head. The beam of his headlamp stabbed sightlessly into the swirling murk that filled the shaft.

And there, ahead—*light!*

Not his headlamp. Not shining out—shining *in*. A beam of light in the distance, a small, round beacon.

The trite phrase bloomed bright and beautiful in his mind. *Light at the end of the tunnel.* The mouth was there! He could see it. He began to stagger to his feet. Surely, he could make it that—

His ears popped.

A thunderous roar ate up all thought. Will felt himself flung through the smoke into a darkness where there was no light in front of him anymore. No light anywhere at all.

◊ ◊ ◊ ◊ ◊

"GRANNY, LOOK!" JoJo cried, though she didn't need to. Granny was looking the same place she was, saw what she saw. Miners had appeared in the smoke, coming out the mouth of the mine! Stumbling out. Folks was running toward them, rescue squad people and EMTs, hurrying them off to the side quick as they could out of the stream of smoke that poured from the entrance. But the miners was walking! Some of them was limping, but they was moving under their own steam. That meant at least *some* of the miners had been far enough away from the blast to survive it, and they'd got out quick enough not to suffocate in the smoke.

Granny grabbed JoJo's arm, her grip so tight her fingernails bit into JoJo's flesh. "I ain't got eyes to look that far. I can't…can you see Jamey Boy? Or Will?"

It was an absurd question, of course. From here, the people were smaller than baby mice. JoJo couldn't see anybody's face, and even if she could have, the emergency personnel had swarmed all over them so quick she couldn't have identified anybody.

"No, Granny. I can't tell."

"You go find out, child!"

"But how—?"

"Walk…*run.* You take that little phone of yourn and you go down there and find out. And you call me. No matter what you find out, you call me. Now git!"

JoJo turned, took the porch steps two at a time and raced down the road.

HOB BASCOMB HAD been standing so close to the mine entrance he seen the first of the miners, seen their headlamps bob in the darkness. Ran in there with some other fellows and helped pull them out. Now, he went from one to the other, searching.

Jamey Sparrow wasn't there. Neither was Will Gribbins.

Hob knelt down beside the miner man, who was leaned up against the wall of the lamp house with an EMT holding an oxygen mask over his face.

"Where's Jamey? He make it out with you guys? Did you see Will?"

The miner man shoved the oxygen mask aside and rasped in a hoarse voice. "Will went lookin' for Jamey. Ask..." He burst into a fit of coughing then and the EMT shoved the mask back over his face. So he finished the sentence by pointing at the scoop operator, laid out on a stretcher. EMTs on both sides were about to lift him up into an ambulance but Hob got there before they could get him inside.

"Will and Jamey! Where—?"

The scoop operator pulled the oxygen mask off his face.

"I told 'em." He pointed to the outside foreman who was huddled with the rescue team that had just arrived from Big Sandy. "They was both alive last time I seen 'em," he started coughing but waved the EMT away when he tried to replace the mask on his face. "Jamey's leg had this big ole splinter in it. I thought he was right behind me, but you couldn't seen nothin' in that smoke..." Then he shook his head. "And that second blast coulda got 'em."

The EMT pushed the mask onto the scoop operator's face and shoved the stretcher up into the ambulance.

Hob marched over to the foremen and the rescue team, butted right into their conversation.

"Will went in after Jamey and—"

"We know that," the foreman barked, "The team's going in to start hanging curtains soon's—"

"They won't last in that smoke 'til you hang curtains!" Hob literally spit the words out. With no teeth, when he got excited he sometimes sprayed his listeners. "They ain't far in. I know it."

He looked at the crew from Big Sandy, then turned and picked up a self-rescuer. The team had just unloaded a box of them and set it beside the office door.

"I'm goin' in after 'em," Hob said.

"Oh, no you *ain't!*" the foreman bellowed. "You ain't certified in rescue. You can't go…"

Hob realized the other rescue team members—five of them—had grabbed self-rescuers and put on nose clamps, too. Without another word, the six men plunged into the black smoke that billowed out of Harlan #7.

A HISSING SOUND.

A beep.

Another hissing sound.

There was a rhythm.

Will seemed to recall that rhythm, but he couldn't remember where. Didn't matter.

Then the sounds and the world faded away.

He was a bubble dislodged from under a rock in a creek, floating up and up and up toward sparkling bright light, diamonds of illumination refracted into sequins of brilliance by the water. He broke the surface into the light and there was air and noise.

He opened his eyes, saw blurry images, closed them again.

"I think he's awake." JoJo's voice.

"Leave him be, child." Granny's voice. "Let him sleep."

"I'm not asleep." His own voice—only hoarse, damaged and painful.

"How long you been playin' possum, laying there listenin' to us talk about you?" Granny again.

He opened his eyes and left them open, the blurry images resolved into the faces that matched the voices. Granny and JoJo. So where was…?

"Jamey!" He tried to sit up. "What happened to Jamey?" Speaking slashed his throat with razor blades.

Granny shoved him gently back down on the bed. "Jamey Boy's just fine." The look on her face said that might not be entirely true.

JoJo was more blunt. "It was a near thing, though. When I called Granny to tell her they'd got you both out, I wasn't even sure he was—"

Granny shot her a glance, then said a little too cheerfully. "You shoulda seen the line of folks waitin' to give him they blood. I never seen the like."

Will looked at JoJo. "Where is he?"

"Up Lexington."

"Then where..." He glanced around. "...am I?"

"Harlan. The Appalachian Regional Hos—"

Will suddenly turned back to Granny and sputtered, "Granny... you're *here!*"

"Ever-body's got to be somewhere."

She couldn't quite pull off the humor, though. Her soft voice had a tremor in it. Will saw then how tight her hands gripped the railing around his bed, watched her hummingbird heartbeat in the big vein in her neck.

"Oh, don't make over it none. It's easier when you's *indoors.* 'Sides, I already been to Lexington." A shadow passed over her face, like the memory took her breath away. "I only done it 'cause I had to. Ain't gonna make no habit out of it."

"The other miners?" The pain in Will's throat kept his questions brief.

"They all made it..." Granny paused, and in the moment of silence, Will felt that sense of foreboding—of something hurling at him in the dark. "'Cept Lloyd." She drew in a deep, shaky breath. "He's gone."

That was the first time it occurred to Will that Lloyd should have been in the mine with Jamey and the others. He'd said that first morning, when he and Will almost came to blows, that he was changing shift, going from nights to days.

"Don't none of what happened make sense," Granny said. "Miners said they seen curtains down on the rail line—*pulled* down. And nothin' 'bout Lloyd makes sense, neither. He told the crew he was goin' back out to speak at the ceremony and nobody ever seen him again. But he wasn't speakin'. He told us he'd turned 'em down when they asked him to speak, said you'd ought to do it, instead. Remember?"

Will noticed that JoJo had an odd, hard expression on her face. He looked a question at her.

"I got some'm here you need to see," she said. "I been waitin' to show it to you." She turned to Granny. "Why don't you go—"

"They got a sody-pop machine down the hall." Granny let go of the bed railing. "Costs a whole dollar but I'm gonna get me one anyway." She nodded toward JoJo. "Then me 'n you need to get on back to the holler."

It was impossible to miss the yearning in her voice.

As soon as the door whispered closed behind Granny, JoJo pushed the button to lift the head of Will's bed up to a sitting position. Then she picked up an object wrapped in newspapers off a chair beneath the ceiling-mounted television and placed it in Will's lap. It was heavy. Cold.

Will's heart began to pound.

JoJo went to the window and closed the blinds, then turned off the bright overhead light and crossed back through the darkened room to his bedside.

"What…?" Will began.

But he already knew—wasn't really surprised when she pulled back the newspapers and took out the jet mural Jamey had carved of the three miners drawing rocks out of a helmet. Still, he couldn't stifle a moan at the sight of it.

"I know this is hard, but you got to see."

She drew a cigarette lighter out of her pocket, flipped the switch, and held the flickering light near the mural. She pointed at the area to the right of the relief sculpture of the kneeling miners, to the coal wall that formed the background of the scene. "There. Look right there."

Will looked. He didn't see anything. He moved his gaze slowly back and forth across the shiny surface. Nothing. He couldn't make out any more than he saw the first time he...

His sudden gasp sucked air down his raw throat so abruptly he almost choked. It was like that one optical illusion picture where he'd actually seen the second image. Once he located the image, it leapt out at him, stood out in stark relief, was so obvious it seemed that it was the focus of the artwork and the rest was background.

An intricately elaborate scene had appeared in the finely etched lines in the black rock. The detail was stunning. You could see Lloyd's face, a perfect likeness. You could see the UK painted on his helmet. You could also see the deranged, maniacal twisting of his features, the knotted muscles in his forearms and the texture of the rope he had wrapped in a hangman's noose around Ricky Dan's neck.

For a moment the room spun around Will in the familiar motion of the state of inebriation just past a pleasant buzz and not yet slobbering and staggering—the place where you could carry on a conversation if it wasn't a complicated one, could flirt fairly effectively if the girl was as drunk as you were.

Ricky Dan's features were distorted in an awful cramp of desperation. His eyes were bugged out, his face swollen in a frantic effort to suck in air as his fingers clawed at the rope that dug into his flesh.

Will couldn't speak. Neither could he tear his eyes away from the stone. The image seared into his mind like a brand; he could almost feel the heat, smell the raw, burning stink. Every line, every detail of it would remain with him, in photographic clarity, for the rest of his life.

He looked up at JoJo, his eyes pleading, as if she could somehow make it not so.

"Granny *knew*," she said in an awed whisper. "All these years. Lloyd come to the house for supper, fixed my car when it broke down, took Jamey sangin'…and all that time, she—"

The door opened, spilled bright light into the dim room, and the image vanished. Granny stood frozen for a moment, a Dr. Pepper can in her hand. Then she flicked the light switch and crossed to Will's bed.

"I wanted her to wait, but she wouldn't hear none of it," she said softly.

Wordlessly, JoJo picked the stone up out of Will's lap and began to wrap the newspapers back around it.

"Now, you listen here to me, Will Gribbins." The old woman shook her finger at him as she spoke. "You need to put all this 'bout Lloyd in a sack by the door for the time being and concentrate on gettin' well. It'll be there a-waitin' for you when you're ready. You hear me?"

Will nodded dumbly, too shocked to speak.

"You know there was three explosions in #7 this time," Granny said in an obvious effort to drag the conversation off in another direction. "Third time was the biggest. I heared they had roof falls all over the new section they just dug. It's gonna be like it was before. They'll yank Black Gold's permits same as they done Wilson Cooper's. I 'spect they won't never reopen #7." She paused, then drifted back in spite of herself. "And maybe that's as it should be. Maybe the whole thing needs to stay buried under the mountain."

JoJo picked up the conversational ball then and tried to run with it.

"It was Hob Bascomb pulled you and Jamey out. Him and the rescue team. You's not but about two hundred yards in."

"I 'spect Hob'd a-kept goin' if you'd been a thousand," Granny said.

"That was two days ago," JoJo said. She must have seen Will's eyes grow wide in surprise. "They kept you all doped up 'cause you's on a respirator for a while. They took Jamey off yesterday. Aunt Ruth Ann and Aunt Charity's with him now." She paused. "He ain't hardly stopped cryin' about that bird since he come to."

Will remembered then. "Jamey said he'd *killed* ValVleen."

JoJo explained why.

"That took a lot of cour—" Will's voice gave out.

"Courage," JoJo finished for him. Her eyes shifted from Will to Granny and then back. "Yeah, there's been a lot of that going 'round lately. Must be some'm in the water."

The world began to grow fuzzy again. Will heard the sound of the bed cranking back down, but he never heard it hit bottom.

◊ ◊ ◊ ◊ ◊

WILL STOOD ON the porch beside Granny as Jamey carried the last of JoJo's clothes out to the car, folded up neatly in a black garbage bag. A harsh November wind had sent the temperature down close to freezing, and Will was shivering in his windbreaker. Granny wore only a light sweater, but she didn't seem to notice the cold at all.

"She'll be fine," Will said, just to have something to say. They'd been over this half a dozen times.

"If this here's some'm she needs to do, she best get it outta her system," Granny said without looking at him.

JoJo had surprised Will about a week after he got out of the hospital, asked him if she could go with him when he left Aintree Hollow.

"You don't even know where I'm going," he'd blurted out to cover up the relief that threatened to bring tears to his eyes.

"Don't matter. Long's it's away from here."

She'd turned and looked out over the valley. "Granny told me once you could see the whole world in just this one little holler if you knew how to look."

Will said nothing.

"Still, I guess I need to see me some of the wide world for my own self. Need to do some livin'…" her voice trailed off, but he heard the silent *before…*

They'd been sitting together on the low limb of the mulberry tree that had caved in the roof of his father's house. Will had invited her to take a walk with him and they'd ended up there, but she'd cut him off at the pass before he could launch into the speech he had all prepared.

She turned to him then and said softly, "I'm scared."

Will reached out and squeezed her hand.

"So am I."

They sat quiet for a few minutes before JoJo spoke again. Will didn't let go of her hand.

"Why'd Lloyd kill my daddy?"

"For the air. He thought I was already dead and he wanted it all."

Once Will had recovered from the initial shock, he discovered he wasn't really surprised by the hidden scene in Jamey's arts. Will had been so guilt-ridden he'd never let his mind go to those last hours, that time in the curtained break. When he did, he saw what the boy he'd been then didn't see, what the man he was now could interpret and understand. Lloyd had orchestrated it all, manipulated both Will and Ricky Dan to ensure his own survival.

Will believed Lloyd had orchestrated the explosion in #7 that killed him, too, that he'd pulled down the curtains the miners said were missing. Maybe the MHSA investigators would figure that out, but Will doubted it. The crime scene was buried under a million tons of rock. There was no proof, just an image carved in a piece of jet.

Will, JoJo, and Granny had studied Jamey's explosion mural for hours, trying to understand why the real event hadn't happened the way he'd carved it. What they figured out was that it had. The arts had shown the future...*and the past*. The only miner in the mural wearing an armband was the one in front. Though his face wasn't visible, there were scratches on his arms and neck that he'd gotten when he fell through a rosebush trellis. The miners in the background, just outlines still buried in the rock...when JoJo counted them, it all made sense. There were 27. Twenty-seven miners killed two decades ago.

Jamey had pointed out something else in the mural the others didn't see.

"I'm down in there," he'd said. And it was true. If you looked deep into the carving, you could see it—a mirror. "I seen me smilin' in the arts the night I finished it, so I knowed I was down in the center of it and I wasn't askeered of it no more. Not ValVleen, though. She was on my shoulder. I shoulda seen her in the reflection. But she wasn't there. I didn't pay it no mind then, but she did. That's how she knowed what was comin'. The end."

Will had come to one final conclusion about Lloyd. He had no more proof to back it up than he did that Lloyd had caused the explosion. But his gut told him that Lloyd had been the poacher in the woods. Lloyd had tried to kill him.

Why?

Because he was mad that Will had run away? Or mad that Will had come back? Or maybe he was afraid Will had seen what he did to Ricky Dan. No way to tell. No way to understand why he killed himself, either, or why he had tried to take another dozen men with him when he died. It was all wound up in the reopening of #7 and Will's arrival in the hollow, but the only person who could unravel the mystery had finally joined the rest of his crew in the silent, forever night under Black Mountain.

The cold wind ruffled Bucket's shaggy coat as he padded up the porch steps in front of Jamey.

"That's the last; it's all loaded up," the boy said, looking down and away. His lower lip was trembling, but he didn't cry. Lately, he'd been trying to be a man about things. Will was proud of him.

JoJo came out the front door with her purse over her shoulder and a determined set to her jaw. Her eyes were red and swollen. There'd been a lot of tears this morning.

When Jamey had wailed, "I don't want you to go! Neither one of you," Granny'd put her arm around his shoulders and told him softly, "They'll be back, Sugar. Ain't no hillbilly can leave the hollers forever."

Will hated prolonged goodbyes. He pulled Granny wordlessly into his arms and hugged her. Tight. Kissed her lightly on the cheek and saw the silent tears spill out of her cinnamon eyes. Then he took JoJo's arm and started down the steps. But Jamey stepped in front of them.

The boy stood tall. He didn't look away. He grabbed Will's gaze with his bright green eyes and held fast.

"You take care of her, hear," he said in a deep voice. A man's voice.

Will heard Granny gasp. JoJo's eyes were huge.

This time, Will could speak. "I will. I promise."

THE END